D0960477

The CREEPING

The

CREEPING

alexandra sirowy

SIMON & SCHUSTER BFYR

NEW YORK   LONDON   TORONTO   SYDNEY   NEW DELHI

An imprint of Simon & Schuster Children's Publishing Division
1230 Avenue of the Americas, New York, New York 10020

SIMON & SCHUSTER BFYR is a trademark of Simon & Schuster, Inc.
For information about special discounts for bulk purchases,
please contact Simon & Schuster Special Sales at 1-866-506-1949 or business@simonandschuster.com.
The Simon & Schuster Speakers Bureau can bring authors to your live event. For more information or to
book an event, contact the Simon & Schuster Speakers Bureau at 1-866-248-3049
or visit our website at www.simonspeakers.com.
Jacket design by Lizzy Bromley
Interior design by Hilary Zarycky
The text for this book is set in Adobe Jenson Pro.
Manufactured in the United States of America
2 4 6 8 10 9 7 5 3 1
Library of Congress Cataloging-in-Publication Data
Sirowy, Alexandra.
The creeping / Alexandra Sirowy.
pages cm
Summary: Seventeen-year-old Stella has no recollection of the day her best friend disappeared while
the two, then six, were picking strawberries, until the corpse of a similar girl turns up and Stella not only
begins to remember, she learns that something dark has been at work in their little town for generations.
ISBN 978-1-4814-1886-7 (hardcover)
ISBN 978-1-4814-1888-1 (eBook)
[1. Missing children—Fiction. 2. Murder—Fiction. 3. Amnesia—Fiction.
4. Brothers and sisters—Fiction. 5. Monsters—Fiction. 6. Mental
illness—Fiction. 7. Mystery and detective stories.] I. Title.
PZ7.1.S57Cre 2015
[Fic]—dc23
2014018405

FIRST
EDITION

For Joe

Chapter One

I'm the lucky one; or at least that's what they say. I'm here to squint up at Independence Day fireworks under an orange-hued moon; to fidget in the violet organza of my junior prom dress; to toast under the midwestern sun while sipping peach fizzies lakeside. But sometimes the luck is harder to see.

I was relieved when Jeanie's parents moved to the opposite side of town; when they stopped going out in public. Finally, their sideways glances, forever sizing me up, would stop. Naturally, they wondered why I'd been spared and Jeanie hadn't. Was I growing up to be something special? Was I worth it? By the way their faces always pinched together—mouths pursed, brows touching, eyes narrowed into slits—it was obvious they found me lacking. But who wouldn't be?

Remember that when you judge me too quickly. Remember that I'm a product of something scary and mysterious. People who didn't even *know* Jeanie won't stop talking about it. I lived it. How else could I have turned out? There's a burden to being the one left behind, even though I don't remember a pinch of it. A weight always pressing down on me, like Jeanie's lifeless body is forever hitching a piggyback, steering me with her sticky hands coiled in my hair. I can't escape her, and I resent it.

Because if I'm being honest, Jeanie probably would have grown up to be nothing more than average. She was chunky at six, her fleshy cheeks nearly swallowing up her pinprick eyes. While all the other kindergarteners were learning to read, she couldn't write her own name. She was the alto with a lisp in a pack of singsongy chirping little girls. I know you shouldn't say nasty things about the dead, but since she never had the chance to become something, it's unfair that everyone assumes that if she had, it would have been bright and shiny. At six Jeanie was one of those dull pennies forgotten on the sidewalk that everyone steps over but no one stoops to pick up; she wouldn't have been a diamond at seventeen.

Even still, if I could remember her at all, I'm sure I would miss her. I'm told I loved her.

But since I don't remember her, and everything I know about her is because of what others say, the best I can do is gratitude. Jeanie's a ghost I owe my life to. After all, if I'd been alone that day, it could have been me who was taken. Jeanie is why I'm here, resting on the banks of Prior Lake, watching my three best friends propel their bikini-clad bodies from a rope swing, practically buzzing with giddiness over the promise of a whole two months with no school.

"So let me get this straight," Cole squeals with delight over the scent of gossip. "You don't remember one single freaking thing about that day? Zip. Zero. Nada. Nothing?" She tilts her head and gawks at me incredulously from where she stands toeing the water. Michaela and Zoey continue hiking up the rocky bank. They've spent the afternoon scrambling to the top of a large boulder to swing through the air shrieking as they drop into the crystalline lake from a fraying rope. Besides, they've heard this story a million times. Every parent in Savage has whispered it as a warning to their kids, voices hushed and foreboding. Every kid rolls their eyes like it could never happen to them.

"Seriously. I don't remember a thing," I repeat for the third time, forcing a smile. Cole's only been in Savage for four weeks, and she's a breath of fresh air with her diamond nose stud, ex-hippie parents who smoke pot on the weekends, and the breathy enthusiasm she says everything with—like the world's a dazzling present laid at her feet. I've been chipping my coral-colored nail polish off during Cole's third degree, and I brush the shards from my lap. I look dejectedly at the frumpy lavender swimsuit I'm wearing. I couldn't find my new white halter, and I hope Taylor and his boys don't pick today to sur-prise us.

Taylor Martinson and I have been flirting for months, and I've been playing it distant and disinterested. Zoey says playing hard to get is the only way to sink your talons in a boy. And she would know. Zoey's gone out with as many guys as me, Cole, and Michaela com-bined. But I am interested. Interested in his lazily crooked smile; his stormy blue eyes; his velvety laugh that leaves my stomach flip-flop-ping; the way he pours himself into chairs, reclining, stretching long, tan limbs out to take up every inch of space, head cocked back, half laughing like nothing is ever for real.

The only iffy thing about him is the couple of lacrosse boys—the "scum brigade"—he hangs out with. They're basically like dogs: Any girl's leg will do. And while that alone wouldn't eek me out, how dishonest they are about it does. They prey on underclass girls with promises of prom and happily ever after. Once the girls give it up, the boys give them the ax. I don't hold that against Taylor, though. He probably bonded with those boys over tetherball and roly-polies on the playground in kindergarten. If you consider that, he's loyal to stay friends with them.

It's doubtful that Taylor and his "bros" could find us here. This is Zoey's and my special hideaway. We're at least a mile away from the nearest cabin, way off the beaten path, and across town from the beaches of Blackdog Lake, where our classmates go for bonfires and swimming. We spend every summer in this spot, dallying away the afternoons, sunbathing topless to get rid of tan lines, and sneaking hard lemonades.

When we were younger, Zoey's brother Caleb used to bait fishing lines for us in this exact spot. It's where I had my first kiss in the summer after the fourth grade with Sam Worth. His palms were sweating so profusely he kept wiping them on his jeans. His eyes were scrunched closed, and his lips hovered an inch from mine until I grabbed his shirt collar and pulled until our mouths met. It's where I had my second kiss, which I lied and said was my first, with Scott Townsend three years later. It's where Zoey went to third base for the first time and was covered in poison oak blisters for two weeks. It's a special spot, sheltered from prying eyes and anyone's expectations but our own.

Cole plops down on her beach towel next to mine and dips her head back, basking in the sun. Thousands of miles from the ocean and she manages to have beach-wavy hair, as if her enthusiasm is generating static electricity. "I mean, oh my gosh. How do you not remember anything?" The cadence of her voice makes her California accent exaggerated. I think she does it on purpose, but it's cute rather than annoying.

"No idea. For the first few years they sent me to shrinks, therapists, psychotherapists. Eventually, the cops talked my mom into bringing me to a hypnotist who was a total wacko and made me lie on a purple velvet couch as she burned incense and pretended to delve into my mind." For some reason I lower my voice as I continue. "But no dice. I never remembered a thing. Just like it happened to someone else." And in some ways it did. I was six years old then, and now I'm just past my seventeenth birthday. I don't remember anything from that entire day or anything specific from any day before. It's like someone reached inside my head and scrambled my memory from that afternoon, leaving me with only my name and my parents' faces.

My earliest memory is of Zoey, stealing a chocolate marshmallow egg out of my Easter basket, the year after it happened. That's more fitting than you know, since Zoey is a total savage. But she's my savage, and I love her more than I love anyone and anything.

"But doesn't it frighten you to be out here?" Cole gestures encompassingly at the wilderness around us.

I want to answer: *not usually.* "Not at all," I say instead. "The trees didn't spring to life and eat Jeanie. Whoever took her didn't have anything to do with the woods. If I wanted to avoid the forest in Savage, I'd have to be a hermit."

Zoey swings on the rope and screams, "Boring conversation!" as she plunges into the water.

Fat droplets of lake rain down on us, and Cole sniffs indignantly. "Well, excuse me if this is *the* most fascinating thing I've ever heard. I mean, two little girls are playing in the front yard, they vanish, and then only one comes back. Creepy." A chill runs from the nape of my neck down my spine. I glance over my shoulder and squint into the woods. I'm usually an unshakable pro at recounting this story—even as a precocious third grader narrating the tale for show-and-tell— but there's something about today that makes me want to whisper its details, hushed and mumbled so the trees can't hear.

"Don't forget the bit about Stella's hair being braided. Her mom swore it was in piggies when she dropped her off, but she came back with a French braid." Zoey smacks her lips salaciously as she wades through the shallows and out of the lake. Her blond pixie-length hair hangs in her eyes, and she adjusts her too-tiny bikini top. Zoey has huge boobs; her favorite hobby is making them look even bigger by wearing the scantest triangles to cover up little more than nipple. Zoey is my oldest friend. She was supposed to be there that day, picking juicy red strawberries from the tangle of vines that lined the dirt lane in front of Jeanie's house, the day Jeanie disappeared. Caleb came down with chicken pox the night before, and their mom put Zoey on lockdown. Funny that an infectious virus likely saved Zoey's life. I can't help but wonder what saved mine. The vines of berries were all hacked down soon after Jeanie went missing, like their fruit was poisonous or somehow to blame.

These are the things I focus on: Zoey home that day; Jeanie being taken; rotten strawberries smashed into the ground. I don't like to focus on my part in the story. Not because I'm traumatized; I'm not. It gives me the creeps, though, that ultimately, somewhere in the never-never land of my brain is what happened to Jeanie. No matter how much I want to, I can't help her.

There are already too many things in the world that are out of the control of a seventeen-year-old girl. I don't need another.

Zoey winces, tiptoeing over the pebbled shore. "You know, now that I think about it, you look a lot like Jeanie did." She props her hands on her hips, examining Cole. "Maybe whatever skeeze grabbed her will come out of hiding and try to snatch your slutty ass. Maybe you'd like it." Zoey runs her tongue over her lips suggestively before combusting into giggles. Cole manages a laugh, but her eyes cut to the tree line.

I nail Zoey on the forehead with a green gummy bear. "You look nothing like her," I tell Cole. "Jeanie had bright-red hair and freckles. And anyway, the police think it was a crime of opportunity or something. Nothing like that has happened since, and they couldn't find any suspects, so they don't think whoever did it was local. They're long gone, and Savage is safe and boring again."

"You've got the boring right." Zoey rolls her eyes and bites the head off the recovered gummy. "And the cops are total jerk-offs, since I can think of at least two handfuls of creepies in this town that I'd consider suspects solely based on how pervy they look." Michaela cannonballs into the lake and Zoey screams, "You slutarella!" I shield my soda from the splash.

"Change of subject now, please, because this scary drivel is all anyone is going to talk about tonight," Michaela groans as she wades to shore. She's wearing a conservative black one-piece; her long, dark-brown hair is plastered to her head, making her large, cat-shaped eyes look like giant mutant almonds. Michaela's gone to school with Zoey and me since her family moved from Michigan in the eighth grade. She's on the honor roll, is an insanely talented web designer, and is the founding member of the Female Leaders of Tomorrow club at school.

Michaela is the polar opposite of Zoey in just about every way. She's reserved and chaste and believes in getting ahead by following the rules better than everybody else. She's also ridiculously pretty in that blazer-and-jeans-wearing sort of way. Zoey either goes braless or wears a push-up; she thinks all first dates should end with making out and doesn't think a skirt can ever be too short. Zoey doesn't follow the rules; she breaks them right in authority's face, with so much gut that teachers end up stifling smiles. Zoey lives for now, now, *now*; Michaela lives for tomorrow. I ping-pong between these two poles.

"It'll be all séance BS and horndog jocks telling scary stories so they can get close and dry-hump you," Michaela adds, wringing the water from her hair. It sounds morally bankrupt, and maybe it is, but every year for as long as I can remember, the upperclassmen at

Wildwood High have called today the Day of Bones. At about this time eleven years ago, I was wandering back into Jeanie's front yard, where her hysterical mother was screaming our names. At least our predecessors didn't immediately deem the anniversary of this tragedy the highlight of their social calendars. Day of Bones started out with a bunch of drunk seniors searching for Jeanie's bones in a demented scavenger hunt—they actually thought they were helping the investigation. I suppose they would have if they'd ever found anything. But I guess it was too much work and not enough drinking. Next it morphed into a memorial and now it's just a twisted excuse for a keg and ghost stories. A very different kind of "boning" on everyone's mind. Every year Wildwood students go to Blackdog Lake for a bonfire. Whatever the debauchery, I am basically the guest of honor.

"One more question, please, S," Cole begs. She didn't ask if the nickname was okay the first time Zoey brought her to lunch with us. But there was a hopeful quality to the breathy way she said it, and I kind of like it. It's new, like her. I smile and nod. "So um . . . I don't know how to say this, but nothing weird happened to you? Like . . ." The apples of her cheeks burn crimson. I know exactly what she's getting at.

"No, I wasn't molested or anything. The doctors and shrinks said I was totally fine in that department." And it's the truth. There wasn't one caramel-colored hair hurt on my head, although Zoey is right about it being braided. As far as anyone could tell, that's all that happened to me.

Michaela kneels at the foot of my towel and digs through her tote. "I'm staaaarving. Are we doing dinner? My mom is sooo not going to let me take her car after last time."

Her gaze cuts pointedly to Zoey, who rolls her eyes. "Last time" was last weekend, when Zoey thought it was hysterical to tie her push-up bra to the antenna of Michaela's mom's sedan before we drove around downtown. It was pretty epic—C cups like a banner in the wind announcing our arrival—right up until we passed the fire chief, who lives next door to Michaela and recognized her mother's car. Michaela's parents aren't as hands-off as the rest of ours. They're ancient and already have grandkids from Michaela's older sisters. They're retired and constantly breathing down her neck.

Michaela stops rifling through her bag. She braces her hands on her knees and waits for an apology overdue by six days. Zoey makes a point to color code the gummies at the heart of her palm just so it's obvious how much she isn't sorry. "I'll drive," I offer. I don't want the standoff to continue. Most of why Zoey and Michaela work is that they're polar opposites, but occasionally opposites combust. More accurately: Zoey combusts. "I have to eat dinner with the parent, so be at my house by eight," I add.

"But you're never gonna make it with Taylor if you're all stiff and sober," Zoey whines. Cole devolves into giggles as Zoey emphasizes "stiff."

"Maybe we should have him pick us up from Stella's and we can watch him ogle her snowballs?" Zoey says, pressing her boobs—or snowballs as she calls them—together. She peeks up at me through thick lashes and bats them flirtatiously. Cole makes kissing noises.

"Not gonna happen," I shout above their sound effects. Turning tonight into a flirt fest seems disrespectful. And I can't blow my whole disinterested thing now by calling and bumming a ride.

Even Michaela, who I can usually count on as an antidote for Zoey's antics, has this giddy grin on her face. Michaela's sworn off boys until she finishes her early admission apps for college. In the meantime, she's taking living vicariously through us to heart. "I'll be DD with Stella's car," she says slyly.

Cole cheers and Zoey flashes a conspirator's grin at Michaela before turning a pout on me. I take aim and lob a gummy bear at Zoey's cleavage. I lean back on my towel. I can feel Zoey staring, but I ignore her. I've been off all day. Ever since she arrived at my house this morning and I answered the door with dark bulges under my aching eyes. Thinking of today made it hard to sleep last night. I'd hash it out with Zoey—the only one I ever talk to about it, since she's the only one who lived all the aftermath with me—but lately she has zero tolerance for anything that isn't hooking up or going out.

My eyes close, and I let the warmth of the sun wash over me. The breeze rattles the oak leaves, making them chime like thousands of miniature bells. I inhale the air, fragrant with damp soil and pine needles. Everything is still wet and gleaming from springtime showers. Soon the trees will be brittle and dry, nothing more than kindling for campfires.

The others talk about Zoey's end-of-the-summer rager, the Fourth of July, and Michaela's trip back east for college visits. Zoey makes a bad joke about Michaela sizing up the student body at Brown. Cole jabbers on about hosting her first house party next week. I can almost see their vivid expectations for break, brightly colored and shimmering like the fireworks they're looking forward to, against the backdrop of my eyelids. I let their voices melt away and concentrate on the beat of wings. Overhead a large bird, maybe a hawk or raven, circles. I feel its shadow slide over my torso as it flies above us. The faint babble of a stream slices through the rustle of the woods a few hundred feet from where we sit. It's full of skinny silver-scaled fish darting around, sparkling in the sun.

". . . I said I'd totally go, but only if it was a group thing. . . ." I listen in to Zoey. Michaela responds with something agreeable, Cole giggles, and I tune out again.

The bird circles for another loop. The momentary lapse of the sun's warmth on my skin as the bird eclipses it sends shivers through me. I peek through my lashes and try to decipher the featureless silhouette in the sky. Long, straggly black feathers that twitch in the wind and a white hooked beak protruding from a head covered in what looks like orange melted wax.

"Ewww," Michaela says. "A vulture means there's something rotting nearby."

Zoey glares at the trespasser. "Nothing dead better stink up our cove."

"Sooo gross," Cole whines.

Michaela lets her sunglasses dip down the bridge of her nose and studies the feathered creature. "It's circling over us, though," she says matter-of-factly. I shiver again. The bird hovers twenty or thirty feet above. There's a rustling in the brush behind us and the resounding snap of a branch. I whip around and stare into the gloom.

"Jumpy much?" Zoey teases, but her smile doesn't reach her eyes. She'd never admit it, but today always spooks her, too. I sense the bird continuing to loop overhead. The shadows are thick in the woods, and it's impossible to see more than a few feet deep. I keep my eyes trained on the spot where I heard the stick snap. It wasn't the light crackle of chipmunks scurrying over decaying leaves and acorns, but the heavy footstep of a person.

"Who is that?" Michaela whispers. I reluctantly turn from guarding against the woods. On the opposite shore, a hundred yards away, a figure stands between two tree trunks along the edge of the forest. His face is masked in shadows, but by his jeans and short-cropped hair, he's obviously a guy. "Is he spying on us?"

Zoey jumps to her feet and yells, "Hey, jerkwad. Stare much? Eff off or we'll call the cops." Cole grabs for her hoodie and pulls it over her head. I wiggle on my jean shorts and stand with Zoey. Teeny-tiny Zoey, weighing in at not a feather over a hundred pounds, fists balled, ready to keep us all safe in her string bikini. Dread coils in my stomach. It's like I swallowed a viper. The stranger takes a step forward.

"What the . . . ?" Michaela mutters. He's maybe a couple of years older than us and he's vaguely familiar. The kind of familiar that suffocates you with déjà vu, like recalling a nightmare in gruesome flashes. He isn't looking at us. Instead his eyes are glued to the vulture circling above our heads. His lips move furiously, repeating something over and over, but the words are only mouthed, not meant to reach us.

Chapter Two

I force myself to unclench my fists. Michaela and Cole frantically pack their things at my feet. Someone shoves me a step forward, and my towel is snatched from the ground. The stranger stands frozen as a statue, a foot from the trees, eyes trained on the sky. Zoey's shouting. I'm not sure what. She's livid. This is our secret place. This is her safe place, where she thinks nothing bad could ever happen. I know better. I know bad things happen everywhere. The slope of his cheekbones, the squared jaw, the hooded eyes—they all add to the tension thrashing my stomach.

Zoey claws at my elbow. I tear myself away from staring at him to see that the girls have packed up our cove day, the provisions loaded in their arms. Cole and Michaela stand at the mouth of the woods, eager to escape. I snap out of my stupor and let Zoey drag me from the shore. I slip over the moss-covered rocks. Just as we're engulfed by trees, I turn to steal one last look over my shoulder. The stranger stares directly at me, angles his head as if he's studying me, and winks before turning away to be swallowed by a copse of trees. A sly wink that makes me feel like an accomplice. *Like we're sharing a joke.*

"Who the hell was that?" Michaela shouts. She never swears, so I know she's shaken up.

Cole gushes, "I mean, it was sooo weird that he was there staring up at the sky like a zombie." She's too excited to be frightened.

"And he didn't even respond to us," Michaela adds.

Zoey and I keep close behind them. It's only a few degrees cooler under the shade of the canopy, but I'm freezing. Zoey is wearing her own backpack with my tote's leather strap slung across her chest, our beach towels bundled in one of her arms as she reaches her free hand out for mine. I seize it like I'd grab a life raft.

"Probably just some jerk-off tourist camping at one of the sites," Zoey says. "He was just trying to freak us out. I should have gone after him with my Mace." Picturing Zoey taking off after the stranger with her key-chain spray can of Mace loosens the knots in my stomach.

I open my mouth to say that he looked familiar, then shut it. Better not to eek Cole and Michaela out. I'll tell Zoey when we're alone. I'm sure it's nothing. If it had been any other day, I wouldn't have thought a thing about it. We would have laughed and flipped him off; maybe if we'd been buzzed on pink wine or beer, Zoey would have flashed him; Michaela would have called him "crack-atoa," her signature insult. It's only that today is . . . well, *today.* Superstitious, I know. I'm not usually such a mental patient. It's like the more time that passes, the less of a grip I have.

It's totally my fault. I should have left well enough alone, but I got curious last year. The same detectives who were assigned my case eleven years ago come by every September. Detectives Shane and Berry go through the same routine with me. First we exchange hi-how-are-yous, because at this point they've watched me grow up. Then the same old questions: Have you remembered anything new? Seen any faces that look familiar? Dreamed about that day? Recovered any memories from the years before? The answer is always no. It doesn't even faze them anymore.

Sure they were hopeful the first few years, eagerly leaning forward, notepads at the ready; now they're resigned. Haunted, even—if I'm being all touchy-feely about it—with their dead stares. They don't bat an eyelash when I have nothing new for them. It's almost a relief that the whole thing can just be left so far behind us it's ancient history.

But last September I screwed up. I let curiosity get the better of me. I wanted to read the case file from that day. Burly and gray-haired Detective Berry had launched into a rant about moving on and talking candidly with my parents, but Shane, who was only a twenty-something newbie when Jeanie was taken, gave me an infinitesimal nod when Berry bent to stow his notepad in his briefcase.

Two days later, when I reached my car in the school parking lot, Detective Tim Shane was there waiting for me. His dress shirt was rumpled and hastily tucked into his jeans, mustard stains dappled his collar, and a badge hung loosely from his belt. In the sunlight the creases carving up his forehead and eyes had the look of thin and crinkled pastry, like his skin was the buttery top layer of a croissant.

"Don't make me regret this, okay?" he said, slipping me a manila envelope. "And don't let your folks know I gave it to you." I tried to squeeze out a thank-you, but my hand shook so badly taking the envelope that we both fell silent. "You have a right to know," he muttered. I held on to that envelope, unopened, for five days. I don't know why it took me so long to muster the guts. I knew the cops didn't have a lot of evidence. There were only statements taken from me and Mrs. Talcott. No neighbors who shared the private drive were home that day, and no one reported seeing anything suspicious for days before or after. It was as though Jeanie had disintegrated. Or like she'd never existed in the first place.

I finally gathered the nerve on a Friday night when Dad was working late in Minneapolis. Mom left us when I was twelve, so I didn't have to worry about her. I told Zoey I was sick so I wouldn't be expected to make the rounds to weekend parties, and barricaded myself in my room.

At first I was crushed that there wasn't anything I didn't know about in the file. Every detail had been plastered on local and national newspaper front pages. I crumpled up the twenty pages, pissed that I'd been so stupid, until a yellow carbon copy slipped from the envelope. It was the transcript of my interview the day of Jeanie's disappearance. There in my cramped bedroom, wedged between my antique dresser and the wall, I read with mounting terror what I repeated 255 times during the course of my hour-long interview with Berry and Shane. It was Shane who kept count.

It's the only thing I told the cops until I lapsed into a silence that lasted a week. After that week was over, I emerged from my quiet as though nothing had ever been wrong. I started first grade with all the other normal kids that fall, showed no signs of post-traumatic stress, and by all grown-up accounts, developed like a healthy and happy kid. Translation: I'm not nuts.

Maybe it didn't keep me up at night then, but it does now. Now I lie awake beating back the sharp-toothed dread and horror of six-year-old me whispering furiously, "If you hunt for monsters, you'll find them."

I shake my head to clear the thought. Zoey sneaks glances behind us as we trudge through the woods. We've worn a trail over the years that makes it easy to reach the clearing off the road where we park. Once inside Zoey's SUV, Michaela's nervous laugh is like a dam bursting, and we all join in. Snuggling up against the soft leather interior, scrolling through Zoey's iPod, and breathing in the familiar smells of coffee sludge at the bottom of paper cups and cake-scented lip gloss make the freaky stranger in the woods seem far away. I'd expect this from the others; they live for drama-induced adrenaline. But I know better. At least I used to.

"Tonight should be interesting, since we're all total crackheads already," Zoey says with a laugh, steering the car on to the highway and accelerating quickly. The conversation turns to senior trip ideas and boys; within five minutes it's as though our lake day ended just as unexceptionally as it always does.

Six hours later I stand bent at the waist, blow-drying my hair. It's longer than it's been since I was a kid, and I grimace when I think about how easy Zoey's pixie cut is to style. My hair has a natural wave to it that takes hours of styling to coax it into anything not resembling a rat's nest. I flip my head over and am still working on it when the doorbell rings. Dad is home, but he'll figure that it's for me. I hurry through the hallway and catch a glimpse of him hunched over his desk in the office. Only his small stained-glass lamp is switched on.

"Dad, you're going to go blind if you don't use the overhead," I say, popping into the room and flipping the switch. He looks up from the document he's skimming. His wire-rimmed spectacles rest low on his nose, and he looks surprised to see me home.

"You look nice. You and Zoey going somewhere?" he mumbles. This is my absentminded father for you. We had his famous pasta primavera with shrimp for dinner just two hours ago, and he's already forgotten I'm home. A lawyer first and everything else second. I understand that this, plus a bunch of other crap I don't know about, is why Mom left us five years ago. Don't get me wrong, she's still a wicked witch for the way she did it. Having an affair with Dad's partner at his firm and then copping to the affair on their anniversary in front of all our friends and family was deranged. Not to mention—surprise—humiliating for me. But that is my whack-job mom for you. A woman who I only see at Christmastime now that she's busy starting her *new* family in Chicago. She and my stepdad, who I despise as much as I do lice or any other grubby parasite, are trying to get knocked up. *Can you imagine?*

I nod, but Dad isn't even looking at me anymore. "Day of Bones, you know. I'll be late, and the girls might sleep here. Is that okay?"

"Hmmm? Whatever you think, Pumpkin. Love you."

"Love you, too, Dad."

I take the stairs two at a time and run through the foyer. I fling the door open and yell, "I'll grab my bag!" before leaving Zoey alone on the porch.

"You said you'd be ready for us at eight. Michaela and Cole just drove up too," she whines. Zoey doesn't like to be kept waiting, even for a moment.

"I know, I know," I call. The shrill sound of Zoey wailing my name dogs me as I search wildly for my navy Converse tennis shoes. I make it back to the front door, where Zoey is kneeling on the carpet, scratching our cat's tummy. Moscow is a Russian Blue that we've had since I was a baby. Dad jokes that he must have a robotic ticker for a heart.

"Good-bye my chunky prince," I coo, stooping to pet his chubby belly. I snatch my keys off the table in the entryway and lock the door behind us.

Zoey gives me a sideways glance as we walk to the driveway. "You are aware that tennis shoes are only for PE and peasants, right?" I roll my eyes at her, but my cheeks burn a few degrees warmer when I sneak a peek at her red platform pumps. It's like no matter how hard I try, I always come out dressed like a big kid, while Zoey's clothes scream hotness.

In the driveway Michaela's leaning against my car door, and

Cole's sitting cross-legged on the hood. Cole tips a pink flask to her lips, and Michaela says, "Did you drink driving over? James Hammer got a DUI last summer and his college found out and they didn't let him come back for sophomore year. Now he lives in a studio with two roommates and buses tables at a Denny's." Cole winks at her and tips the flask to her lips again. I think (not for the first time) that Cole is a lot more like Zoey than Michaela.

Once in the car, Cole's excitement for the bonfire is infectious. She practically vibrates. Zoey sits shotgun and turns the music up full blast; the thumping bass makes my old Volvo's speakers rattle. Despite the bizarre afternoon, this is normal. This is my comfortable. I smile at Michaela's reflection in the rearview mirror as she studiously applies her lip gloss. Her parents get weirded out by their "baby girl" wearing makeup, so she usually forgoes the argument and does it once she's left the house. She could probably apply flawless eyeliner during a rocket launch after doing it in the car enough times.

We follow Savage's main street through downtown and keep going when it narrows into a snaking two-lane highway, running toward Blackdog Lake.

"So why this one place? Is Day of Bones always at Blackdog?" Cole hollers above the music. Zoey swats my hand when I reach to turn the volume down. She cranes her neck and twists to face the backseat.

"Yes, it's always at Blackdog!" she shouts. She'd rather holler than stop swaying in her seat. "Most Wildwood High bonfires are, even though there are a shit-ton of lakes around Savage. But there's only one spooky cemetery, and it's right along the shore." A chill runs up my arms, and I alternate holding the steering wheel with each hand to rub the eerie sensation away. I hope no one notices me spazzing out before I can get a grip.

"Omigosh, a cemetery? That is so spectacularly morbid," Cole says, straining against the seat belt and pumping her hands in the air.

Michaela pipes up, "You don't know the half of it. It's our equivalent of a lookout point. Everyone drives there to make out, and the place is packed with cars on the weekend. Windows all steamy. Everyone hooking up among the dead."

"Have you ever?" Cole asks Michaela. Michaela gives a fluted laugh and falls into being engrossed in the contents of her clutch. She's the least experienced of us—by choice, obviously—but she's still spent a handful of nights getting groped at Old Savage Cemetery. Who hasn't? She's just not the type to kiss and tell.

"We all have," I say. Most girls are shy talking about hooking up. I refuse to be. Guys shouldn't be the only ones talking about that stuff.

Zoey shrugs and winks at Cole. "Sure, it's actually kind of romantic when there's a big bonfire. Some of the tombs are absolutely to-die-for gorgeous. It's not like we're making it lying on top of a mausoleum, although I'm sure that's happened. We at least do it in our cars."

We wind deeper into the woods, following the serpentine highway to the lake's secluded eastern shore. The pine trees grow denser and taller, their boughs weaving a tight canopy, until they shut out even the pale light of the moon. For miles there are no houses, no signs of life, no buildings, no other cars. After a while I turn off the highway to take a dirt access road. A gleaming white skeleton is fastened to a wooden post marking the drive. It's secured with a thick rope, limbs dangling limply in the breeze. I'd know the turnoff even if not for Scott Townsend's dad's skeleton. Dr. Townsend is a pediatrician, and every Day of Bones, Scott kidnaps the skeleton from his study. It's even kid-size, for God's sake.

"Gross, is that real?" Cole asks.

"That's Scott Townsend's. Our girl Stella here went out with that loser for a whole year," Zoey shares gleefully. "Alas, though, in eighth grade she broke his heart." I roll my eyes at Zoey's melodramatic tone. It was way more sitting at the same lunch table and exchanging locker combos than it was dating.

"Zoey thinks every guy who isn't varsity in at least two sports is totally worthless," I explain.

"Um, and they are," Zoey replies, scandalized. "Why would any of us waste a single minute on someone who isn't killing it in high school? It only gets harder from here on, folks, and if you can't cut it in high school, the world is going to chew you up and spit you out."

I look at Zoey out of the corner of my eye. "You do realize that I could rattle off a list of, like, a hundred names that proves your theory is crap, right? Like, aren't most bajillionaires losers in high school?" But Zoey has turned her attention to reapplying her mascara and stares mesmerized by her own reflection in the rearview mirror. This is my Zoey: absolutely obsessed with bagging the most popular guys and always pursuing her idea of high school glory. And she does a bloody good job of it. Three-time homecoming queen, lead in five Wildwood drama department productions, and most Internet-stalked girl in Savage. Zoey is in it to win it, even if it's not a competition. And she's my life raft, my comfort blanket, the sister I never had. She's kept me sane through my parents' divorce, through years of Jeanie aftermath, through high school, which everyone knows is a living hell without a popular girl as your spirit guide.

Michaela and Zoey don't agree on a lot, but they do see eye to eye about killing it in high school. Michaela just doesn't value prom crowns and social chairs. While Zoey has a monopoly on pursuing *social* glory, Michaela's pursuing tomorrow's glory. She believes her ticket to college, a career as the founder of a monolithic social media site, and marrying some czar's son or a progolfer is to take every honors class in math and science, every year. Michaela is likely the only person on the planet who could have made our twosome a threesome in the eighth grade and not gotten herself kneecapped by Zoey over the last four years. They have nothing in common except me and wanting to be the best at what they do. And thankfully, they want different things.

What I want is a little harder to define, blurrier. I'm not possessed to be the best like Zoey and Michaela. I've tried a bunch of activities— from my childhood stint playing the violin, to freshman year as the world's least peppy cheerleader, to sophomore year in yearbook. Dad says I'm well rounded; Zoey says I have commitment issues.

The only thing that's stuck is writing for the *Wildwood Herald*. Originally, I joined the paper to fluff out the activities portion of my college apps, but when my first article about sex trafficking was printed—very edgy stuff in comparison to the puff pieces on sports teams and marching band trips my colleagues produce—I was hooked. Just staring at my name in bold black font next to the word "by" gave me a sugar rush. Here was an article that was by me instead of about me and Jeanie. Sure our school newspaper is only a four-page newsletter that masquerades as a news-bearing paper, but it's better than no experience if I want to write in college.

Cole—and I'd never say this to her face—is kind of an experiment. Girls have been vying to get in with the three of us for all of high school. It wasn't until Cole strolled through the quad on a Monday morning in white jean short-shorts, strappy sandals, and a DEATH TO HIPSTERS T-shirt that Zoey took notice of a newbie. Every guy in a hundred-yard radius froze as her wavy blond hair caught the wind. I think it's the first time Zoey ever felt fear. Don't get me wrong, Zoey's way hotter than Cole, and that's not just my bestie-love talking. But exotic things have a unique appeal to guys, and a girl from a SoCal beach town is as exotic as it gets. Zoey knew she had a choice to make. When we met up in the parking lot to go off campus for lunch, Zoey had Cole in tow.

I've always thought Zoey could be one of those grand-master—although she'd insist on calling herself a grand-mistress—chess players. She understood that it was better to make a friend than to see the new girl become her rival. Don't wage a war you can't win.

My car groans and shudders as I accelerate over the dirt road riddled with potholes. After a sharp right turn, we emerge onto a gravel lot. There must be sixty or seventy cars already. I park alongside a burnt-orange Mustang that I recognize as Taylor's. Cole jumps out of the car before we even stop. Zoey winks devilishly, leans over the emergency brake, and practically purrs, "You know we won't be mad if you ditch us and end up making it with Taylor."

"Doubtful. I'm still freaked over earlier." She flicks her wrist like it was nothing. "Plus, I don't really relish my first time being in a cramped backseat on the anniversary of . . . you know."

Zoey juts out her pink-gloss-coated bottom lip in a pretend pout and then grins. "I understand. Let's just have the best night ever then, 'kay?"

She tucks a rogue wisp of hair behind my ear as Michaela reaches for my keys and adds, "I'll drive you home the nanosecond you want to go." I smile gratefully at them both.

"Hurry up, lesbos!" Cole yells from outside the car, dancing on her tiptoes.

Out of the car, the pulsating music makes the ground quake; the bass works its way into my bones, and I can't help but look forward to dancing under the stars. A few hundred yards from the shore, we walk through a labyrinth of parked cars. With every step, the details of the bonfire zoom into sharper focus.

The campfire is as tall as several stacked cars and as wide as the length of one. "Crazeballs," Cole whispers in awe. Its heat warms my face from a hundred feet away. All around it stand girls and boys in little more than their underwear.

"Ha," Zoey scoffs. "Amateurs. That's exactly why I wore my swimsuit under my dress." She pulls her sundress up and over her head.

The fire rages on the rocky shore; the sky is open and empty above the massive tower of flames. The surrounding trees are frosted with white lanterns, hooked along their boughs, glowing like mammoth fireflies. The iron fence of the cemetery runs the length of the gravel lot to the left of us, and candles speckle the gravestones and tombs. Cole's mouth flops open as she absorbs the spectacle. I can just make out some kids wearing Halloween masks. Monster-type stuff with messily stitched scars, ghoulish grins, and oozing blisters. Maybe I feel it all more—the heat of the fire on my cheeks, the snap of the cold where it doesn't touch, and the masquerade—because Cole is experiencing it for the first time.

A drunken sophomore staggers past us with fangs in his mouth and fake blood painted down the corners of his lips. Zoey tosses her hair from her eyes and glowers. "Vampire loser. What do these freaks think this is? Effing Halloween?" There are a few plastic corpses hung from the trees, nooses knotted around their necks. Leave it to my twisted classmates at Weirdowood to go above and beyond the disturbing. We're only a couple of yards away when Janey Bear, who is the biggest loose-lipped gossip at school, spots me.

"She's here!" Her shrill cry slices through the thudding music. I freeze as face after face turns expectantly toward me. Their mouths are agape, grinning, muffling giddy laughter, practically salivating like hungry beasts who crave drama. A pack of sadists, really. All high on the mystery of what happened to someone else; of what twisted our little town into knots; of what they get to retell to kids who aren't from here, claiming a little corner of the horror for themselves.

You'd think I'd be used to it by now. The last three years of high school have played out identically. Since my freshman year, my infamy as "the one who got away" has earned me an epic amount of popularity. I guess it could have turned out differently. If I'd been all morbid and gone goth in steel-toed boots and a safety pin through my eyebrow, then it would have turned me into a social pariah. Given that I'm more skinny jeans and ballet flats, am pretty with bright-green eyes, and have a monopoly on the whole survivor thing, my past has only added legend to my social status. It's like those castles and forts you learn about in history that are glimmering museums full of tourists now but used to be leper colonies. That's me, former leper colony.

But this time when the crowd turns, lifting their red plastic cups full of beer and toasting me, actually cheering me for being the one to survive, I see six-year-old Jeanie directly in front of the fire. Her cheeks are filthy and striped with tears; her dress is torn at the collar. It's a blue gingham jumper that I recognize immediately as what she was wearing the day she was taken. This isn't earth-shattering, since that detail was splashed all over the news.

What is strange is that she has a trickle of blood oozing down from her scalp, slithering over the skin between her eyes. And all at once I know that this is not my imagination. I've pulled this from the depths of my charred memory. She's upright in front of me, but by the way her hair is pooled around her head, defying gravity, I get the impression that I'm looking down at her, lying on her back. For the first time, I can remember smelling Jeanie's fear as she wet her pants, while I reached to hold her bloodstained hand.

Chapter Three

A hundred pairs of eyes crawl over me. After the image disappears I'm swallowed by the memory, capable only of staring at the empty patch of dirt where Jeanie was. Zoey shouts something bitchy and sarcastic at the crowd. They laugh like she's kidding. She jabs her elbow into my forearm. Her skin on my skin jolts me aware, and I try to recover with a toothy smile and a wink. Everyone is either as observant as a wall or too drunk to notice my nutso behavior, because they cheer in response. Zoey turns to me, concerned, but before she can say anything, Taylor separates from the crowd, his duo of jock scum as one seething mass of testosterone and cinnamon-flavored whiskey in his shadow.

"Hey, Stella, Zoey," he says. He carries an extra red cup and offers me the beer. I try to get ahold of myself, but it feels like gluing one of Mom's cobalt-blue vases back together after smashing it into a million pieces on the floor. I remembered something. Should I be jumping for joy or sobbing in fear? I don't do either. Instead I take the plastic cup from Taylor, and without saying a word, I pound its contents. Definitely not *beer*. Liquid heat sears my throat.

"What's up?" Zoey takes control. "Hey, guys," she adds, nodding to Taylor's two buddies. Zoey has hooked up in various degrees with both of them. Drew and Dean play lacrosse with Taylor, and for some reason I always have trouble telling them apart. Maybe Zoey does too, which could explain why she's made out with both at random. I'd feel bad for them if it wasn't for how infamous lacrosse players are at Wildwood for being players on and off the field. I suspect that this is why Michaela steered Cole toward less chartered male territory in the direction of the kegs, once the boys sauntered over to us. Taylor is more decent than most: He dates in our grade, his exes never say anything bad about him, and he always opens doors for girls—even the unpopular ones. There's also the issue of that irresistible smile.

"You know, just knocking back some beers and shots," Taylor states the obvious. Okay, so he's not exactly Ivy material, but even through my conflicted haze, he's hot. Over Taylor's chiseled shoulder, Michaela and Cole melt into the crowd. Cole is a social butterfly, and since she spent only two weeks of our junior year with us at Wildwood, she's eager to mingle. Flickering light from the fire dances on the tree trunks. It makes it look like the whole world is moving, swaying and spinning to the music's rhythm. The liquid I chugged spreads fire up my spine from my stomach, and I swear I can feel it seizing my brain, screwing with my equilibrium.

Taylor leans forward, looking at me expectantly. Zoey's blue eyes widen as she realizes I haven't been listening. "Sorry, what?" I ask, shaking my head. Taylor's cocky grin fades. I try to steady myself with a deep breath, but smoke fills my lungs. I sputter as my throat thickens. I'm standing too close to the fire, and Jeanie's face and its curling trickle of blood keep flashing before me.

"I'll—I'll be right back, sorry," I stammer, turning before Zoey can grab hold of me. With the blaze at my back, its dancing flames behind me, I'm better, more solid. I move away from the crowd and let the yips and shouts fade behind me. I veer straight for the wrought-iron gate of the cemetery. If I can just catch my breath, sit down on a bench, I'll be alone with my thoughts. All of this is doable. It's only that I haven't had a moment to process that I'm losing it.

Zoey calls my name once but doesn't follow. I reach the cemetery gate and duck under the scalloped archway. Out of habit I reach above my head and tap the iron heart that marks its apex. Zoey told me once that it would keep unsettled spirits away. Otherwise those that aren't in heaven or hell haunt anyone who enters the cemetery. I know, I know. I'm positive Zoey made it up. But whatever . . . better safe than sorry. Stuff like that really makes my skin crawl.

Anyway, the cemetery is spooky enough without tempting ghosts. It's one of the oldest in the country, with gravestones hundreds of years old. No one's been buried here for over sixty. Zoey said she heard it was originally a Native American burial ground that was dug up by settlers. She could have been full of nonsense, but I don't feel bad repeating it. Weren't settlers always digging up sacred stuff? Distant giggling and a moaned, "Oh nooo," make me focus. I swerve in the opposite direction.

I swat boughs from the low-hanging willows brushing my face. The candles are everywhere to guide me. I pass my favorite marble statue of a weeping angel and caress its broken wing. There's a smooth granite bench rooted to the ground across from the statue and a small, enclosed family plot. I lie down on it. The cold seeps from the stone into my back. I shiver. Blackdog State Park is far enough from the city that the stars blaze like tiny lightbulbs illuminating the sky's blackness. The candles speckling the cemetery have the look of fallen stars nestled in nooks and crannies.

I close my eyes for a moment, but Jeanie's bloodied face is there, like an indelible memory I've always had and not one that just reared its warty face. I open them and stifle a scream. Two brown eyes hover above me.

I bolt upright. "Sam!" I shout. "Jeez, you scared the crap out of me."

He takes a backward step, flicks his hair off his forehead, and shoves his hands deep into his pockets. "Hey, sorry. I saw you take off and wanted to make sure you were okay," he says, ending with an uncertain smile.

I take a deep breath and shrug. "You know . . . it always feels weird to be here . . . on this day." What's *weird* is that Sam—not Zoey, not Taylor, not Michaela, not Cole—cared enough to follow me. "What's with the vest?" I point to the bright-red atrocity he's wearing over his T-shirt. If Zoey were here to see this, she'd roll her eyes and say *I told you so*. Sam Worth used to be one of our best friends. We were inseparable as kids, right up until Zoey decided we wanted to be popular and that Sam was destined to be the King of Loserdom.

Although Sam isn't a Cyclops, he isn't the kind of guy that most girls date. At least not girls I know.

Sam looks down and practically turns green. "Oh crap, it's my uniform," he says, ripping the vest off his shoulders so quickly I think it might tear. "I'm always forgetting I have it on." He wads the polyester nightmare up in a ball and tries stuffing it in his jeans pocket. Half of it sticks out.

The Star Wars T-shirt he's rocking underneath isn't much better. I try not to laugh. "Uniform for what?" I ask, scooting over so there's room for Sam on the bench. Zoey would flip if she saw this, but I'm just off balance enough to flirt with disaster.

"I work at BigBox," he says, plopping down next to me, springy and eager like a puppy.

BigBox is one of those giant you-can-buy-everything-under-the-sun stores. "Since when?"

"Every summer for the last four years," he says, a hint of a laugh in his voice. "It's okay, though, there's no reason you'd know."

I blink at him through the darkness. Is he being sarcastic or is he *really* that nice? I mean, I do the best I can. Zoey erased Sam from her social radar, but when I see him in the halls, I always say hey. No, I'm not twelve years old, sporting a feathered headdress and playing cowboys and Indians in the woods with him anymore. And I probably wouldn't ever in a million years follow him into a spooky cemetery to make sure he was okay. But I keep Zoey off his back.

It's not like I can invite him to eat lunch with us. That's not how high school works. Even my popularity couldn't take the hit of me being seen hanging out with science-fiction-loving, second-hand-clothing-wearing, BigBox-working Sam Worth.

It's kind of a shame, because if Sam ever tried, he could be vaguely hot. In the pale light I can just make out the cluster of tiny freckles on the bridge of his nose—they make me think of sunny days. He has muddy-brown eyes that make it hard to look away. Tousled bedhead hair. That whole I'll-listen-to-everything-you-have-to-say-and-then-write-you-a-love-letter thing. Girls eat that stuff up. Instead he's tragically committed to achieving new astronomical levels of bizzaro-ness. I can't be sure, but I think I glimpse a shoelace as his belt tonight.

"Hella Stella, I said, 'Are you okay?'" Sam repeats himself for what's likely the millionth time.

I bristle at my old nickname. The word "hella" was sooo middle school and plus, I don't need to give people any more reason to talk about me. I scan the cemetery around us nervously. I can see a small group of stoners lighting up twenty feet away. Definitely not worried about them overhearing. But Janey Bear and her bestie, Kate Lucey, are staggering down the path toward us, arms locked, red cups in their hands, jaws clacking. Fan-freaking-tastic. I bet they're only out here prowling for sordid hookups to gossip about. Janey couldn't keep a secret if her life depended on it. Me sharing a romantic moment with Sam Worth in this gloomy cemetery will be the scandal that she's dreamed of her whole life. Before the night is over, rumors will be spreading that we were hooking up between the tombs, Sam calling out my childhood nickname between thrusts, me confessing my eternal love. *Gag me.* And of course, if that happens, I can kiss ever kissing Taylor Martinson good-bye.

I turn back to him and mouth, "Don't call me that."

His eyes widen, and he reminds me of this owl stuffed toy I used to have. "Call you what? Hella Stella? Why?" he says so loudly I know Janey must hear.

I take a shaky breath and glance toward the girls. Janey's staring back at me with narrow-set blue eyes that don't miss a thing. "Sam, just don't," I murmur urgently. "Please shut up." I try to scare him with a nasty glare, but he starts to chuckle.

"What's up with you tonight, Hella Stella?" he asks right as Janey and Kate stop in front of us.

"Hi, Stella," Kate says, her pitch swinging with joy over discovering us. Even she knows they've caught me red-handed. Janey just stares, the mole on her wormy upper lip twitching. We're not exactly friends. Zoey calls Janey and Kate leeches behind their backs. She says they're really nice to the actually popular people so that they can latch on and get invited to parties. I dislike them for different reasons. They're always looking to knock you down a peg. Like they think of being popular as being on a varsity team. Someone should tell them that making other people less popular doesn't guarantee that they'll be called off the bench. It just makes them bitches. I'd like to tell them that this very moment. Instead I take the easy way out.

I hold my finger up to the girls for them to wait a second and then cross my arms against my chest. "I said don't call me that. I'm not ten anymore, Sam. And apparently you need me to spell it out for you. We're. Not. Friends. When are you going to get that through your head?" The words taste bitter in my mouth.

Sam's eyes are glued to mine. His top lip begins to bow like he's going to smile or laugh. I feel my bitchiest scowl falter. He stands with his hands in his pockets—the left one still bulging with his vest—and completely ignores the other two girls. For some reason a little trill of satisfaction runs through me that he acts like they don't exist. He smiles like he knows better—better about what I can't imagine—and says to me, "Did you know that in the Middle Ages people used to write the news on cemetery walls? Cemeteries were the first public parks." My jaw literally drops, I'm so shocked at the random factoid. I guess we are *technically* in a cemetery, but I didn't expect him to respond spouting like an encyclopedia. "Take care of yourself tonight, Hella Stella." And with that, he walks away.

I can barely tear my eyes away from his back. What is he thinking saying something like that to me? And in front of our school's biggest gossip hoarders. Doesn't he understand that I already have enough people whispering about me? I get roller-coaster stomach as I turn back to the girls.

Janey's gawking wordlessly at me. Her eyes are glazed doughnut holes imagining all the headlines she can spin out of this. "Do you have a mint?" I snap. I can practically see the cogs winding tighter in her head. She fumbles through her purse and produces a box of Altoids.

She pops open the lid and holds them out to me. "What was his problem?" she asks, her tone all sugar.

"Total freak," Kate says, smacking her lips.

I snatch two mints and pop them into my mouth to banish the foul taste that's still there. "Biggest freak ever," I mutter halfheartedly. "Whatever, I have to get back to Zoey, byes." I jump up and hurry away from them. I wrap my arms around myself as I go, trying to ease the queasiness that's crept up on me.

"God, you're such a fugly witch," I scold myself. But Sam didn't give me a choice. I practically begged him to shut up. Pleaded with him not to call me that. Maybe it's for the best? Maybe it was the humane thing to do? Yeah, it's better if Sam gives up trying to be my friend. It's been too many years. I mean, he even knows I lied about Scott Townsend being my first kiss because I didn't want to admit it was him. How could he stand me after that?

The mints mingle with the sourness in my mouth. The taste of shame or guilt or remorse. It's rancid like the shish kebab Zoey and I got from a food truck the last time we were in Minneapolis. I spit the mints on the ground just before I exit the cemetery, tapping the heart on the iron gate to leave any clinging spirits behind me. The bonfire is almost exactly how I left it, except that there are more half-naked girls and boys dancing on the shore. Cole has stripped down to her bra and skirt and is gyrating against a senior football player who was a transfer last year too. Michaela's still fully clothed, but she's actually dancing with a guy, albeit two feet away from him—but dancing is dancing, right?

Zoey's on the opposite side of the bonfire, standing on a folding chair, surrounded by guys. She's a queen addressing her subjects from a pedestal. One after another each boy in the crowd takes a shot of something clear, and Zoey knocks her own head back, lips suctioned suggestively around a bottle of booze. I catch her unfocused eye, and she beckons me over with a roundabout, inebriated wave. I motion for her to wait. So that's how the night will end. Zoey will outdance, outflirt, and outplay everyone. I'll have to drag her away from the party. What's new? At least I won't have to hold her pixie hair back when she hurls in the parking lot.

I make a beeline toward the crowd of dancers. I start searching for him before I even admit to myself who I'm looking for. I crane my neck and stand on my tiptoes, straining to glimpse Sam. This foul taste in my mouth isn't going away until I apologize. If I can just tell him that I only said what I said because of Janey and Kate. He has to understand how it is.

Even though the shore is wide and long, my classmates are squished and sandwiched into one another, like invisible walls are pressing them together. His being on the dance floor is a long shot, and I'm not surprised that my search comes up empty. Small bunches of teenagers clot around the bonfire, but he's not with any of them. Maybe I should yell his name? No, my voice won't travel over the blaring music. And that would really get people talking about us.

There's a group of twitchy-looking boys about ten yards removed from everyone else. While the rest of my classmates are half-nude, these boys are in glasses and long sleeves; beads of sweat clinging to their temples. They're like the boys who wear T-shirts at the public swimming pool to hide their concave chests. One is actually sporting a sweater-vest—the kind with wooden buttons my father wears.

I sidle up to them. I don't mean any offense, but they are the only guys present who look like they're friends with Sam. Four moon-shaped faces—three with acne and a fourth with sideburns that defy my understanding of how facial hair grows—gawk at me. The boy nearest actually scurries back, giving the impression of a shivering daddy longlegs, dodging my tennis shoe's sole. "Are you here with Sam Worth?" I shout to be heard over the music. "SAM. WORTH. Have you seen him?"

"He left with Anna Young," Sweater-Vest pipes up, brazenly holding my eye contact while his friends stare at their shoes.

I want to ask, *Who the hell is she?* But in my head it sounds more scorned than it should. I flash an awkward smile and mumble, "Okay," and shuffle away from social Siberia. I fumble through my bag for my cell. A text to him will be better than nothing. Before my fingers can jab the touch screen, someone yanks on my arm, tugging me around to face them.

"Omigosh, you have freakish drunk strength," I gasp at Zoey, rubbing my arm where her fingers dug into my skin. Her hair is disheveled, and a mist of sweat shines on her chest. She's still wearing her bikini, and I feel an overwhelming urge to drape the hoodie I keep in my purse over her. "What's wrong? You look like a possessed pixie," I shout over the music. She's furiously chewing her bottom lip; her eyes are almost watering with concern. I can smell the vodka on her breath. In a flash Michaela is there, towing Cole by the hand. How on earth did Zoey get Michaela's attention on the dance floor?

"You're not going to believe who is back in town," Zoey yells, placing both hands on my shoulders. I don't know if she means to hold me up or steady herself. "Jeanie's big brother." Michaela gasps, and a few junior girls turn to watch us, obviously jealous of whatever drama we're enduring. Zoey pivots to face Cole and zips through the details. "He's a total psycho, went off his rocker after Jeanie disappeared. Their parents sent him to some reform thing, but when he came back in middle school, he basically stalked Stella. Then he got sent away again because her dad complained to the cops. The last time he came back he got some barista pregnant and ran away. He was watching us at the cove today." I hear every one of Zoey's words, but they're difficult to process. Every little bit I make sense of, my brain rewinds, and I find myself unable to get over the fact that Zoey got Michaela's attention in that crowd of grinding dancers.

Michaela laces her fingers in mine, and Cole sympathetically squeezes my shoulder. Of course it was Daniel there at the cove today. I knew he looked familiar. I guess I haven't seen him all up close and personal since I was twelve and he was fifteen. The last time he came back, when I was a freshman, Dad threatened to file a restraining order and the Talcott family became more reclusive than Bigfoot. I never saw Daniel again, although Zoey swore she could feel him watching us.

"Wait for it," Zoey says dramatically. "He's here tonight." Michaela not only gasps this time, she staggers backward like the words have a physical weight that barrels into her. Cole's eyes look about to pop from their sockets. The earth tilts, and my knees bend and straighten like I'm trying to find my sea legs. I close my eyes to steady myself, but all I can see is fifteen-year-old Daniel, holding me against the brick retaining wall that framed my middle school parking lot. Its ragged edges scraped the skin on my back. "Tell me what happened," he demanded for the millionth time, teeth bared. And as always with Daniel, I took a deep breath and promised him that I really didn't remember anything. I was choking on tears, but I managed to get the words out. He asked me again and again, stopping only because Sam heard me howling and came to my rescue, threatening to call my dad. Sam did tell Dad, and Daniel was sent off to another reform school.

Even as a kid I was in awe of Daniel's devotion to his sister. I dreamed of having a big brother who loved me like that. It was only frightening because his boundless suspicion was directed at me. I never blamed him for it. He'd gotten it in his head that I knew more than I let on, and as early as I can remember, he insisted that I was a slippery shit-faced liar. Those were the exact words he shouted at me when I was seven and he was ten, at a school assembly. That got him suspended for the first time, but not the last.

Zoey wraps her arms around me, and for a moment I am completely safe. Zoey is the closest thing I've ever had to a love like Daniel had for Jeanie. I scrunch my eyes closed. Plump drops of water begin to fall. At first it's only one on the bridge of my nose and then another caught in my eyelash. Within a few seconds the pitter-patter of random drops crescendos, and sheets of warm rain cascade down on us. The party erupts into chaos.

"You've got to be effing kidding me!" Michaela shrieks, futilely shielding her pin-straight hair with her palms. "I just blew my hair out." Zoey releases me and holds her head back, catching drops in her mouth. Her cheeks are flushed pink; her lip gloss is smeared. Groups of drenched teens stampede toward the parking lot, hooting and laughing. Others stay put, swaying to the music still shaking the ground. Zoey lets rip a witch's cackle and claps her hands in delight. She lets the seriousness of the moment wash away with her mascara. A senior footballer whose neck is as thick as his head chants for a wet T-shirt contest, and Zoey disappears into the crowd on the shore.

"Zoey!" I shout after her. "You're not even wearing a T-shirt." The rain pounds on relentlessly. My sundress is completely soaked, and the insides of my shoes are soggy. "You guys go to the car and I'll get her," I yell as our faces are illuminated by a bolt of lightning.

Cole and Michaela take off running. I watch them disappear into the rush of cars swerving over mud and around underclassmen begging for rides. The thunder follows quickly, and the roaring clap is so loud it's everywhere, surrounding me, a part of me. You'd think that thunder and lightning lakeside would send more of my peers searching for shelter, but when I turn to find Zoey, the number of dancers bumping on the shore has multiplied. The bonfire sizzles to nothingness, the flames extinguished. Only the battery-operated lanterns and the moon cast light. In the dark the dancers' limbs and torsos dissolve together, becoming a rhythmic shadow creature, shuddering and pumping.

Bottles of alcohol soar from open hand to open hand. I catch sight of Zoey's slender fingers groping one. The gold bangle she's worn since she was a little girl winks in the light at me. She's a good fifteen people deep in the crowd. I shout her name, but I can barely hear my own voice. Elbows jab my sides. My toes crunch as a heel grinds into my wet sneaker. I curse and fight forward. Hands grope my butt, and I try to slap them away. By the time I squeeze through the drenched and drunk cluster of bodies, she isn't where I thought she was.

I push free from the crowd. These kids have gone completely crazy. Day of Bones my ass. This has nothing to do with Jeanie Talcott. This is an excuse for them to get hammered and live without inhibitions for a night. Well, who am I kidding? Isn't that the reason for every high school party, and don't I usually L.O.V.E. it?

I whirl away from the dancers and trudge as quickly as I can through the mud up the shore in the direction of the car. Twenty more minutes of this downpour and Zoey will wade through the parking lot like a drowned kitten, begging to be let into the car. All we have to do is wait her out. My legs are wobbly, reminding me of the alcohol in my bloodstream. How much was in that cup Taylor gave me? Three, maybe four shots? Thank God Michaela's DD. My stomach lurches thinking about sitting shotgun as she careens down the narrow highway in the rain, but it's better than driving drunk and Dad finding out. Not that he'd even notice if I stumbled into the house handcuffed and singing like a drunken sailor. From behind, a calloused hand grabs my shoulder; its index finger slides under the strap of my dress. I spin around, even though I don't really need to look to know who it is.

"Daniel," I say, wiggling out of his grasp. The thud of my heart hitches. He takes a step closer. I don't move back, letting his face linger only six inches away from mine. The lightning splits the sky, revealing green eyes, grassy and speckled with brown like the swamps west of the cemetery. They're eerily similar to mine. His eyebrows were bushy when he was a kid; now they give him a wild-man look like he cave-dives and kills all his meals. They match his auburn hair.

"Didn't you turn out pretty?" He clenches his teeth too much for it to be a compliment. He's so close I can smell the alcohol on his breath. His words aren't slurred but lazy, buzzed. The only thing that frightens me more than grown Daniel is grown *drunk* Daniel. He grabs my arm, and I shudder at the heat of his skin and his words.

"Why were you watching us?" My voice is steady, to my surprise. He leans in even closer. To anyone around us we must look like boy-friend and girlfriend, or just two people about to make out in the rain. "Why did you come *here?*" I demand.

"What? You thought I wouldn't come back to see *you?* To see how you ended up?" There's mock flattery in his tone. "You think I wouldn't check on the bitch who survived instead of my sister?" He tightens his grip, and his expression darkens. "I watched you and your perfect friends playing in the water today, and all I could think was that even if Jeanie were alive, she wouldn't be there with you. She wouldn't have been good enough for you. Or hot enough. Or skinny enough." There's only malice dripping from his words. Does he know I've thought that before, that Jeanie would have grown up to be average? "Do you deny it?" His hand pulses around my arm. "You telling me you would have kept her around?"

The rain hammers down on us, its sheets of water making me blind to everything more than five feet away, everything except Daniel. He came looking for me like he always does, and instead of me scared in the parking lot like the last time, I was with a group of girls the age Jeanie would have been. He probably watched Michaela catch air before she splashed into the water. He saw how alive we looked; how unlike Jeanie. I want to swear to him that it isn't true; that Jeanie would have been there with us. But Daniel's right. "You aren't supposed to be talking to me." I try to yank my arm free, but he holds me still. "You shouldn't even be near me," I say louder.

Daniel's mouth is right at my eye level. "I kept saying, 'See, Jeanie? See, Jeanie? See? Look what you were spared. Those girls can't hurt you.'"

I lock my sagging knees and resist the urge to cover my face. As we fled the cove, Daniel was whispering to his dead sister. I know that he doesn't really mean that Jeanie's better off dead; this is the endless grief talking, the sorrow that inspires conversations with ghosts.

"Daniel, why would you come home *today?*" I already know the answer. My eyes dart upward. We're unwittingly standing under a dummy corpse. Its clothes are saturated with rain, and rivulets run from its boots. Staring at it, tears well in my eyes. I doubt he notices because my face is already slick with water. "You're here for this." I motion with my free hand. Vaguely, I register screaming coming from behind us. Not the celebratory yips about the storm or the manic laughing of the drunk dancers, but something shrill and full of alarm.

The fine lines on his lips stretch and vanish as he opens his mouth to speak. Of course he's here to see how his sister is being remembered or forgotten, how I turned out, how his parents are doing across town. He's here today for the same reason I had trouble sleeping last night; for the same reason I asked Shane for the case file. Who knows? Maybe Daniel has come back every anniversary with no one other than his parents the wiser. Before he can rumble all this at me, a sharp cry like a siren carried on the wind reaches us: "There's a body! A body!"

Chapter Four

I don't know how we go from the charged moment where I'm afraid of Daniel, to tearing through the mud and spitting rain toward the screams. One second he's clutching my arm to keep me from running, a captive to his sadness, and the next he's holding me up as I slip and slide over the eroding sludge the ground has become. We turn in unison, both of us instantly filled with dread that a body might mean something intimate to us. It could be decomposed Jeanie. It could be grown and killed Jeanie. It doesn't matter which; all that matters is that we are both running because of Jeanie.

Daniel's fingers lace tightly with mine, but it doesn't feel like holding hands. It's more like being handcuffed to him. A confusion of colors and shapes spirals around us as a dizzying crowd surges toward the cries for help. Water splashes from the ground and the sky as though we're underwater, and I wonder for a second if we should be swimming rather than running. We're in slow motion, wading through the mud to reach the cemetery. All the while the screams find us on the current of the wind.

As I reach to tap the heart on the iron gate, my tennis shoe snags the uneven rocks lining the path. I stumble forward, my hand missing the heart. Daniel's arm wraps around my waist, his left hand clings to my right, and he hoists me to my feet.

My stomach churns as we draw closer, the girl's cries getting louder as we move toward the edge of the cemetery nearest to the lake. The candles are still lit, powered by batteries like the lanterns. Their wash of light makes it possible to see Tara Boden, a sophomore who shouldn't even be here, hunched over an uprooted gravestone. Her voice is worn and ragged now, barely more than a hoarse whimper. Her shirt is unbuttoned, revealing her yellow lace bra. A junior boy is shirtless and rubbing a wide circle with his palm on her back.

Only a handful of my classmates have reached the site, teetering unsteadily on the disrupted soil. All hang back and gawk at where Tara's quivering hand points. The pelting rain washed away a ten- or fifteen-foot segment of the wrough-iron fence that separates the cemetery from the shore. Where there used to be a gradual slope down to the pebbled bank, it looks as though a giant monster took a bite.

All the things that should stay hidden at cemeteries are unearthed by the mudslide. Coffins exposed, either swept downhill by the slide or jutting at sharp angles from the ground like compound bone fractures piercing skin. Jaundiced partial skeletons litter the soil. Relief swells in me as I hope that we're only seeing the remnants of those who died a hundred years ago. Tara Boden is a drama whore;

of course she'd seize the opportunity for attention. I squirm out of Daniel's grasp. On unsteady legs I inch forward, toes of my sneakers narrowly missing ancient bones as I work my way into the shallow crater the slide left. Daniel doesn't follow. I drag my arm over my top lip, wiping off water and snot from the run.

I go from hobbling to crouching when I reach the bottom. I squint at the sludge in front of me, the votives' pallor hardly enough to see by. Gnarled tree roots. Crumbled graves. A fractured Virgin Mary statue that rests headless on its side. The clouds drift away, and the moon's light penetrates the gloom around me. A flash of yellow cloth sticking up from the mud. A nest of brown lichen or matted hair. A rubber-soled sneaker. Fuchsia-painted fingernails. Bits and pieces of a body visible in the weak light. She rests diagonally on the lid of a coffin at the bottom of the crater. Before the storm she might have been righted, hands folded and crossed on her chest, sleeping deeply on the top of an ancient grave with the look of a princess waiting to be awakened by a kiss. I suck in my breath, afraid to exhale.

I must look like I've lost my mind as I sink down to my hands and knees. The slimy soil squishes and bubbles under me. I crawl carefully, so the earth doesn't swallow me up. I choke back vomit as my hand brushes what I know is a human skull. Bones. Decomposed flesh. Eyeballs. Brain matter. Maggots. All the gross things that are likely in this soil seep into my hands and knees. But I have to get to that body. I have to make sure that it is a body and that I'm not seeing things. That I haven't lost every last ounce of sanity I had.

Out of the voices behind me I hear Zoey arguing. Demanding

that the cops be called. Barking orders in a way only Zoey can get away with. A few more feet to go. I still hold my breath. I try to let it out very gently and to draw it back in without the dead noticing. I don't want to breathe them in either.

I can see her now. Hair, hands, torso. For a second I'm grateful the body isn't dismembered, but that fades once I note the size of the features. Small and doll-like. *A little girl.* Ivory skin taut over her bones; hair is matted on her forehead. It's impossible, but my tongue presses to the roof of my mouth to say Jeanie's name. Of course it's not her. I haven't taken anatomy yet, but who doesn't know enough about decomposing corpses from watching *CSI* reruns to know that someone buried eleven years ago wouldn't be in this condition? But still. She looks young. She looks six.

I reach for her—I don't know why, since the last thing I want is to actually touch her. My hand splayed wide, fingers stretching against the joints. Three inches. Two. In the instant before I make contact, the sludge shifts and bubbles under me and I'm knocked forward against the coffin lid. The jolt rocks her head to the side, but the red hair and the flap of skin that is her scalp stay put. "Naked" is the word my brain vomits. Her head is hairless. Skinned. *Scalped.* The membrane that she should be wearing as a crown is disconnected, limp in the mud, only placed near so it might look as though she's in one piece.

"Zoey." I must say her name a hundred times in the minute it takes her to crawl, drunk and in her bikini, through the demolished graves. She reaches me, hands fumble to pull me away.

It takes twenty minutes for the police to arrive. During that time I'm a nonverbal animal completely consumed with watching and listening to those around me. Zoey torpedoes Tara Boden with insults until she leaves and returns with a blanket from her date's car. It smells of mildew, but I let her wrap it around me anyway. As we huddle together in the dark, her arm pressed against mine, I close my eyes and wish away the scene unfolding in front of me.

Daniel stands where I left him. His shoes have sunk into the mud like quicksand swallowing him up. I don't think he'd mind. He's completely still: no flinching, no twitching, no wailing. His eyes never leave the matted hair sticking up from the upturned earth, spindly as a grubby little shrub climbing toward the light, lonely away from its head.

Michaela and Cole aren't here. Probably taking cover from the rain in my car. It isn't pouring from the sky like the heavens have burst open on our heads, but it sprinkles. Yes, that's it. Jeanie went to heaven eleven years ago, and tonight they spit her back to earth. Thank God I can't form a sentence, because Zoey would have me committed.

I've come full circle since she dragged me from the mud pit of corpses. And she had to *drag* me, looping her arms under mine and guiding me away. The body's tiny hand, outstretched and decorated with peeling nail polish, momentarily rotted my sense. I was certain she was connected to Jeanie. It felt too cosmic that on this day of all days a corpse would show up. How could there even be another hurt little girl? The frosting on the cake, albeit a twisted cake made from guts and demon horns, was that Daniel and I were both here to witness it. There's no way this is not some bigger-than-all-of-us reckoning. But the farther away Zoey hauled me from the body, the bossier the voice of reason in my head got. What was I thinking? Did I have gruel for brains all of a sudden? What happened to the reasonable girl who grew up in the shadow of hysteria and learned that the color of madness wasn't for her?

By the time Zoey plastered a perma-smile on her face and created a cocoon out of the blanket for us, I'd talked my inner psycho off the ledge. This was a coincidence. Ridiculous happenstance. Maybe I even imagined that the body looked fresher than it was? Maybe some fluke global-warming voodoo preserved the body for the last hundred years until she was freed from her coffin during the storm? Maybe it only looked like she'd been lying on top rather than inside the tomb? Maybe her hair detached from the skull because that's what happens when bodies decompose? All the explanations in the world won't banish the nagging in my stomach that this can't be, won't be, the case. Sure there is the whole inconvenient fact that they probably didn't have hot-pink nail polish a hundred years ago. But also, there is this writhing inside me, like I've been infected by a tapeworm of doom. As the police sirens sing louder, I feel the parasite nibbling away my reason to make room for fear.

The blue-and-red lights of cop cars reflect on the surfaces around us like glittering disco balls. Zoey leaves my side, cradling my face in her hands and brushing her lips to my forehead. She mumbles a few words and then is gone. My classmates leave too, drawn toward the flashing lights or away from them, depending on how drunk they are. I crane my neck to watch the stream of police descend on the cemetery. Detective Shane shoves through the uniforms and angles to where I sit.

"Stella!" he shouts above the commotion. I rise on jittery knees. Zoey is hot on his tail. She went in search of someone who'd be familiar to me. Of course she did. My best friend who crawled through corpses for me. The concern scrunches up Shane's face, and offhandedly I think he looks like a shar-pei. The comparison makes me guilty. He's a youngish older guy, and it's probably my unsolved case—unsolved because of my screwed-up memory—that's made him look more ancient than he is. Either that or he's a chain smoker. "Are you hurt?" he asks. I must look like I've been run into the mud by a bulldozer. Then Zoey comes to stand by my side, and we look like we climbed out of the bowels of the planet.

"No. There's a body of a little girl. It's Jeanie," I blurt out before I can stop myself. Zoey shoots me a worried glance and throws her arm over my shoulders. Shane chews the inside of his cheek for a moment before turning and surveying the mudslide in front of us. Uniforms are setting up giant fluorescent lights to illuminate the ground.

"Why don't we get Stella back to her car, and I'll come out to the lot as soon as I can. I don't think she needs to see this," he says to Zoey. His expression and tone are loaded. Zoey nods knowingly. They think I've lost it. They're probably right. I don't resist as Zoey tows me through the pandemonium of uniforms, equipment, radio chatter, and sopping-wet teenagers. I wonder halfheartedly where Daniel disappeared to.

"Did Sam come back?" I murmur. Zoey smiles sadly at me. She must think I'm delirious and asking for my old friend. "He was here earlier," I squeeze out, but I don't have the energy to explain. Once at the gravel lot, we duck under police tape. Michaela rushes away from where she was in the throes of an argument with a cop. Cole's close at her heels with her cell out.

"Oh my God, are you guys okay? They wouldn't let me through or tell me anything. It's a police state out here," Michaela says, glaring at the uniform over her shoulder.

Zoey's eyes don't move from Cole, who can barely contain herself from the full-on rapture attack she's having. She points her cell at the flashing lights to snap a photo. I want to tell Zoey that Cole doesn't get what's just happened; she doesn't feel the weight of it. "You are not posting pics of this," Zoey says, a death threat for disobedience implicit in her tone. Cole mutters a confused apology as Zoey shoulders by her and tucks me in the backseat of my car.

My eyelids are heavy, too heavy to resist; I cave to delicious nothingness. The darkness floods the car, and only after ten or fifteen minutes do I blink to focus on the windshield. The swoosh of the wipers brings me back to the land of the living. Cole watches me from the front seat. We must be cutting through neighborhoods, since a wash of light illuminates her blond mane in intervals as we pass under streetlamps. Cole chews her lip as my torso rocks at the slight pumping of the brakes, signaling that Michaela's driving. My head's cradled in Zoey's lap, and her fingertips are tracing tiny shapes on my temple.

"I am so, so sorry, S. I didn't realize—I would never ..." Cole trails off. My hand fumbles at the center console, trying to pat her arm.

"Hey, sleepyhead." Zoey's face is a moon blotting out the rest of the world as she hangs over me. "There's nothing to worry about. We're taking you home. Michaela told Detective What's-His-Face that he could talk to you in the morning."

"Mmmkay," I mumble. I let my eyelids flutter shut again, relieved that I can return to the realm of nothingness. They reopen briefly as Dad tiptoes up the stairs, carrying me like he hasn't since I was a baby.

Hushed voices. The creak of the door to my bedroom. The squeak of my mattress's coils compressing under weight. Soft-sounding words float to me from down a very long tunnel. I swat the sound away, letting their tinny ring fade as sleep pulls me under.

The morning is bright. Too bright for half past six, but I can't coax myself back into that sleepy dreamland where the eeriness of last night is awash with honeyed light and the fluttering of butterfly wings. The rumble of a newscaster's baritone wafting from downstairs hypnotizes me, and before I can even change from the crumpled, filthy thing I used to call a dress, I gallop down the stairs and sink in front of the TV as though my life depends on it. Maybe it does. I shake my head violently to shoo away the morbid thought.

"Morning, Pumpkin," Dad calls from the kitchen. Dishes clatter against the counter; he lets a frying pan clang on the gas stove. Of course he's in the kitchen, concocting a meal that he thinks will be an antidote for all this trouble. Dad was raised by his nana, who was a strict believer in the cult of comfort food. She didn't believe in an ailment that couldn't be cured with her fried green tomatoes or apricot streusel. Screw you, cancer. She'd kill the nasty disease by adding more habaneros. Although Dad is a reasonable guy—and Nana actually did die of cancer—his first instinct is always to run to the kitchen for solutions.

"Morning, Dad." I turn all my attention back to the balding, overly tan newscaster. The Oompa Loompa is being broadcast from the edge of Old Savage Cemetery. The ticker on the bottom of the screen recounts short, abbreviated details from last night. With each I feel less and less hungry. *Jane Doe found in cemetery. Possible connection to eleven-year-old cold case. Victim of cold case discovered body last night.* They're calling *me* a victim. Am I? Everyone always says I'm lucky. My mouth goes dry when I think that people might be talking about me like I'm broken. The newscaster waxes on, spewing details of Jeanie Talcott's disappearance. There are crime scene techs in white plastic suits scurrying around in the background of the picture. It makes the cemetery look alien. Like the awfulness is happening on a different planet with astronauts. I wish.

"The body was found yesterday evening at approximately half past eleven. The sole survivor of the Jeanie Talcott abduction made the discovery," the newscaster drones on. I glare at him through the screen. I did not make the discovery. Tara Boden did. But I guess that's not the spooky coincidence they're after. Isn't it horrible enough? "Events of yesterday evening unfolded during a fluke storm." The reporter presses his ear, listening to his radio feed. A smug smile tugs at his mouth. "My meteorologist has just informed me that a similar summer storm occurred on the night of Jeanie Talcott's abduction. Possibly another strange connection between the crime eleven years ago and the recovered body." My stomach lurches, and I've completely lost my appetite.

Fifteen minutes later I'm watching the same reel as Dad puts a piping-hot stack of pancakes on the coffee table in front of me. I smother my breakfast in syrup, hoping to make it irresistible. I take an unseemly bite; so big I can barely chew with my mouth shut. But there's no fooling my stomach. The news footage segues to clips of Savage residents reacting to last night's discovery. An elderly woman with a hooked nose and curlers in her hair crosses herself with her right hand over and over again. The newscaster interviewing her asks if she suspects cult involvement, since the discovery of the little girl's body in the cemetery could be construed as religious sacrifice. The woman grabs hold of the wooden crucifix around her neck and rushes back into her house, slamming the door behind her. I nearly choke at the mention of cults.

"You want to talk about last night, Pumpkin?" Dad asks, his own mouth full of food, and syrup staining his lips. Rather than answer, I motion for him to dab with his napkin. "Just as well." He shrugs. "I've seen it all on the news, and Detective Shane called last night to brief me. Speaking of Shane, he'll be here at eight thirty for your statement."

I nod without making eye contact. I'm relieved that Dad gets why I don't want to rehash everything with him this morning. How could I when I barely understand what happened myself? What I do understand is that I acted insane last night, clawing through a stew of mud and bones. I did not survive eleven years of Jeanie aftermath by going nuclear. I can't imagine what it is, but there is a perfectly reasonable explanation for all this. No cosmic voodoo, no monsters, no crazy cults seething under the surface of Savage.

I shove the panic down so that the hotcakes don't find their way back up. I succeed in polishing off a second bite before Jeanie's face flickers before me. With all the gore of last night, I forgot that I finally recovered a memory. Not that I've been sitting around waiting for the memories to be salvaged. There wasn't a mash of severed silhouettes, or a jumbled sequence of events, or dialogue so garbled that it's a foreign language, floating in my mind. My memory wasn't just a featureless landscape, it was a black sea—liquid, shapeless, and azoic. I resigned myself to having lost those years, and I haven't been crying about it. My idiot brain just couldn't leave well enough alone.

The sight of Jeanie's pale face, freckled from the summer sun, contorted in fear as blood so dark it's black crawled down her forehead, doesn't give me peace. Would it give her parents peace? Or Daniel? Doubtful. Her parents convinced themselves a long time ago that Jeanie either went painlessly or was growing up somewhere off in the horizon with a picture-perfect family who loved her. It was only ever Daniel who was eaten up by the wondering. That seems saner than hiding from the truth and pretending that the sky is full of rainbows and that child molesters don't exist. I guess what made

Daniel desperate and crazy was what made him saner than his parents. How unfair is that? Not for the first time, I feel a stab of pity for him.

So what would be the use of me telling the cops what I remember? Knowing that something or someone hit Jeanie's head and that she peed her pants in terror wouldn't help them solve the case. Anyway, I might be wrong. Even as I entertain the tempting thought, I don't buy it.

Dad leans forward and taps me on the nose. "Earth to Stella. Did you hear me, Pumpkin? I said I have to go into the office today." Worry twists his mouth, and his graying eyebrows nearly touch, they're so drawn.

I shake the jumble from my head. "Sure, Dad. No worries."

"You'll be okay here? You could always come into the office with me. I'm sure we could find an empty desk and a computer for you to mess around on."

"I'll be completely, totally, utterly fine." I nod to emphasize my point. "I'm sure Zo will come over."

He clears the plates from the coffee table and carries them clanking to the kitchen. "All right, but call if you need anything. Remember that the police will handle this and that you don't have anything to worry about. I'm sure your mother would like to hear from you." I roll my eyes. If she wanted to hear from me, wouldn't she just . . . oh, I don't know . . . call? A minute later he waves from the front door, leather briefcase in one hand, a coffee mug in the other that still has my mother's lipstick staining the rim. No matter how many times

I run it through the dishwasher, I can't erase the red traces of her. Despite them, or maybe because of them, Dad has sipped his coffee from that mug every morning for five years.

I stay curled on the carpet in front of the TV, legs drawn up to my chest, as I text Zoey. I hit send as a female newscaster with a velvety drawl interrupts Mr. Oompa Loompa's interview.

"This just in," she buzzes excitedly, her shellacked blond curls frozen in place like a helmet. "The county coroner has confirmed that Jane Doe has been dead no more than thirty-six hours. Cause of death is trauma to the head. Medical experts estimate Jane Doe to be between five and six years old. Please be advised that the picture we are about to show is of a graphic nature, but in an effort to identify this little girl, we have decided to broadcast it." The feed to the blonde is cut, leaving only a photograph taken by the coroner.

The girl's eyes are closed and her skin is pale. She lies on a sterile stainless-steel table, her body covered by a papery blue sheet. Her hair is damp, arranged so it covers the wound that severed her scalp from her head, but the red locks are unmistakable. She looks exactly like Jeanie. I jump to my feet but only have time to reach the kitchen before I retch my two bites of breakfast into the sink.

Chapter Five

I'm clean and dressed a minute before Detective Shane pounds on our front door. I used up all the house's hot water cowering on the slick tile floor of the shower, trying to flush the similarities between Jeanie and Jane Doe from my mind. *Coincidence.* I say it over and over, hoping to drum it into the universe, hoping to make it true.

"Morning, Stella," Shane says as I swing the front door open wide and step back for him. "Your dad said he'd be at work this morning. He already take off?"

"A little while ago."

He follows me to the living room, where I curl in the corner of our large floral couch. It's one Mom bought the year she left. She used to say the flowers looked like birds that were trying to escape through the window. I thought that sounded like a fairy tale at the time. Now I think I should have taken the hint. She was looking for her own escape from us. I keep meaning to make Dad replace it, but he never has time to shop for a new one.

"How you doing this morning? Sleep any?" he asks, folding his long limbs into Dad's leather recliner.

I ignore his questions. "Why isn't Detective Rhino Berry here?" I've called Detective Frank Berry "Rhino" since I was seven. I was going through a major Serengeti phase when they came to question me that September. All I wanted to talk about were safari animals. Berry told me to call him Rhino from then on. Shane drops his gaze to his boots, cemetery mud still caked on their soles. "Where is Frank?" I repeat, stiffening on the couch.

"Ugh." He rakes his hands through his thinning hair. "He had a heart attack two months ago. Then another three weeks back." He leans forward, resting his elbows on his knees. "It finished him off, kid." My stomach plummets again, but I know I won't vomit. Nothing's left in there.

"But he was only fiftysomething," I whisper. "Not much older than my dad."

Shane heaves a sigh and pats his shirt pocket absentmindedly. I can make out the shape of a pack of cigarettes. "This job . . ." He trails off.

"Unsolved cases," I supply. I've grown up watching the strain of a cold case on these two men, seen the years round their shoulders forward, the stress coat their hair in white like a fine dusting of snow.

"But enough of that and back to business." Shane straightens up, puffs his chest out. "I'm lead detective on the Jane Doe case for obvious reasons, so let's get down to brass tacks." Shane speaks with a drawl that elongates his vowels and makes waste of consonants. He got the accent growing up in a big city in the south. I told him once that he's crazy to live in Savage over a place with sun year round. He didn't deny it. He just said that moving to be a cop in Savage, where his dad's side lived for four generations, seemed like an adventure at the time. I don't like to think about why Shane stays. I don't want to think that it's unfinished business like Jeanie's unsolved case that he can't walk away from.

He draws a notepad from his coat pocket, and I tell him everything. Well, my version of everything. I leave out Daniel, because if Shane doesn't know he's in town yet, it's not for me to stir up more trouble for Jeanie's brother. Yes, I realize I need to watch my back. Live like a paranoid schizo until he leaves town again. That I can handle. I also leave out the memory of Jeanie. Everything else, cross my heart, I am honest about.

"The little girl looks like Jeanie," I say once he's stowed his tablet. "I saw her picture on the news." He caps his pen like it requires a lot of concentration, but I know he's stalling for time. "Does this have something to do with her? I thought you said whoever took her didn't live here." My voice trembles. So much for staying calm. "Shane," I plead. "I'm really frightened. Say something. Have I been walking around smiling at the guy who took Jeanie?"

I try to blink the tears away, but a few escape. I didn't even realize how scared I was. It could be anyone. Forever ago the police ruled out local suspects, but what the hell do they know? It could be red-faced Mr. Robins working in the office of Wildwood Elementary; or leering Jeremy Rangle filling up your gas tank at the Chevron station;

or the silver-haired mailman who waves at every single kid he passes. The only way I ever felt safe in Savage was that I believed that the man who took Jeanie was gone.

Shane leans his head back against the recliner and rubs his temples. He blinks up at the light fixture on the ceiling. "I don't know for sure, but we may be close to making a connection with Jeanie. The little girl, she had something tucked in her fist." I picture a scrap of fabric torn from her attacker's clothing, the mildewy arm of a teddy bear, a fistful of smashed ladybugs that were dancing on her palm the moment she was attacked. "It's a finger bone."

The words meld in my head. I stare at the seat cushion next to me. A ripple runs through the birds. It crimps their spines, twists their necks until they're deformed, broken, dead. My breath is uneven, unpredictable. "Whose?" I wheeze. But why do I even ask? I know who it must belong to.

"We're working to identify it. But unless their DNA is in the system, we won't be able to find a match." If I thought he looked ancient before, he looks like he's aged about a hundred years in my living room.

My brain works slow and clunky. "Do you have Jeanie's DNA?"

He averts his eyes. "Yes, we saved a hair sample when she disappeared. If it's hers, we'll know."

I gather up a throw pillow and hug it to my chest. It occurs to me that I can't decide which would be worse: the finger being Jeanie's or a stranger's. "Could it belong to whoever took Jane Doe?" I have the fleeting sense that my own appendages could be stolen away, and I make fists to keep them safe.

He shakes his head. "It's picked clean. Whoever it belonged to has been dead for at least eight years. That's how long it takes for skin and tissue to decompose."

The finger of someone who has been dead for years. *Someone like Jeanie.* I shrink back into the cushions. It's not that I ever thought we'd find her alive. Now, sitting in my living room, it seems weird that I don't do a double take whenever I spot a redhead my age. I don't search the bleachers at away football games, *just in case.* I know Jeanie's not somewhere, seventeen and sunburned, laughing so hard soda's gushing from her nose. But I never thought we'd find her dead, either. Maybe it was easier to think of Jeanie like vapor, as though eleven years ago, she turned to dust and blew away.

I catch the tail end of what Shane's saying. "What I can tell you, *promise you,* is that we will keep you safe. Whether there is a connection or not, I will keep you safe."

I nod, believing him, but not comforted. "It was crazy last night. What happened to her scalp . . . it was like a nightmare. Is that how she died?"

He rubs his forehead and averts his gaze. "The medical examiner confirmed it was trauma to the head. It's too early to speculate on what caused it, but he believes the scalping was postmortem." I can tell he doesn't want to elaborate. I rub my arms, the hair standing on end. I don't really want him to anyway.

With one last heaved sigh, he stands from the recliner, then tilts his head, studying me. "You never called about what you found in your case file. I worried I made the wrong decision giving it to you."

My eyes trail to his in a roundabout way. *If you hunt for monsters, you'll find them.* "It was the right thing to do," I say. "I needed to know." He doesn't look convinced, and I don't sound certain.

He runs his hand over his jaw. "And it didn't jog a memory?"

Is that why he gave it to me? Was he hoping it would knock something loose in my mind? "I didn't suddenly remember that Jeanie was taken by a giant purple monster, if that's what you mean," I say.

He shakes his head slowly. "What you said . . . it was probably nothing."

I stare at my bare knees; faint white lines crisscross them from skinning them as a kid. My gaze shifts to Shane's face. "But I repeated it over and over. It must have been important."

"Kids see monsters everywhere," he says automatically, his tone dismissing it as nothing. His eyes stay focused on mine, though. "With everything being dredged up in the news, it might make it harder for you to . . . you know . . . move on, keep getting over it."

"I was the one who wasn't taken, remember? I'm the lucky one," I say softly. The echo of the newscaster calling me a victim ping-pongs in my head.

"I tell myself that every time I walk onto a new crime scene." He strides toward the front door. "Don't dwell. You're lucky this wasn't you. Be grateful." He glances over his shoulder. "It never makes the fucked-up shit I see any easier to handle. Call me if you want to talk," he says gruffly. I stand rooted to the spot as he lets himself out. The rumble of his unmarked sedan comes to life in the driveway, and his tires squeal as he reverses too quickly.

I focus on my cell to stop the room from spinning. It's already quarter after nine. Zoey will be here by ten. I pour myself a glass of water to settle my stomach. The doorbell chimes as I take a sip, and I hurry to the door. Maybe Zoey skipped giving herself a morning facial to get here sooner? I peer through the peephole. Rather than Zoey, Sam stands uncertainly on my doorstep.

"Hey," I say, throwing open the door, probably looking like a grinning jack-o'-lantern, I'm so relieved for the distraction. His eyes go round for a second, surprised. The constellation of freckles on the bridge of his nose shows bright in the pale morning. There's a corner of red vest poking from under his black hoodie. "You on your way to work?"

"Yeah." He bobs his head, eyes narrowing. "Some of us don't have rich lawyer parents." I can't help but wince. He takes a deep, struggling breath and jams his hands into his pockets. "Look, I heard about last night and just wanted to make sure you were okay. You're obviously in one piece. So I'll go now." He steps backward off the porch.

"Oh," I say dumbly. He's leaving. My throat tightens. I don't want to be alone with thoughts of dead little girls. "You want to come in?"

He stops, one foot suspended in air, eyebrows drawing together for a confused half moment, like he thinks he's missed the punch line of a joke. When he realizes that I'm not messing with him, he shrugs cautiously. Slipping past me, he says, "This place looks exactly the same." He scans our living room, a slow smile warming his expression as he turns back to me, staring a beat. I fidget, self-conscious. Why did I invite him in again? "Some furniture's been moved around, but other than that, it hasn't changed in years."

"Other than the broken-home part," I say.

"Well, yeah, other than the fact your mom is gone." It doesn't sting when he says it. It's matter-of-fact. "You talk to her a lot?" I shake my head. The thing is, Mom didn't just leave Dad when she went, she left me, too. I visit at Christmas every couple of years, but it's like visiting a stranger's house, where you recognize nothing and sleep in a nondescript guest bedroom that smells of potpourri. She's not even the kind of divorced parent who attempts to buy my love; last Christmas she gave me a turtleneck sweater. I repeat: *a turtleneck sweater.*

I try not to be obvious keeping an eye on the mantel clock; pleeeaase let Zoey arrive after Sam is gone. He shrugs off the black hoodie like he means to stay awhile, and I confirm that he really is using a white shoelace as a belt. He catches me looking. "What? You're not up on this trend? Just give it a month, Hella Stella, and you'll be begging to know where I bought this stylish shoelace." His laugh is full at his own joke. "You still play the violin?" He jerks his head at a studio portrait of me hanging above the mantel, violin in hand, smiling in the orange glow of pillar candles. It's a melodramatic pose for a twelve-year-old; my tight-lipped smile was forced. Mom insisted. It was taken a few months before she left us. I haven't touched my violin or sheet music since she stopped making me practice.

"God, no," I answer. I suspect he's attempting to make casual conversation and already knows I wouldn't be caught dead in the school band room. I eye the throw draped over the love seat. I want to tunnel under it and disappear. Something about Sam being here dredges up things I don't want to think about. Instead I let out a puff of air and push on. "Listen, Sam, I tried to find you after . . . after I was such a bitch last night. Some guy said you left with some girl." I can't remember names, but he should really be appreciative that I went to the trouble of searching for him at all. "I only said what I said because . . . *you know*." The lame excuse spills from my nasty mouth; it's hollow-sounding, and I end up flicking my wrist like Zoey does when she can't be bothered to elaborate.

His eyes dart over my face like he's searching for hidden meaning. "I received about a hundred messages from the guys, saying you asked about me. You almost gave Harry an asthma attack." Of course Sweater-Vest and company relayed my excursion into social Siberia to Sam. My stomach flips thinking about this Harry guy hunched over his inhaler, wheezing about it at the bonfire, and Janey Bear getting wind. Sam blinks at me with a serious expression. "But I don't understand why you said what you did or why you wanted to find me after."

I try diffusing the situation by shrugging and allowing him to interpret it how he wants. It isn't enough to end the most awkward staring contest ever, though. I wish I hadn't invited him in. I wish that I could actually disappear under the blanket. "I mean, Janey and Kate were *right there*," I say finally.

"So?"

I fidget, uncomfortable with totally having to spell it out. "Us sitting there in the dark . . . and you with your nickname that no one calls me anymore." He still shakes his head, not getting it. "I just . . . I was worried what they'd think. Because of what they would tell people." I cover my mouth, trying to muffle the confession that I care what someone like Janey thinks or says. "And I was worried what you thought. I mean, I have my own group of friends and you . . . you have your own stuff." I motion at his vest. "And besides, I don't really date anyway. You're just sooo nice to me, and I don't want you to get the wrong idea."

He's quiet for a long time. I perch on the love seat's arm, waiting for the hurt feelings to erupt out of him like a PMSing volcano. His eyes are glued to the framed pictures displayed on the marble mantel. Most likely he's considering the irony that there's still a photo of us from an apple-picking field trip during the fourth grade tucked into a papier-mâché frame he made for me.

"I'm too nice to you?" he asks, turning to study my face. "You'd rather I pretend to forget your name? How about if I hit on your friends in front of you? Or if I said I'd text and then didn't?" There's nothing biting in his voice; it's thoughtful, like his eyes searching mine. I try to stop the shock I feel from reaching them. His jaw is relaxed, his brown irises cool as they figure me out. "I know what the guys you hang out with are like. I think you deserve better than that."

I don't know if I want to scream or cry at what he says. It wasn't what I was expecting. Instead I smirk and vomit up a "Whatever."

With that one little word he stiffens, and his head jerks back like I hit him. Three long steps to the front door, and he pauses at the threshold. Anger makes his whole body rigid. "You want to play nothing but games with guys who don't give a shit about you, who don't even know *you*. And that 'stuff' you're talking about that I have—friends who don't choose who I talk to, who are my friends regardless of who my other friends are—you'd be lucky to have stuff like that. You had a friend like that until a minute ago, despite how little of *you* there is left." He leaves, closing the door so quietly I don't hear the latch click. Somehow that's worse than if he'd slammed it.

I'm speechless. I've never ever seen Sam angry before. I was trying to make things better. How did he end up even more pissed? *I'd be lucky to have friends like his? Despite how little of me there is left?* He doesn't know anything about me anymore. He doesn't have an inkling as to what kind of guys I like or how much they care about me. I haven't even had an actual boyfriend in years. And it's not like it's not my choice. Loads of guys are interested—*Taylor* is interested. But being interested in dating is different from sticking your hand in the fire and expecting not to get burned. I don't do the "feelings" that the whole boyfriend-girlfriend thing involves. What's the point? I'm seventeen, and it's not like things will last. Someone always ends it. I don't need to experience that for myself to know it's true. I've seen too many girls hoovering up whole cans of Funfetti frosting to know that's not for me.

And the bit about my friends? Okay, so it's not total BS. At twelve, Zoey told me that I'd have to choose: her or Sam. It was the summer before seventh grade, and Zoey had plans for us. It was a hard choice to make, but in the end it was always going to be Zoey. Zoey is savagely tempered, but she's my best friend. Mom used to laugh at Zoey's antics. She said that if the devil existed, he was a teenage girl. Well, Zoey is *my* devil, and I love her. If Sam's so effing smart, why can't he see that?

I pound my fist in the soft stuffing of the love seat, pretending it's Sam's face. It doesn't help nearly as much as it should. I'm doing him a favor. I'm sure there are tons of perky little band geek or show choir or auto shop—or whatever it is that Sam's into—girls who'd be all over him. Girls who he actually has a shot with. Girls like this Anna whatever-her-last-name-is he left the bonfire with last night.

I huff and puff up the stairs to my bedroom. I feel cruel. I also feel burned, more hurt by his words than I should be. What gives? With everything going on, why would I let Sam Worth under my skin? Why am I even so effing aware of the way he treats me?

I flop down on my bed, roll over on my back, and text Zoey, jabbing my thumbs into the touch screen of my cell. I get no response. I try to relax, but when my mind wanders, it veers toward Sam. Do all his friends dress like that? I bet even the girls in his group walk around with shoelaces laced in their jeans. I picture the shuffling, twitchy group of guys from last night that I immediately identified as catastrophically clueless enough to be his. I snort. *With friends like that, he'd be better off alone.* I don't even know who Harry with asthma is or where they eat lunch at school. Probably in the bio lab, or the library, or the band room. What is Sam even into? How do I not know if he's in auto shop, or any sports, or any clubs?

To stop myself from obsessing, I roll off my bed and flatten myself on the floor. My navy violin case is under the bed, where I deserted it ages ago. And eons' worth of dust bunnies and grime cover it now. I take the instrument out and spend the next thirty minutes plucking its strings until they're tuned. There's something so predictable about the way it works; how the pegs feel smooth under my finger pads as I twist them. I forgot how much I like the way it looks resting on my shoulder, its neck supported by my palm with fingers curled on the strings. *Fingers.* I stare at my bent index finger. Was it a child's that ended up in Jane Doe's little fist? I shove the thought from my head and dust the violin with a cloth, carefully uncovering the grain of the wood with each swipe.

"What's with the cello?" I whirl around. Zoey stands in the doorway, leaning against the frame. She pops a handful of gummy bears into her mouth from a bag she's cupping. "You didn't answer when I knocked, so I let myself in," she says, multicolored gummy carnage visible in her chomping teeth.

"Careful not to choke." I kneel on the ground, swiftly stowing the instrument in its case. "And it's a violin, not a cello."

She rolls her eyes. "Same difference. I get PTSD thinking about the dying animal noise you made when you used to practice. I stopped at Powel's." She swings the bag of gummies in my face. "And it took me forever to drive here, because there are cops everywhere." I snatch the bag from her and ferret out the green ones. They're the only color I eat. "Are you listening to me, Miss Piggy?"

"Continue." I grin, revealing a mouthful of green gummies. "Do I look so hot, Zo? Should I go over to Taylor's looking like this?" I tease, alternating winking one eye, then the other.

She tries to cover my mouth with her outstretched hand, but I stick my tongue out, licking her. "Gross. Just shut up for a second, you sticky bitch!" she says, laughing. I try to look serious wiping the candy oozing down my chin, but I'm reduced to giggles when I see how hard she's trying to choke back her own laughter. "Stella! I'm trying to tell you something important." I roll back on the floor, holding my stomach. It's such a release to laugh after hours of crap. "Stella, listen to me. It's Jeanie's mom." I gulp the gummies down instantly. I sit up, staring at Zoey, waiting for the other shoe to drop.

"They found her this morning. She's dead."

Chapter Six

"Dead" is a funny word. For ages I've said that Jeanie is probably dead, but it's different to hear that it's unequivocally true about someone. Dad's nana died when I was ten and both Mom's parents long before I was born, so I don't have a lot of experience with death. Zoey says it like a dirty word; something that can't be taken back. I've always said it like it's a get-out-of-jail-free card. Like Jeanie being dead is the best-case scenario; it's freedom from whatever monster took her. Mrs. Talcott being dead isn't like that.

The morning and afternoon pass quickly. Uniforms fill my house. It takes them an hour to arrive, but once they do it's as if they're breeding like bunnies to produce more cops that take up every spare inch of space. More badges whispering about me from the corner of my living room; more badges' radio static; more badges coming and going. Since it storms again, they track mud on the carpet, a funeral procession of footprints carving up the living room floor. If Mom still lived here, she'd throw a fit over the stains and mess, but Dad doesn't notice incidentals. I curl on his recliner, lost in blankness, my vision tunneling until all I see is a tiny keyhole of light in front of me.

At first I don't get why they're all here, and then one word says it all. *Homicide*. Mrs. Talcott's death is ruled a homicide almost immediately. A rookie with acne and a lisp speculates loudly that he thinks it's Jeanie's killer come back to tie up loose ends and to off the witnesses. Then he and the dark-skinned woman cop he's talking to peek in my direction. As though they half expect me to be finished off already.

Detective Shane arrives just as the news crews set up camp on our lawn. They bring plastic tarps and giant umbrellas to shelter their equipment from the rain. Shane barks for them to move on to the sidewalk as he grinds his soiled boots into the welcome mat. He sniffs the air, face softening at the scent of Dad's turkey meat loaf wafting from the kitchen.

"Everybody who doesn't live here, out," he orders. I close my eyes as Shane settles on the love seat across from me. I'm not questioned this time but briefed. Every detail he keeps brisk and clinical: Mrs. Talcott strangled; her body dumped along the road on the outskirts of town; they suspect a connection to Jeanie's disappearance and the discovery of Jane Doe.

"Are there any suspects?" Dad asks, his voice tense but controlled.

"You know I can't discuss possible suspects, Joe," Shane answers.

"Jeanie's father is obviously at the top of your list," Dad continues.

Shane sighs loudly. "Kent Talcott claims to have been home all evening with his wife. He says they went to bed at quarter to eleven, and that's the last time he saw her. A gossipy neighbor heard about Jane Doe and phoned Bev Talcott to tell her a little after midnight. That's the last anyone spoke with Bev. The neighbor called us this morning once she heard Bev had been found. There was no sign of forced entry in the house. Kent said his wife often had trouble sleeping and would take late-night strolls. Neighbors corroborate this, and her key was found in her pocket."

He sets his chin and continues, "As you know, Kent Talcott had a similarly questionable alibi for Jeanie's disappearance. He was still working as a park ranger at Blackdog State Park and was patrolling the fire trails that morning. There was a two-hour gap where no one saw him. Not surprising, since the trails are remote. His connection with the park where Jane Doe was found is hard to ignore."

"Is there anything to indicate that Stella might be targeted next?" Dad asks.

There's a long pause and then, "We're linking the current crimes with Jeanie's disappearance—at least for the time being. Bev Talcott is Jeanie's mother, and Jane Doe looks extremely similar to Jeanie. There's also the issue of timing. Both murders took place either on or very near the anniversary of Jeanie vanishing. Given that Stella likely saw Jeanie's abductor and he or she is at work in Savage once more, Stella could be in danger. We're taking Kent Talcott into custody for questioning, and once my team can gather more forensic evidence, we'll know if we can keep him." Shane recounts the details as neatly ordered clues that are bound to add up to one rational and inevitable conclusion: Jeanie's father.

I keep my eyes closed, wishing this nightmare away. Why is this happening? Why now? Why at all? Haven't Dad and I been through enough? "I'm in danger because I'm a witness to something that I have no memory of," I say.

"Possibly, yes," Shane says.

I look at Shane. "But other than blathering on about hunting monsters, I don't know anything."

"Pumpkin." Dad leans forward. "What are you talking about?" He is confused, of course; he didn't know I was aware of what I told the cops that day.

Shane's eyes flick from my dad to me. I worry that I'll get Shane in trouble, so I add, "I've known for a few years. Zoey heard it from someone a while back and told me." Shane flinches ever so slightly at the lie, but he doesn't correct me.

"I see." Dad nods gravely. "I wish you had told me you knew."

I'm impatient now. "Why would I have? You kept it from me. You lied."

"Stella"—he reaches for my hand, but I yank it away—"I apologize for that, but your mother thought that it would disturb you too much."

I sniff and stand from the recliner. "Disturb me too much? You've got to be freaking kidding me. She wasn't too worried about that when she left us. My *whole life* is disturbing." I look to Shane. "I was a living, breathing echo that afternoon, repeating only one thing over and over again. If it was Mr. Talcott who took Jeanie, why wouldn't I just say so? I could obviously speak. I would have recognized him, right?"

"Stella." Shane motions for me to take a seat. I stay standing. "I wish I could tell you that we understand why you chose those words. We don't. I don't." He sounds defeated by the admission, but I'm already too incensed to care.

"So am I on lockdown or something? Are you going to have cops watch me?"

"That's something we need to discuss," Shane says calmly. "I'm keeping a patrol car out in front to watch the house, and until we've straightened this out, I think it's best if you stay at home or in public places with your friends. When you do go out, it's important you tell your dad exactly where and for how long." I cross my arms against my chest and raise an eyebrow. He knows as well as I do how pre-occupied Dad is with work. He nods, receiving my silent message loud and clear. "How about you tell the officers stationed out in front when you leave?"

I roll my eyes. So I'm going to be babysat by cops now? "Whatever," I mutter, turning and leaving the living room. Shane and Dad both call my name, but I hurry up the stairs and lock my bedroom door behind me. Immature, I know, but at least I resist the urge to slam it. I can't think near the two of them.

Mr. Talcott's been taken into custody. Well, of course he has. He's the perfect suspect, except for the fact that there's not a snow cone's chance in hell he did it. The whole "hunting monsters" gibberish aside, I spent years looking into his face, and the only thing there is a grief so big it has its own heartbeat. Besides, I seriously can't imagine Mr. Talcott with his gigantic calloused hands and his jean jacket knowing how to French braid hair. Huh. How many men know how to braid, let alone French braid? Even I fumble through it. I've never considered that Jeanie's abductor could be a woman. I can't really picture a woman taking Jeanie. Men are the ones who commit crimes like that. Male sickos.

I like to believe that even if the memories are lost, I'd still *feel* something in the presence of the person who took Jeanie. My nerve endings would tingle or I'd become really dizzy. There's not a bit of that with any of the Talcotts. Not even psycho Daniel. Poor Daniel. Where is he now? First his sister, now his mother. He'll be devastated. Frantic. I'm the only person who can help him. Somewhere in the black hole of my mind is the proof of his father's innocence and his sister and mom's killer. I throw myself down on the bed, gathering up the loose fabric of the comforter in my fists. Jane Doe, Bev Talcott, Jeanie, the finger bone. They're related somehow. Knit together by a common killer.

Whatever is happening, I won't be safe until I remember who took Jeanie. I need help for that. Help from someone who remembers the events of that summer; who remembers Jeanie. I know we were only six, but Zoey has a way better sense of who Jeanie was. Maybe something she knows could help? It's not much to go on, but it's all I have right now. I snag my cell off the nightstand. The phone rings twice before Zoey answers.

"Took you long enough," she whines. "I've been going craaazy waiting for you to call. I can't believe your dad sent me home. Next time I see Joe, I am sooo giving him a piece of my mind, and for that matter—"

"Zo, just listen. I need your help."

"Interrupt much? What, you need me to break you out of the prison cell your bedroom has become? Mom just got home and said your block has more cop cars than the Fourth of July parade."

"No, not yet, anyway. Shane and Dad are still downstairs talking. But listen, they're pinning Mrs. Talcott's death on Mr. Talcott. Jeanie and Jane Doe, too."

She gasps on the line. "I always thought he had rapey eyes!"

I sputter, "No, Zoey. He doesn't have . . . What are rapey eyes?" I shake my head hard like she can see me through the receiver. "Whatever they are, he doesn't have them. He didn't do any of it. I would know. I swear *I would know*."

"Okay, but you don't remember anything, so *how* would you know? Maybe he's got a thing for little girls and diddled the one in the cemetery? Maybe the old ball-and-chain found out that he hurt Jeanie and Jane Doe, so he offed Mrs. Talcott to keep her quiet? I mean, you don't even know if you saw who took Jeanie for sure."

"I know I saw something, and I don't believe it was Mr. Talcott." I want to tell Zoey about the finger bone found on Jane Doe, but Shane was clear that the detail wasn't being released publicly. Also, it doesn't really feel like my secret to tell.

"What, now you have some sixth sense for guilt? Like a super-tingle in your tits telling you whether or not Mr. Talcott did it? How could you possibly know?"

I sigh. This is what I've been dreading. Spilling the truth. I steel myself for Zoey's wrath. "Because I told the police something the day Jeanie was taken. I don't think I would have said it if I'd seen Jeanie's dad take her. I knew Mr. Talcott, you know? Wouldn't I have recognized him taking his own daughter and told the cops?" Okay, so that's half the truth, but not the part that she'll be pissed about.

She sniffs. "That hardly proves anything, Slutty Sherlock. The cops could have misinterpreted what you said. Maybe you were trying to tell them it was Jeanie's dad and they didn't get it?"

"No, Zo," I explain. "I repeated myself two hundred and fifty-five times. There was no mistaking what I said."

"You're killing me with suspense," Zoey says, distracted. I can tell she's probably giving herself a pedi by how disinterested she sounds. "Drumroll . . . what were you saying?"

I take another deep breath and swallow. "I was saying, 'If you hunt for monsters, you'll find them.'"

A loud clatter on the other end of the call. Plastic against tile. Zoey curses and then fumbles with the phone. She shouts, "You've got to be fucking kidding me, right? What the hell, Stella? If this is a joke, you're a real twisted psycho-slut and you just made me smear nail polish all over my new jeans."

"This isn't the kind of thing I'd joke about. *Two hundred and fifty-five times*, Zo. Shane counted."

"OMIGOD . . . I mean, what does that mean? Why was six-year-old you talking about monsters?" She sounds so concerned that for a moment I let myself believe she'll only be supportive and that it won't matter that I kept it from her. "Wait a tampon's bloody second.

How long have you known? I mean, you don't remember anything from that day, so how do you know what you said?"

I close my eyes. "I asked Shane to let me see the case file last September. I don't know why or what I was looking for. My dad was never going to tell me. . . ."

A long pause. "So you've known for nine months and you didn't tell *me*?" her voice is quiet, laced with venom.

"I didn't tell anyone," I rush to explain.

"Anyone? What the hell, Stella? I'm your best friend. I'm not just anyone. We're supposed to tell each other *everything*, and instead you're keeping something this juicy from me for nine effing months? I told you when I went down on Patrick Hoser. Stinky effing Patrick Hoser! I tell you my most mortifying secrets."

But all I hear is Zoey calling my deepest, darkest secret "juicy." Of course she would see this detail as tantalizing. Of course she'd be livid with me. How could I have been such a fool as to think she wouldn't be? "It just kind of freaked me out, and I didn't know what I thought about it. It blindsided me. How could I tell you? You would have made up your mind about what it meant instantly. You would have told *me* how to feel about it. Maybe I just wanted to figure things out on my own for once?" Tears pour down my face. Is that really why I didn't tell her? It rings partially true, but not completely.

"Please, Zo, don't be mad. I'm telling you now and I need your help. I'm desperate for your help." I hiccup out the last word.

I imagine Zoey sitting rigid on her bathroom floor, seething at the betrayal. "Yeah, whatevs. My mom's calling me for dinner, so I've got to go." Before I can beg her to stay on the line, she's gone. Only silence left.

I stare moon-eyed at my phone. Zoey has never hung up on me before. Shouted, berated, cussed, screamed, pulled my hair, and even thrown food at me, sure. But never once has she just fallen silent and refused to fight. Is it really so unforgivable that I kept something that scary to myself? Can't she fathom that I might have been frightened to tell her? That I might have been worried what she'd think?

"Shit," I hiss, glaring at the ratty and worn stuffed bunny that rests on my pillow. Now who's going to help me remember Jeanie? Obviously Daniel could, but do I want to be alone with him? I doubt he'd be willing anyway. He's so freaking certain that I know more than I'm letting on. I mentally run through the list of those close enough to me that I could ask such a bizarre thing of. It's shorter than I'd like. What would I say anyway? *Hey, do you think you could help me remember who took Jeanie Talcott eleven years ago while her murderer is on the loose offing new victims and her body parts might be showing up one by one?* Yeah, right. I'm sure people would be banging down my door to help me with that morbid journey into the past. Especially now that I basically have a target on my back. Michaela's the only other person I could ask, but she never knew Jeanie, since she moved here in the eighth grade. Wait . . . Sam. Sam Worth went to kindergarten with me and Jeanie. The only reason he wasn't there the day she disappeared was that it was a girly playdate set up by our moms.

"Crap." I smack my forehead with my palm and glare at my bunny's smug whiskered face. Even my bunny with stuffing for brains knows that I screwed up any chance of Sam helping me. He'd probably hang up on me the instant he saw my name on his cell. Or he'd answer to tell me just how little of me there is left. In which case I could assure him that I'm next on a kill list, so there'll be even less of me left if he refuses to help.

I scroll through my contacts quickly before losing my nerve. I stab my finger at his name. Once I hear ringing, shame washes over me. I have no right to call Sam for help. No right to ask him to do anything for me. Ever. By the second ring I'm in a cold sweat. I hit end before the third can finish me off.

I roll off the bed and lie crumpled on my white shag rug. When my parents remodeled the house, Mom argued with me for days about my choice of carpet. She said it wasn't practical. She didn't understand that it was soft on my face and I wanted something to curl up on doing homework and talking on the phone. Even though there's a glaring green stain from a guacamole debacle, I'm glad I didn't let her talk me out of it. I wish I could crawl into the shag now and hide.

A buzzing above my head makes me jump. I sit upright and look eagerly at the offending cell. Let it be Zoey calling to give me a chance to explain. It's not, though. The screen glows blue with Sam's name in bold black letters. They look angry.

"H-hello," I stammer. "Sam?"

"You prank calling me now?" His tone is quiet but not angry.

"No . . . I mean, I guess I did, since I called and then hung up. Sorry."

"Sorry about calling during dinner and then hanging up, or sorry about what you said to me earlier?"

"Both." I've recovered my bunny from the pillow and wrap my arms tightly around his mottled gray body. I hope he'll keep me afloat through this.

"Well, apology accepted, but I have to go—"

"Wait a sec. Please," I squeak. "I—I have no right to ask you this, especially after earlier, but I need your help." A noise halfway between a snort and a chuckle from the other end. "Did you hear about Jeanie's mom?"

"Yes."

Another deep breath on my end. "Okay, so the cops have been here, and they think whoever killed her is the one who took Jeanie and is also connected to the body in the cemetery."

"And? Hate to break it to you, Stella, but my Hardy Boys phase is over, and I'm not much of a detective."

"The cops think it was Jeanie's dad, but it's not." Panic makes my tone too high. "I don't know how I know, but there is no way it's him. I just know it's not. I—"

"Okay, I hear you. It's not Mr. Talcott."

I take a long, silent breath and let it out slowly. Sam believes me just like that. Zoey doubted me, but Sam doesn't. "Daniel is back in town."

"Since when? For how long? Have you seen him? What does your dad say?" He's louder with each question. "Do the cops know? You don't think it was him, do you?"

"Sam," I shout over him. "Of course it wasn't Daniel. Just like I know it wasn't Jeanie's dad. Daniel was just a kid when Jeanie went missing, and no matter how much of a freak you think he is, you can't actually believe he'd ever kill his mother. What matters is that the cops are arresting Jeanie's dad for something he didn't do, and they're worried whoever's responsible might target me next. I have to remember, Sam. And if I can't remember, then we at least have to prove it wasn't Jeanie's dad."

"*We?* What we, Stella? Just this morning you told me I was too nice to you. That we each had our own friends." He half sniffs, half snorts. "No, sorry, you told me I had my own 'stuff.' Can't Zoey help you on your crusade to save an innocent man? Can't your dad, you know, the *lawyer?*"

"Zoey won't help. She's angry, and I can't ask Dad. He'll tell me to stay out of it. You're the only one who remembers Jeanie. You can help me figure out what happened. Look, it sucks that I'm asking you. But I'm asking anyway." I stop, brimming so full of shame I imagine it leaking onto the floor and turning my white carpet brown. I cover my stuffed animal's face so he doesn't have to witness how horrible I am.

"You are completely out of your mind for calling me like this after everything." I wince, bracing myself for Sam's next words. "I'll be at your house tomorrow morning at eleven. Be ready, because I'm not coming in. I'll honk." With that, he hangs up. Leaving me with my mouth gaping open, searching my bunny's face for the same shock I feel.

Chapter Seven

True to his word, Sam's horn blares at 10:59 the next morning. I race downstairs, purse slung over my shoulder, scouring the floor below for my violet ballet flats. I'm hopping on one foot, then the other, slipping each on, as I burst through the front door. The news crews left late last night, the hum of their engines jolting me from sleep. A single police car sits idling. I hold up an index finger for Sam, who peers at me through the windshield of his beat-up teal station wagon—one of the many reasons Zoey's dubbed him the King of Loserdom—and hurry over to the cops.

The officer with pimply skin—who somehow manages to look even younger in the sunless morning light—rolls the passenger-side window down. He smacks his lips loudly, chewing a massive wad of gum.

"Good morning, Ms. Cambren." His voice is artificially low, trying for older but failing miserably.

"Good morning." I wave to his partner slouching behind the

wheel, devouring a bagel and lox. "Umm . . . I'm headed out." I angle my head toward Sam's car. "We're just going to the mall and then coming right back." I spin on my toes as soon as I've finished and run for the wagon. He calls after me, but I don't stop. They can follow us if they're that worried.

"Hey," I say to Sam, throwing myself into the passenger seat of the wagon.

"Morning." Sam avoids my eyes and devotes all his energy to backing the car out of the driveway. One of those cheesy car fresheners in the shape of a tree swings from the mirror. Cedar, I think.

After a block of Sam keeping the speedometer at ten miles under the speed limit, I laugh. "So not only does your car smell like an old lady's closet, you drive like one too?"

He looks at me out of the corner of his eye. "Be sure to add that to your list of complaints about me. I don't really want to get a ticket from your illustrious police escort." Some people can pull off sarcasm; Sam can't. It's forced and clunky, like my accent in Spanish class. He tilts the cracked rearview mirror toward me. Sure enough, the cops follow at a car-length's distance. "We won't be in any high-speed chases today, but maybe you should put on your seat belt?"

I struggle with the belt, sneaking a peek to see if Sam is upset. His face is unreadable, neutral. After five more blocks, I can't bear the silence. "I really appreciate you helping me, and I just want you to know that I'm really sorry and—"

"Stella. Stop." One hand temporarily strays from the wheel as he holds it between us. "I'm helping you because that's who I am. I'm someone who helps friends. Even if it's an old friend and even if they don't deserve it."

"'Kay, thanks," I mumble, staring at my hands. I swallow the ten other apologies I feel the need to vomit at him. Dependable Sam. Kind Sam. A friend who I've thrown away, over and over again. I don't deserve his help. He knows it; I know it.

The wagon makes a sharp right turn into a massive parking lot. BigBox's glowing red cube emblem could probably be seen from space, it's so bright and huge. Sam parks the car and jumps out. He ducks his head, regarding me frozen in place. "Come on, let's go lose our tail," he says with a wink. I follow, nervously glancing over my shoulder. The police car idles in a handicapped space, but the officers don't move to pursue us. A rush of cold air bathes my face once we're through the automated doors. The store is packed with carts and families, the quiet drone of elevator music its white noise.

"What are we doing here?" I call to Sam, who strides briskly a few feet ahead of me.

"You'll see." We snake through the crowded aisles, dodging crying toddlers and yelling mothers. A few red-vested employees nod greetings to Sam as we dash by.

"We can't lose the police in here because they didn't follow us in. They'll be at the car when we leave," I say.

"That's what I'm counting on." He takes a sudden left, and I have to backtrack a couple of steps to shadow him through a doorway in the store's rear wall labeled EMPLOYEES ONLY.

"This really isn't a great time for you to take me on a tour of your work," I grumble, just before Sam grabs my wrist and tows me down an even darker corridor. "Okay, this is kind of freaking me out." Sam drags me for a few more yards before slamming his shoulder into a door and bursting through. White light blinds me. I squint, trying to get my bearings.

"We're outside," I exclaim. We stand on a paved loading dock; the cement extends twenty or thirty feet before dying into the woods.

A ribbon of light from the sun seeping through the clouds illuminates Sam's face as he smiles slowly. "I figured we would need to lose them, and since the wood runs into Jeanie's house, we can walk. It's about three miles," he says, appraising my shoes. "You okay in those?" I nod, mutely in awe of Sam. I only asked him to help me remember, and that's all it took for him to devise a plan. I didn't even think about where we'd go today. Of course, the dirt drive by Jeanie's old house is exactly where we need to start. It's where she vanished.

"Sam, this is . . . amazing." He shrugs the compliment off and turns to start into the woods. I follow after a moment's hesitation, watching him go. From behind I wouldn't recognize him. His shoulders are broad and his arms less lanky and more muscular than they used to be. He isn't wearing a shoelace as a belt today, although a UFO is centered on the back of his T-shirt, and there are patches ironed on its front with words in Latin. Hanging off his jean's waistband is a pair of suspenders.

He doesn't look like the little boy I kissed at the cove the summer before fifth grade. All knocking knees and front teeth big as white

Chiclets. We'd had sex ed earlier that spring, and ever since then I'd felt some weird buzzing down deep in me. Gag me, but it's true. I was curious. And Sam was my guinea pig, since he was basically the only boy I talked to—other than Caleb, who's too brotherly to think of like that. The kiss was all teeth-clattering awkwardness, Sam leaning in most of the way, me pulling him the rest. It was sweet.

"Hey, you okay?" Sam calls. I look around, having totally spaced out. He waits for me to catch up so we're walking side by side.

"Yeah, sorry." I'm horrified by what I'm going to say but totally unable to stop myself. "I was just thinking about our first kiss."

Sam's steps falter. He opens his mouth to speak, then closes it, then opens it again. He raises an eyebrow and prods softly, "I thought your first real kiss was with Scott Townsend." Somehow the fact that he doesn't sound bitter or angry or pissed makes it sting worse.

"I don't think you could call any of my kisses with Scott Townsend *real*," I admit. After that, I try not to hear the familiar rhythm of Sam's steps as I watch a blue-winged sparrow with iridescent feathers swoop low overhead. I try not to see the droplets of sweat pooling at the base of his neck as the heat of the sun burns through the canopy of branches. I inhale deeply the scent of decaying leaves as enchanted bits of light play on Sam's shoulders.

In the back of my mind I never stop searching for anything to bridge the divide between us. Or at least to distract him from it. "I remembered something the other night at Blackdog." I take a deep breath, preparing myself to admit it out loud. "I saw Jeanie. I mean, I didn't actually see her there, but I remembered what she looked like that day, and then I imagined her standing by the bonfire."

Sam adjusts his pace so we're walking abreast. "That might not be a memory. Even I can think of what Jeanie looked like the day she disappeared from hearing about it on the news."

"But I remembered things that no one knows. Like that Jeanie was afraid, really afraid, and that she wet her pants." I lower my voice. "Something, I'm not sure what, had hit her in the head, and there was blood dripping from her scalp."

He catches my eye. "You didn't tell anyone?" he asks.

"No. You're it," I say, a little jitter in my voice as I look away. "Something happened to Jane Doe's head, too. It looked like her whole scalp was torn off," I finish in a whisper.

"I'm sorry you saw that," he says.

I bob my head and try to concentrate on pleasanter things. Sam swings his arms as he walks. Each step is animated and alive with energy. His hand nearest to me looks really empty, and I wish I had the courage to reach for it. What a joke. After all, he doesn't think there's any of *me* left. He'd pull away, reject me. And what the hell is wrong with me anyway? There are about a trillion reasons why Sam Worth is not the kind of guy I flirt with.

We walk without speaking for thirty more minutes. Every few paces I cave to paranoia and glance over my shoulder. But nothing's following us. Shane is going to be furious when his officers tell him we ditched them. If Dad actually comes home from the office tonight, he'll be angry too. Although Dad's anger won't last. By the time he's done baking a batch of his snickerdoodles, he'll forget he's not speaking to me.

As we near Jeanie's, the wood grows denser with birch, the trunks covered in thin, peeling white bark like the shedding skin of a snake. There are rogue flashes of rust-colored brick walls and white picket fences through the slim trunks. We're close to neighborhoods now. Belts of forest crisscross the town of Savage, a patchwork of trees cutting up the roads and houses. It's possible to travel from one end of town to the other completely sheltered by woods. If we turned northeast rather than northwest, we'd end up in Zoey's backyard.

"Hey, I didn't realize that Zoey's and Jeanie's were so close," I say. Sam ignores me. I try again. "Do you like working at BigBox?"

He answers without sparing me a glance. "It's not exactly my dream job, but it does pay enough for me to save."

"Save for what?"

"College tuition."

"But won't your parents . . ." I let the question trail off, because it sounds ruder than I expected.

"They would if they could. Not everyone has money to go to whatever school they want." There it is again. I know I'm lucky. But it's not like Sam to be sour about anything.

"Sorry," he says, half turning to me as he smiles hesitantly, "That was unfair. It's been worse over the past year since Dad was laid off. He picks up odd jobs, but it's not really enough." I haven't thought about Sam's parents in forever. Now I remember his mom telling jokes and his dad working long hours at Halper's Cannery, where he managed the warehouse. Sam's dad is a large, burly man; although

Sam has his size, they were never anything alike. His dad was gruff and quiet, kind of frightening to a kid.

I catch up to Sam, pushing myself to twice my comfortable speed, bumping over the mush of pine needles and moss, dabbing sweat from my forehead. "I didn't know."

"I know you didn't. Why would you?"

I fall quiet. Again, Sam's right. Why would I know? He's asked me stuff almost every chance he gets, and I've repaid him by never asking back. I've shrugged off all the little thoughtful things Sam's done for me over the years. I frown at the perky yellow dandelions sprouting from the forest floor. They look smug; they make me feel like an abominable snowgirl. For a few paces I go out of my way to stomp on the little blossoms. I chose Zoey five years ago, but here I am, hiking through the woods with Sam, the only friend who has my back.

He takes off in an easy jog. "It's just up ahead."

I can't run without losing my shoes and pant, "Wait up!" I'm so busy watching where I step that I emerge from the trees without really noticing. There's compact dirt under my feet and the warmth of the sun on my head. I turn slowly in a circle. It didn't occur to me that bursting upon Jeanie's house after so many years would unsettle me, but seeing it makes my throat close. I have the sense that the house and the drive snuck up on me, rather than the other way around.

If it's possible for a place to look sinister, it does. The house's facade is warped and decaying as though turned rotten by Jeanie's disappearance. Maybe it saw what happened to her? It has its own dark memories. The paint is discolored and chipped, flaking onto the dirt lot. Shutters hang by single nails. The front windows are shattered, with the look of gaping eye sockets. A small aged vigil of candles and rank stuffed toys lines the porch steps. I can practically smell the mold poisoning the air inside its walls.

Sam appears at my side. "Hard to imagine why her parents stayed here after she was gone. I'd want to get as far away as possible. They only moved away three years ago."

"I haven't been here since it happened," I say, standing in the shadow the roof casts. "It looks like it's been abandoned forever."

Sam leaps over a puddle of sludge and onto a crumbling footpath leading to the house's ramshackle side gate. "I heard it got bad the last year they were here. Mr. Talcott's drinking was worse; he'd go into town drunk, get kicked out of bars. The state park fired him. They couldn't pay for the house. It's why they ended up in a trailer across town."

My bottom lip quivers, listening to what became of Jeanie's family. I can't reconcile the memory of Sunday-dress-wearing ladies fresh from church waddling from door to door taking up collections for the Talcotts in the few years after Jeanie disappeared with what Sam is saying. I guess people got sick of their tragedy. "I was happy when I stopped seeing Mr. and Mrs. Talcott," I admit, face heating up. "I didn't think about why they stopped coming out."

Sam pauses just before the rusty hinged gate. "I saw Mrs. Talcott a couple of times. She always looked like she'd been crying."

The gate swings open with a loud creak, narrowly missing Sam. "That's because she *was* always crying," Daniel growls, shouldering through the gate into the front yard. Before I can scream for him to stop, he swings his broad fist through the air and sinks his knuckles into Sam's face.

Chapter Eight

The force of the punch knocks Sam back a step.

"Daniel! Stop!" I shoot toward them, my shoes lost along the way. I make a mad grab for Daniel's arm as it swoops through the air for a second strike. "We want to help you," I shout. I throw all my weight into hanging on his arm. I foul him up long enough for Sam to regain his balance.

"I never pegged you for rabid," Sam says, rubbing his beet-red cheek. Daniel shakes me off, staggers back, stares at us a bit dazed. He looks as stunned by his reaction as Sam. Daniel's surprise doesn't last.

I stand between them, aware of a stinging sensation in my heel from where something sharp punctured the skin. I'll probably die of encephalitis or scabies or whatever it is you catch from rusty metal.

"Have you been staying here?" I ask Daniel, waving toward the house.

Daniel sets his jaw belligerently and crosses his arms. When he scowls, his bushy brows dip so low they almost cover his green eyes. "Yeah, so what? You going to call the cops and have me sent away again? Maybe if you're lucky they'll lock me up just like my dad."

Sam works his bruised jaw from side to side. "We didn't even know you were here," he says. Daniel snorts scornfully.

Even in grief he wants to pick a fight. But I won't let him, and I won't run scared. I sigh, shake my head, and hobble to where my shoes lay discarded. The violet suede is totally ruined. I free them from the mud and give them a futile shake. Zoey has matching ones, and we try to wear them on the same days. I brush my feet off as much as possible and jam them into the ruined flats.

"Whether you believe me or not, I'm so sorry about your mom." I approach him like you would a feral animal. "I didn't tell the cops you're in Savage, and for what it's worth, I know that your dad didn't do any of this. That's why we're here. I want to remember so that they can arrest who's really responsible."

Daniel tilts his head skeptically. It takes him a minute to respond, as if he's been caught off guard. "What the fuck is he doing here then?" He jerks his thumb at Sam. "I remember what a snitch you were, running off to Stella's dad every time I was in town." He takes another threatening step toward Sam.

"Enough, Daniel. Sam's helping me." I try to look too severe to cross. "He's the only one willing to."

Sam pushes his hands in his pockets and shrugs. "C'mon, man, it wasn't as if I ever meant you harm, but you were really intense with Stella."

Daniel whips his head back and forth. I cut him off before he can argue. "Is this where you came after the bonfire?"

"That's great." He scrubs his hands over his sneering face. "Rub it in that if I'd gone home to that rat-infested trailer, my mom might still be alive. I could have stopped whoever hurt her." He groans, and his arms drop limp and heavy at his sides. "I didn't want to be with them, okay? Not after you found that kid . . . not after I saw how much she looked like Jeanie. I needed to be in our old house."

If he were someone less volatile, I'd throw my arms around him. Daniel didn't go home to his parents' after the bonfire because he wanted to be where Jeanie had been alive. If Daniel had driven across town to the trailer instead, would he have arrived before his mom went for a walk? He might have gone with her, and Mrs. Talcott would be alive.

"What's your plan?" I ask. "You just going to camp out in your old abandoned house while your dad goes to jail for crimes he didn't commit?" I sweep my arms, indicating his outfit. "Or a neighbor calls the cops on you for looking like a homeless squatter?"

A muscle ticks in his jaw as he mulls over his answer. There's something he's holding back, unsure about trusting us with.

"Let us help," I plead.

Finally, he groans in surrender. "I was about to go talk to someone who was a witness the day Jeanie was taken."

I shake my head. "I was the only witness. Me." I touch my chest for extra measure just so there's zero confusion. "The case file says so."

He clears his throat and spits a fat wad on the ground between his dusty Vans. "Yeah, 'cause cops never lie." If it's possible, his expression becomes even surlier. "A neighbor was home, and those pigs interviewed her but decided she wasn't credible. They left her statement out of their reports."

I prop my hands on my hips. "Shane and Berry wouldn't do anything dishonest. You don't know them. Berry died a few weeks ago because he was such a stress-ball. And Shane . . . he would never."

Daniel laughs an acidic-sounding laugh. "You think you're the only one Detectives Douchebag and Dickless check on? I know all about them. And I know that they interviewed Mrs. Griever that day. If you two junior detectives actually want to help, let's go." Daniel's expression isn't exactly welcoming as he stomps across the marshy front yard, but what else can we do other than follow? What other option do I have? We trail after him down the drive bordered by strawberry plants. Wait. *Strawberry plants?*

At first glance they appear to be thorned. I angle closer. Their glossy leaves and green stalks that curl and bow almost disguise a waist-high mass of bramble. The bramble's half-inch-long barbs have the look of talons or claws. The two vines, one laden with red fruit shinier than what we get from the grocery store and the other with the look of barbed wire, have intertwined as one snarl.

"I thought they tore these up," I say to anyone with answers. I glare suspiciously at the healthy torrent of vines.

"Dad tried," Daniel says. "He hacked them down every year since Jeanie, but they grew back stronger. I guess their roots were too deep, and they just resprouted each summer. Then the bramble started growing through them, taking over. It drove him nuts. He'd shred his arms on their thorns trying to get the whole mass out." He kicks a bulbous berry from the trail. "None of the neighbors would touch the fruit, because they're convinced it's poisonous. Without Dad here, no one's slashing them down anymore."

The confusion of vines seem darker and greener than the muted shrubbery along the drive. I can't tell if the bramble's strangling the strawberries, or boosting them up as a lattice would and protecting them from greedy hands with their thorns. I'm seized by an awful fantasy that the bramble's protecting the fruit from something worse. I shudder and duck around Sam so he's between me and the plants. The scuff of my flats on the trail grows quieter. I have the sense that we're sneaking up on what doesn't want to be found.

"You okay?" Sam whispers, nudging my arm with his elbow.

I nod and then shake my head on second thought. "This place doesn't feel right, does it?"

"No, it doesn't," he mutters. The lane narrows the farther we get from the abandoned house. The trees lining either side grow diagonally over us, their branches tangled and woven together in a tie-dye of browns and greens. We pass what I thought was the last house on the drive, a large two-story Victorian wearing a wraparound porch like a hula hoop, but Daniel marches on. The lane is no more than a path now, barely wide enough for Sam and me to walk alongside each other, let alone for a car to make it through.

"How much farther?" Sam calls ahead to Daniel.

Daniel whirls around, his face shadowed with stubble. "As a kid

I thought there was something off about Old Lady Griever. She's all over these woods, and if anyone knows what happened to Jeanie, it'd be her. Don't freak her out before she answers my questions, okay?" We stare at him blankly. "Got it?" he demands. Sam nods and I mimic the gesture, too baffled to be original. I can't imagine what about a little old lady would make Daniel think she was keeping details of Jeanie's disappearance from him.

I take a deep breath, stifling another shudder, and follow. Moss-covered stones that fit like jigsaw pieces make up the pathway. Thick bramble etches both sides, and sharp branches extend with the look of tentacles threatening to pull me into their hungry mouths. One catches at my camisole, and when I tug free, it tears the silk.

I glare at the offending branch as Sam reaches for it, snapping its bony finger off. He grins as he makes a show of stomping it. I can't help smiling embarrassingly large in response. "I feel like we're Hansel and Gretel making our way to the witch's house in the woods," I whisper.

"I hope you're not picturing me in lederhosen." Sam laughs. He's close enough behind me that his heat spreads down my spine, beneath my shirt. There's something so familiar, so comforting, about being near him. It's an irresistible taste of a home that's no longer mine. I let my eyes flutter shut, pulling the sensation over me like a blanket. My face collides with Daniel's back.

"Watch it," he growls. I shrug off his vileness and follow his gaze up to a shabby gray house.

Calling it a house might be too generous. It's more a shack than anything remotely houselike. It's a room or two large, with busted steps leading to the front door. Haunted-house-worthy cobwebs hang thick from the porch eaves. The windows are blackened with soot. There's not one living thing within a perimeter of several yards; the trees and brush actually grow as if they're trying to escape it. There's a perfect circle of blue sky directly above the roof, making me feel too exposed, like we're bugs under the lens of a magnifying glass. Inky smoke snakes from a crumbling chimney, filling the air with the stench of burning fur or hair. To the left the entire front yard has been freshly churned for planting; when I look closer, I see it's really separate small mounds that have been tilled just close enough to look like one large plot.

"What the . . ." My words fade as I catch movement out of the corner of my eye. The shack's front door swings inward, revealing a rectangle of pitch blackness beyond. Daniel straightens his shoulders, steps forward holding his hand up in greeting, and squares his feet to brace himself.

"Good afternoon, Mrs. Griever. It's Daniel Talcott," he calls, eager and polite, the ragged edge of his voice gone. "My parents and I used to live down the lane. We've spoken before, remember?" Silence. A light breeze spirals around us as if trapped in the clearing, causing the shack to sway. I take a small step backward into Sam. His chest doesn't give, and I don't restore the space between us. Just for a minute I want to be warm and safe touching him. His heart tap dances its rhythm into my back.

"I've nothin' more to say to you," a voice like a meat grinder growls from the open door.

Undeterred, Daniel steps closer. "Mrs. Griever, do you remember Jeanie? She brought you cookies once with my mother. The ones with little jam thumbprints in the middle? She used to play near here." Daniel's tone is raw and vulnerable. I catch a sob in my throat that comes out of nowhere. His memories of Jeanie are so intimate. They're difficult to hear. I've been busy convincing myself that Jeanie was nothing special, but to him she was. I want to ask him what it was about her that he loved so much.

A knotted hand protrudes from the doorway. It braces the door frame and wrests its owner slowly from the dark. As if she's emerging from a pool of black tar, she's revealed piece by piece: the saggy transparent skin on her forearm; crookedly formed bare feet; a shrunken skull with loose white skin and deep scores under her cheekbones; clumps of silver hair patchy over a navy-veined scalp; earlobes that hang lank; and a hunched spine in a ratty black shawl tied over a mauve-pink dress, which reaches her ankles.

"I told ya to never set foot on my property again. I told ya I didn't know anythin' about your missin' sister." The last piece to emerge from the darkness is her other hand, gripping a shotgun. Daniel puts his hands up slowly as though involved in an old-fashioned stickup. Sam steps in front of me so quickly I barely know he's moving. She jabs the barrel of the gun toward Daniel. "Yous have till the count of three to get outta my sight. I don't want no trouble. Stop bringin' it round."

Daniel holds perfectly still. "You're the only one who lives out here, and it's been years since I asked you. I thought you might have found something . . . evidence or a sign of what happened to her."

"One," she bleats.

Daniel clasps his hands like he's praying or begging. "Have you found a toy or a shoe or footprints or any . . . *any bones?*" he squeezes out.

"Two!" Griever shouts as a bitter lump rises in my throat. Daniel's looking for what's left of Jeanie, and he believes her body never left these woods. With his whole family falling apart, Daniel only wants to put Jeanie to rest.

Sam turns and tries to push me down the trail.

"Please," Daniel cries.

"Boy, I don't have no business with monsters. Three!" Her voice echoes in the clearing. Her words sear hot in my eardrums. *Monsters.* I fake left and then slip right around Sam to make a wild dash in front of Daniel.

"I'm Stella Cambren," I scream, like it might save me from the gun pointed at my head. I'm breathing hard. Chest heaving. Hands tingling.

The old woman inches farther from the door, still training the shotgun on us. "You're the one who wasn't taken?" she rasps. I nod desperately. She considers this for a long minute, nose twitching, until she shifts the gun so it's on Sam. "I won't talk to your boys, but you come on up here, girl."

"Stella, no," Sam bursts out. Daniel stays quiet, but I can feel his eyes, like iron pokers left in a fire, jabbing me ahead.

My gaze flits to the mounds of dirt, and then unsteady legs carry me forward. "Don't you move, boys," she orders. I make it to the busted steps. "Up here." She indicates the porch by tapping her knotted foot. I kick my leg over the two ruptured boards and lunge up to her. The cut on my heel stings. My God, we were *stupid, stupid, stupid* to lose the police tail.

This close I see that one of her eyes is milky, the iris clouded over, its pupil gray rather than black. But the other is clear and alert, watching me. "What you said about monsters," I whisper, because I don't trust my voice to keep steady any louder. "Why did you say that?"

"You're helpin' this hooligan find who stole his sister, are ya? Better you run from this town. Don't ever look back." Saliva gathers in the corners of her mouth, and her unseeing eye twitches. "There ain't no getting' any of 'em back. Best you give thanks it wasn't you."

Every atom of me wants to recoil as I inch closer. "Please. Daniel's mother was killed, and his father is being blamed for what happened to her and Jeanie. He didn't do it." My eyes cut to Daniel for a moment. "I know he didn't. Is there anything you can remember from that day? If the police spoke to you, why didn't they include your statement in their report?" My hands shake violently; the porch wails under my weight.

She grunts, letting spit bubble on her lips. "The police? I told 'em I was here that day and for the one before."

"I'm sorry, the one before? You mean the day before Jeanie was taken?"

"I didn't see her, but I was out here when his li'l redheaded sister was taken." She jabs the gun at Daniel. "And I was here when the li'l redhead before her was snatched up too."

Confusion snarls in my head. This woman is old and obviously crazy, with her shotgun and cottage in the woods. She must be senile, and Daniel is so desperate for information he doesn't see that she couldn't possibly know anything. She can hardly walk to her porch; she definitely isn't hiking through the forest and coming across Jeanie's body. Her mention of monsters is coincidence. I only interpret it as meaningful because I'm desperate for clues.

She leans forward and clucks her tongue. "I see ya think I've got a head full o' worms. But Jeanie ain't the first or last. This town has a short memory for what happens to its children. I was sixteen when the Balco girl was taken. Hair so red it was like drunken molasses cookies. She lived a little ways down the lane. Grabbed right from under the clothesline in her front yard." She drags her trigger hand across her frothing mouth.

Something cold washes over me as I listen to her. It's that looking at this woman, I know I shouldn't believe a word she's saying, but I do. My mouth is flooded with acrid saliva, hearing her. It tastes like the truth. "How is that possible? Anyone who took a little girl that long ago would be dead now or too old."

Her lips pull back in an almost snarl, so the remains of her decaying teeth are visible. Yellow and black nubs like tiny gravestones. "Well, aren't you a bright one," she sneers. "Now get off my land before I fire a round of iron into one of your boys' guts." I take a clumsy stride forward and then jump down from the porch. Just before the front door clatters closed, she says, "You keep squintin' in Savage's dark corners, you gonna wish yourself blind."

Chapter Nine

Numbness. I move toward the boys, unaware that I'm propelling myself forward. Rubbery knees bending and straightening on their own. Daniel is pale and still as a statue. Sam's mouth twists in a corkscrew. "Go," I order, waving for them to start down the path. I want to get away from here. Away from the woman with her tales and her shotgun. Away from the sensation creeping up on me. I'm no longer sneaking up on what's hiding. I feel pursued by an invisible force—hunted even. But I don't dare run. Everyone knows that running from monsters makes them chase you more.

Halfway back to the Talcotts' abandoned house, Daniel begins muttering under his breath. First cursing and then repeating "impossible" over and over again. "You can't stay here," I tell him. "You have to go to your dad's." The trees lining the path nod in the wind, agreeing with me, feeding my panic. "It doesn't feel *right* here. It can't be safe." He doesn't respond. I whirl around. "Do you hear me? You can't stay anywhere near here!" I'm losing it. Suddenly this dirt lane is the most dangerous place in the world to me.

My mind races. Monsters. Other little girls have been taken. Other little girls who look like Jeanie. *Redheads.* My stomach churns. "The body from the cemetery was a redhead. I puked when I saw her picture, she looked so much like Jeanie." I try to connect the dots. My horror multiplies. "Do you know they found a *finger bone* in her hand?" If anyone deserves to know, it's Daniel; after all, it might be Jeanie's. "The news said something about a sacrificial killing. I thought they were crazy, but maybe it *is* a cult? That could explain the disappearances spanning generations. You know, because there would have to be multiple people taking the girls? Maybe it's a religious cult?" My pitch climbs, my words spewing out fast and messy. "Although I don't know what religion sacrifices little redheaded girls. Jane Doe was one, and her scalp was torn clean off. Maybe that's why I wasn't taken? I don't have red hair." I tug hard on a clump of my honey-brown locks. "Neither did your mother. She must have been on to them."

The path widens as we pass the large Victorian. I clench my mouth shut. Daniel doesn't need to hear the harpy song of my innermost fear screaming that the finger bone found is going to be—*has to be*—Jeanie's. That Jeanie and the tiny redhead in the graveyard will be linked for certain. My thoughts are a hysterical snarl, yes, but they are also perfectly reasonable.

After a minute of quiet, Sam says, "What was with all the little heaps of dirt in her yard? Do you think something was buried?

Animals? They're too small for children." He averts his eyes quickly when I give him a horrified look.

"She didn't say anything about the others before," Daniel says. He buffets his arms against his sides as he walks, like he's punishing them for something. "I went to her a few years ago, asking if she'd found any sign of what happened to Jeanie. She was in the woods a lot, and I thought . . . I thought . . . maybe she saw more than she was letting on. Maybe she found signs of a body? But that crazy old hag never said there were more. Why now?"

Sam answers more to himself than to us. "Why any of this *now*? Why did Jane Doe turn up dead? Why was your mom *murdered*? Why after eleven years of nothing has so much happened in only twenty-four hours?" He flicks hair from his wide eyes. "And Mrs. Griever didn't tell *you*. She told Stella," Sam adds pointedly. "It sounded like a warning meant only for Stella. She's probably just an old lady with dementia who's been alone too long. The police were right not to take her seriously, and if they suspected her of anything more than being senile, they would have investigated her."

I stop, rooted to the spot. "Do you know what I told the cops when they questioned me after Jeanie disappeared?" Both boys swivel to face me. I look from Sam to Daniel; one gnawing on his lip as if faced with a confounding puzzle he'll think through, the other pulsing his hands into fists like he'll beat the answer free.

Sam backtracks to stand near me; he rests his hands on my shoulders and squeezes softly. "It doesn't matter, Stella. You were only six."

I shake him off. "That's where you're wrong, Sam. I was saying,

'If you hunt for monsters, you'll find them.' I said it two hundred and fifty-five times." Daniel sucks in a breath hard.

My eyes brim with tears. In this moment I understand Daniel's instinct to pummel the trouble rather than solve it. I want it out of me: everything I've held back, every word I've ever spoken about Jeanie, every bit of me that exists because of that day. There have to be parts, right? Parts born out of whatever I saw without me even knowing that that's where they came from. I don't want them anymore. I plow onward, certain that if I can say everything, then those parts won't have to belong to me.

"All these years you've thought I was holding something back. But I have only one memory of that day, Daniel. Something I remembered at the bonfire right before you showed up. Jeanie hit her head. She was bleeding. She peed her pants. That's it. That's all I've managed to remember over eleven years." I half laugh, half sob. "No wonder you hate me. I'd hate me too."

For once Daniel looks at me without glaring; his eyes are swimming in their sockets. "I don't hate you," he whispers. "It just should've been you and not my sister." You'd think that would make me cry more—especially the conviction he says it with—but it doesn't. Daniel loved Jeanie. I understand.

We march in stunned silence until we reach the abandoned house. All along the way I glower at the strawberry vines. Dad had a vegetable garden two springs ago, and these prehistoric-looking weeds kept popping up in the arugula. For weeks he kept hacking them down rather than yanking them up by their root-balls. Each time, the weeds resurrected themselves with knobbier and thicker stalks. They began to resemble miniature spinal columns. Their bristles catching at my skin was why I stopped picking the vegetables myself. These strawberries remind me of them; feral and stronger for being half murdered over and over again. Nature even lent a hand and sent the bramble as armor.

I go out of my way to stomp on the juicy berries that rest on the lane. The way they rupture, popping red pulp under my shoe, is oddly satisfying. With each miniature explosion, I get a firmer hold on reason. The bone will be Jeanie's; she was bound to turn up at some point. The little girl will have been the psycho's next victim. Serial killers have types, and he must like redheads. Bev Talcott will have been on the verge of discovering the killer's identity. The cops will hunt him down—there are two bodies now covered in evidence and clues—and he'll go to jail forever. Mystery solved.

"Look, man," Sam says to Daniel as we spill back onto the Talcotts' marred lawn, "I know we've had our differences, but if you need somewhere to stay, you're welcome at my place. My mom and dad won't have any idea who you are, and they'll be cool with a friend from school crashing. If you're avoiding the cops, then going to your folks' isn't a great idea. And Stella's right about you not staying here."

Daniel's lost his edge. The older boy with his unruly hair, five o'clock shadow, and sharply defined arms looks sunken in. Deflated by the afternoon. He nods slowly and says, "That's decent of you, thanks. I've got to clean up here, but I could head over tonight." Sam gives Daniel his address, and I wave a silent good-bye to him as we trudge back into the bleak woods. There were birds cawing, toothy rodents scampering, the buzz of swarming bees before. Now it's eerily quiet. The sky's clogged with clouds and there's a stormy cast of light. I'm not even sure what time it is, since I left my purse and cell in Sam's car.

With each step the water filling my flats gurgles and my fingers turn bluer. Our pace slows to a crawl as my feet grow sore and tired. "You look cold," Sam says after he helps me over a rocky stream. He pulls his T-shirt up and over his head, revealing a white sleeveless undershirt, his skin showing through the thin fabric. His shoulders are tan and freckled from the sun. "Here." He offers it to me.

"But you'll be cold," I say. There's a purple welt on Sam's cheekbone from Daniel punching him. Zoey dated a freshman in college for a week last year; their relationship lasted until the black eye he'd been given at a party healed. Zoey said that bruises do to guys' faces what makeup does to girls'. I think she was on to something.

"I won't. I run warm, remember?" Sam says. I take the T-shirt reluctantly. His big muddy-brown eyes on my face as I do, my gaze sticking to his. He grins when I pull the still warm shirt over my head. It hangs low, to my mid-thigh, and smells of my childhood. I can't pinpoint it exactly . . . maybe chlorine from his pool, coconut sunblock his mom made us wear, and something vaguely mint. Shampoo or peppermint iced tea.

He jams his hands into his pockets and wades forward through the mucky woods. I slip and slide after him, too tongue-tied to talk, an old sensation sneaking on me. It reminds me of gardenias. For a month before homecoming freshman year, Zoey and I obsessed over getting senior guys to ask us. When Lucas Fitzpatrick, senior class royalty, waved a homecoming flyer in my face and grunted, "You wanna?" I was ecstatic. Believe it or not, the actual night was just as swoon-worthy.

I noticed when Sam showed up because he came stag with a bunch of boys, their adolescent bodies sized all wrong. For all I know, they were younger versions of Sweater-Vest and company. I remember Zoey dragging me to the bathroom to adjust her push-up bra so her boobs looked extra big. Zoey's all about being desired, especially by those who could never get her. Sam had this little plastic box with him: a single gardenia wrapped in a blue silk ribbon. Once I saw it, I knew it was for me, as much as I knew that my date hadn't given me one.

You see, there used to be this photo on our mantel of my mom wearing an identical corsage at prom. She looked glamorous in the picture; grown-up for only seventeen. I wanted to be her. I told Sam I wanted a corsage just like it someday. Being Sam—years later—he remembered.

Sam stood with his group of friends most of the night. They danced in a wide circle, laughing and smiling way more than I was, and he never put that box down. He wasn't staring at me or anything. Nothing stalkerish. But when my Neanderthal date went out to the parking lot for shots with a bunch of jocks, Sam found me. I was standing with Zoey and a trio of junior girls she was trying to impress. They were the kind of popular girls who are cruel because they enjoy it. Zoey's only nasty as a means to an end. Trust me, there's a difference. Zoey saw him first and purred, "Hi, Samantha, you hoping to be deflowered tonight?" The juniors burst into mean fits of giggles. He ignored them.

"Hey, Stella. I brought this for you," he said, opening the container and removing the corsage. "I remembered you always wanted one like in the picture." I was horrified. I could sense Zoey mentally screaming at me to chuck it; that this was our chance to prove that we belonged.

It was stupid, but the only thing I could think to say was, "Gross. I'm not deflowering you, Samantha." Lucas walked up right then and slapped the corsage from Sam's hand. The trio of juniors laughed like hyenas. Sam didn't say a word. He looked right into my eyes, smiled like he felt bad for *me*, and walked away. When no one but Zoey was looking, I scooped up the flattened corsage and tucked it in my clutch. A year later, Zoey dethroned those three junior girls—who were seniors then—by seducing each of their boyfriends into dumping them over the course of a month. I'm sure she didn't remember us trying to impress them at Sam's expense. Popularity's just a zero-sum game to her.

There have been a lot of chances since then to prove that Zoey and I belong. And I've taken them mostly. This time I don't want to. I don't cave to the bazillion what-ifs. What if Janey Bear sees us walking out of the woods together? What if Taylor hears I wore Sam's shirt? What if Zoey gets pissed that I spent the day with Sam? What if the rumors start and I get more stares than I already do? I bat the what-ifs away. I'm not twelve anymore. I can have both Zoey and Sam in my world.

"Do you want to do some research on past abductions and disappearances?" Sam asks abruptly. "Because of what Mrs. Griever said about there being others. If we could show the police a pattern, they'd have to take her seriously. Right?" His body is angled toward me, the arm nearest to me extending each time we navigate over a log or a stream, in case I need it.

"I think that's brilliant," I say. "But I'll probably be on lockdown after going rogue today." Without thinking, I pull the collar of his T-shirt to my face and inhale deeply. Oh. My. God. What is happening to me? I veer to allow more space between us. Was I this psycho when we were young playing together? It's as if I've been poisoned by the nostalgia of remembering us as kids and I'm losing brain function.

I manage to control myself for the duration of the walk—not without having to defeat the urge to take one more whiff of the T-shirt to prove that I only imagined that it smelled like childhood. After nearly twice the time it took us to travel to Jeanie's, we arrive back at the cement loading dock. I follow Sam around the perimeter of the giant building he works in to the parking lot. I can only imagine the holy hell I look, with twigs and leaves sticking from my hair, soiled shoes, and muddy jeans. We probably look like a pair of mountain people setting eyes on civilization for the first time.

The teal station wagon is right where we left it, and to my sublime relief, the police are not. Taped to the passenger-side window is a folded piece of paper. I climb into the dry interior of the wagon and unfold the note to behold Shane's frantic chicken scratch:

Stella Cambren, call me the INSTANT you get back to this car.

I frown at Shane's obvious fury and pass Sam the note. I wiggle out of his T-shirt and toss it to him once he's done. He tugs it over his head and grins. "Smells like you," he says. There's a bizarre stirring in my chest. It's suddenly tighter, making me work harder to breathe. I close my eyes and count to ten.

Sam's voice cuts me off at seven. "There's something familiar about what you told the cops that day. I can't shake the feeling of déjà vu."

"If you hunt for monsters, you'll find them," I speak slowly.

"Yeah, I swear I've heard that before, or maybe I've even said it," Sam says thoughtfully. I look at him, startled. The late-afternoon sky is dark with clouds, and Sam's edges are silver as he shakes his head. "I didn't mean to upset you." His eyes click to me before returning to the asphalt in front of us.

I rest my head against the seat back. "There's a whole lot of twisted crap that's upsetting me lately, Sam. Anything you can remember helps."

"Here's the thing." He steers us out of the parking lot. "You were six, right? Six-year-olds believe in monsters and all sorts of things: Santa Claus, the Tooth Fairy, the Easter Bunny, werewolves. But that doesn't sound like something a kid would come up with." His eyes gleam with electric thought. "At least not a kid that young. To me it sounds like a warning someone else told you, and then you repeated it because you were traumatized."

My eyes are suddenly damp hearing Sam say it. I was *trauma-tized*. I watch the houses pass by, their shapes smearing and bleeding like watercolors as I let a few tears fall. *I was the lucky one, and I was traumatized.* It's hard to make sense of. I try to focus only on the houses and trees streaking by as we pass, to let their shapelessness numb my mind.

"Do you see what I'm seeing?" Sam asks. I squint through the windshield at a corner house. I roll down my window for a better look at the vague outlines crowding the lawns on the block we've turned up.

Every few houses there's one decorated with symbols and candles. Porch lights illuminate rosaries dangling over front stoops. Bunga-lows are lit up like birthday cakes in the gray dusk. Eaves are fes-tooned with loops of daisy chains. Wood crosses spear apron lawns and tidy flower beds. We pass a ranch home with a clot of white pillar candles and a framed picture of Jeanie at the center. Orange ribbon knots, like those worn in remembrance of Jeanie for months after her disappearance, are tied around doorknobs and car antennas. Big, clumsy bows are secured around tree trunks; candles, photos, and newspaper clippings are displayed at their bases. Everywhere I look there are vigils for the dead, displayed in front yards like tiny lawn-gnome funerals.

Chapter Ten

Everyone's heard about the body in the cemetery and Mrs. Talcott's murder," Sam says quietly. "It's a small town. This place was messed-up enough over Jeanie's disappearance. Remember how long it was before we were allowed to trick-or-treat? People are bound to lose it again."

I turn away and burrow through my purse for my cell. Sam's right. I don't like to recall what Zoey refers to as "the lost years," the three years after Jeanie was taken. Three Halloweens canceled—trick-or-treating actually outlawed. Three years of town curfews, police patrolling, flashing lights seeping through the blinds. Three years of students hustled from classrooms to their parents' idling cars, teachers yapping into walkie-talkies at the sight of a stranger. Three years of mandatory weekly town council meetings in the church's pews—the fire-and-brimstone preacher sharing the pulpit with the mayor to outline safety measures the town was taking. Three is how many years it took Savage to stop being afraid. I can't face what's happening outside the car window, time reversing its course. I'm not ready to see the stitches on that collective wound torn open. Not yet at least.

I have only two texts. The first is from Shane. And although he uses a few more curse words, it's basically the same as the note he left. The second is from Michaela.

Parents have me on lockdown today, but I will break out if you need me. XO

Poor Michaela. Her parents are always griping about her needing to spend time with "constructive influences." Ron and Helen don't mind me so much, since they judge all of Michaela's friends by how many As they earn. Me: I get a lot. It helps that Dad plays golf with Michaela's dad. But Michaela's parents condemn Zoey whenever they get the chance. According to them, she's some kind of anarchist. They're probably injecting Michaela with one of those GPS microchips as we speak and brainstorming ways Zoey is likely to blame for Mrs. Talcott's demise.

"My dad didn't even call." My voice is a near whine. "And I thought Zoey would text for sure." How is it that I'm left with only Sam?

The next five blocks leading to my street are exactly the same. Crucifixes of all sizes, candlelight vigils, framed photos of Jeanie Talcott, rosaries, dream catchers, piles of acorns, tiny mountains of salt. Anything that anyone believes will ward off death has been rounded up and displayed. I hope my neighbors haven't lost it too.

But once we turn onto my street, I can't even see the surrounding homes. The sidewalks are filled with reporters; news vans line the drive; nosy neighbors huddle together; kids circle their parents, kept near with invisible leashes of fear. The lights of cop cars cast a red, white, and blue wash on the carnival. Before I can beg Sam not to stop, he wrenches the wheel and makes a sharp U-turn.

"Thank you." I exhale, eyeing the glittering mess in the rearview mirror.

"No problem." He shoots me a sympathetic look. "You don't need to be there for that." A long pause. "How do you feel about chicken piccata?"

I smile weakly. "I am decidedly pro chicken piccata."

We navigate the ten blocks that separate our houses. With every block put between us and my house, I breathe easier. Sam's is a brick two-story on a quiet court. No reporters or meddlesome neighbors in sight as he pulls into the driveway. I push out of the car and regard the house for the first time in years. The ivory paint on the shutters is peeling like my nail polish; the waist-high lawn has splotches of brown; the picket fence is sagging and creaking rhythmically. It's not what I remember.

As if reading my mind, Sam says, "Dad's picking up odd jobs whenever he can. I try to keep it up, but between school and BigBox, I don't have much time."

The outside of the house may look shabby, but once inside it's obvious that Sam still has a family-sitcom kind of home. Sam's mom practically floats from the kitchen, donning a ruffled apron to welcome us.

Mrs. Worth's eyes linger on Sam's bruised cheek and then on me. She doesn't ask, though, and I'm sure she assumes the injury has everything to do with me spontaneously reappearing in her home after a five-year absence. "You've been missed around here," she whispers close to my ear as I'm wrapped in her soft arms. She avoids mentioning the news and tells us that dinner is in a half hour. I follow Sam up the narrow carpeted staircase; its shag is squishy and familiar under my soles. The dimly lit hall is lined with framed family photos. I'm in a few taken at picnics, field trips, and school plays.

I stop halfway up the stairs, tapping on the glass of one picturing Sam clad in green tights for his role as Peter Pan in the fourth grade. "I wish you still had this outfit. I'd like to see you running around school in those tights," I tease.

He pauses a few steps above me, leans one hand on the railing and, with the other, points to a scrawny nine-year-old in a blue leotard and fairy wings in the corner of the photo. His voice is soft but serious. "I'd like to see you in this, Tinker Bell." He holds my gaze with his. The words are light enough, but there's an undercurrent to them that makes heat rise in my cheeks. Who knew that Sam Worth could . . . uhhh, flirt? I catch my breath and jog up the stairs after him.

The second floor is warm with stale air. Sam lifts a hall window up a crack before opening his bedroom door. He stands to the side so I can enter. I hesitate. "We can keep the door open if you're worried about not being able to control yourself so near a bed with me," he says with a laugh. I brush against him, even though there's plenty of room to avoid touching him. Umm . . . alternate universe much, am I flirting back?

Sam's bedroom brings on a deluge of memories. It's almost exactly as I remember: walls painted in forest green, with the silhouettes of pine trees in brown; his twin bed draped in a navy comforter with white piping along its edges; two nightstands stacked precariously with books; and a giant bulletin board above his desk, covered in photos, pictures of cars from magazines, and band logos. It used to display photos of us; now I'm not in any of them. I inch closer to see who is: a group of boys on a camping trip; a mousy brunette sitting on his lap grinning at the camera; a bunch of girls and boys in matching yellow T-shirts huddled in a pyramid; a perky blonde in a low-cut tank top with her arms wrapped around Sam's waist. I don't recognize a single person in any of them. It makes me feel left out; ridiculous since he's the one who should feel that way.

I prop my hands on my hips and try to imitate Zoey's purr and honeyed smile. "Well, I guess now you wouldn't need me to pull you in for a kiss, since it looks like you've had loads of experience." Sam fills the doorway, where he's leaning watching me. "Who are these sluts?" Inwardly I cringe at saying "slut." Zoey says it a lot, but only because she tries to own the word. You know, take it back from all the people who put girls who like sex down? I use it in the bad way. I'm instantly ashamed.

"Who are you talking about?" Sam asks.

I flick my hand toward the bulletin board, completely aware of what a wicked witch I'm being. "Is Anna what's-her-face up here?" I ask. Just thinking it makes me want to rip the pictures down. *Nice to meet you, jealousy.* I seriously need to get a grip. I shouldn't even be *here.* Who am I kidding? Zoey will lose her shit over today. And how is this fair to Sam? Once this nightmare is over, we'll go back to the way we were. I'm *Stella Cambren*; he's Sam Worth.

Sam's jaw tightens as he stares at me. There's no trace of the glint in his eye or the smirk that guys get when trying to make you jealous. He actually looks . . . *angry.*

"Stella, you've had nothing to do with me for five years. For five years I've tried to show you that I care about you, and you've shot me down every single time. I've made friends. Was I supposed to wait for you just in case you changed your mind?" He shrugs with his hands. "I went out with other girls. Don't call any of them that word. Better yet," he adds, steady and low, "don't use it at all."

I bite the inside of my cheek. I'm a monster making Sam explain anything to me after I deserted him. What did I expect? That Sam wouldn't be able to make friends? That there would never be a girl who saw what ten-year-old me saw that day at the cove? And why do I care anyway? Why do I feel like the girls on the bulletin board stole something vital from me, when really, I threw it away?

I drop to the edge of his bed, covering my face with my hands. I wish I could make my awfulness disappear. Why can't Sam just get it? *I didn't choose him.* He was supposed to hate me, not spend the last five years proving that I chose wrong. Proving that even though I threw him away, he would never ever do the same to me. Believe me, *I get it.*

Sam drops to his knees at my feet. "It's okay. It's been an insane couple of days." He pats me lightly on the knee and then withdraws his hand.

I wallow in the darkness of my palms. "I don't know who any of those people are. I only guessed who your friends were at the bonfire because of how they were dressed. I don't know if you have a girlfriend . . . or if she's the girl you left with the other night." Jealousy threatens to choke me as I inhale. "I used to know everything about you. With my eyes closed, I could pick your footsteps out during silent reading whenever you got up from your desk, and I'd ask for a bathroom pass and we'd talk out in the halls." I stare at him. Only Zoey's face is more familiar than Sam's.

Sam knits his brow and rocks back on his heels. "I might not always like you, but I could never hate you." I try to blink away the tears; they're too fat. Sam jumps to his feet and taps a photo on the bulletin board.

"You see all these losers in the yellow shirts?" His eyes laugh. "We were in a science camp the summer before sophomore year. A few go to Wildwood, but mostly they're from all over Minnesota. They're all at camp this summer, but I couldn't take the time off from work. This girl here"—he points to the blonde—"this is Anna. We met a year ago at BigBox. We dated for four months and are strictly friends now. I gave her a ride home because she was there with another friend of mine—Toby from school with the thick-framed glasses and braces—and she wasn't into it." He grins like it's a funny story. "This is Harry." He taps a photo of two boys sitting on the hood of a vintage car painted cherry red. "I helped him rebuild his Dad's '67 Mustang last summer. We're going to take it to a track in a few weeks. This brunette is Sarah. We dated for all of eighth grade. It wasn't serious and we had nothing in common, but she was my first girlfriend, after you." He freezes. Did he just call me his girlfriend? Well, maybe that's what we were. We were just kids, but we were every bit as much of a couple as I've ever been with anyone. Obviously minus the sex stuff. When I don't object, he launches into a short bio of every person pictured on his board.

Fifteen minutes later Mrs. Worth shouts from downstairs that dinner is ready. I've been quietly listening, gradually letting my guilt wane as Sam tells me about his life, post–Hella Stella. It's difficult to hear he's been mostly happy without me, but I guess it would be worse if he'd been pining away. I drown the jealousy by picturing every guy I've made out with over the past five years. The only problem is this makes me queasy. Every one of those kisses took me further and further away from my first kiss with Sam. The only kiss that ever *really* meant anything.

"Wait a second, there's one more here." He shuffles through papers in a desk drawer. "Here we are. This is my oldest friend. She's a raging ass most of the time, but I just can't get rid of her." He winks at me and tacks up the photo in the center of the board. It's one his mom took while we were swinging in his backyard forever ago. She captured us mid leg pump as we were reaching to grasp hands. Our arms splayed in the air, like once our fingers touched we would take flight. Vaguely, I remember believing we would.

"And you're right"—he nails me with a solemn stare, the sort of stare you fall into—"I wouldn't need you to pull me in for a kiss. All you'd have to do is say the word and I'd be all over you."

Chapter Eleven

think Sam's mom can hear my heart thumping, wildly trying to free itself from the cage of my ribs, during dinner. Sam's words bounce around in my head, and I can't quit being completely turned on by them. Gag me, but somehow it's the hottest thing anyone's ever said to me. Epically random, since I don't even think Sam's hot. I appraise him slyly over a spoonful of rice. Okay, so maybe that little crease between his eyebrows from concentrating too much is adorable, and maybe there's something kissable about those freckles, and maybe the lean muscles corded in his arms are quiver-worthy?

But *hello?* How can I be falling for Sam with all that's going on? *Or at all?* That is what's happening, isn't it? Am I falling for Sam Worth? Falling *back* into Sam Worth?

Sam's dad never comes home, a knowing look exchanged between Sam and his mom, so it's only the three of us at the round kitchen table.

"Stella, tell me what you've been up to." Mrs. Worth launches her first of many questions. I tell her everything I think a mom would want to hear. She beams proudly when Sam says we compete against each other for the second spot in our class—Michaela usually comes in first. She tilts her head and listens when I tell her about the last article I wrote for the *Wildwood Herald*. She applauds when I tell her I might work as the *Herald*'s editor senior year. She coos sympathetically when I share that I haven't seen my mother since Christmas Day. It reminds me of long summer afternoons spent by Sam's pool, with his mom serving us lemonade and teaching us to backflip into the deep end. She's always been the kind of mother I wish I had.

That is, until she scrapes her fork along her plate and finishes her last bite. "Do you have a boy you're seeing?" Her voice is low and velvety, but her words needle my eardrums.

I stare at the points of my fork; if I jammed them into my arm, would she be too distracted to make me answer? "No, not really," I say after too long.

She leans forward, resting her elbows on the table. "Really? It's hard to believe that such a pretty girl doesn't have a boy."

"Mom, stop," Sam groans. "You don't have to answer, Stella."

I fidget in my chair. Mrs. Worth keeps her eyes on me, waiting for more. I swear the grandfather clock ticking in the living room has been turned up ten decibels. It's all I hear as I say, "I don't really date much. I mean, I go out on dates, I just don't have boyfriends." I stop. I've already said too much. This apron-wearing, stay-at-home mom will not understand. The fabric of my camisole pulls uncomfortably against the itchy skin on my chest. Great. I'm breaking out in hives, red welts rising as they watch.

Mrs. Worth scoffs at Sam, "Don't be silly. It's a harmless question." She smiles warmly at me. "You'll get no judgment from me. I barely know what I want and I'm . . . well, let's just say I'm older than you. I can't imagine knowing what you want when you're your age." She shrugs and slides her chair back from the table.

She shoos me out of the kitchen when I try to carry plates over to the sink. "You two go watch a movie or something."

I follow Sam through the house, up the stairs, and into his bedroom. My purse is on his bed where I left it and my cell rattles, vibrating against a compact. I snatch it from the bag and glare at the screen, hoping beyond hope that it isn't Shane calling to chew me out. Taylor. Really, now? It's been days since the bonfire and no word. Plus, we usually text, so what's with him calling all of a sudden?

"You should answer it." Sam surprises me, looking over my shoulder. I avert my eyes, worried that they'll reveal too much, and fumble for the end button.

"No, that's okay. I don't know why he's calling."

"I do. Aren't you going out with him?" He laughs a bit nervously, mostly to himself, when I don't answer right away. He perches on the edge of his desk. He's still wearing his UFO shirt, but it doesn't look silly to me anymore. I take so long to answer because I can't get over the fact that even though Sam assumes Taylor and I are together, he didn't bring it up when I was throwing a jealous tantrum earlier.

"No, I'm not." Thinking about Taylor makes me frown. "We've

never even been out together. You know, not without a group."

Sam stares at his socked foot as he taps his toes on the carpet. I crawl back onto his bed, crossing my legs. "I don't get it then," he says, shoulders drooping.

I start to get blushy as I realize I'm sitting on his bed. "Don't get what?" I sound too breathy.

"Everything, really." He smiles crookedly. "But in this moment, I don't get why you never seem to have a boyfriend, but I always see you with guys. Granted, the infamous lacrosse or football players at Wildwood aren't my type either." He waggles his eyebrows before continuing, "But I see you out with them. And . . . I hear things." He finishes quietly, eyes intent on my expression.

I pretend to fawn over my polished nails to stall for time. The tactic doesn't deter Sam, who stares at me unflinchingly, patiently. Always patient. I sigh and admit, "I go on first dates with a lot of guys. I like flirting; guys act really interested when you're just flirting and you're still . . . you know, not giving it up. But I don't have boyfriends."

"Why not?"

I stare at the ceiling as I answer. "Guys lose interest once you show you're interested. They only want what they can't have. Once they get it, they leave. Everyone knows that."

"I don't know that," he says firmly. I risk a quick look at his face when he says it. The crease in his brow is a parenthesis mark.

I shrug, turning my attention back to the ceiling and its whirling fan. It's safer to stare at. "Then you must be the only person on the planet who doesn't."

I'm aware of him moving closer. I resist the urge to run. He stops directly in front of me, his head blocking my view of the ceiling. "Any guy who doesn't want you because you don't play hard to get is an ass. Those guys aren't good enough for you." I chew my bottom lip. Zoey would totally pitch a fit to know this: I've always wondered what it would be like to kiss Sam again. You know, after I've kissed handfuls of boys. I wonder if it would still stack up.

For a moment I think I might find out. I'm aware of my bottom lip parting from my top. My phone vibrates again, just as he moves to sit next to me. I glance down to see Dad's office number on the screen.

"Dad?" I answer, breathless. Sam backs off, leaning against his desk, whistling softly.

"Hey, Pumpkin. I'm swamped at the office but wanted to check in and let you know I'll be late tonight. Are the police still in front of the house?" Typical. Dad doesn't even know I'm MIA.

"Not certain. I'm actually at Sam Worth's house. His mom made dinner and we're watching a movie."

"That's nice, Pumpkin. He'll make sure you get home safe? Give me a call once you're back." The call ends when good-bye is just rolling off my tongue. I can't help sighing as I toss my cell back into my purse.

"He still works a lot, doesn't he?" Sam asks.

"All the time. He keeps saying he'll cut back with Mom gone and all, but you know how it goes. Plus, I think it makes him sad to be home without her."

"It must be hard for you too," he says gently.

I wrinkle my nose. "I'm mostly used to it. What else is there to do but accept it? She left us." My shoulders rise and fall. "Was Harry wearing a sweater-vest at the bonfire?" I change the subject.

One-half of his mouth hitches up. "Yeah. Don't you remember Harry? He's been in school with us since the eighth grade." My fingers knit in my lap as I picture a twelve-year-old in a sweater-vest. "He wore headgear to school every day for two years?" Sam prods. I shake my head. He groans. "Zoey called him Dirty Harry."

My hand flies to my mouth as I try to smother a laugh. "Oh my God. Dirty Harry is your BFF?" He smiles at the teasing in my tone. "Jeez, I thought he moved or something."

"Nope. He got rid of the braces, started using dandruff shampoo, and became a Jedi Master at avoiding Zoey." I cringe and laugh at the same time. "Really," he says, stroking his chin, "Dirty Harry was not her best work."

"No, it wasn't," I agree.

Sam moves to sit on the bed next to me; the mattress squeals under his weight. He's serious all of a sudden, and it kills the laugh gurgling up from my throat. "Stella, about what I was saying before." He turns to me, lips parted, the pulse in his neck beating steadier than my own. "I want you to know that—"

"SAM!" Mrs. Worth yells from the foot of the stairs. "The police are here to speak with you."

"Oh crap." I leap from the bed like it's on fire and jam my feet into the ruined flats. "It'll be Shane. I should have called him back." I grab my bag and rush down the stairs. Sure enough, Detective Tim Shane fills the foyer with his broad shoulders and menacing frown.

When I'm halfway down the stairs, he says, "In the car, please, Stella," in his best cop voice.

"I'm sorry, Mrs. Worth. Thank you so much for dinner. Bye, Sam!" I shout without turning to see if he's followed. My cheeks and thoughts are feverish. I want out of here. I'm not prepared to hear what Sam wants to say. Mostly because I'm not sure how I'll respond. I also can't stomach being chewed out by Shane in front of him.

I duck past Shane and through the door, jumping off the porch and jogging to his idling sedan. Heavy droplets of rain plop from the sky, and I hurry into the car's cloth interior. It reeks of cigarettes and greasy fast food. After another minute, Shane joins me, silently backing the car out of the driveway. Mrs. Worth stands on the porch waving, her back-lit silhouette somehow warm and inviting. Traveling away from her sends a pang deep into my chest.

We drive without speaking. I crack my window, hoping that some fresh air will vanquish the nausea rising in my stomach. When it doesn't work, I try apologizing.

I twist to face him, hands imploring. "Look, I know today was bad. I understand you had those cops follow to keep me safe. But I was totally fine with Sam. And there was something we needed to do without them."

Shane grits his teeth and growls, "Stop calling them cops. It's disrespectful. They're police officers who would risk their lives to keep you safe." I clasp my hands in my lap, trying to look remorseful. "You scared the shit out of me. I've been looking for you for *hours*. The DNA results came back on the finger bone." I hold my breath, waiting. Waiting for him to hiss Jeanie's name. Waiting for all the strangely shaped jigsaw pieces to snap together as something obvious—horrible, yes, but instantly recognizable, like a kiddie-porn pervert. "It's not Jeanie's," Shane says instead. The words are raw, screechy. My head droops to the seat.

"The lab says the bone is old—older than Jeanie's would be. They called a bone-dating specialist in to give us an exact age. Techs combed through the graves disrupted by the mudslide, and it didn't come from any of them."

For a block there's only the beat of rain as I imagine techs counting the toes and fingers of skeletons, humming this little piggy went to market, as part of some deranged lullaby.

"We've got something really ugly on our hands, and then you go and ditch my officers like that. What were you thinking?" Shane's volume builds. "Or is that the problem, you weren't? You wanted to run off with your boyfriend, everyone else be damned."

This ignites my temper. Yes, anger is easier than fear, so I grasp at it. "He's not my *boyfriend*, and I'm trying to do everything I can to figure out what happened to Jeanie and the poor little girl in the cemetery and whoever she had a piece of." I jab my finger into his shoulder. "You're the one wasting time with Jeanie's dad. Do you understand that?" I glare at him accusingly. "You've got an innocent man while the real perv is free."

Shane brakes hard at a red light; the tires shriek on the wet pavement. "What are you talking about? Kent Talcott is a likely suspect.

What do you mean he's innocent?" His baritone booms in the confined cab like we're inside a beating drum. Anger must be easier for him too.

"I'd know if it was him. Don't you get that?" I clutch my hands to my chest. "I'd feel it here when I look at him, and I don't. He's a good dad who's never done anything wrong. Like mine. You've taken the only family Daniel has left." My voice cracks as I clamp my mouth shut. OHMYGOD. Why did I bring up Daniel?

"Daniel? Have you seen him? We reached his aunt in Portland, and he hasn't been there in months." Shane's like a zombie scenting blood. "Stella, if he's in town, he's a suspect. We've been operating under the assumption that he's estranged from his family." A car behind us at the stoplight honks. The rain is heavier now, almost hail.

I avoid looking at Shane. "Obviously I haven't seen him. You know I've always felt bad for him. I just mean that his dad is all he has left, and I get that." Desperate to change the subject, I rush on. "Why didn't you include Mrs. Griever's statement in the case file you gave me? She was home the day Jeanie was taken, and not just that, she says there are others."

Shane pulls the car into my driveway. Only two news vans remain, their reporters huddled under a tarp strung up between trees. "Griever? That old drunk who lives down the Talcotts' lane? She was barely coherent when we interviewed her. So old that she probably couldn't make it out of her yard. She said she didn't see either of you. Stella, she's just an old woman who tells tales. There haven't been any other child abductions in Savage in the last sixty years. Whoever the bone belongs to, they aren't from here."

The fury drained out of him, he pats his pockets, looking for a pack of cigarettes. "I don't blame you for looking for answers, but Old Lady Griever will fill your head with nonsense. *I'm the police.* I can't solve a disappearance that there's no record of." He leans forward and adds in a gentler tone, "Maybe . . . maybe you should talk to your dad about staying at your mom's during all of this? It could be good to remove yourself from it. This town is only just beginning to react. You see all the vigils."

It takes all my willpower not to slug Shane in his globe-shaped face. Go stay with my mom? That's literally the only thing worse than all this Jeanie Talcott gruesomeness. I kick the car door open. There's nothing else to say tonight. He doesn't believe Mrs. Griever, but I do. "You shouldn't smoke or eat fast food," I yell right before I slam the door in his face. I sprint to the house and jam the key into the door's deadbolt. Inside I flick all the light switches on and trudge up to my bedroom.

Safely stowed in my bed after showering, I curl beneath my comforter, twining my fingers in the sheets. My insides buzz. I lie awake for a long time with my eyes wide open, too electrified for sleep to find me. I didn't act like me today. I didn't do the things I was supposed to. Nothing happened as it should have. Everything that makes sense is dissolving. And yet, somehow, even with the visions of amputated fingers and missing children on a carousel loop in my head, I feel more me than I have in forever. As if I haven't been *me* in ages, and I'm just remembering how.

Chapter Twelve

Wake up, my sleeping angel." There's a Zoey-sized heap straddling me. I try to push her off, worming my head under my pillow, refusing to open my eyes. She wrestles the covers from me and tosses the pillow on the floor. "Get up. I miss you," she whines, squeezing my ribs with her knees.

It was only yesterday that I hiked into the woods with Sam, but it seems more like a century ago. "What are you doing here?" I whisper, mouth dry and sticky from sleep.

"Open your eyes and look at me, Stella!" She pinches my cheeks until I give up and peer into the light. She throws her head back, laughing, as she slides off me.

I push myself to a sitting position, rubbing the sore spots where her knees dug into my sides. Zoey's turned on the overhead, and it's blinding me. "What is it, Zoey?" She's probably mistaking my glare for squinting at the light, so I cross my arms against my chest to make certain she knows how annoyed I am with her. She didn't call or text me yesterday. Cole texted a couple of times—granted, the texts were begging me to meet her and Zoey at a house party.

"Haven't you missed my adorable face?" Zoey asks, batting her long lashes and framing her cheeks with her hands.

I roll my half-lidded eyes. "You're the one who hung up on me. You're the one acting pissed."

"You know how hard it is for me to admit when I'm wrong," she says. "But . . . I was at least fifty percent wrong in hanging up on you." Her blue eyes are wide and solemn.

"So you're saying we're both to blame?" I struggle not to laugh at the half-assed apology she's delivering. It is actually half an ass more than she usually gives.

"No, I mean yes. That's what I'm saying. That I'm responsible too. Let's just move on." She buries her head in my comforter. I sigh loudly.

"Okay, I'm sorry too."

She pops up, smile bright and victorious. She really is a manipulative heathen. "Get your skinny ass out of bed then, because we're overdue for a cove day." I let her haul me from the covers and watch patiently as she digs through the closet in search of a swimsuit she approves of, discarding every other article of clothing on the floor.

"What about the police?" I peek through the blind slats but can't see the cruiser on the street. "I don't think they'll want me going out to the middle of nowhere."

"What cops?" She scowls at a pink floral one-piece like it's mortally offended her. "There wasn't anyone outside when I got here, and your dad didn't say anything about them." She drops the suit and smiles angelically at me. "I even told him where we'd be going. He thought that taking your mind off all this dead-people mumbo jumbo was a good idea." Only Zoey could make something so serious sound sooo insignificant. And what's with my police escort being gone? Is Shane really that furious with me?

Zoey babbles on, "I had the most awetastic night ever. I got totally wasted at Scott's house, and we hooked up." She tosses her hair and smirks. "Can you effing believe me? And I thought there wasn't enough vodka in the world." She drops the lavender frumpy number I wore the other day and kicks it across the room. It lands precariously on the seat of my desk chair.

There's a pinch between my eyebrows as I try to catch up with what she's telling me. "Wait, Scott *Townsend*?"

She speaks in a lousy Russian accent. "Yessss, your ex-lover." Then normally, "That's okay, right? I'd usually classify girls who do other girls' exes as leeches or barnacles, but since it is Scott Townsend and all, I figured you wouldn't mind."

As she turns back to the closet, I try to decipher what exactly I do think about it. If I'm being honest, I only went out with Scott because I missed having Sam around. Minding isn't the issue; it's just too bizarre for words. "Are you running out of guys? Are you going to have to start recycling?"

"HA! You know it." She winks over her shoulder. "We're in desperate need of new blood. I think a trip to U of M is in order once school starts." She tosses me my white halter bikini. "Change and we'll head out. Michaela and Cole are meeting us there, and we have a surprise for you."

As I change, Zoey goes on and on about how psycho the whole town is acting. It becomes evident on the drive to the lake that for once she isn't exaggerating. Overnight the crosses, rosaries, vigils, and charms have multiplied. Downtown a crowd of adults wave signs with doomsday slogans like REPENT or BURN IN HELL, BEHOLD SATAN, and FEAR GOD'S WRATH inked on them. One displays a blown-up picture of Mr. Talcott from the newspaper, and pasted above it are the words DEVIL WORSHIPPER.

"Sheesh. Has everyone lost their mind?" Zoey says, flipping off one of the picketers as he steps into traffic, furiously waving his sign. "Whack-job Jesus thumpers who should be locked up. Leave it to this hick town to go all medieval. Next they'll be burning witches."

I grip my seat's edge tightly. "Has it been on the news that they took Jeanie's dad into custody?" I ask.

"Yep." She flips her mirror down at the next stop sign and purses her lips, checking her gloss. "My mom said they were forced to release him because there wasn't any . . . um, what is it called when the perp leaves spit and junk on his victims?" She snaps her fingers.

"Forensic evidence," I supply.

"Yeah, there wasn't any *forensic evidence* proving he attacked his wife or Jane Doe. The cops had to set him free."

I watch the mob scene fading in the rearview mirror. "It doesn't seem safe for him with the whole town having already made up their minds that he's guilty," I say. Unease spreads in my stomach like I've got a handful of creepy-crawly worms wriggling around down there. I hope that Daniel made it to Sam's last night and that he doesn't see or hear what these people are saying about his dad. I know I'd go nuts if people accused mine of something so horrible. I slide my phone from my pocket and angle it so I can text between my seat and the car door.

"Who ya texting?" Zoey asks. Nothing gets by her.

"Ummm . . . Sam, actually."

She taps the steering wheel to the pop song turned on low. "Sam who?"

I roll my eyes. She knows who. "Sam Worth."

She turns to me in mock horror. "I leave you to your own devices for one day and you're texting the King of Loserdom, Sam Worth? Random," she sings. "What gives?"

I was hoping to avoid this. I hardly know "what gives" myself. "He helped me out yesterday. I wanted you to help me remember Jeanie, but you were giving me the silent treatment, and he was the only other person I could ask. And please don't call him names."

"Wait . . . you actually went somewhere with him?" Zoey sounds appalled. "Like outside, and people could have *seen* you?" Her eyes are saucers of disbelief as they click to me. "I know you're going through some messy shit right now, but do you have to eff with Sam Worth mere months before senior year? What if Taylor had spotted you guys together?" she laments.

"So what if anyone saw us together? Us being seniors is the point. Aren't we a little old for all this peasant stuff? Isn't being friends with whoever you want the point of being popular?" I ask, throwing my hands in the air.

Zoey's eyelids drop like hoods, making crescent moons of her eyeballs. That's the surest way to tell that you're in for it with Zoey. She brakes on the side of the road where we usually park to hike to the cove. She twists the keys from the ignition and turns to face me, slow and mechanical. "Please. Stop. Don't ruin our last year of high school. If you want to screw losers in college, it's all you, but can you just give me the senior year we've been working for? This is *our* time." She leans forward, cupping my face with her hands. "This is our year to be the best at everything. The last year we'll be together before college. *Please.*"

Her pleading makes me doubly guilty. Zoey's been a good friend. No, better than that. The best. "I'm not screwing anyone. He's only helping me figure this whole Jeanie thing out, 'kay? We're friends."

"That's all? You swear?" she whines. She pouts and makes her eyes wide. I dread this expression of hers almost as much as I do the last. It makes her look like a frightened child. For some reason it works on most people. Especially guys. Kind of pervy, if you think about it.

I open my mouth to answer. I have no idea what I'm going to tell her, but by the grace of a shooting star or a unicorn or whatever saved my butt I never get the chance to say anything, because someone's blaring horn interrupts us. It's like a shade snaps down on Zoey's face. She's sad one second and then all at once has a flirty smirk painted on her mouth. Michaela, Cole, and four guys pile out of Cole's SUV, whooping and cheering that they've arrived. Taylor is obviously one of them. *My surprise.*

"Ste-lor is back on." Zoey winks at me. "Get it? Stella and Taylor: Ste-lor." When I don't smile, she rolls her eyes. "Kidding! As if I'd be that stale. Laugh much?" She hops straight from the car into the arms of one of Taylor's lacrosse minions, either Drew or Dean, I can't tell which. It gives me the thirty seconds I need to text Sam, asking him if he's with Daniel and telling him I'll call later.

"Hey, babe," Taylor says, throwing the car door open so I almost fall out from leaning on it. He's wearing blue board shorts that match his eyes perfectly—definitely no accident—and is shirtless.

"Hey." I steady myself and grab my things, shoving the cell into the pocket of my jean shorts. Suddenly, I wish I was wearing more than just my white halter bikini top. His gaze flicks over me and he grins, practically licking his lips. Usually, I like this kind of attention; today it makes me queasy.

"I called you last night," he says.

"Yeah, I saw. You didn't leave a message."

"We were all headed to Townsend's. His parents are in Chicago. Total rager. We had a sick beer pong tournament. Too bad you missed it." I shrug in response and try to focus on the gap between his two front teeth rather than his defined abs. I imagine all the spinach or broccoli that could wedge itself in there. His mouth moves to add something else dazzling, when someone pinches the crook of my elbow hard.

I turn, ready to lay into one of the Ds. Caleb, Zoey's brother, stands there, smiling a Cheshire cat's grin at me.

"Oh my God, why didn't you text you were coming home?" I squeal, throwing my arms around his neck.

"I just drove up last night," he says, squeezing me. "Are you okay?"

He pulls back and studies me. He definitely isn't checking me out; this is *Caleb*. Caleb, who's the closest thing to a brother I have; who taught me how to ride a two-wheeler; who beat up Mike Walt in the sixth grade when he called me an abomination for surviving what I did; and who saved my life in Chicago last winter, by springing me from the mind-sucking awkwardness of Mom giving me the silent treatment and her husband drilling me on Dad details. I slept in Caleb's dorm room from the day after Christmas to New Year's Day, when my flight left for Minneapolis. Mom never even called looking for me or told Dad I was MIA. I guess she felt the unscalable wall between us as much as I did and figured I'd booked it home.

Caleb bobs his head finally. "You could look a lot worse for what you're going through."

"Gee, thanks," I laugh, punching his arm softly. "But really, why aren't you in Chicago? You had that internship thingy."

He claps a hand on my bare shoulder. "Sometimes things don't work out, doll." He does an old-timey newscaster voice. When they were kids, Zoey and Caleb treated falling into weird accents as an art form. Zoey only relapses when we're alone and she's trying to get out of trouble by being cute. "It fell through, and I had a few weeks to kill. And then I saw the news. I needed to be here with you guys." Half his mouth smiles sadly. I hear Taylor sniff from over my shoulder.

"Let's go posse!" Zoey yells, waving toward the wood.

With a wink Caleb ducks his head and whispers, "We better listen to her like good little soldiers or else." Side by side you'd think Caleb and Zoey were twins, they look so much alike—they basically even have the same haircut now.

I fall in step with him and the girls, perfectly aware that I'm ignoring Taylor. Cole jabbers on about how worried she's been since the bonfire, and for one guilty second, I fantasize about holding her mouth shut so I can talk to Caleb. Caleb was always a way better listener than Zo. Zoey would die to know that I told him about my first kiss (the real one) a full hour before I told her. More importantly, Caleb was in the same grade as Daniel. All of us played together, and if anyone can help me remember, it's Caleb. And just like that, there's one more person I can depend on, and he's had my back most of my life.

Chapter Thirteen

Michaela locks arms with Cole and steers her a few feet ahead, winking at me as she distracts her from Caleb's dimpled smile. I've never had even a fleeting crush on Caleb, since he's really just a much taller, more masculine, more benevolent version of his sister. By the way girls respond to him—by how Cole yanks her beach cover-up over her head and glances at him coyly over her shoulder in one deft move—I know he has largely the same effect on the opposite sex as Zoey does. He tilts his head to mine and whispers, "Watch it, Zoey's in one of her moods. You guys fighting?"

I grunt noncommittally and check that everyone else is a couple of yards ahead. I keep my voice low. "I've been trying to remember what happened . . . you know, the summer of Jeanie."

He freezes midstride, with one foot suspended over a fallen trunk. His eyes dart to mine before he resumes the step and offers me a hand to help me over. "Sorry. That took me by surprise. I always thought you didn't want to talk about it."

"You're right," I admit. He is. I'm not certain Caleb and I have ever discussed that summer directly, even though he indirectly shut up a lot of guys—including Mike Walt—for teasing me when we were younger. "I definitely wasn't into obsessing over it. But with the dead little girl and Mrs. Talcott and the cops suspecting Mr. Talcott . . . how can I go on my merry way, pretending everyone's salvation isn't trapped in my screwed-up brain?"

"Salvation?" One blond brow lifts up, and he swats at a swarm of gnats we're traveling through. It's an unusually buggy afternoon.

"Okay. Maybe that's melodramatic. Mr. Talcott's freedom and probably Daniel's sanity hinge on me doing something."

"Seriously, Stella, don't you think it's safer to stay out of it?" he asks. I open my mouth to argue before he cuts me off. "Just hear me out. You matter to me. Zoey matters to me. My mom matters to me. That's not a lot of people. You're like my less bitchy kid sister." He elbows my side playfully before sobering up. "Whoever took Jeanie, whoever killed that kid in the cemetery, whoever killed Mrs. Talcott, you don't want a piece of them." His shoulders rise and fall, and I can tell he doesn't want to keep talking about it.

The way he refers to Jeanie's, Mrs. Talcott's, and Jane Doe's killers separately rather than saying *the* killer . . . It nicks my imagination. I get these sudden glimmers of yesterday at Griever's, and Jane Doe's body in the cemetery. I'm sure Caleb doesn't mean anything by it, because he doesn't know about the Balco girl. Caleb doesn't know that the crimes are stacking up and they couldn't possibly be the work of one person.

Zoey spins to face us for two backward strides. "Hurry up, slackers," she yells, staring daggers at Caleb and waving her middle finger in the air. He picks up the pace instantly. I trot to stay at his side. We're coming up on the others, and I'm losing my chance.

"Caleb," I hiss under my breath, and reach out to tug on his T-shirt—there's a grinning adolescent pop star on the back. I'm sure Caleb thinks he's oh-so ironic wearing the T-shirt.

Before my fingers make contact, Caleb stops suddenly and spins to face me. "I know what you're gonna say. You're asking me to help you." He sweeps his hair off his forehead and blinks, daring me to argue.

I step toward him and keep my volume low. "Yeah, I am. Just talk to me about that summer and about Jeanie."

He steps away and says too loudly, "Why? So you can pick up the trail of a killer? So you can get closer to a homicidal maniac? So you can get yourself killed?" There's desperation in his pale-blue, rounding eyes. "This isn't rescuing you from your mom's so we can bum around Chicago for a week. This is *dangerous*." His voice takes on a pleading quality that echoes mine.

"Please."

"No. I love you too much for that. And don't make me—"

"Don't make you what?" I cock my hand on my popped hip.

"Tell your dad what you're doing. I'll tell the police, too." He says it uncertainly. He doesn't want to cause me trouble. He cares about me, and what can I say in response? If I push it, maybe he really will tell Dad. Maybe I really will be sent to my mom's. And there will be no Caleb there to whisk me away.

I sigh. "Just forget it, okay? It was stupid of me to ask. Stupid of me to think I'd crack a case the police can't." I walk around him to catch up with the others. I think he calls my name, but I don't stop. Eventually, he joins the group, and I try to shake off being annoyed with him. How can I be angry because he wants to keep me safe? Wouldn't I want the same for him? I'm disappointed, though. Caleb was my last chance at recruiting another to help Daniel, Sam, and me.

When we're halfway to the cove, Drew or Dean says, "My boy saw that psycho Daniel Talcott back in town." I cringe at hearing Daniel's name in this jerkwad's mouth.

"Dude, it was probably Daniel who hacked up his mom and sister. Or a father-son crime," Taylor spits. He saunters up and flings his arm across my shoulders, binding me to his side as we walk. "That whole family is screwed up. I heard they're into incest." His skin is clammy, venomous sweat seeping into mine. I throw his heavy arm from my back and stomp forward. I grind my teeth, willing a billion verbal lashings silent. For Zoey. Only because I know Zoey brought Taylor to make me happy.

I look to Caleb for a distraction, but he's making gooey eyes at Cole and asking her about California. I drop to the ground, pretending to be engrossed in tying a shoelace to lose him. It doesn't work, since Taylor waits for me to finish. "Are you afraid 'cause Mr. Talcott is out of jail? We could pay him a visit for you, kick his ass." I look up at Taylor, disgust rising up with bile in my throat. His head blots out the sun like a lunar eclipse. Drew and Dean hoot in agreement, arms waving like a couple of monkeys. *No, monkeys are smarter.*

"Jeanie and her mom weren't hacked up. And the cops let Mr. Talcott go because they didn't have any evidence that he did it," I snap, getting to my feet and jogging to catch up with Michaela. "Anyway," I add, "Daniel loved Jeanie. Neither of them are guilty. I would know." I hope I sound convincing enough. They lose interest anyway and drone on about the logistics of luring a hog into the pool of a rival school as a senior prank as we empty out onto the shore. I spread my towel next to Cole's, and Taylor beats Michaela to my other side. Just fan-freaking-tastic. I'll be stuck with him all afternoon. How on earth was I completely into him seventy-two hours ago? He's still hot, but it doesn't come anywhere near to making up for his personality.

"I brought shots," Cole squeals, retrieving a bottle of raspberry-flavored vodka from her purse. She passes out little lime-green plastic shot glasses and begins pouring the first round. Zoey strips her shorts off and wades into the water. Caleb shouts for her to cover up. Drew and Dean follow like eager puppies after a bone as she waggles her finger at both of them.

Taylor lies on his side, facing me. He pops a giant wad of gum into his mouth and says, chewing noisily, "You want to swim, babe?"

I grab a filled shot glass from Cole and knock it back before she can even pour herself one. "No thanks, I want to sunbathe for a while," I say. He shrugs and cracks his gum loudly.

"Whoa there, bobcat." Cole giggles. "Want to wait for me to take one too?" I thrust the glass out for her to refill. Cole raises an eyebrow and then shrugs, filling me up again and topping off a red party cup that Caleb offers up. If I have to pretend to have a good time while the rest of the town goes mad and Daniel loses his whole family, then I'm going to need a good buzz. Luckily, I don't drink much, so I'll be nice and fuzzy after two or three.

"Pace yourself, slutini!" Zoey yells from where she sits atop one of the D's shoulders. "We're going to have a bonfire when it gets dark." I grin back at her, showing way too many teeth for her to think it's sincere. There's no way, no how that I'm spending my whole day here. I need to remember things. I need to research past disappearances. I need to check that Daniel's okay. I need to see Sam. Cole clicks her shot glass against mine and throws her head back, gulping the cloying vodka that goes down like maple syrup. I do the same, letting its warmth spread in my stomach.

"Maybe you should eat something?" Caleb calls from Cole's other side. He's unwrapping what looks like a turkey sandwich and offers me half, spilling wheat crumbs on Cole's midsection. He moves to brush them away, stops, and blushes crimson at almost touching her.

Cole plucks one of the crumbs off her stomach and pops it into her mouth—she is definitely more a Zoey than a Michaela. I don't see Caleb's reaction, because Zoey shouts out for me. "Stella, get in here! Let's play chicken." I shake my head mutely. "Fine. Cole, c'mon and bring Taylor!" Taylor shrugs and sprints into the water. Cole gallops after, emitting a burst of high-pitched noises as she hits the lake. Five minutes later Zoey's and Cole's shrill screams are likely heard across town. Michaela brings the magazine she's been reading and reclines on Cole's towel, talking off and on with Caleb about her early admission college apps as I force the last bite of sandwich down.

"You okay?" Michaela whispers to me after a few. I incline my head in a way that could mean anything. "I guess that's a stupid question, because how could you be?" I muster a smile for her. "Let me know if you need anything. My sister just had *another* baby and my parents are gone for the next two nights, and I will totally throw you a pink wine slumber party." Michaela might be pursuing her idea of the glory that lasts—*tomorrow's glory*—but she isn't one of those stuffy girls who are all pasty and cross-eyed from too much studying.

This rare combination of being fun and obliterating the scholarly competition was one of the reasons we became friends. Here is a girl who spent honors eighth-grade math drawing a graphic novel about our teacher's love life and still managed to pull off perfect scores on the quizzes. Mr. Ralph—picture Mr. Potato Head with a lazy eye and a vintage Beanie Babies collection on his desk—never had a clue the entire class eagerly awaited Michaela's Monday installments, which featured his weekend adventures in dating. It was obviously a comedy.

That's why *I* fell in love with Michaela. For Zoey, it was practically love at first sight. It was the first week of eighth grade, and Zoey attended the informational meeting for all the kids who wanted on student council. She had her sights set on social chair—*obviously*. Michaela wanted class treasurer—*shocking*. They hadn't met because they didn't have any classes together, and Zoey wasn't the omnipresent force she is now. They locked eyes across the classroom full of brace-faced kids, bouncing in their seats. *They just knew.* Zoey seconded Michaela's nomination for class treasurer without missing a beat, and Michaela returned the favor. They campaigned hard for each other—okay, Michaela campaigned and Zoey made bribes and threats. The rest is history.

I smile at my pink-wine-loving friend. "Thanks, M. I may need it." She turns back to Caleb, and they continue talking about his experience applying for schools. Michaela's being generous, since Caleb's college is fathoms less competitive than the programs she's interested in. Caleb isn't exactly an overachiever; his group in school was a hodge-podge of stoners, skateboarders, and wannabe musicians. Senior year he scored high on the SATs and got into a small college in Chicago. Zoey's never forgiven him for it. Rather than her average grades being the standard Caleb was measured against, it was the other way around. Zoey became the loser of the family in her mom's eyes, overnight.

"Shot?" I ask them, pouring myself a third. Michaela shakes her head and withdraws a rose-colored bottle with dolphins on the label. She rarely drinks anything but pink wine—oh, and pink *sparkling* wine. Caleb wags a chastising finger as I tip the glass to my lips but doesn't say anything to mother me. I try to sip the shot slowly, but the sickening-sweet taste makes that impossible. After I choke it down, I check my cell to see if Sam's responded. He has.

With Daniel. At library. When/where should we pick you up?

I'm instantly all keyed up and can't sit still on my towel bunching under me. Daniel and Sam are at the library, most likely researching past disappearances in Savage. I should be there. *I'm* the *Wildwood Herald* reporter with supersleuth research skills. And here I am: in a bikini, drinking girly vodka, and getting ogled by lacrosse players, while Sam gets his hands dirty in our town's history. But as the seconds tick by and the alcohol takes effect, the sense that I'm penned in lessens, and my frustration loses its edge. I text back:

At cove. Pick me up at 1.

It's just before eleven now. Putting in a good two hours should appease Zoey. Yeah right. Who am I kidding? There's no appeasing Zoey. She'll be livid. But there's nothing I can do about it. I close my eyes, letting the sun's rays make me drowsy and unfocused. After ten or fifteen minutes I clumsily spray sunblock on, hoping that I don't turn streaky. I dig out a bag of gummies from Zoey's purse and pick through for the green worms.

I turn my attention back to the water, where Cole and Taylor are ganging up on one of the Ds. The other has vanished with Zo. I can't help the smile on my face. She does work fast. Taylor catches me watching and waves. I wave back halfheartedly, and he takes it as an invitation.

He stands dripping over my towel. A sheen of water makes his chest and stomach sparkle in the sun. It's hard for me to force my eyes from being glued to his body. Downing three shots in less than an hour was not my best idea ever. My lips tingle, and my nose is numb. I sense my reservations about him ebbing.

"Will you come for a swim?" he asks. I let him pull me up from the towel and to the left along the shore before I answer. Before I really register the question, we wade into the jade water, ripples and minnows scattering. The icy temperature sends a jolt of awareness through me. Sam. Sam is why I don't want Taylor anymore. What do I want with Sam, though? And how do I know that Sam even wants me? Why would he? I assumed last night that he was going to say something about still being interested, but what if it was the opposite? What if he was going to say that he's finally over it? That he'll never bring me a gardenia corsage again, or send me a valentine chocolate-marshmallow heart, or follow me into a spooky old cemetery. I'd know if I hadn't run like a coward.

I go deeper. The water laps at my knees, my thighs, my waist. I stop shivering once it hits my chest. The water's clear today, with little sediment masking the lake's sandy floor. The minnows dart near, then double back abruptly but not entirely, so that they gradually close the distance between their silver, glinting bodies and our ankles. Taylor dunks underwater, swimming around my feet and bursting through the surface directly in front of me. I laugh. He looks like a wet dog and he shakes like one, wildly whipping his hair back and forth. I shield my face, still laughing. I totally know this is the alcohol talking . . . no, *giggling*. I am buzzed. *I know it*, but somehow it doesn't make much of a difference.

I push off the bottom and swim forward to the deepest point; on this side of the cove, a thin peninsula of rocks juts out of the water and shelters us from the others. The rope swing sways in the wind off to the right. Taylor glides through the water gracefully, seeming more fish than boy. I tread water, watching him dunk to swim down to the lake bed. He's under for almost a minute before he kicks to the surface with a handful of brightly colored pebbles.

He paddles closer and holds his palm open, showing me. I toss away a fishing hook with a plastic worm attached. He has two rocks the color of crème brûlée and a handful of bloodred-speckled ones.

"I'm glad you came today," he says, suddenly even closer. We're shaded by the lacy canopy above, and I can't see or hear the others on the opposite side of the rocks. He sinks his hand into the water and releases the stones. Sadness nudges me as I watch them fall. With his hands empty, he reaches for me. His palms are warm compared to the water as they skate around my waist. I float into him, my swimsuit grazing his chest. He tightens his grip and leans forward, brushing my ear with his lips. It sends a shiver down my spine. I close my eyes, waiting for him to kiss me; *wanting him to kiss me*. In the second before his lips find mine, I picture Sam's face.

Muddy-brown eyes that stick with you. Freckles like splattered honey. A smile like he knows better. I worm out of Taylor's grasp, giggling the close call away. I am definitely buzzed. Maybe even a hint drunk. "I—I bet I can hold my breath longer than you," I stammer, trying to dash away the awkward moment. He grins in response. He thinks I'm playing hard to get. I've done it to guys before. This is different, though; I don't want Taylor anymore, whether Sam wants me or not.

"On the count of three. One, two"—I take a deep breath—

"three." I plunge my head underwater. Taylor follows. He paddles nearer to me, so I dive down to the sandy floor. It's only twelve or thirteen feet in this spot, and the pressure isn't too much for my ears. At first I try to keep track of the passing seconds, but after I hit twenty I lose count. Taylor hovers a few feet to the right. I doubt I can actually beat him. Winning doesn't matter, though; I need a few seconds to sober up.

The water presses into me from all sides, and a dull burning in my lungs mounts. I let my eyes flutter shut to absorb the calm. I beat my arms to stay on the ground and cross my legs. A slimy plant tickles my ankles, and I snap my eyes open to make certain it isn't a fish. The big ones gross me out if they touch me with their scales. There's algae the color of rust all around me. It starts to lengthen and grow, twining up from the sandy bottom and extending as a jungle in front of me. The color deepens and brightens until it's a blazing red. I close my eyes and shake my head, preparing to surface. If I'm imagining things, I've been under way too long.

When I open them again, I can see that the redness all around me isn't algae, it's hair. Long strands of red hair. Jeanie's there. I'm no longer under water but standing knee deep in a thicket of thorned brush. I'm a kid again. The trees and hedges tower over me, even when I stand on my tiptoes. I can taste the sweetness of strawberry seeds on my tongue; my fingers are stained with their juice. Jeanie struggles on her back like an overturned potato bug. A massive gnarled hand is twisted in her hair, clamped on a fistful, holding her down or dragging her away—I can't tell which. I'm frozen, though, unable to move to her. Try as I might, my short legs are useless and stiff. My arms won't budge from my sides. I can't help her. I open my mouth to scream, but I only gulp water. My eyes fly open, the calm of the blue lake all around me. I kick off the sandy floor.

Chapter Fourteen

I hit the surface gasping. My head throbs as I splash frantically, trying to get ahold of myself. "Whoa, whoa." Taylor is by my side. His hands slip over me, trying to get a grip on my flailing arms. "I was about to come down for you. You've been under almost a minute and a half. Steady." I give up fighting. With his arm hooked under mine, he swims toward the shore. My chest heaves as I fill my lungs again and again with giant mouthfuls of sweet air. Jeanie on her back. Distorted fingers laced in her hair. Who was it? Why didn't I see a face? I couldn't look up. The person's arm and everything beyond it was out of the picture. It was as if I were peering through a telescope, everything outside of the lens unseeable and a million miles away.

Taylor stumbles forward, hauling me to my feet. We're waist deep, but my legs won't work. I cling to him, willing the sensation back into them.

"I can't believe you stayed under so long. You're ballsy for a girl." He wraps his arms around me, mistaking my nearness for flirting.

"I'm okay." I stagger backward, forcing my legs to support me. I make it to the shore and crawl over the slippery rocks, slithery like eels under my feet, to get back to the beach where the others are sunbathing.

"Hey, hey," Taylor calls, catching my arm. "Let's not go back to the others yet. We could take a walk or . . . you know."

I whirl around. The pervy way he says *you know* makes my temper flare, sending adrenaline into my limbs. "No, I don't know," I say tartly.

He tries to deliver a suggestive wink but ends up looking like he has a gnat in his eye. I hope he does. "Come on," he half whines. "Stella, you've been leading me on for months. There's not going to be a more perfect time to hook up. Plus, you've messed around with a ton of other guys." He reels me in closer. "Don't be a cock tease."

I slap his hand from my arm. "You'd have to have one for me to be able to tease it," I say venomously, turning and hurrying over the rocks.

Zoey and one of the Ds are still missing, probably making out in one of the nearby coves. Michaela is wiggling her toes and humming to the music streaming from her earbuds. Caleb's towel is still next to Cole's, but he's gone, probably headed to yank a horny lacrosse player off his sister. I blink back tears. If only he'd been there to haul Taylor off me. I wrench my cell out of my jean shorts to check the time. Just before one p.m. THANK. GOD. I can't stand another minute of Taylor. "Michaela," I whisper, trying not to disturb Cole, who I'm certain is sleeping under the magazine covering her face.

"Hmmm?" Michaela lifts her glasses off her nose, peers at me, and shrugs off her earbuds.

"I'm sorry, but I have to go. Sam Worth is picking me up."

Her neck lengthens as she gazes over my shoulder at a fast-approaching Taylor. She frowns and then nods her understanding at me. "I'll tell Zoey you weren't feeling well," she whispers. "And just so you know, Sam's been my lab partner a bunch of times in physics, and he's way nicer than Taylor." I smile gratefully before grabbing my things and jogging into the trees. My nerves are completely shot as I hurry through the woods. I check nervously over my shoulder every few seconds to make certain Taylor isn't following. Fat chance. He'll never look at me again. What a jerk. I haven't messed around with that many guys, and even if I had, so what? Even if I'd made out with a billion guys, it wouldn't make him entitled to anything. In a burst of understanding I know that it's not only loyalty keeping him friends with jock scum; he's just like them, except he's smarter about hiding it.

The snap of a stick, and a flock of sparrows take off from the forest floor. I run. The impact of my feet hitting ground makes my head pound. I drank too much. I should have known better. I *do* know better. Now I'm alone in the woods with a killer on the loose. The air smells dank; it's the scent of rain, and the bugs have multiplied like they're drinking the moisture out of the atmosphere. I was just under the glaring sun and there wasn't a cloud in the sky. I'm running from Taylor and to Sam. It's as if the whole universe is out of whack.

The cell vibrates in my pocket. I ignore it. I'm not slowing down for anything. There's the whoosh of cars passing along the highway up ahead. Another few yards and flashes of the teal station wagon waiting for me, parked alongside Zoey's car. I'm out of breath, but I urge myself on. With each stride I am closer to Sam. Closer to being safe. I explode out of the woods ten yards from him. Sam paces, jabbing at the buttons of his old cell. He looks up immediately, probably because I'm moving with the grace of a hurricane, huffing and puffing.

"Stella! I was worried when you didn't answer." He holds up the cell. I barrel into him, throwing my arms around his neck and burying my face in his shoulder. His arms are slack at his sides at first and then slowly they wrap around me. I fold my arms as tightly as I can around him, desperate to escape what I remembered; what Taylor's lips felt like on my skin; what his hands felt like on my waist; the insulting things he said to me. Sam doesn't even grope me when I'm practically naked hugging him.

"Are you okay?" His breath tickles my ear, and I lift my head so I'm looking up at him. I don't want to untangle the rest of my body, though. Not yet.

"I remembered more of that day." I hiccup and bury my face again. "I think I had too much to drink." Sam tenses; his arms go rigid around me, and I know he's about to pull away. "Please, just hold me," I say, my voice muffled by his T-shirt. He stands perfectly still for another minute. It's like embracing a tree trunk. I can't stand it and shove him away. "Whatever, Sam, you'd think I was asking you to jab a fork in your eye or something."

I allow more room between us, hyperaware of my relative

nakedness. At first I fold my arms over my chest to cover myself, but Sam's eyes trained only on my face infuriate me. He's such an effing gentleman. Always so *grown-up*. Just once I'd like to see him lose it. I drop my arms to my sides. "What is your problem?" I snap.

He shoves his hands into his pockets and blinks at his sneakers. His T-shirt is in Greek, so I have no idea what it says. Probably Greek for King of Loserdom, Zoey would say. "I don't drink," he mutters.

"So?"

"My dad has a drinking problem. That's why I don't drink." He shuffles his feet, eyes glued to the rising dust cloud he's creating.

"But I've seen you at a bazillion parties. Why go if you don't drink?"

He lifts his head slowly. A wash of satisfaction soothes my temper as he tries to avert his eyes from me but can't. The tips of his ears redden. "I like hanging out with the guys, and they like hanging out with the kind of people who get invited to parties." He gives a self-deprecating laugh. "Also . . . you're usually there."

My breath hitches. Of all the insane things he could have said, nothing could be crazier or sweeter. "I didn't know about your dad. I'm sorry." I take a step nearer. "Do you really look for me at parties?"

He scratches his head and grins slowly. "Yeah, about ten percent of my brain is permanently programmed to keep a lookout for Hella Stella." He laughs like he isn't embarrassed at all. "Bonfires, parties, school dances, football games, lacrosse matches. I'd get a lobotomy, but you know, side effects, complications."

"The unglamorous reality of being a drooling vegetable," I say, mock gravely.

He grins wider. "That too, obviously. It would really cramp my style with the ladies."

My hand brushes his, completely independent from my brain. "Really, though. I didn't know."

"How would you? I never told you." The laughter is gone from his voice, and the tips of his ears deepen to cherry. He breaks eye contact. "C'mon, let's get out of here." He steps away and opens the passenger-side door.

The car's leather sticks to my butt as I slide in. I awkwardly tug on my shorts and will away the lingering sensation of touching Sam's hand.

"Where's Daniel?" I ask as he steers us on to the two-lane highway.

"He had to meet up with his dad. He was all cloak-and-dagger about saying any more than that." Sam flips the sun visor down and settles back into his seat. "We went to the library this morning to use their online newspaper archives. My laptop broke during finals, and I haven't had a chance to get it fixed." By the way he emphasizes "chance" I know he means he doesn't have the money to fix it.

"Did anyone recognize Daniel?" I say.

"No. He wore a hat, and it's been a few years since anyone saw him." I nod. If I didn't identify him immediately, I doubt a random librarian would.

"There wasn't a lot online from before 1972 because of a fire at the *Savage Bee*'s headquarters that year. Everything they have before then came in as donations from Savage's residents. It's mostly yellowed newspapers people saved in attics. So even though there isn't a complete record, there are random records dating back to 1910 that the librarians have scanned into their online system."

I bob my head. Although I usually write articles with a slightly more global perspective—and I have access to everything I'd ever need on my laptop and cell—I ventured into the town library once. Honestly, up until now, Savage was this Jeanie-shaped town on the map I didn't need to know more about. I'm not saying I planned to leave and never come back after graduation. Everyone I love is here. I just mean I wasn't eager to learn about Savage's history, because in my mind, Jeanie is its history. The one and only time I visited the library was to ask about records they keep on Blackdog Lake for a climate-change article I wanted to write. No dice. They gave me the same line about a fire, and I never went back.

"Since Mrs. Griever said she was sixteen when the Balco girl was taken," Sam continues, "we looked up her birth records online to approximate the year of the girl's disappearance."

I grin at him. "That was really smart."

"You have no idea what a huge nerd I am," he says, laughing. Then more seriously, "So it was 1938 that she would have gone missing. There were only a few newspaper clippings that had been scanned into the library's electronic system from that year, although the archivist is checking their boxed archives for me. I guess there are still records dated 1972 or before that haven't been entered yet. There are also way more entered from the 1950s, sixties, and early seventies than the decades earlier, since the longer a newspaper hangs around in an attic, the likelier it is to get trashed. The archivist said to come back tomorrow morning."

"I'll go with you," I offer. "Shane said they can't identify Jane Doe." My fingers twist the hem of my shorts. "How is that possible? How can someone lose a little girl and no one know about it?" I feel the tension in my solar plexus. It's not too different a thing from losing a little girl and not knowing how or why. "The finger bone doesn't belong to Jeanie either. Not her DNA," I say haltingly. It's the first I've let myself think about it since last night. It isn't that I wanted Jeanie to have suffered being cut up, only that it would have meant that there wasn't another victim. It made sense. Two eyes and ears, one nose, one mouth, and teeth sense. Shane dashed that orderly explanation into a million pieces, rearranging the face into an unrecognizable ghoul.

Sam looks at me sideways and then back at the road. "Jane Doe could be from another state or she could be a foster kid or an orphan. The finger bone could be the Balco girl's. If Jane Doe had it, their deaths must be connected."

My thoughts hum. First Griever connected Jeanie's disappearance with another that happened decades ago, and now the bone connects Jane Doe's. Suddenly, there's a ribbon of clues, trailing through generations, leading us deeper into the forest rather than out of it.

"How is it possible?" I whisper.

"It might not be," Sam says softly. "We haven't found proof that there were any past disappearances yet." I try to smile at the reassurance but fail. I'm about to share the gnarled hand—at least gnarled in my memory—twisted in Jeanie's hair when Sam adds, "There's something else."

"What?" I ask, guilty with the relief of not having to regurgitate the memory that found me under the water. If I don't say it out loud, it doesn't have to be real. Those twisted fingers don't have to be real. They don't have to be wound in Jeanie's hair, pulling clumps by the root from her bloody scalp as she struggled.

"It's more something that I have to *show* you." He cracks a smile that is more hopeful than suggestive. "Can we go to your house?"

"Sure, as long as you don't mind that I'm a little tipsy." I lean my temple against the cool window and close my eyes, letting the car's easy rhythm on the highway rock me. "When do you have to work?"

"Tomorrow. I have shifts Thursdays, Fridays, and Saturdays from three to nine. I've been trying to pick up more, but everyone else needs extra hours too," he says. I place my hand on his knee and shift my weight to lean against him rather than the window. I don't know why . . . I just want to show him that I understand it's hard.

He chuckles softly. "What?" I ask, glancing up at his profile.

"You're sweet when you're drunk."

I straighten up, my hand to my chest, mouth open wide in mock outrage. "Why, Sam Worth, are you saying you like me better under the influence of alcohol?"

He leans over the steering wheel and stares at the graying tufts of clouds. They've accumulated in the sky since I stampeded through the woods. They explain the smell of rain in the air. "No, just that you're the only person I know who doesn't transform into a much uglier person when they're drunk."

My face falls and I chew my lip. "Does your dad change when he drinks?"

Sam tips his head. "He fights with my mom. Says things he shouldn't. He never drank at home when he worked. He tried to hide it from my mom before. As a kid I knew what it smelled like when he came home and hugged me. I guess now he needs a way to cope all the time, but . . ."

"But it's not what you and your mom deserve." I lean into him again. It occurs to me that I'm not usually this affectionate when I drink, and dimly I contemplate that it is Sam bringing it out in me and not the cloying vodka. I try to bat that train of thought away. So what if the concept of personal space loses its meaning around Sam? We basically grew up together; of course being near him is a little like digging up our fifth-grade time capsule. I may crave the simplicity of being ten—I may even feel the familiar ping for unicorn stickers—but I'd lose interest after five minutes. I'd get bored with all the artifacts of my childhood.

I stare at the darkening clouds, smothering the sun completely, washing everything in plum and gray. Hopefully, Michaela's noticed them and hustled everyone back to the cars.

I fiddle with the radio, trying to find something upbeat that comes in clear this far out in the sticks. There's nothing but some religious talk-radio show, rattling off forty ways to survive the rapture. I flip it off. I can't shake the sense that Sam isn't like the sticker books I grew out of. It doesn't feel as if I left him with two feet firmly in the past. I wonder why that is, and it becomes sharp and clear. "Sam? Do you remember what you said a few days ago about you having friends who don't care who you're friends with?"

His lips part, and his eyes cut from the road to me. "Yeah, but I shouldn't have said that. I was upset."

I consider this for a second. "It was true, though. How did you know that Zoey didn't want me hanging out with you anymore?" See, I didn't outgrow Sam or give him up willingly. I lost him to keep someone I loved more.

His jaw clenches and then unclenches. With that little tick of his muscle, the sky cracks open and dumps rain. "She told me," he says.

I was lounging back, feeling kind of soupy. Now I sit straight up. "What?"

He takes a drawn-out breath. "Right before she told you to choose, she told me you only had room for one best friend and that she was going to make you decide who you wanted to keep. Zoey never liked me, and when you weren't around she was a real . . . well, she was mean-spirited, even as a kid. When you didn't show up to swim that Sunday afternoon, I knew." His big, sensitive eyes flit to me like he's checking that he isn't hurting *my* feelings.

He knew. Twelve-year-old Sam knew that given the choice, I didn't choose him. I swallow a big gulp of air. It slides down my throat, choking me. If not for it, I'd cry; the sky already is. "Why didn't you tell me that you knew? That I was horrible for picking Zoey?" I ask, barely louder than the drops pelting the windshield. The car veers off the highway and on to Main Street, cutting through downtown Savage.

"Because you chose Zoey. What was I supposed to say? Should I have begged you not to?" We pull to a stop at a red light. He runs his hands through his hair, heaving a huge sigh, and holds them up, defeated. "*You chose Zoey*. And she was the one who made you choose. I would never have asked you to give up a friend. Especially right after—"

"Right after my mom left," I supply. I have to admit that even at twelve the timing of Zoey giving me the ultimatum seemed really cruel, really messed up.

I glare at our reflections in the window. I see a half-naked drenched girl who's a miserable shadow of who she used to be. I see a boy who's been burned by her over and over again. But for some bizarro reason he doesn't leave like everyone else.

"I understand what you meant about there being so little of me left," I whisper. The light turns green and he accelerates. I wonder when whatever magic elixir that made me *me* started to dry up. I have an inkling it began with Jeanie. The droplets of water ping against the glass, and I see they've morphed into hail. *Hail in June*. I remember learning that hail forms in clouds, where the air is much cooler, making it possible during summer months. Still. The universe seems off-kilter, addled. The windshield wipers don't even come close to defeating the ice that rockets down on us. I fantasize that a comet-size chunk will burst through the glass and pummel me out of existence.

We turn down my street. I reach for my shoes in the backseat and struggle to get the wet canvas onto my feet. Sam stares straight ahead; he can't stomach looking at me. The instant the wagon pulls into my driveway—before we're even parked—I leap from the car.

"Stella, wait!" Sam shouts. I don't stop. All I want to do is hide from him. He's the only evidence of the hurtful choice I made. But he follows. I struggle with the key in the lock and explode through the front door. Moscow's lounging on the back of the sofa. He raises his head, lackadaisically regards me, and then settles back in for a nap. I kick off my soaked shoes. Their moisture leeches into the carpet as a swelling shadow.

Finally, I turn to Sam, who sloshed through the front yard and stands dripping and muddy in the doorway. His hair is plastered to his head, and his eyelashes are clumping. He slams the door, making the whole house and my insides rattle.

"If there wasn't any of *you* left, why would I be here? Why would I be helping you? Why would that ten percent of my brain always be hoping that you're at the party I am? That we'll see each other and we'll talk and you'll smile because I made you laugh." He steps closer, and I mirror it with a step back. He shoves his hands deep into his pockets. "I've had it bad for you most of my life. *You*. The fearless you who stepped in front of Daniel when Griever aimed a shotgun at him. The you who used to do backflips off my diving board. The you who I knew would realize sooner or later that you chose wrong."

I tug my hair furiously into a knot at the base of my neck. "Zoey's my best friend. Don't you get that?" Even now the urge to defend Zoey stomps out everything else. "I didn't choose wrong."

I hold my breath, waiting for his response. He leans forward rather than away. "Stella, don't *you* get it? I'm not saying you should have chosen me. *There was no right choice.* You shouldn't have chosen at all," he says softly. There are no words. It's the simplest, most obvious thing, and it never occurred to me. "You did, though, and I don't care that you did."

His eyes are so intent I imagine them crackling like embers in a fire. He's waiting for a response. There's this humming between us, making the hair on my arms stand on end. I take another hasty step back and try to look unaffected as I gather up stray hairs and tuck them into my knot. "What did you want to show me?" I breeze over everything.

Sam hesitates for a second, holding my gaze. My hands fall to my sides; they feel awkward there, purposeless. He reaches into his hoodie and pulls out a white envelope. "I couldn't get the part about monsters out of my head. I even dreamed about it. And then it hit me this morning. The spring before Jeanie was taken, we played at Jeanie and Daniel's a lot." Sam levels his gaze with mine. "We were always playing in the woods." I go absolutely still.

His brow creases, and he rubs his chin with the effort of remembering. "We were pretending to slay dragons and play-fight as cowboys and Indians." He frowns. "We weren't the only kids playing in the forest—the woods are everywhere in Savage." He's right. The woods and their shadows are all around us. "There were always urban legends going around school. Bloody Mary stories. Goblins and ghosts in the woods." I incline my head. I remember a lot of those from slumber parties. "But in the months before Jeanie went missing—I can't remember exactly when—a group of older boys swore they saw something in the forest—I want to say cannibals. Then the rumors spread, and more kids said they'd seen stuff in the woods; all different creatures that couldn't exist. You know how kids are with rumors and made-up stuff. I remember us at Jeanie's, and we were going to drive something out of hiding. I wasn't sure any of that mattered, though. Then I found this." Sam slides a single photo from the envelope. I take it and slump down to the couch.

It's a Polaroid snapshot of five kids. Weird that I recognize myself only after I spot Sam, Caleb, Daniel, and Jeanie in the photo. We're lined up like little soldiers, and everyone but Jeanie is grinning fiercely at the camera. I'm more growling than smiling, with one arm slung over Sam's shoulders.

"Remember that Zoey ran around with a Polaroid camera all of first and second grade?" Sam asks. I nod. "Well, she had it in kindergarten, too. She must be the one taking the picture. The four of us would have been six, and Caleb and Daniel would have been finishing third grade. This is the spring before Jeanie was taken."

I bob my head dumbly again, running my finger over the objects we're gripping in our chubby-knuckled hands. "Sam, are those what I think they are?" I ask quietly.

He sinks down next to me. "Yeah," he says, his breath tickling my ear. "Those are spears that Daniel and Caleb made from sticks and arrowheads they found in the woods."

Our savage expressions, the crude weapons, the smears of dirt on our cheeks, those strange words I chose when Jeanie was taken, all add up. I take a shaky breath and whisper, "We were hunting monsters."

Chapter Fifteen

My hands tremble as I bring the picture closer to my face. I tilt it from side to side. I even examine its back. I don't know what I'm looking for—maybe some clue to appear like the images in those Magic Eye books—but there's nothing find.

"Do you remember this day?" I ask, pivoting on the couch to face him.

"Not really. But I remembered hiding a few pictures away. Feeling like they were my secret treasure. I stuck this one in the pages of a ratty copy of *Where the Wild Things Are* hidden under my box spring. It was still there when I looked." His brow pleats as he prepares to explain more. "After Jeanie was taken, my parents talked to me about strangers who kidnap children, and that whole conversation is scar tissue on my memory." He taps his head as if to indicate exactly what part of his brain he's talking about. It wouldn't surprise me if he knew. "It was traumatic and made everything surrounding Jeanie's disappearance vague. I remember the bit about the rumors, and I sort of remember being afraid, but there's nothing clear or specific about it. I'm sorry," Sam says. He leans back into the couch cushions. I angle forward slightly as though there's a string attaching us.

"You were only six. And you found this." I pat his knee. "Wait a sec." I point to the older boys in the photo. "We were only six, but Caleb and Daniel were nine. I have *loads* of memories from being nine."

"You're right. Daniel and Caleb should be able to remember this." Sam tugs his cell from his pocket and begins dialing as I'm going for mine. "They should be able to remember the rumors, too," he adds. He's right. When I asked Caleb to help me remember that summer, he should have mentioned it, right? But why would I expect Caleb—Caleb who up until two years ago hung out with *stoners*—to remember every game of make-believe and goofy adventure we had? And to be fair, he wouldn't understand the significance of it, because he doesn't know what six-year-old me muttered 255 times.

I dial Caleb and an instant later hang up. He told me he'd rat me out to keep me safe. I'm pretty certain sharing that we uncovered a forgotten photo from that summer and letting him know that I enlisted Sam's help would send him snitching. A second later Sam says, "Hey, Daniel, it's Sam. I know you might be spending the night with your dad, but give me a call. It's important. I think we're on to something, man." He returns the cell to his jeans.

"I can't ask Caleb," I explain. "He was with us earlier, and I tried to get him talking about Jeanie. He said it was too dangerous for me to be involved."

"It's okay. Daniel will call back," Sam says.

My eyes linger on the five faces in the photo. All of us look feral, glowing from the thrill of whatever hunt we were on—that is, everyone but Jeanie. Her eyes are angled downward at this rust-eaten coffee tin tied with string around her neck. The tin cylinder hangs just above her waist. Her mouth is pressed into a thin line. "What is that around her neck?" I ask, tilting the photo for Sam.

His jaw works back and forth as he thinks. "It looks like a homemade drum, like we were soldiers and she was the drummer of war," he says. "I remember making one out of a milk carton."

"Yeah, I guess," I say. I have trouble looking away from its shape, how she's wearing it as a necklace, and her downcast eyes. I know I've seen it before, more than once, more than just that afternoon. The coffee tin's lid is snapped on, and I can imagine her tiny hands beating it as a percussion instrument. There's a quality to her expression, though—bleakness and dread—that makes me doubt it's a toy. It makes me think that Jeanie was the only one who understood that whatever game we were playing at wasn't a game at all. She was smarter than the rest of us.

"What do you think we were looking for?" I ask, moving on to my likeness. I don't know what it is. I look different from all the other pictures I've seen of myself as a kid. I look wild. And happy. Maybe that's what I looked like before Jeanie was taken?

"I don't know. There might not have been anything. I remember seeing a couple of homeless men walking in the woods near the train tracks."

"The police searched the woods for drifters who might have

taken Jeanie. Hundreds of volunteers walked the woods for weeks afterward looking for any sign," I say. "But they never found anything."

"The woods run into Blackdog State Park. It would be easy for someone to stay hidden up there for a long time. Hundreds of square miles of nothingness and only a couple of rangers who patrol," Sam says thoughtfully. He focuses on my frown and adds quickly, "I'm sure that's not what happened, though. Why do you think you said that stuff to the police?"

I take a deep breath and let it out slowly. "At first I was sure I didn't mean it. There obviously weren't really monsters in the woods. I just figured that I was confused or that I was talking figuratively. Like I meant that the *person* who took Jeanie was a monster. I guess that's dumb. Six-year-olds don't think that way." I wrap my arms around myself, the house suddenly cold. "Kids see monsters everywhere." I echo Shane's words.

"Maybe," Sam says. "But maybe there was actually something there to see." My eyebrows pinch together. He holds his palms up. "Remember that I'm a science nerd, and so far the evidence suggests that the perpetrator doesn't have a normal human lifespan."

I shiver, fidgeting in my now stiff and filthy jean shorts. "I think you're confusing science with *science fiction*," I murmur. "And all signs point to this being more than one *person*." I emphasize the word, but I can't shake a gnawing inside me. Sort of like a homework assignment you forget to complete before you go to bed at night, and you get that maggot of suspicion squirming inside your head that your work isn't totally done.

Sam slides the photo back into the envelope. I'm about to tell him that something isn't stacking up when the doorbell rings.

I hop up and cross my fingers that it's Caleb back from the cove. He's had a couple of hours to think about it, and he's realized we have a responsibility to help Mr. Talcott and Daniel, even if it puts us in danger. He's realized that I'm *already* in danger. Two steps through the foyer and I twist the bolt and yank it open.

No one's there. "Hello?" I call. There's only the pouring rain and the bruised sky of pre-dusk. I take a step onto the porch, and my toe nudges something. It's a wicker basket full of anemic-looking strawberries the color of dead flesh; it's as though the life's been sucked out of them. I stoop for a closer look. It has. White maggots writhe from holes in the berries.

Sam charges out the front door, over the soggy lawn and down the sidewalk. I brace myself in the doorway. My hands shake. I kick my bare foot into the basket, sending the berries and maggots scattering down the porch steps and into the rain.

After five minutes of scouring the block, Sam jogs back. "I didn't see anyone anywhere," he pants. He hops over the mess. "Let's get inside and call the police."

I nod but can't will my legs to move. Sam gingerly maneuvers me back into the house and walks me to the love seat. I sink down into the cushions. "Are we overreacting? Maybe a neighbor just left a gift? *They're just strawberries.* Maybe they didn't know the fruit was rotting?" I whisper, desperate for it to be true.

Sam finds my cell on the coffee table and hands it to me. "Everyone in Savage knows that you and Jeanie were picking strawberries when she disappeared. Everyone knows that Mr. Talcott mowed those vines down every year. People used to talk about him breaking down in tears in the hardware store while he was buying a machete to use on them."

My mouth goes dry as I scroll through my contacts.

"Stella?" Shane answers after the first ring.

"Shane. Hi. Can you come over? Something's happened," I say, a little quaver in my voice.

There's the rustle of papers on the other end and a muffled apology made to someone, Shane's hand probably covering the receiver. "Sorry, Stella, I'm back. Are you hurt?"

"No . . . I just . . . Someone left a basket of strawberries on my front porch. They rang the bell, and when I answered no one was there. . . . They're covered in maggots."

Shane is quiet for a long time and then, "I'll be over in five." The line goes dead.

Four minutes later, Shane knocks. I stay planted on the love seat as Sam, who's wearing a beach towel from the linen closet over his sopping-wet clothing, jumps to let him in.

"Glad you're not alone," Shane says, wrinkling his forehead at Sam and stomping his feet on the mat. He's trailed by two uniformed police. I recognize the acne-faced cop and his lady partner. I curl my legs under myself and nod hello.

The two uniforms are quietly arguing under their breaths. Their faces are animated and flushed. Shane explains that they've been watching my house from an unmarked car parked down the street. "You gave me no choice yesterday," he adds defensively. "What were we supposed to do?"

The idea of strangers watching me makes me feel ill, even if they are police. "Did they follow me to the cove today too?" I ask. I peek at them sidelong. Did they see me and Taylor swimming? Did they hear what he said to me? The lady cop elbows her partner in the ribs. Both shift their weight uneasily.

Shane clears his throat, wipes a handkerchief he pulls from his pocket over his lips, and turns toward them. It's clear by their reluctance to meet his eyes that they missed me leaving this morning.

Sam plops down next to me and wraps his arm and the towel around my shoulders. Our sides press together.

Shane has some harsh words for the uniforms after they admit to showing up late and assuming I was inside until they saw otherwise when Sam and I arrived home. I learn their names are Reedy and Matthews, and they took the most horrifically timed coffee break known to man, fifteen minutes ago. They were ordering caramel macchiatos—I know because Shane demands to hear what was so important that they risked my life, and Matthews *answered*—as the basket of strawberries was being delivered. Shane dismisses them once it's obvious he's going to burst a blood vessel if they continue pissing him off with excuses. He drops down onto the sofa with an exhausted groan once they've left the house.

"They'll be more careful about watching you from now on," Shane assures me. Sam snorts. "They're going to bag the berries, worms, and basket as evidence. It's doubtful, but we may be able to get a partial fingerprint off the basket," Shane adds.

He rubs the scruff shadowing his chin. "We're dealing with a real sicko. Please don't go anywhere secluded. No more cove and no more woods. I hoped I wouldn't have to tell you this, but I think the time's come." He pinches the bridge of his nose as if the thought is giving him a headache. Sam's arm tightens around me. "Not only was Jane Doe's scalp severed from her head, but not all of it was recovered with her body."

I try to ask, "What do you mean?" but it's more of a jumble, my brain outdistancing my mouth, my mouth sounding out words too late or not at all.

"A small portion, about twenty-five percent, of her scalp is missing. Our lab techs can tell that the piece was severed postmortem, as was the rest of the scalp. She didn't suffer. We have to assume that the killer took it with him as a souvenir." My throat tightens, each breath labored like Shane's standing on my chest.

"*Him?*" Sam asks.

"We don't know anything for sure, but crimes of this nature are usually committed by men," Shane says. "Predators victimizing both little girls and adults are rare. This is one reason we think it's likely that the perp is linked to the Talcott family or the community at large. We're operating under the assumption that Jeanie's mother was collateral damage. Either she got too close to the identity of the person who took her daughter or the killer revealed himself in some way with Jane Doe. Mere hours after the little girl was found, Bev Talcott was killed. It's safe to assume it was to keep her quiet." All of this is what I've assumed, but there's no satisfaction in hearing it.

I press my palm to my chest, my lungs constricting. "But Jane Doe wasn't . . . I mean, no one abused her in a different way?" I blink hard against the black holes in my vision. *Breathe.*

"No, no signs of sexual abuse," Shane assures me.

"Our expert was able to date the bone found with Jane Doe," he adds after a long pause. His spine stiffens, and he laces his hands together, thumbs punctuating his words. "Understand it's not the final word. We're in the process of getting a second opinion. But it's old, very old. And we're considering it a coincidence that Jane Doe had it. Totally unrelated. Not every clue leads somewhere." He sounds very far away as he continues, "Radiocarbon dating puts the bone at between a thousand and twelve hundred years old." I don't hear anything he says after that. The synapses in my brain fire slowly, as if they're the cogs of a rusty steam engine or those cell phones as big as people's heads in reruns from the nineties. A thousand years old.

"That's freaking biblical times," I cry, interrupting whatever Sam and Shane are saying minutes later.

Shane's lips part, but Sam speaks first. "Actually, it was the peak of scientific discovery in both Chinese and Islamic civilizations." His cheeks redden as he mumbles, "But I'm not certain what was happening in North America."

Shane snorts. "As I said, we're getting a second opinion. And don't forget that these details haven't been made public." He points a stern finger from me to Sam. "There could be a real backlash from folks. Kent Talcott has been released. I put a protective detail on his house at night after someone launched a brick through his window, but we can't spare the manpower during the day. He's still a suspect."

I shift my weight and try to smother the current of anger rising up through me. All this horror and Shane still thinks it could be Jeanie's dad. "You think Jeanie's dad took the scalp off a little girl and then kept a chunk? What's the matter with you?" I blurt.

Sam makes a quiet noise of surprise. Shane leans forward, staring at me hard. "I understand the inclination to want to think the best of someone you've known for a long time." His brows lift up, softening his face. "But you can be *that* wrong about people. You understand? You can't see what's really on the inside."

I don't say so, but I think Shane's the one who's wrong. Even if people try to hide who they are, I think there are always indications, clues, and it's just a matter of recognizing them.

For the few remaining minutes Shane is here, my body is on the couch, but my mind is wholly somewhere else. It's across town, in the basement of the morgue, in a cold metal drawer with the birdlike frame of a five-year-old girl who was found murdered, scalped, and clutching an ancient bone in her dead little fist.

I give my head a jerk. Shane is shaking Sam's hand and trying to smile reassuringly at me, but it's lopsided. As he leaves, he calls over his shoulder for me to put a sweatshirt on.

Sam locks the door behind him and walks heavily back to my side. "Why didn't you tell him about the Balco kid? He could have helped us. It could have convinced him to stop looking at Mr. Talcott."

I stand from the love seat, hands steadying myself on Sam's arms. I'm suddenly so tired I have to focus to stand. "Shane's looking in all the wrong places." My voice is dead, drained. "You heard him; he won't even believe how old that bone is, and he has an expert telling him. He's going to think that the stress is getting to me if I start talking about missing kids from 1938 and monsters that take little redheaded girls." After all, it's what I would think.

"If he worries I can't deal, he'll tell Dad to send me to my mom's." I glare defiantly at my parents' wedding photo that's still on the mantel, daring Mom to argue, as if she'd actually waste her breath on me. I release Sam and force my spine straight. "I want to remember what happened to Jeanie. I can't screw it up by being sent away. *I owe her this.*" I startle myself saying it, how it's bubbling up as words before I think it, how much I feel it, and not just crushed by the burden of being judged as the one left behind once it's said.

Sam reaches for the flannel blanket hanging from the back of the couch and wraps it around my shoulders like a cape. Still holding on to the corners, he tugs me a foot closer. There's the faint whistle of his breath between his teeth. "Okay, we won't say anything to Detective Shane until we have more proof. But if this gets more dangerous"—he angles his head until he's certain he has my attention—"if something else happens where you're targeted, I'll tell him myself. I'll say it's my theory; I'll show him the picture, and if he wants to act like I'm crazy, fine."

Sam leaves soon after with a wave. It makes me feel disappointed somehow. Empty. But I can't obsess. Whatever I'm *feeling* will have to wait. There's too much to process. And I have the sense that I've been disassembled and put back together, but none of my pieces fit seamlessly anymore. I stare at the blank space between the lines of a book for an untold amount of time. My whirring mind won't concentrate on what's in front of me. I force myself to wash up for bed even though it's early. After one text to Dad telling him I'm home, I turn my ring tone to silent.

Something occurred to me as I showered, and I prop my laptop on my thighs. Killers and kidnappers don't always limit their crimes geographically. Sam's only looking for a girl who went missing in Savage. I jump from search engine to news database, looking for disappearances of young girls with red hair throughout Minnesota. I hold my breath speed-reading an article that appears to be a report of a six-year-old strawberry blonde vanishing during a walk home from school. Two paragraphs down I discover she turned up with her estranged mother in California. That's the closest I get, and in the results of every search—no matter how I try to filter them—Jeanie Talcott always pops up in the first few names. I snap my laptop shut and drop it to the carpet below.

I curl up around my bunny and try to find peaceful sleep as Jeanie's name runs across the ticker of my eyelids. Sleep comes easy, but peace doesn't.

Mom hasn't taken my summer clothes down from the attic yet, so I'm wearing my Easter dress, even though next week is the last of school. I pinch the dimples on my elbows as I sun my bare arms in Jeanie's front yard. Their Christmas lights still frost the house, but they don't light them up anymore. Too bad, since they're the twinkly kind. It was a rainy week, and I'm a bottle rocket ready to explode with pent-up yips and hollers. The hum of the TV wafts into the front yard. Sometimes Mrs. Talcott lets us watch her grown-up shows. Mom never lets me watch TV.

"Can we ask your mom for a juice bar?" Zoey calls on the upswing of a leg pump. Her hair is in long pigtails, their strands getting stuck in the rusty chain of the swing looped over a low-hanging branch of a tree. Once she tipped backward, whacked her head on a rock, and bit hard on her tongue, so she doesn't swing as high as I do anymore.

Jeanie and I kneel, surrounding a red mound of dirt. There used to be ants streaming out of it. Yesterday Daniel sprayed it with water until all the little black specks were drowned and washed away. Jeanie and I pick a ladybug family out of the strawberry vines. They're going to live in the anthill, and we won't let Daniel know.

"Can we, Jeanie?" Zoey whines louder. I look up from stuffing the mama ladybug into the tiny tunnel the ants dug. Best thing about Jeanie's is the Popsicles. Jeanie isn't answering Zoey, though. She was trying to feed blades of grass to two little green winged bugs she said were baby boys. Now she's staring over my shoulder at the line of strawberry bushes bordering the woods. Her eyes bulge and water. Her bottom lip quivers. There's a streak of snot under her nose. I turn to see what the matter is.

The slender strawberry vines quiver as if something's just escaped their cover, the red berries wagging back and forth. Beyond them there are only shadows in the wood. It's almost time to go home, since the sun is tucking itself behind treetops. I turn back to Jeanie. Tears, silent except for her breath slipping through her gap-toothed smile, stripe her cheeks. She's panting, her fists wadded into balls and shaking.

"Is it the witch?" I whisper. Daniel says a witch lives in the wood, but Jeanie says she isn't a bad one. She walked Jeanie home one time when Jeanie got lost and Daniel left her out there. But Jeanie doesn't answer. She doesn't even look at me.

"Is it the monster?" I ask even quieter. Daniel says it can leave the forest, but Jeanie thinks he's wrong. She said so to his face last week. He told her that the monster can smell that she doesn't believe it can leave the woods. He said it's going to come show her.

I think it might be showing her now. A stream of stinking water trickles downhill from Jeanie. Hot on my legs. I hop from the ground as a current of it carries the ladybugs between my sneakers, whisking them away. Jeanie stays cross-legged in pee. She opens her fist slowly, cradling it in her lap, trying to shield it with her other hand. *But I see.* I see mangled green wings and black guts staining her palm.

"They're dead," I say.

I haul myself into the shower at a little past eight. My eye sockets ache, and a throbbing pain gores my head. I dreamed only one dream, but it played over and over again. Waking up between each, heart racing, lying in the dark convinced that what I was dreaming wasn't a dream at all. It was a memory. Jeanie was taken in June, mere days after summer vacation started. But more than four weeks earlier, she was acting strange. I don't know if she always acted like a schizo staring out into the woods, but I doubt it. I can't say why I know that that afternoon was the start of everything, but I know with a certainty that hurts that someone was there in those strawberry bushes. Jeanie, slack-jawed, guarding against the woods. So freaked out she crushed the ladybugs in her fist. Jeanie *loved* ladybugs; all of a sudden, this is a truth I know.

I avoid my reflection in the bathroom mirror as I get ready for Sam and the library. There's some flash in my stare that unnerves me, that's entirely other to me. Did Jeanie know that something bad was going to happen? Was she being watched for weeks before? Hunted from the strawberry vines? Did they see what I didn't? Their branches were thin, satiny, and a haven for ladybugs. Now the bramble pervades their patch, its thorns guarding the vine's swollen fruit. Did someone stand in those vines to watch her? Did the bramble grow slowly toward the strawberries to protect them? "Nutso, get a grip," I tell my reflection, forcing myself to stare me down.

The strawberry vines grew thick and sturdy over time. The bramble that grows intermingled with the strawberries must have skirted them before. It was a casualty to Mr. Talcott's machete wielding too. All sorts of species of plants and animals develop means of surviving. If Sam were here, or Michaela, they'd launch into a mini lecture on evolution. Mr. Talcott brought those vines to the brink of death for eight years—the time between Jeanie's disappearance and her family's move—and each summer they returned more determined to live. When I think about it like that, I can't help thinking that those strawberries and I have something in common. We refuse to vanish. If Jeanie were being watched, she would have told someone. Her mom. Her dad. Her brother. Maybe she did tell someone, and maybe that person was me?

My hands shake harder as I throw clothes on and run a brush through my hair. A long time ago I got over a slice of my memory being gone. I figured that my recollection of that afternoon, and every day before it, disintegrated like dust along with Jeanie. Turns out neither were as gone as I thought. I refuse to bawl my eyes out like some melodramatic amnesia patient, but what if I could have stopped the person who took Jeanie and didn't? Never, not even for a wisp of a second, have I considered that I might be to blame.

I grab my cell to turn the ringer on fifteen minutes before Sam is set to arrive. I have a crap load of missed calls and texts. One each from Michaela and Cole, checking on me. The other seven texts are from Zoey, each bitchier than the last.

M said you've got cramps?
Call me k?
Where R U?
WTF S?
R U w/Sam?
Lose my #.

And ending with, **FU bitch!**
To tell you the truth, I expected worse. Once Zoey egged my

car because I stayed in to study rather than go to a Scott Townsend house party. She helped me clean the yolk and shells up the next morning, but still, *not so nice*.

I hit Zoey's name on the screen and hold my breath, waiting for an answer. After the fourth ring Zoey says, "Now you call? You call at eight-freaking-thirty in the morning, but you couldn't be bothered to call your best friend all day and night?"

I let out a puff of air. "Can we meet today? I have a lot to tell you, and I can't say it over the phone."

Zoey sniffs. "Text it then, bitch."

I cringe at how callous she sounds. "No, I mean I want to tell you in person."

"What about Taylor?"

"What about him?"

She sputters and chokes on whatever she's drinking. "Cooome ooon, Stella. You go hard after Taylor for months. I'm a bitch to every other girl who wants him, so they stay clear, and then you blow him off like that. What the fuck? Why would you spaz right before senior year?"

"Umm, in case you haven't noticed, the whole town is spazzing out. Dead little girls are turning up. Jeanie's mom is dead. There's a killer on the loose. There are bigger things happening." She's quiet on the other end, but I can picture her flipping her cell off. "Zoey, please. Meet me at the library at nine. 'Kay?"

"Yeah, whatevs. Caleb's using my car because my mom's taking hers to work, so I'll have to see if I can bum a ride from him."

"I'll pick you up. I'll be there in twenty," I say, rushing to hang up before she can tell me no.

I decide to wait on the front porch for Sam. The rain and the uniformed cops washed away any remnants of the rank strawberries. I scan the block warily to make certain there aren't any reporters lurking. None. They've probably all relocated to the Talcotts' house. The unmarked cop car parked two houses down is the only thing out of the ordinary. I wave to Officers Reedy and Matthews from afar, figuring that they're probably spying on me. I wonder if they use binoculars. I text Shane to let him know I'm making a quick trip to the library with Sam and Zoey, and then it'll be straight home for me.

Sam *and* Zoey. Zoey's going to *murder* me when I show up at her house with Sam. I sniff . . . bad word choice.

Ten minutes pass, and I start to fidget. What if Sam got home last night and realized what a massive mistake helping me is? What if he's headed north to the border to live a life of crime, all to escape me and the impending doom I bring along? Okay, that's unlikely, but waiting for him makes me queasy.

I focus on my shady street. Gradually, the eeriness hits me. There are barely any cars on the block. Everyone's shades and curtains are drawn, houses wrapped up tight as presents on Christmas morning. Their porches are littered with talismans to ward off evil. Horseshoes, bells and chimes, wreaths hanging above doorways. Crucifixes sticking out of manicured lawns. It looks postapocalyptic. This is what the lost years looked like. Deserted tricycles and basketball hoops rusting in cul-de-sacs. More wild turkeys bumping along the road than cars. Empty buses headed to school. Kids didn't go anywhere without their parents. And everyone went to church, because people find God fast when stuff scares the crap out of them.

I try to laugh it off. People just being paranoid and superstitious. So what? It's like I'm on the set of a B-movie horror flick. But all I can think is: *if they only knew*. If they only knew that this happened before . . . over seventy years ago. If they only knew what Jane Doe was clasping in her dainty hand. If they only knew she was scalped. If they only knew what six-year-old me was saying when I came back that day. If they did, they'd be sitting on their porches with shotguns rather than leaving a couple of violet rabbit's feet to do the job.

Chapter Sixteen

Sam's wagon roars into the driveway, and I book it a little too quickly to climb into the passenger seat.

"Good morning," he says with gusto. He smells vaguely like mint and toast. His cheeks glow pink, and the fringes of his eyelashes arch as he smiles. "Sorry it took me so long. Mom wouldn't let me leave before I ate breakfast with her."

"No worries." I settle back into the familiar seat and suppress a sigh. "Could we stop by Zoey's on the way? She's going to come with," I say.

Sam's wide eyes flit back and forth between me and the road. "Zoey agreed to be in the same room as me?" he asks dubiously.

I act preoccupied with my reflection in the mirror. "Mm-hmm." I try for nonchalance.

"Huh. I guess there's a first time for everything," he says in a pluckily optimistic way that makes me feel guilty for lying. "Daniel never called me back last night. I'll try him again after the library. He's probably just lying low with his dad." I shrug. Daniel is the least of my worries. First I have to survive Zoey; then I have to figure out a way to tell Sam and Zoey what I remembered.

Zoey lives on the opposite side of downtown from me, and even though fifteen blocks are all that separate our two houses, it's like traveling from one world to the next. The homes get dollhouse small, and on every other street there's a cluster of trailers. Pretty ones with plastic pink flamingos and fake green hedges, but still . . . houses on wheels. If the train tracks actually ran through town, this would be the wrong side of them. Zoey will antagonize just about everyone for just about everything, except not having a lot of money. Once I caught her in the locker room when she thought she was alone, telling her reflection that money can't buy popularity. I think it probably can in most places, but not at our school, not under Zoey's watch.

"I'll be right back," I say to Sam when he throws the car into park in Zoey's gravel driveway.

It isn't raining, but the sky is still brimming with clouds. Not the wispy kind, but the ones that look like sponges soaked with water, begging to be squeezed. I ring the doorbell rather than use my key. Zoey's lost five spare keys to my house; I've hung on to hers since I was ten. Shuffling on the other side of the door, and then the lock clicks open.

"Hey," Caleb says as he flings it open. He drags Zoey's yellow Lab Nanny back so that I can squeeze through and shouts, "Zoey! Stella's here." Nanny lunges forward, snorting furiously and sniffing my shoes like she means to inhale them. I scratch Nanny behind her ears, where the fur fades from gold to white. She's fourteen and the reason we spent so much time at Jeanie's as kids. Jeanie was allergic to dogs, and both my parents worked. That left Jeanie's house for playdates.

"Calm down, girl," Caleb croons to Nanny. Then to me, "You left yesterday without saying good-bye. Are you really that pissed at me?"

I shift my weight from foot to foot. "I'm not mad at you." I smile sheepishly. "It got awkward with Taylor, and it was either fight or flight." I wink at him, trying to make it a joke so I don't have to give him all the gory details or talk about where we're headed and why.

"You and Zo really know how to pick douchewads," he says, chuckling, as Zoey stomps from the hallway.

She rolls her eyes and purrs, "And you pick such lovely young ladies, don't you, Caleb? Didn't your last girlfriend drop out of school after screwing a professor and posting the pics on her photography blog while she was dating you?"

She nails us both with critical stares and then walks out of the house without another word. "So if you're not pissed, where are you guys going and why wasn't I invited?" I catch an undercurrent of hurt or suspicion in his breezy tone. "Zoey isn't in a sharing mood," he adds.

I hang in the doorway. I've never been more grateful for Zoey's gripe with Caleb. I don't like lying to him, but it's an unpleasant necessity. "I've been hanging out with Sam Worth." I say it like I'm telling a scandalous secret—how I would have whispered it only a week ago. "We started talking the other night at the bonfire . . . before everything happened, obviously. And I don't know . . ." I try to will on a blush. Make it convincing, Stella. "It just made me want to keep talking to him." I wave vaguely. "It's not going to turn into anything. I just want to see if Zoey can play nice."

He snorts loudly. "Good luck with that." He's totally buying it.

"Yeah, I should really go supervise." I walk backward, flashing an apologetic smile. "Text me tomorrow, 'kay?"

"You got it, Cambren." The front door clicks shut as I spin around and jog down the gravel path.

Zoey is frozen halfway between the station wagon and the house. She's staring daggers at Sam with her hands on her hips as she shouts, raspy-voiced and outraged, "What is *he* doing here?" Red-faced and shaking, she rushes to the car and flings the passenger door open, practically crawling into the car on her knees and stabbing her finger at Sam's chest. "Why are you trying to ruin Stella's senior year? Do you realize that she blew off Taylor Martinson for you? Taylor effing Martinson. Captain of the varsity lacrosse gods! Every girl at Wildwood would kill—literally kill—to hook up with him. And he wanted her."

She pauses for the full weight of her words to sink in. Instead Sam cranes his neck, looks past her, and smiles at me. That slow smile he gave me when he offered me the corsage and after our first kiss and in the cemetery the night I shouted at him in front of Janey Bear. The one that says he knows something that no one else does. I can't stop it; I smile back.

Zoey ducks out of the car and looks around hurriedly, like it's just occurred to her that someone might see her in the throes of an argument with a peasant. She smooths her tank top, straightens her mini-skirt, and tucks her pixie hair behind her ears. Satisfied that there's no one around but her obese neighbor rocking on her porch swing, Zoey looks back to me. I give her a helpless shrug. Her jaw drops.

"Oh. My. Fucking. God," she says. "You like him."

I cover my mouth to hide that I'm still smiling. "Zo, please come with us. I need you."

"What gives, Stella? I'm your best friend *forever*." She waves her palm at me furiously, showing off the hardly there scar from where we pricked our hands with tweezers to be blood sisters in middle school. She backtracks until she's right in front of me and holds me by my shoulders. "How did this happen?" she whispers like I've contracted some rare and tropical disease. Sam strains his neck to hear.

"I don't like him," I whisper back. I'm unnerved by how feeble it sounds.

"Uh-uh, Stella Cambren, I know you better than anyone does, and I have never seen that flushed gooey-eyed-bullshit-I-want-to-have-your-babies look on your face. Ever." She presses her fingers to her temples, as if I'm giving her a migraine. "Okay, look, I love you. You love me. How about you avoid Sam for senior year, and then you can do whatever you want to him after?"

My smile fades. "Zo, I might not make it to senior year, let alone survive the whole thing. Jeanie's killer is out there. Whoever it is might know that I'm trying to remember. There are cops watching my house twenty-four/seven. Do you understand?"

First she rolls her eyes and juts out her bottom lip. When I don't cave, she exhales loudly. "Fine. Whatevs." She crosses her arms and pops her hip. "I don't approve of this kinky thing you've got going with the King of Loserdom. But I love you, and I'd go banshee on anyone to keep you safe."

"Thanks, Zo." I lock my arm with hers and have to give her a little tug toward the station wagon to get her feet moving. This momentary cease-fire is really the best reaction I could have dared to dream.

As she climbs into the backseat, she grumbles, "But I call dibs on selecting your senior prom date. I am not going to let you ruin the single most important night of our lives. And did you guys hear that the cops took Daniel Talcott in for questioning late last night?"

Sam and I both whirl around. "What?" we say in unison.

"You know I don't believe in watching the news—too depressing," she says, pointedly not looking at Sam. "But Cole texted me at the butt crack of dawn this morning. I guess Daniel just strolled right into the police station and announced who he was. No one squealed on him for being at Day of Bones, and now the cops are calling him a suspect because they had no idea he was here—which BTW, makes zero sense since he turned himself in." She waves again, dismissing the topic. "So tell me one good reason why we're wasting an awetastic day in the library."

As we drive, Sam fills Zoey in on everything. She slouches low in the backseat so no one sees her riding in his station wagon. Her upper lip, shimmery with coral-colored lip gloss, curls in distaste at speaking to him directly. But for the most part, she listens to him. As they talk, I worry about Daniel. I guess he figured it was only a matter of time before someone who recognized him told the police he was here, and it's better to talk with the cops voluntarily. With Savage's residents in a tizzy over the crimes, maybe the safest place for Daniel is with the police? Maybe it'll keep all the bible-thumping wannabe vigilantes, who probably have arsenals full of apocalypse-ready firearms in fortified basement bunkers, away from Daniel and his dad? Maybe Daniel will be able to convince the police his father had nothing to do with any of this?

The library parking lot is underground and deserted. We hurry up the stairs to the surface to escape the sulfur smell that Zoey worries will stick to her clothes. The library is empty too, except for the librarian. She looks up, penciled-in eyebrows scowling as we make the turnstiles shriek walking through them.

"I'll check with the archivist if you guys want to get us a table," Sam offers, angling toward the reference desk.

Zoey sashays forward, batting her eyelashes as she snickers over her shoulder, "Yeah, we better hurry, 'cause the place is so effing crowded." I follow her through the stacks, trying to ignore how dark it is between the shelves. "What a dungeon. Anything could be lurking in here," she adds, practically reading my mind. "Hell, Jeanie's killer has probably been hiding out in children's books diddling himself for the last decade."

"Don't say that," I hiss-whisper, taking a seat across from her at a table. It's against the farthest wall from the door. I watch her remove a tiny packet of wet wipes and swab the dust from the table before she leans her elbows on it.

"It's weird," she whispers, eyeing where Sam stands across the library at the reference desk before she continues, "I think I kind of remember that day we went hunting for monsters." I frown. When Sam asked her in the car if she remembered the spring before Jeanie went missing, Zoey grimaced and massaged her temples like he was a trumpeting pygmy elephant. "The thing is"—she crumples the soiled wet wipe and tosses it over her shoulder—"it's like I remember *more* than one day. I knew we played outside a lot at Jeanie's, but the memories are fragments rather than whole."

I fight the urge to peer deeper into the shadowy corridors around us. "I bet Caleb would remember," I say, keeping my volume low. "I want to ask, but yesterday when I tried to ask him about that summer, he told me it was too dangerous to be hunting for Jeanie's killer." I lean over the table to be closer to her. "He said he'd tell my dad on me if I didn't stay out of it."

"Well, duh," Zoey says. A half roll of her eyes, because Caleb doesn't even warrant a full roll, in her opinion. "My handi-capable brother is not exactly known for his courage. He needed a night-light until he was thirteen." She flicks her hair from her eyes and taps a disjointed melody on the table. She's instantly impatient when Caleb's the subject. A hum buzzes from her throat, and I'm about to lose her completely to the lyrics of an unidentifiable song.

I reach across the table and hold her hands. "You could ask Caleb. Don't mention me, just act like it's something you're wondering. He'll probably remember."

Zoey's face crinkles with mean-spirited amusement. "He smoked so much pot in high school I'm surprised he doesn't forget his own name." Her mouth cuts a neutral line. "You'd think if he or Daniel remembered us hunting something in the woods, one of them would have had the brain cells to mention it at some point during all these years." Her eyes settle on my hands over hers. "If it's that important, I'll ask."

Having exhausted the subject, Zoey gives me the rundown on what I missed yesterday—Caleb ogling Cole, the Ds ending up in a shoving match over Zoey, Michaela noticing the rain clouds gathering, Caleb ditching the others, and Zoey refusing to go home until the hail pelted her in the water. Imagining the bedraggled group, shrieking and sprinting through the wood toward the shelter of the cars, does bring a smile on. Zoey tactfully—so tactfully that I suspect an alien hijacked control of her brain—doesn't mention Taylor.

"Why did Caleb ditch you guys?" I ask.

She drums her sparkly painted nails on the table between us. "He probably had one of his stoner-ific boys pick him up. He came home reeking of stale beer." She pinches the tip of her nose and sticks her tongue out.

Sam lets two beige folders thud on the table between us. "Been in a library much? Keep quiet," Zoey purrs. I give her a chastening glare until she adds, "Kidding. What've you got there, Wikipedia?"

"Clippings the archivist pulled for me."

Zoey shoves the folders toward Sam, who catches them before they glide off the table. He takes the chair next to me and starts thumbing through the pages. All photocopies of newspaper articles.

He divides the sheets into equal stacks and slides us each one. After the task of combing through articles of unrelated missing children last night, I feel too gutted for it today. But sometimes you have to suck it up. I look over my pile, keeping one eye slightly squinted as though it helps buffer me from the awful details. The *Savage Bee* covered crimes that were big news throughout the state, and many of my articles are on the missing children I read about last night. Zoey's luck isn't any better.

"Look at these," Sam murmurs excitedly, his hair a wayward pile from all the absentminded rubbing as he read. He arranges three photocopied articles in front of us. "This one is Betty Balco, the girl in 1938 that Mrs. Griever told us about. She was playing in the front yard. Her mom went inside to grab laundry for the clothesline and when she came out, Betty was gone. And these"—he points to the others—"are for two other missing girls. In 1930, Rosalyn Jensen disappeared while hiking in Blackdog with her brother. He said she was lagging behind and then vanished. She was five. And this one, Penelope Petersen, disappeared when she was six in 1936. Her family was picnicking somewhere called Norse Rock."

Zoey snatches up the articles on Penelope Petersen and squints at the faded black-and-white photograph. "All this proves is that there were sickos in the olden days," she says. "I have an entire stack of articles testifying to that fact. Big surprise."

"Read the second paragraph," Sam tells her.

Her eyes skim quickly over each line. As she reads, the blood drains from her cheeks. "They're little gingersnaps too." She places the page down delicately as if she's afraid of disturbing their sleep. "Redheads just like Jeanie," she adds in the barest of whispers.

"There's nothing in these clippings about their remains being found or any serious suspects or arrests ever being made," Sam says. I reach for the articles, hands shaking. I scan them for the details Sam says aren't there. I have to make sure. As I do, Zoey rests her head on her folded arms, and Sam stares over his shoulder at the bank of front windows. Their panes give the forest across the street the look of a cubist painting. I imagine his gaze sticks to the dark mesh of trees, searching for the monstrous explanation. The articles are short, and it doesn't take long for me to drop them on the table. Sam was right: no bodies, no suspects, only fruitless leads.

Sam's irises are darker as he turns back to us and says, "They vanished just like Jeanie."

Chapter Seventeen

t's too much to be a coincidence," Sam says for the third time. I slump in the passenger seat and cover my face. Since we left the library, I've been trying to stitch my words into anything believable, anything less horrible than the evil taking shape in Savage. Griever warned us, didn't she? She said I'd wish to be blind if I kept looking in Savage's dark corners. I'm not ready to gouge my eyes out, but I'm close.

Sam turns onto the two-lane highway heading toward Old Savage Cemetery.

"Wait a sec, let me get this straight. I almost lost it in the library I'm so eeked out, and now you're taking me to the cemetery?" Zoey asks, a nervous laugh fluting her voice. "We should be heading home to pack. We should be booking it to make the first flight to Chi-town to stay with Stella's whorebag of a mother. And I mean whorebag in the worst way possible." She leans forward and wraps her arms around me and the seat. I hug her arms back;

Zoey took my mother leaving me almost as hard as I did.

"There could be more little girls, Zo. The newspaper archives weren't complete. If we find a bunch of headstones for kids, then that's even more of a pattern to show Shane," I explain as she rests her chin on my shoulder.

"Otherwise he'll say it's a coincidence or that it doesn't mean anything," Sam adds.

Zoey pops up and wags a finger triumphantly. "But what if the families never added a headstone? Hello? No kiddie corpse, no grave, mathemagicians."

Sam tilts his head, mulling it over. "That's possible, I guess. But I bet that if families held out hope, they'd still want their daughter to have a headstone in the family plot."

Zoey stomps her heel against the back of the driver's seat. "Fine, but at the first sign of any monsters, I'm out. I just wish the Savage PD wasn't so epically snowballs incompetent. I'm not effing Nancy Drew."

The sky darkens as we get closer—kind of an ominous sign— and tiny drops of rain speckle the highway. The air in the wagon sweats. I wrap my hair in a knot on the nape of my neck and concentrate on deep, calming breaths.

As we come to a stop on the gravel lot adjacent to the cemetery, Zoey says, "About all this monster randomness, nothing like that actually exists, right?" She sounds young and scared.

"No, Zo. Of course not," I say, my stomach flip-flopping in a way it wouldn't have if she'd asked me a week ago.

She leans forward, tugging on my sleeve. "So why were you talking about monsters? Why did that dumpy old lady mention them? Why were we hunting them?" Panic makes her pitch rise.

Sam twists to face her. "People are always looking for someone or something to blame for the bad that happens. It's just the scariest thing people can think up."

He probably can't see it, but I can spot her vulnerability fading as she tips her head and blinks lazily at him. "It's not the scariest thing I can think of," she says smoothly.

"What do you mean?" I ask, suspicious.

"The devil," she says in a singsong voice, slipping out of the car, into the rain.

A white-hot flash of anger sears through me. Zoey knows it freaks me out to talk about stuff like that, especially *here*, of all places. Our one and only major fight—more like all-out war—was over her insisting that we use a Ouija board to—get this—contact Jeanie's ghost on Halloween night freshman year.

I jump out of the car and shout, "Why would you say that? We're about to go searching through a graveyard, Zo. Why can't you ever keep your big mouth shut?"

She stops abruptly; her white tank top already has Dalmatian spots from the rain. In the dim light her edges blur, making her a shimmery specter under the iron heart of the cemetery gate. She calls over her shoulder, "Isn't the devil just the ultimate monster?" A chill travels up my spine.

"You sure you want to do this?" Sam says at my side, making me start. I nod a little and then grab his hand, lacing my fingers with his, trying to feel his skin on mine more than I feel scared.

Zoey disappears into the cemetery, after tapping the heart, and we follow. "Talking about supernatural phenomena still freaks you out, huh?" Sam asks. I try to focus on a gray van and a beige four-door parked at the opposite end of the lot. Most likely deserted cars from the last kegger.

"Maybe it freaks you out because of how mysterious Jeanie's dis-appearance was?" Sam continues. "Or maybe it's because of the way people talked afterward? You remember that pastor in Rascan they used to interview on the news? He'd rant about the evil hocus-pocus at work in Savage. I remember my mom hustling me out of the gro-cery store because some out-of-towner in produce was shouting that we were all devil worshippers and brought this on ourselves. All that stuff would freak any kid out, especially since you were so close to it all."

"I guess," I answer flatly. The truth is I don't have a clue. While other little girls giggled infectiously over ghost stories and got adrenaline-junkie highs over scream-fest slumber parties, I hated them. Super dumb, if you think about it. What's real doesn't eek me out, but what couldn't possibly be makes me totally crazy. I know better than anyone that people do beastly things; my mom deserted us, remember. That I can stomach. But just whisper Grim Reaper to me before bed, and I won't sleep a wink.

It hits me that I didn't tap the iron heart once we're a few yards deep in the cemetery. Whatever. It was just one of Zoey's scary stories meant to screw with me. I tighten my grip on Sam's hand. Strange how perfectly our hands fit together.

"Do you believe in the devil?" I ask quietly. *I know*, it can't be good karma or cosmic juju or whatever to ask about the devil in a graveyard. But at the risk of cursing myself for life, there's something about what Zoey said that coaxes that strange, nagging feeling from my gut.

Sam strokes my hand with his thumb. "Not in a religious sense. Actually"—he feigns a horrified expression—"I agree with Zoey. The devil is just a scary monster that people dream up. And who says there's only one?"

"*Devils*, you mean?" I shiver, scanning the haggard gravestones surrounding us.

He gets that parenthesis mark between his brows. "Yeah, why wouldn't there be? There's more than one bad person in the world. Why wouldn't there be more than one monster? Even more than one *kind* of monster?" I scrunch up my nose. "Sure there is." He chuckles. "You've got those that aren't bound by space and time, spirit types. And then you've got those that are more animal than ghost, like werewolves, yetis, and vampires. They may have longer life spans, but they can die. Let's hope we're dealing with the latter." He's smiling in jest, but there's a wistful quality to his voice that makes me doubt he's kidding.

The raindrops bead on the patchwork of emerald moss and soil. Neon-green lichen hangs straggly, like Silly String from the dark boughs of trees. The cemetery is unchanged and peaceful except for the hundreds of footsteps left between graves. All sizes crisscrossing, like a parade or a funeral procession marched through.

"The oldest graves are along the fence, facing the shore. It makes sense to start on the opposite side, since we need to check the most recent," Sam reasons. I catch a flash of Zoey's blond head in that direction, so light it glows white as a halo. When we reach her, she's refastening the strap of her sandal, perched on a crumbling gravestone that reminds me of a giant molar.

"I don't think you're supposed to sit on those," Sam says. Zoey makes a show of jumping down and curtsying. She falls in line next to me.

We work our way from the left to the right. It's morbid work sorting through the dead. Well, the *very* dead, since the last person buried here died in 1946. The only noises are the sigh of the wind and the rhythm of raindrops.

"These names sound made up," Zoey complains as she stands in the middle of a family plot surrounded by a waist-high wrought-iron fence. "Gottmo, Bbjorstrand, Faltskog—they sound like characters from those online wizard games guys play when they're too fugly to get laid." She bats her eyelashes innocently at Sam. "You know the type, Sam—everything they know about girls they learned from porn and music videos?"

Sam flicks his hair from his eyes, ignores the slight, and answers, "Many of the families that industrialized Minnesota were of Scandinavian decent."

Zoey blinks at him. "Come again?"

"Like, descendants of the Vikings? That's why there are so many Scandinavian names here." His eyebrows arch up, and he looks from me to Zoey. "You know, that's probably why there are so many blond and redheaded families in Savage," he muses. I chew the inside of my cheek, nodding thoughtfully. I've never lived anywhere else, so I haven't considered that Savage has more redheads, but it makes sense that someone who kills them would gravitate here if it's true.

"There are some families in Savage that are descendants of the original settlers. Not my family, but hasn't Mayor Berg's been here for six or seven generations?" Sam adds. Zoey starts humming to herself to tune him out. She stops at a massive tombstone with a shield and an eagle engraved. "That's the coat of arms for the US Navy," he says. "There are graves of military families here, since the navy built ships before World War II just a few miles up the Minnesota River."

Zoey snaps to attention. "Guys in uniform?" She smacks her lips. "Yum."

After thirty or forty graves, it takes me longer and longer to calculate ages from years of birth and death. Many of the headstones are weathered, crumbling, turning to dust, like the bodies buried underneath. I kneel down at the base of a tall, pointed column engraved with a faded epitaph. I run my fingers along the grooves, able to make out only half the message before I trace the shape of vanishing letters with my finger. It's easier to feel them than see them. SWEET GIRL, HERE YOUR SPIRIT SHALL REST UNTIL THE HOLY FATHER DELIVERS THEE HOME.

"Sam. Zoey," I call. They backtrack quickly. "Look at this one.

The date and name are too faint to read, but the epitaph could be about a missing girl. 'Until the Holy Father delivers thee home.' They were waiting for her to be found." I run my finger over the eroded surface. There are striations and grooves made in the stone where the dates and name should be.

Sam crouches next to me and leans forward, examining the headstone. "It's like they've been filed or scratched away. It must have happened decades ago, since even the scratches are smooth and weathered to the touch. Their edges have been rounded by rain and wind like the rest of the grave."

"But if she went missing and she was never found, at least not when the epitaph was written, why put a year of death?" I say.

"For the same reason her parents made her a headstone at all. They knew she wasn't coming back, and they wanted to memorialize and mourn her. It's probably just the year they lost their daughter," Sam says.

"So why would someone remove the date and name on a headstone?" Zoey whispers. My hand feels extra empty not holding Sam's, so I take hers.

"They didn't want her grave to be identified," I say. I feel Zoey's shudder travel up my arm.

"But who did it?" she asks.

I shake my head and admit, "I don't know."

"Let's check to see if any others have been removed." Sam's already starting forward. After ten minutes we discover four more graves with names and dates that have been filed away. The vandal grew sloppy as his work continued, and on two of the graves it's possible to discern the dates of birth and death through the scratches. One of them was six and the other seven. The years of death—or disappearance—are in the 1930s.

Zoey's started to shiver. Her teeth chatter as she says, "Can we get out of here? I'm getting a really bad feeling."

There's a distant grumble of thunder. I look up, and my face is splattered with more raindrops.

"Sure. You ready, Stella?" Sam asks.

I nod and then hesitate. "Wait. I want to see something." I turn on my heels, dragging Zoey along, heading to where the little girl was found. Our shoes slip and slide in the mud. The gold straps of Zoey's sandals are speckled with dirt. The yowling wind picks up, and the willows rock angrily back and forth. A flash of lightning illuminates the sky and a clap of thunder comes right after. I follow a stone path that twists and turns through the core of the cemetery. We snake around the corner of a large mausoleum. Fluorescent yellow police tape marks a perimeter around the mudslide.

"It's just upturned earth," Sam says behind us. "They removed all the bones and fragments from the coffins so they could reconstruct what was destroyed. I heard that the anthropology and forensic science departments at U of M are going to restore the skeletons."

Sam's right. It's nothing but black and wet collapsed earth, edged by the mossy bank of the cemetery. "I guess it was silly that I wanted to see it again. I just thought that maybe it could help," I say. Zoey drops my hand and wraps her arm around me.

"It's okay, doll," she says. I let her lead me a few steps before something bright catches my eye. I pull away.

To the right of the slide, where the wrought-iron fence washed away with the mud, is a cluster of white candles at the base of an old oak. The tree's roots, with the look of knuckles poking up from the dirt, obscured our view of the wax pillars as we approached the slide. The flames have been extinguished by rain, but the heady char of smoke is still in the air. The candles form a perfect circle, and at their center is the corpse of a tabby cat.

Chapter Eighteen

Tripping forward, I call back to Zoey, "Don't look." She's at my side, squatting by the strange altar, a moment later. The tabby's rust-colored fur is threadbare, and its tiny rib cage pokes through the mangy coat. The circle of candles allows for a few inches of space around the cat's prostrate body. There are no other objects within their borders, but there is a smear of red at the base of the oak's trunk. It's bright and wet.

"Blood," Zoey breathes, staring at the same charnel graffiti. "The cat's?"

"Probably," I whisper. A jagged tear rings the cat's neck like a bloody necklace. I gently nudge the head and it rolls, unattached from the body, pupils focused on me as it tumbles. It rocks to a stop, the creature's little pink spongy tongue sticking out.

"Ewww!" Zoey screams, throwing herself backward, landing on her butt in the mud. She scurries to her feet and ducks behind Sam; one watering eye peeks out from behind his shoulder.

"Stella, come on. Let's go back to the car and call the cops." Sam speaks steady and slow. I shake my head for a moment. How can I leave this helpless little animal alone? I scour the ground for anything I can use to cover the cat. There's nothing but a loose wad of police tape. I edge toward the head, trying not to see the purple-and-red jelly of its wound. I fold the tape over the head, nimble fingers becoming fat and clumsy, brushing a damp ear. I choke down a whimper and whirl away.

I tail Sam and Zoey through the cemetery. Everything is watery from tears and pounding rain. I try to rub away the sensation of the cat's fur on my palm, but I can't. I feel it under my skin rather than on it.

We sprint through the gravel lot and rush inside the station wagon. I wipe the steam from the window and squint out to where the other two cars were parked. They're gone.

"W-who would do something like that?" Zoey stammers. Sam fumbles with the buttons on his cell, fingertips slippery and blue. I cross my arms over my face and close my eyes. I try to take refuge in the blackness, but the image of the cat's rolling head is burned on the insides of my eyelids.

Sam's on the phone with the police station. "Yes. That's what I said, a dead cat . . . No, not hit by a car . . . Excuse me, but someone butchering a pet *is* a serious police matter. . . . Hello? Hello?"

With a clatter, he tosses his phone on the dashboard. "They hung up on me. With everything going on, you'd think they'd take something like this seriously."

My arms droop to my sides, and I stare at the worn ceiling of the car. A yellowed spot stares back. I want to call Shane. Spill everything we've been up to. But I can't risk getting sent to Chicago, not when human lives are at stake. "Everything going on is probably why they're *not* taking it seriously, Sam. They don't see that everything is connected," I murmur, drawing imaginary lines from stain to stain just like connect-the-dots. "There were cars parked over there"—I tap against the window—"and now they're gone. We didn't see anyone in the cemetery." I pause. Look back up at the stains. "You don't think they were doing that to the cat while we were in there, do you?" My stomach lurches.

"No, I'm sure it—uh—he or she had been dead for a while." Sam sounds hopeful, not certain. He turns the key in the ignition, and the wagon springs alive.

"I've got to drop you guys off so I can get to my shift at BigBox." He indicates the car's digital clock.

I know Zoey is traumatized, because she misses the opportunity to say something snide. Instead she murmurs weakly, "Bring me home. I'm going to puke."

The ride back is mostly quiet. Zoey gives me a quick hug and nods to Sam before running into her house through the dumping rain. I focus on the canvas of my tennis shoes as we cut through town. I've hit my threshold for twisted today—not just today, for a lifetime. I don't need to see my neighbors patrolling the streets in armed posses or building bonfires to burn witches.

"Is your dad going to be home tonight?" Sam asks as we pull into my driveway.

"Probably not until late." A little spike of terror runs through me. I don't want to be alone. There'll be too much time to think. Too much time for nightmares—real and imagined.

"I get off at nine. If you want, I could come over."

"I'd like that," I say speedily, too relieved to care about playing it cool. He smiles a little sadly as he leaves me waving from my porch. I exhale deeply and force myself to push through the front door.

Two hours later, showered, fed, and a little less ragged, I curl on the couch with my laptop.

"Okay, back to it," I say to Moscow, who's purring loudly from the opposite end of the couch. I need answers, and this is the only way I know to find them. Since all evidence points to a multigenerational cult at work in Savage, and the cat, butchered on a makeshift altar, screams twisted sacrifice, I search three terms: "cult sacrifice," "animal sacrifice," and "child sacrifice." I start with general searches on Wikipedia and Google.

After snowdrifts of bizarro articles, I'm too queasy to wade through all the dementedness anymore. I need to narrow results, since it's unlikely that Savage residents are performing an obscure ancient Chinese ritual of sacrificing people to the river deities or that the fictional Cthulhu Mythos has been brought to life in our small town. I get the point: There are sickos out there, and they believe all sorts of warped things.

Next I search the same terms but limit the results geographically to Minnesota. Using search engines, I come up with a load of indie bands and heavy metal groups with the terms in their names.

I switch to searching news databases and subscription websites like LexisNexis, which we use for the *Herald*, but I don't find a single article about any cults, legends, or lore in Minnesota that says an iota about sacrifice or redheads.

No shortage of death and dismemberment, though. This area's history is grisly, not the oasis-in-the-wilderness fantasy I remember learning about in school. Fur traders settled their outposts here and massacred the wildlife. Pioneers drove the natives from their villages. Colonial wars left mass casualties. And outbreaks of tuberculosis, called "the white death," wasted the population. I gulp. Maybe there's something to the name of our town after all? Yet none of this has anything to do with Jeanie or the tortured cat in the cemetery.

Moscow arches his back, showing off his chubby tummy. "You brilliant little pig," I coo to him. I bring up the Savage Public Library's webpage and click on the news archives. All of the town's records aren't available, but it's worth a try. I search "animal sacrifices." Zero results. I glower at the screen. *I was so sure.* I'm about to close my laptop and give in to my sulk and that pint of ice cream in the freezer when something occurs to me. I type "animal disappearances"; holding my breath, I hit enter.

I blow out the breath in a whoosh of dismay. I was right. Seventy-three entries for missing pets in the *Savage Bee*'s classifieds fill the screen. The newspaper still devotes its last four pages to community classifieds: rummage sale notices, job postings, houses and cars for sale, and missing pets. I hunch over the laptop and scroll through them, my throat getting tighter with each. There are holes in what's available, multiple-year blocks where no search results are yielded, but there's enough for it to be a kick in the chest. There are entries dating from 1910 to 2014. Some entries are even from the same week. Families missing dogs and cats, local farms missing livestock, the nursery school missing a goat from their petting zoo, all posted in the classifieds in the hope that someone will find their animal and return it.

I drag Moscow into my lap and cradle him protectively. There's even one article published in the newspaper on a bizarre number of dog disappearances in November of 1938. This isn't shocking; ten Fidos going missing is the definition of small-town news. For the seventy-three missing pets that are posted in the classifieds, there must be tens that went unreported. I bet if I went to the library and spent hours looking through the archives, there would be scores more that haven't been scanned into the system—just like Sam's articles about the missing girls.

"Why would someone do this?" I think of the butchered tabby cat. Someone went to the trouble of making an altar of candles and sacrificing the poor cat in the place where Jane Doe was found. Aren't sacrifices usually meant to appease some awful thing? To stop something bad from happening? If all these animals were taken to be sacrificed—I suck in my breath hard—then there were bad things happening around them.

I search for violent crimes and deaths in the archive. With a notebook and pen I chart a time line, staring at the computer screen until my lids are like sandpaper on my eyeballs and my mouth is almost as dry. It isn't comprehensive. I don't have time to read every boxed-up and disintegrating newspaper in the archives at the library to flesh it out. I also remember what Sam said about there being more newspapers donated from the years closer to 1972 than further back in time. The distribution of dots on my time line tells the same story. There are even more dots after 1973, since the *Savage Bee* was rebuilt and the records preserved.

I sit back against the couch and behold the ten-page time line spread over the coffee table: tragic deaths and accidents and their corresponding clusters of animal disappearances.

"Oh. My. Freaking. Gosh," I say to Moscow. He yawns loll-eyed. My phone buzzes loudly from where I kicked it across the living room floor an hour ago. I crawl toward it; a little current of anticipation runs through me as I spot Sam's name on the screen.

"Hi," I say, sounding too jittery.

"Hey. I'll be there in ten and didn't want to scare you ringing the doorbell without warning. I brought supplies to cook dinner if you haven't eaten." I stare bewildered at the laptop's clock. How is it past nine?

"Thanks. I totally lost track of time."

Once the call ends, I dial Dad.

He's worn-out answering, his voice thin. "Hi, Pumpkin. Everything all right?"

"Yeah, I just wanted to let you know I'm home and that Sam Worth is coming over to make food and watch a movie."

"Oh, good. Listen, Stella, I'm really sorry I haven't been around much for you with everything going on. I'm working on a complex tax evasion case that's demanding most of my attention, and I can't let any of the details slip through the cracks." I mouth the next part along with him, because I've heard it a billion times before. "You know the devil's always in the details with cases like this." Goose bumps spread up my arms.

"It's okay, Dad. Really. So you'll be pretty late?"

"We've got the whole team working through the night."

"'Kay. Well, love you and drive carefully," I say, knowing full well I sound buckets more like a parent than he does.

At least I don't have time to mope. I sprint upstairs to change the clothes I've been marinating in all afternoon. Right as I swing open my closet, the doorbell rings. I swap my hoodie for a black tank and wrestle on a pair of jeans.

Thirty seconds later I'm breathy but there to let Sam in.

"Hey," I pant, flinging open the door. Sam stands on the porch, one arm around a bag full of groceries, the other around a bouquet of flowers. He shakes the thatch of hair off his forehead.

I stand half-dazed in the doorway, trying to blink the stars from my eyes. It's not only that he brought flowers, that I don't want to be alone, that he said he'd be here and now he is and few people actually stick around when they say they will. It's that I haven't looked at Sam—or maybe anyone—this way since I was little. Everyone else's insults and opinions fall away so that he's only Sam to me, and my whole body hums to be near him.

"Hi." He glances awkwardly from armload to armload. "I know

this isn't a date or anything," he adds quickly. I imagine a muddy boot stepping on the papery-winged butterflies fluttering in my chest. Whoa there, tiger, rein the roller-coaster emotions in.

"Sorry," I blurt. "I mean, c'mon in." I step clumsily back on a pair of Dad's running shoes by the door and almost sprain my ankle trying to hide what a klutz I am.

"These are for you." He offers me the bouquet of delicate ruffled pink rosebuds.

"Non-date flowers," I say before I can stop myself.

He frowns at the bouquet. "I'm confused." He looks from the flowers to me. "I thought you didn't want this to be a date." I swallow hard and twist my finger in the hem of my shirt, sure that my cheeks match the flowers. "If it were up to me, it *would* be."

I take a shaky breath, inhaling too much of the bouquet's perfume, drunk off nerves. "You said that I would just have to say the word and you'd be all over me." I speak carefully, like I'm in a verbal minefield. The ceiling lights suddenly beam down on me like strobe lights. But rather than let my resolve melt, I steady the hitch in my breath. "What word is it that I need to say?"

The corners of his mouth twitch up as he leans in until our noses practically touch. The flowers press against my chest. I want to look away but can't. "Why do you want to know?" There's laughter and heat in his voice.

"Oh, just for future reference." I shrug a shoulder and breeze on, "You know, so that I don't say it by accident." I can't help smiling like a fool.

The warmth rolls off him. With his free hand he reaches toward me, coiling a strand of my hair around his finger, brushing my shoulder with his arm. "I lied before. It's not just a word but a sentence." His eyes twinkle mischievously.

"Okay, what is this magic sentence?" I fight to stop my gaze from traveling to his lips.

He tugs my hair lightly. "You have to say, 'Sam, I want you to be my boyfriend.' And then *poof*, I'll do the rest."

I withdraw. His hand drops away from me. "Sam, I—I don't have boyfriends. I told you that." I look down at my bare feet, wishing I had at least put socks on. With socks on I wouldn't feel so exposed.

His lips form a perfect O shape. "Stella, I'm telling you I want you. I—I'm in *love* with you. I've always been."

For some reason my chin trembles as he says it. I don't know why it sounds so terrifying to me. Dad tells me he loves me all the time. Mom says it when we talk on the phone. Even Zoey tells me. But coming from Sam's mouth, the words turn me into something wild and skittish.

"That's what you say now, but Sam, you won't. You'll get tired of me and being my . . . *you know*."

He closes his eyes and shakes his head. "I haven't gotten tired of you for as long as I've known you." His voice gets deeper, huskier. "I won't be someone who leaves you. I'm not your mom. I'm not your dad. I'm not Jeanie. I won't go."

I blink up at him. If anyone else said those things, I'd probably scream bloody murder in response. Sam's right, though, I've lost a lot of people. I keep everyone at a distance except for Zoey, and that's only because it's too hard to tell where I stop and she begins.

"Are you hungry?" he asks suddenly, the flush in his cheeks receding. I remember the grocery bag still in his arms and nod, grateful for something easy I have the answer to. "Great. I'm not as good a cook as my mom, but my specialty is pasta and turkey meatballs." He slips around me and moves toward the kitchen. From behind there's no sign that he's been rejected. I follow after a few moments of nerves paralyze me. When I do, Sam's already unpacked the bag of groceries and is searching through drawers of cooking utensils.

"Hey, tell me what you remembered yesterday. If you're up for it," he says, bumping through the cabinets.

I stow the flowers in a vase I snag to stall for time. I'm not eager to fill Sam's head with the nightmarish memories I recovered. When that's done, I twiddle my fingers on the counter, playing an imaginary keyboard. "How was work?" I ask.

He shrugs, hunched over a giant sauté pan. "It was okay. I remembered to take off the red vest this time." One brown eye winks at me, and he turns back to cooking.

I jump up to sit on the counter and dive into rehashing the ugly things I remembered. I start with the ladybugs in Jeanie's front yard.

Sam stops washing mushrooms to listen, and when I'm done, barely skipping a beat, he says, "In the dream, you knew Jeanie was afraid of something, but that's because you're not six anymore. You might not have understood what you were seeing while it was happening." Then more firmly, "You're not to blame."

I grip the countertop and nod. What he says makes sense, it just doesn't make me feel as innocent as it should. I start telling him about the disfigured hand twined in Jeanie's hair. Obviously, I spare him the parts where I was up close and personal with Taylor.

I stare at the lines on my palms. "You don't think what happened to Jane Doe's head happened to Jeanie, too?" A shudder runs through me. "Her scalp, I mean."

Sam stands at the chopping block, studiously slicing an onion. He smiles ruefully at me. "I wish I could tell you no, but I can't. None of the other little girls' bodies were found either, and they all had red hair. There's a connection there. The scalp injuries . . . the red hair. What did Zoey say about what you remembered?"

"Umm . . . I didn't tell her. She took off with one of the lacrosse boys she hooks up with, and I didn't get a chance." He raises an eyebrow over the lemon he's zesting.

"Why were you holding your breath underwater? Didn't anyone ever tell you that oxygen deprivation and alcohol don't mix?" He dumps the chopped onions in the pan, and they hiss in the hot oil.

"I was with Taylor," I admit as quietly as possible. Maybe he just won't hear? The knife he's washing in the sink slips from his hands and clatters against the other dirty dishes. "I didn't invite him, Zoey did." I'm flustered. "I was underwater to escape him. And it wasn't just Taylor but other guys at the cove too." I've made it sound like a party Sam wasn't invited to; that's the case, though, isn't it? All of high school there's been an impassable line between us, albeit one I helped create. I'm trying to vault over it, when what I wish I could do is erase it. I'm indignant for Sam; he is so much *more* than boys like Taylor.

Sam leaves the knife where it lies in the sink and adjusts the stovetop. He fiddles with the onions and adds meatballs he rolls between his palms. The silence is earsplitting. I sound too defensive when I say, "Nothing happened with Taylor. Sure, he would have liked it to, but I'm not interested in him. I made that clear."

Sam turns abruptly to me. "You don't need to explain." His smile is slow and sweet. We don't speak again until we sit down to eat. He grins at me over our food and takes a gigantic bite of spaghetti.

"Your dad won't mind if I'm here when he gets home?" he asks midway through dinner.

I scrunch my nose up. "My dad isn't that kind of dad. He probably wouldn't even care if you slept over." I blush once the words have left my mouth.

Sam chuckles them off. "Good to know."

"I just mean he trusts me to make my own decisions. It's nice to be treated like that, most of the time." I twirl my fork in the pasta. "Will your mom care that you're out late?"

He covers his mouth with a napkin. "No, once she heard that I was coming here she didn't even give me a curfew. I'll have to use you as cover every time I go out."

I stab a meatball with my fork. "I missed your mom."

"I think she missed you," he says with a full mouth, smiling with bits and pieces of food in his teeth.

"Oh, sooo hot." I throw my napkin at his face, laughing. "What about Daniel? Did you call him?"

"I texted him what we found at the library and cemetery and finally got a text back saying he was crashing with his dad. He was vague, but I guess the police questioned him and then sent him home. He said he'd call tomorrow."

I nod. "I've been thinking a lot about Jeanie," I admit absently. "I can't remember what she was like, and all I really know is what Zoey says."

"You want to know what I remember?" he offers. I swallow and nod. He leans back in his chair. "She was funny. She kind of wobbled everywhere, like she was dancing rather than walking. That really got me at six." He laughs under his breath. "She had a lisp, and she loved rattling off in gibberish. I'm not sure if she made up her own language or what, but she'd dissolve into giggles after a few sentences of nonsense." I stare into the middle distance of my kitchen, like I might be able to look back in time and see what Sam does. "She always wanted to play outside . . . always in the front yard or the woods." We don't speak for a long time.

"Do you think I'd be friends with her now?"

He blinks at me carefully; he can probably see how thinly veiled my guilt over the imagined answer has become. "Who knows? Everything could be different if she were here."

I know exactly what he means. Who would I be without the disappearance sending ripples through me? If Jeanie were a person with laughter and habits rather than a diamond or dull penny to me, who would I be? In an alternate universe, where Zoey made me choose between herself and Jeanie, might I have chosen Jeanie?

Would we be in orchestra? Would we date best friends who took us to the Cineplex every Friday night? I like the idea of three alternate realities for me to exist in: one where I've chosen Zoey, one with Sam, and one with Jeanie. Perhaps that's because Sam is right: I shouldn't have chosen. Jeanie shouldn't be dead. We're all disembodied from the way it *should* be.

Sam rises to clear the plates. I dump them in the dishwasher once he's rinsed. "Thanks for making dinner. Do you want to watch a movie or something?"

Sam heads to the front room. "You don't have to do that. It's okay if you want me to leave," he says, stooping for his keys on the coffee table.

I watch helplessly as he walks toward the front door and pulls it open. He'll leave, travel into the darkness between our two houses, accept that I won't say the magic words to make him mine, convince himself that I don't want him, and this moment will be gone forever, snatched away from me like the gust of wind from the open door is scattering the pages of my time line to the floor.

Before he gets any farther, before I lose him, I blurt out, "For the last hundred years a secret group has been sacrificing animals every time something horrible happens in Savage."

Chapter Nineteen

You remember those heaps of dirt at Mrs. Griever's? Well"—I wave for him to follow me into the living room—"I think they're buried animals. I don't know if that means that she's one of the people sacrificing them, or the only one, or that she's cleaning up after them and hiding the evidence. But I found a pattern—well, most of a pattern, since the online library archives are incomplete."

I hand him the notes, and his eyes skim rapidly back and forth. "See." I point to the first page. "We know that none of the missing girls from the thirties are in the online archives yet, but in December of 1938 there was an article about ten dogs going missing. That's only months after Betty Balco disappeared and a few years after the others in the articles you found." I flip to the second page. "In 1956 the town's first cannery burned down, trapping and killing three men who worked there. They burned alive. Four people reported missing dogs in the month after." I thumb through the pages and put another on top of the stack for Sam to read. "The *Savage Bee* burned down in 1972. The paper's secretary was killed in the fire. Two weeks later, three families reported their dogs and cats missing."

I try to stay calm, but my palms break into a cold sweat. "In the summer of 1960 a houseboat sank in Blackdog Lake, killing the family who was vacationing on it; in 1980 two hikers were mauled by a bear; in 1984 a school bus collided with a delivery van, killing a teacher and two students; and eleven years ago, Jeanie Talcott disappeared while playing in her front yard." I take a second to catch my breath after the grim list. "Since the newspaper began reporting in 1910, there have been twenty-one disasters or accidents that have happened in Savage. Those are just what showed up in the online archives and don't include the disappearances we know about in the thirties. Do you know what seventeen out of twenty-one of them have in common?"

Sam drops the stack of papers on the coffee table and tucks a frenzied wisp of hair behind my ear. His mouth sets into a gloomy line. "There's a bunch of animal disappearances afterward," he supplies.

"Right," I say, waving my finger in the air. "As few as one and as many as ten have been reported missing in the weeks after these bad things. I could only find the one article from 1938 talking about a rash of lost dogs, and people just figured there was a large animal hunting in the woods."

"But you don't think so?" Sam asks.

"No," I say fiercely. "Those animals had the same end as the cat from the cemetery today. I wish it weren't true, but I know it. Sacrificed on a makeshift altar by some sicko who thinks they're making an offering to stop the horrible things from happening."

"Making a sacrifice to who, though?" Sam motions skyward. "To the gods? This isn't ancient Greece. Accidents happen. It's horrible that all those people died, but fires burn down buildings, people die in accidents. Nothing's causing those things to happen but terrible luck."

"I know that and you know that, but whoever is doing this thinks they're not accidents. I get that it's padded-room-worthy, but whoever these people are, they think someone or something is causing all of it."

Sam chews the inside of his cheek. "So you're saying that you don't think whoever killed Jane Doe, Jeanie, and her mom killed the tabby cat?"

I shake my head hard. "I don't. I think that we're looking for multiple psychos. Whoever is killing the little girls and whoever is killing the animals are different groups. More than one monster." I lower my voice. "More than one devil."

"And you think it's a clandestine group? Like some order of men and women trying to protect Savage from evil happening by sacrificing animals over generations?" I jerk my head yes. "How could something like that stay secret?"

"I have no idea, but it has." I run my hands from the roots of my hair to the ends. The hitch of my heart picks up. "And maybe it was going on way before the newspaper started reporting in 1910? Maybe the finger bone fits in somehow?" My words fall faster. "There have to be more records of Savage, ones that go back further in history, even before the town was founded in 1902." Sam's face is neutral, reflecting none of the frenzy I feel. "Before 1902 there were settlers here."

He shrugs. "A small group of fur traders came in the 1600s. Then Scandinavian settlers after that." His feet shuffle restlessly. His brows pinch together as he opens his mouth, closes it, opens it again. "Stella, whatever is going on, it's bigger than Jeanie. I know there are bad people in the world, but this"—his eyes search the room for the right word—"this is *more*. It's *unnatural*." His hands flop at his sides, and he huffs with the admission.

I get what Sam is saying; why the muscle in his jaw is clenching; why his shoulders round forward; why the web of blue veins on his neck is showing through pale skin. There's a coldness in my bones telling me there's something else to all of this too. Like a thin layer of dust coating a fresh body. Something that twists the mind. Defies sense. But unlike Sam, I have a name for it: fear. And unlike Sam, I believe there are people out there—people so bad their organs are as shriveled and rotten as the strawberries left on my front porch—who could have killed all those little girls. I don't need to invent monsters.

I rub the goose bumps from my arms. "All I know for sure is that I have to keep looking. If that means digging up Mrs. Griever's yard to find tiny graves of the sacrificed, so be it. There's nothing I won't do," I say recklessly.

Sam's eyes get big. "Hold on. There's no way I'm letting you go back out to Mrs. Griever's. Remember her? The one with the shotgun aimed at us? And while there's a serial killer on the loose scalping children and a cult that's murdering innocent pets? All so you can dig up their bodies?"

I move closer, desperate to make my point, hands wringing as I do. "Don't you get it? This is the first piece of the puzzle that we've had any luck with. Other than my creeptastic memories, we're no closer to figuring out who took Jeanie. If we could find out who's taking the animals, then maybe they'll talk to us. They know more than we do. There wasn't just a cat on that altar, it was a cat with *red fur*. And it was near where a little *redheaded* girl was found, mutilated and dead. Sure they're nuts, but they'll at least be able to tell us what they're so afraid of." Having a plan makes me braver. I stand taller sharing it.

"I think it's time that we go to the cops with this. *With everything*." He motions to the door like he might leave to get the police this very second.

"The cops?" I cry. "You mean the cops who hung up on you today when you reported a beheaded cat? You think *those cops* will help?" It sucks to admit it, but I don't think Shane would buy one bit of this. I'm not sure if anyone would believe me, except for Sam. My chest rises and falls fast. Sam's pulse flutters under the skin on the curve of his neck. I rub my collarbone, suddenly warm and itchy with splotches. There's a shift in the air, a charge different from anger between us.

Sam wavers, the crease between his brows lessening. "You always kicked my ass at staring contests," he grumbles, a hint of a smile playing on his lips. His hands disappear into his pockets, and he stands uncertainly in front of me. But he's still here—not just in my living room but *near me*—and it occurs to me that he shouldn't be.

"You don't have to go to Griever's if you don't want to, Sam. I understand that this is all . . ." I search for how to say it.

"Horrific? Bone-chilling? Terrifying? Shaping up to be preternatural?" Sam offers.

"A lot to ask of you," I whisper. "This is *dangerous*. Just being near me is dangerous."

"Stella, haven't you heard anything I've said?" His hands cup my face; his thumbs brush my cheeks, leaving warm streaks in their wake. "I'd let you bury me in Mrs. Griever's front yard if you wanted to. I'd camp out in the cemetery or the morgue or in Jeanie's abandoned house. I'd do anything for you," he says wildly, his giant brown eyes earnest.

You see, this is the moment. If I was ever going to free Sam from whatever hold I had over him, this would have been it. In the wreckage of a second I imagine sending him away, finding the lies he needs to hear to leave me. There are a billion things I could say. And he'd be safer if I said any one. For once I'm glad Mom is in Chicago; she's safe there. I'm glad Dad practically lives at his office; he's safer there. But Sam . . . he's standing too close to the campfire, and he doesn't even know it. Instead I let the moment slip away and cave to wanting him.

"Please don't leave," I say, placing my hands over his, eyes begging like every hope and wish I've ever had depends on Sam staying. Like my life depends on it. Maybe it does? After a beat I turn and walk upstairs. And of course, a moment later, Sam follows.

His padded steps trail after mine on the stairs. By the time I enter my bedroom I'm shivering, the chill of the house sticking to my skin. Sam is calm and quiet as he strides through the doorway. He moves as though he belongs here, like it's his room rather than mine. I watch as he leans close, eyes blinking solemnly, crescent mouth curving in a smile, to study the photos and drawings tacked up on my walls. I shiver harder, feeling too revealed in front of his careful stare. I don't think he misses anything. "Do you want to watch a movie?" I ask, sitting on the foot of my bed. I grip my hands together making white splotches on my hot skin.

"No," he says softly, eyes not straying from the photo he's examining.

"No?" I peep.

He turns his head slightly and nails me with a serious look before turning back to read a bunch of quotes I printed out and stuck to my bulletin board ages ago.

"What do you want, then?" I whisper, a little breathless. He doesn't answer at first. I watch him reach up and unpin a photo. He tilts it toward me and raises an eyebrow. It's one of Taylor and me from an end-of-the-school-year bash. Sam was there too. I noticed him from the corner of my eye with a coed group in Scott Townsend's backyard, throwing his head back, laughing. But lately, aren't I always at least a little aware of where he is in relation to me? Even then I remember wondering what he thought was so funny.

Sam drops the photo in the wastebasket to the right of the desk. "I want you," he says, and moves on to my bookcase. A spasm passes through my chest. *I want you.* It's as simple as that. The syllables come easy and sure, a quiet bravery at their core. I used to know what it felt like to be that certain. It's how I felt about Sam at the cove when we were ten.

Sam angles his head to read the titles of my books, his broad fingers running over the spine of each as he goes. His lips move ever so slightly, mouthing each one.

He turns to me, and I'm caught staring at him, my own lips parted, a bit dazed.

"I have a lot of the same books," he says.

"Oh?" is all I can think of to say back.

A crooked smile from him. "Stella?" His tone swings up in question.

He crosses the room and stops over me, running his hands through his hair, tugging on it. I stand quickly from the bed, light-headed and springy. The heat of him reaches me from a few inches away, prickling and tickling my skin. Truthfully, I'd say anything so he'd touch me; so I could feel certain and fearless again.

"Be my boyfriend," I say, so out of breath I can hardly get the words out. He moves lightning fast. We're not touching, and then suddenly I'm reaching for him and his arms are encircling me. I gasp as he pulls me hard against him, and his lips press firmly to mine, the heat of his skin burning me everywhere. I sway into him, toes barely staying on the ground, caving to the buzzing thing inside me.

It's the most seamless kiss I've ever had. Not the fumbling make-out sessions I'm used to. Every move is natural. One of his hands slips into my hair, entangling itself until I think it'll never be freed. The other keeps pressing on the small of my back like it means to break me in two. I can hear my own heartbeat pounding deep in my eardrums and his hammering into my chest. Their beats mingle. My skin is feverish. My face and chest are probably red and blotchy. I wouldn't mind if I combusted completely, burning up like a toasting marshmallow or something more romantic, like a dying star. Sam's mouth separates from mine, and he stares down at me.

"I love you," he exhales, like the words are something he's been holding in with the kiss. I try to hide the shock from my face. Here we are, practically ripping our shirts off, and Sam stops to tell me how he feels. *He loves me.* What does that even mean? My head is full of an earsplitting call for *more.* But more of what? Okay, I want more of this heavy-breathing, wild-haired, clinging-to-each-other thing, but how do I *feel?* The only thing I know for sure is that even with all the danger and uncertainty around us, I want Sam to stay.

"Will you stay with me tonight?" I ask.

He smiles wide in answer. He moves away from me, flicks the light switch off, and closes the bedroom door. I hear the lock, its click loosening the muscles in my chest. A minute later the mattress whines under his weight. After a moment's hesitation, paralyzed by nerves that for the first time ever postpuberty I am going to sleep beside a boy, I crawl beside him, resting my head in the crook of his arm. He pulls me in closer and presses his lips to my forehead.

"Good night, Hella Stella," he whispers in a hoarse voice.

I half moan, half giggle as his mouth dots a trail of kisses from my forehead into my hair.

"Good night." I sigh, closing my eyes and saying a silent thank-you to whoever brought me back to Sam.

Chapter Twenty

Early-morning light seeps through the slats in my blinds. I'm burning up wrapped in Sam's arms. My back is to his chest and we're spooning. If Zoey were here, she'd make gagging noises. I stifle a laugh. Her reaction will be a hybrid of astonishment and horror. Kind of like when Janey Bear showed up with her belly button pierced the week after Zoey had hers done, and Zoey made Janey remove it at lunch in the bathroom. Like that, but worse.

I wiggle onto my back and stare at the ceiling. Sam's arm rests on my chest. He's breathing softly, a faint whistle through his parted lips. Five days ago I was scoping out Taylor's sun-kissed abs, and now I'm lying in bed with Sam Worth. The ceiling starts to spin, and I close my eyes to stop the roller-coaster stomach from taking hold. It's not that I'm having second thoughts. I'm not. I want Sam here, in my bed. I want to stay wrapped in his arms until the next ice age, frozen in a glacier with our lips still locked. It's a huge shift in my world, though. I tug the comforter to my chin and take deep breaths. My bunny lies discarded on the floor. He's on his stomach, plush head facing me, a knowing twinkle in his black button eyes.

"Hi," Sam whispers. He starts to withdraw his arm. Instead he brushes the hair from my forehead. He blinks solemnly at me.

"Hi." I fight the impulse to duck under the covers and hide. Why do I suddenly feel naked in a T-shirt and leggings? "Did you sleep okay?"

He nods. "What about you, are you okay?"

"Yeah. Better than that."

Sam's whole face bursts into a grin. He presses his lips to mine. "That was the most incredible night of my life. I love you," he says close to my ear. I shudder and bury my face in his chest. A few tears squeeze out, and I wipe them away hastily.

We lie in bed kissing and giggling like little lovesick idiots for the next hour. A quiet knock on the bedroom door breaks the trance.

"Stella, Pumpkin? Could I see you for a moment?" Dad calls softly from the hall. I jump from the bed like I'm on fire. Sam's legs get tangled in the sheets, and he falls from the mattress, banging his head against the bedside table and landing with a thud on the carpet. I wildly pat my clothes smooth. I wave for Sam to hide in my bathroom, and he scurries across the room and slams the door behind him. There is no way Dad didn't hear all that commotion. I take the sort of deep breath you'd take going in front of a firing squad, smooth my hair over my head one last time, and open the door a crack.

"Could I have a word with you downstairs?" Dad asks, eyes glued to my toes. I nod and follow, closing the door behind me, hands trembling as I head down the stairs. Dad's in a freshly pressed suit, with his briefcase in one hand and a muffin in the other. He stops at the front door and faces me. Again he speaks directly to the tops of my feet, like I've sprouted eyeballs there.

"Pumpkin, if your mother were here, she'd be the one talking to you right now. This is extremely uncomfortable for us both." His finger hooks and tugs on the inside of his collar like it's slowly strangling him. "I realize that we haven't had a frank discussion about male and female . . . *relationships*. You know if you have questions regarding *intercourse*"—he coughs out the word—"you can always ask me. Or maybe there's a school counselor you could speak to?" His tone trails up hopefully. I'm struck completely silent and find myself staring at his shiny brown shoes as if they're the most fascinating things ever.

"If I hadn't recognized the Worth boy's station wagon in our driveway when I arrived home last night, I might not have been so discreet." He waits for a response. I try not to look as guilty as a kid with her mouth stuffed with candy right before dinner or a girl hiding hickeys under a turtleneck. How could I have forgotten Sam's car in the driveway?

"Dad, I'm—I didn't want to be alone with everything going on, and . . ." I move my lips soundlessly.

He tips his head forward and holds up his hand for me to stop. "Sam is welcome to our couch in the future. Just . . . be safe, Pumpkin. Again, if you need to talk with someone about methods of—"

"Dad," I cut him off. "I got it."

He pats me on the shoulder and nods, satisfied. "Well, okay.

Glad we talked." He stops just over the threshold. "Please don't leave home today, Pumpkin. It's safer for you here." I stand dumbstruck for a minute more after he leaves. That was literally the most awkward conversation I have ever had. Obviously, I'll be too embarrassed to look Dad in the eyes ever again.

I bound up the stairs, and by the time I reach Sam, my mood's brightened and I'm jouncing with giggles.

"You aren't grounded, are you?" Sam says, perched at the foot of my bed. "I can talk to him. I'll tell him it was my fault I stayed."

I leap onto the bed and hug him from behind. "My dad doesn't know what grounding is, and no, I'm not in trouble. He says you're welcome to the couch in the future."

Sam covers his face. "There goes my making a good impression on your dad."

"Dad sort of already knows you, Sam."

"Yeah, but it's been years, and now I'm your boyfriend."

The roller-coaster stomach is back, and I get the sense that I'm free-falling as I hug him tighter.

"I picked up a shift today, so I have to work in an hour." He twists in my arms and turns to look at me. "Is that okay? I shouldn't have, huh? Now I won't get to see you the whole day."

I brush the hair from his eyes. "It's fine, really. I should see the girls today anyway. Zoey was pretty messed up yesterday. And I miss Michaela and Cole."

"Tonight then? Do you think your dad will mind if I come to actually watch a movie?" he asks, the tip of his nose brushing mine.

"Don't forget that we're digging up graves in Mrs. Griever's yard tonight. Will you text Daniel the plan?" I'm undeterred by his reluctant grunt.

Sam leans in for a kiss, and I get this perfect toe-tingling closed-eye moment where I realize I want a bazillion more kisses just like that from this one boy. "Thank you, Sam," I whisper.

He tilts his head quizzically at me, face still only an inch from mine. "For what?"

"For the corsage." I hop up from the bed and run to the bookcase. Between my Wildwood junior and sophomore yearbooks there's a small leather-bound journal. I pluck it from its shelf and hand it to Sam. The book falls open. Pressed between its pages is a flattened gardenia corsage, wrapped in a blue satin ribbon, its stem impaled by a long pearl-capped pin.

Sam blinks at it like it's the last thing he ever expected to see again. "Is this . . . ?" he asks.

"I saved it," I say, more shy than I was about sleeping next to him. "I'm so sorry for the way I treated you . . . for not telling you how beautiful I thought the corsage was."

For once Sam is speechless. I peck him on the cheek and tow him downstairs. After an embarrassing amount of stalling, he leaves, one of Dad's pumpkin muffins in hand, waving good-bye.

Now the hard part. An hour later, having showered, called Zoey for a ride, and fed Moscow, I'm scaling the wood fence in my backyard. While Dad telling me to stay home on his way out the door didn't exactly inspire me to listen, I do experience a pang of guilt at completely disregarding him. I'd call him and explain that I need to be with the girls today, but I worry he'll tell Shane. I don't want to contend with the uniformed minions tailing me. I have to confess to Zoey about Sam and me, I have to convince her to dig up graves at Griever's, and I have to remember what happened the day Jeanie was taken.

"Ouch," I whimper, snagging my arm on the ridge of the pickets. I'm sure there's a cluster of evil splinters sticking out of my flesh. I jump down into my neighbor's yard—the Howards don't have kids and they work, so their house is dark—and scramble to their side gate. I emerge onto the street that runs parallel to mine.

Zoey's SUV waits idling under a mammoth oak. The lowest branches have the look of arthritic skeleton hands reaching greedily toward the cab. Zoey's already popping gummy bear after gummy bear into her mouth.

"A little early for gelatinous sugar, don't you think?" I say, climbing into the front seat.

She taps the lid of an extra-large coffee in the cup holder. "This is breakfast, and these"—she waggles the candy bag in my face—"are dessert."

"Oh well, in that case." I hold my hands up in surrender.

She tosses me the bag. "And don't eat all my green ones this time, Secret Agent Slut."

Mouth full, I raise an eyebrow.

"Don't get me wrong, I liked the old Stella, but I'm in looove with this new badass Stella who scales fences and ditches cops."

She throws the car into drive, and the wheels spin taking off.

Zoey doesn't usually have a lead foot; she told me once that looking eager equals looking desperate. Today she must not care. I hastily snap my seat belt on as we careen sharp around a corner. It's supposed to storm this afternoon, but you wouldn't know it by the blissed-out sun rays making everything glow.

"I'm thinking the sun wants us to have a cove day," Zoey says. I squirm under the seat belt at the thought of heading back to our spot after everything that's happened there.

I open my mouth to protest; Zoey shoots me a warning glare. Usually, I wouldn't give in so quickly, but I don't want to piss her off, especially before I confess and ruin her chirpy mood.

"The girls are already there waiting for us, and I brought an extra bikini for you," she adds.

"'Kay, sounds fun." I muster a teaspoon of enthusiasm. "Zo, I have something to tell you." I pause, trying to work my words out. How do you tell your bestie you're shacking up with a guy she calls the King of Loserdom?

Before I take a stab at it, she says, "We're making a quick stop. We have to meet Drew's older cousin by the garbage bin at the back of the drugstore."

I'm grateful for the momentary reprieve. "What kind of back-alley deal are you dragging me to?" I ask.

She pantomimes tipping a bottle to her lips. "He's hooking us up with hard lemonades and a bunch of pink wine so we can have fun this summer." I give her a sideways look. She flaps her hand at me. "Spare me. I mean, after all this Jeanie *stuff* blows over, obviously."

The loaded way she articulates "stuff" inflames me. I can hear her insinuating Sam's name, as though he is only Jeanie blowback and I'll move on once the killer is caught. "I asked Sam to be my boyfriend," I blurt.

Zoey slams on the brakes. The car screeches bloody murder, almost turning sideways in the middle of a deserted residential street.

"Tell me this is a really effed-up joke, Stella!" she shouts.

I shake my head. "We made out last night." I don't add that the kissing continued this morning, because I'm not suicidal.

She stares at me, mouth agape like a dead person, lips stained from candy. "Then tell me that you just wanted to mess around with someone who wasn't a total skeeze and that you were only using Sam because he's a peasant and therefore STD free."

My arms cross against my chest to shield myself from Zoey: from her judgment, her anger, her biting words. A car honks and then drives around us, the driver shooting us a dirty look before speeding up. Zoey flips him off until he disappears around a street corner.

She takes her foot off the brake and we continue toward downtown, where the alley behind the drugstore waits, bearing gifts.

"Well," she snaps, "say something."

"Why'd you do it?" I watch her profile change as she puzzles out what I mean. "Why did you make me choose, and why would you tell him? My mom had just left and you thought that was a good time to make me pick between my best friends?" I fight to keep control; all the sticky resentment finally gushing out.

"Oh, I'm sorry," she says sarcastically, flipping her hair from her eyes. "Did you want high school to blow? Did you want to be stepped on by girls less pretty but more popular than you? Did you want to beg for a dribble of attention from some guy who stank of BO and couldn't remember your name? I didn't realize that Stella Cambren wanted to be a desperate freak. Because let's be honest, people think you're a freak for surviving what you did. And without me, without being popular"—she checks to see that I'm looking at her before she smiles wickedly—"people wouldn't be too afraid to tell you so."

Bleary-eyed, I stare at my best friend, the urge to punch her bitchy upturned nose so strong I form a fist. I've never heard Zoey say anything half as mean to one of her so-called peasants. I take a shaky breath, fighting the vomit washing up my throat. "What you did was shitty, Zoey. It was fucked up. To me. To Sam. We were his best friends."

She runs her tongue over her shimmery bottom lip. "Whatever, Stella. Tell yourself what you need to. But I made you choose because you were too much of a coward to do it on your own. You *needed* me to make you." She presses her finger to my forehead right between my eyes. "Just like you need me to be the pusher. If I'm the pusher, then you can do whatever you want without feeling bad about it. Without ever taking responsibility for what you are. Ohhh, poor me"—her lip juts out and she whines in a baby voice—"Zoey makes me treat people like crap to be more popular. Now I have the hottest guys wanting me. Every girl wants to be me. Poor Stella." She spits my name out.

Zoey's words resonate in me. They bounce around in all the dark corners. I try to resist them; I don't want them to stick; once they stick, I won't be able to ignore them. "Being popular was never important to me," I whisper.

"Sure, Stella." She laughs cruelly. "Who would you be if I hadn't pushed you? Who the hell do you think you'd be without me? You'd finally have to accept that you're not a nice girl." We come to a stop sign in front of the massive white building that Savage's city hall and courthouse share. We're a block away from Drew's cousin. Vaguely, I'm aware of a large crowd on the courthouse steps and the faint roar of them chanting. Men and women, shoulder to shoulder, pumping their fists in the air.

Zoey leans across the emergency brake so she's a few inches from me. Her face softens, and she takes my hand like she's breaking really horrible news. "I made you choose once. But you chose over and over again. Every time Sam came around with some sappy bullshit corsage, or valentine, or playlist, or pathetic excuse to be near you, you chose all on your own." She catches my wrist as I pull away. Her skin is porcelain and flawless this close; her voice becomes full-throated and velvety. "And if it wasn't for me, you'd have to face it. You're a fucking monster, Stella. You're *just* like me."

At that moment I make sense of what the mob is chanting, a single word decipherable from their bloodthirsty howls.

"Guilty! Guilty! Guilty!" they chant. I tear my eyes away from Zoey to see Mr. Talcott, in shackles, escorted by a dozen cops up the courthouse steps.

"What the . . . ?" I mutter. Before I think better of it, I swing the SUV's door open.

When I look back to Zoey, her expression has changed, its control melted away, her head wagging at what she knows I'm about to do. She grabs hold of my seat belt just as I'm unbuckling it. "No, no, no." Her voice goes shrill, losing the venom that laced it a moment ago. "It's a shit-show out there!" She tries to shove the buckle fastened, but I slip out from under it.

"I have to help him," I shout, jumping out onto the sidewalk.

"Stella Cambren, you get back in this car," she cries after me.

I push forward into the mob, trying to get to its core, where Mr. Talcott is handcuffed like a criminal. Fragments of Zoey's voice follow behind me, cursing and shouting, trying to keep at my heels. I don't have a plan, and by the time I realize that this was a horrible idea—like pounding-a-strawberry-milk-shake-before-you-get-on-a-roller-coaster brainless—the people around me have started to recognize me. One by one, pairs of eyes attach to me. Some strangers murmur condolences, others scream, "Guilty!" louder, like it's *my* battle cry. Everyone smiles this brainwashed fiend's grin at me, like I'm no longer a seventeen-year-old girl but the main attraction in their circus of horrors.

All the reporters must communicate through some insect-y silent sixth sense, because as soon as one reporter notices me, the whole army turns to torpedo me with questions. I try to spot Shane as I fight forward. If I can find him, explain to him what's really going on in Savage, they'll have to let Mr. Talcott go.

The blond reporter with the shellacked helmet of curls is nearest to me. "How does it feel to know that the man who victimized you and your childhood friend will finally be behind bars?" she yells above the chaos.

My stomach thrashes. This is my fault. *Doubly so.* If I'd been able to tell the cops what happened that day, this wouldn't have gone on for years. If I had told Shane about the other missing girls, they'd know that there's no way Mr. Talcott is involved. Instead I was selfish, spoiled, stubborn. Too worried that I'd be sent off to Chicago. Now Mr. Talcott is being sent off to prison.

Hands reach out, palms petting me, patting me, squeezing me. Everyone trying to console me, not giving me any room to breathe. I can't wade through the crowd any farther. A wall of reporters has formed—at least they won't be hassling Mr. Talcott now—and I can't get past their swarm of cameras. The blonde sticks her microphone in my face again and says, "Any comment on the judge moving Kent Talcott's trial to today?"

Mr. Talcott and his police escort reach the top of the stairs, and the beast of the mob cries louder, working itself into a tizzy. Jeanie's dad's shoulders are hunched, and he's being careful not to look anywhere but at his shoes. Someone in the crowd throws a full soda can at him; it thuds loudly between his shoulder blades. Zoey comes out of nowhere, elbowing and kicking to make her way to my side. Her hand slips into mine; her bony fingers make me braver. The crowd writhes and cackles as Mr. Talcott stumbles to regain his balance.

In that faltered step, in the instant I see the yellow and violet stains on his face from where people—probably neighbors he's shared meals and laughs with—attacked him, it hits me. There's only one thing I can do.

I grab for the blond reporter's microphone, wrenching it from her faux orange grip, and yell at the top of my lungs, "I remember what happened. It wasn't Jeanie's dad. Jeanie's dad is innocent."

Chapter Twenty-One

I t's amazing how quickly the fury drains out of the crowd. One minute the mob is an angry beast, and the next they're sheepish adults looking nervously around like they hope no one will remember that they were here.

Once I scream the lie I look to Zoey, for I don't know what. She inclines her head almost imperceptibly, and I know that I did the only thing I could have, the thing she would have done. The police find us, and we're propelled forward through the now docile crowd. I gulp one last breath of fresh air before being ushered into the courthouse.

Mr. Talcott sits against the far wall, slumped on a wooden bench, red hair sticking to his sweaty forehead, still flanked by cops. The officers turn toward me, mouths twisted as they watch me, noses scrunched like my lie reeks. And then I spot Daniel.

Daniel's dressed in a pair of gray slacks and a button-down shirt, like he's going to homecoming or a funeral. He's nodding, arms crossed against his chest and speaking under his breath to a paunchy older guy clad in a suit and the kind of spectacles my father wears. A wash of relief and I sink back onto my heels. He's probably already told the police everything Sam told him. They know about the generations of missing redheads, and they've likely sent a patrol car out to Mrs. Griever. She'll give a statement, an official one this time, and Mr. Talcott will be home for dinner.

I step forward, lips forming Daniel's name. But then Shane, who pushes through the crowd of uniforms, comes to rest at Daniel's side, clapping a hand on his shoulder. I hang back uneasily, struck dumb. The thinly veiled distrust that Shane has always had for Daniel—my restraining order against Daniel had even been Shane's idea—is gone. In its place is a fatherly smile, an encouraging bob of his head, and a thumbs-up. Gradually, I recognize the man in the suit as a lawyer with the courthouse, one who prosecutes criminals rather than defends them. But ultimately it's the fact that Mr. Talcott is in shackles and Daniel is getting a pat on the back that sets off a keening siren in my head.

Shane starts toward me. "Stella, what's going on?" he asks tersely. "This is serious," he adds just in case I'm a total moron and the least observant person on earth.

"I think she gets that," Zoey says saucily, hands on her hips.

"What is Daniel doing here?" I ask, craning my neck to catch his eye. We're fifteen feet apart, but I can't seem to snag his attention.

"Not here, Stella," Shane warns.

I look from Shane to Daniel, the earth abruptly tilting under my feet. Shane protecting Daniel from me rather than *me* from Daniel. "I said, *what is Daniel doing here?*" I raise my voice.

Shane frowns down at me. "That's official police business."

I toss my hair over my shoulders and glare at him until his resolve falters. He lets out a puff of air. "Daniel's giving us a statement. As you can see, his father's been taken into custody, and Daniel's corroborated our evidence."

Shane's words are like the shriek and hiss of a machine seizing right before it breaks down. I shake my head. "Corroborate? Daniel knows his dad didn't do anything. Daniel went to the police station to tell you guys that, right? To tell you what's really going on."

Shane crosses his arms in a lousy attempt to look official. "The details of his testimony are confidential."

I move to go around Shane, but he catches my arm. "Daniel," I shout, struggling against his grasp. Through gritted teeth Shane pleads under his breath for me not to make a scene. Finally, Daniel looks up, features sharp, clean-shaven chin set. "Sam found a picture of all of us in the woods before Jeanie went missing," I call. "We were out there looking for something." He keeps his eyes on me. His irises are usually the same tie-dye of green and brown as mine, but today they're darker. He tilts his head. For a brief, half-confused moment I think he's glaring at me. But I'm wrong, because why would he be angry with me? "Griever was right. Your dad has nothing to do with this. There's something bigger going on."

Daniel takes a step forward. "The only thing going on is that my dad killed my mom and sister," he says, his voice dead, features slack. But the Daniel I know is a rabid animal: boundlessly suspicious, quicker to bite than bark, and definitely too feral for the lavender shirt he's wearing and the close shave.

I'm hot-faced as more and more sets of eyes focus on me. "Don't you remember what we were doing in the woods?" I try.

The lawyer with the pillowy middle rests his hand at Daniel's elbow and begins to usher him away, giving me a sideways look of disapproval. "I don't know what she's talking about," Daniel says, hushed.

Desperate, I yell at his back, "We were hunting monsters. You told Jeanie it could leave the woods, remember?" The gentle hum of conversation in the hall goes quiet. I lunge forward to go after Daniel, but Shane holds me in place.

"Not here," Shane whispers harshly in my ear. I reluctantly look away from Daniel's retreating figure. "We need to speak in private."

Shane's hand is replaced by Zoey's arm looped in mine. "Stella isn't giving her statement until her father, her *lawyer*, is here," she says icily.

Shane's face deepens a few shades, and he opens his mouth— probably to have Zoey arrested. I cut him off. "She's right." I try hard not to flinch at the hurt obvious in his eyes.

He takes a long breath and says, "You're a minor, so I can't question you without your dad's permission anyway. But we can speak, just me and you, off the record. Anything you say will stay between us."

Zoey shakes her head adamantly, but I nod. After five minutes of her protesting, she finally relents and slouches against the wall, dropping to the ground, letting loose a string of curse words that make the nearby police blush.

I follow Shane down a beige corridor, carpets and walls the same drab color, fluorescent lights sighing like they're alive, until we find an empty office.

"Start talking," he orders after I sit. And I do. I tell him everything—minus my plan to trespass tonight on Old Lady Griever's land—and he listens.

When I'm finished, I fold my hands neatly in my lap and try to look as sane and believable as possible.

He leans forward, elbows resting on knees, blue bags bulging under his eyes. "I understand why you think there's something else going on here. What you've recounted for me are a lot of strange occurrences, and I agree that it seems too much to be coincidence. But Stella, this is me. I know you. If you told this story to any of the department's other detectives, they'd think you were on drugs or a kid looking for attention. They'll call the memories hallucinations from stress or dismiss them as the products of an active imagination."

"What about Daniel? Whatever he said, he's confused. It's this town. Everyone convinced that his dad did it. It got to him. He's been helping us figure out what happened. He's been searching for Jeanie's body. I know he'll remember hunting in the woods. If you would just talk to him again."

Shane sits back in his chair and eyes his wristwatch. "Set aside the fact that you lied to me—to the police—about knowing Daniel was back in town. There's nothing I can do to stop this. Kent Talcott confessed, and he's going before a judge in fifteen minutes."

"N-no," I stammer. "Your officers are wrong. He wouldn't have confessed to something he didn't do."

He tilts forward, sticking his face right in mine. "I'm the one who took his confession." He thumps his fist to his chest. "Me. Late last night. He pled guilty to all three charges. Jeanie, Bev Talcott, and Jane Doe. He says she was a runaway in the park. We still haven't identified her. But he knew about the finger bone. There are numerous Indian burial grounds in Blackdog. It's something he came across; nothing more than a little misdirection to throw us off his trail."

I whip my head back and forth. "Don't you get it? I told Daniel about the finger bone. Daniel knows. He must have told his dad. Daniel knows about her scalp, too. He knows everything."

"Stella, there isn't even going to be a trial by jury, only a sentence agreed to by his defense attorney, the prosecution, and the judge. Daniel came to the station the night before last. He wanted us to know he's been in town and investigating the murders himself. He came back to the station with his dad when Kent turned himself in. Verified that his dad doesn't have an alibi for the window of time our medical examiners say Jane Doe and Bev Talcott were murdered. Do you hear me? Jeanie's father murdered her."

I close my fingers around the chair legs to brace myself. Here Shane is, with a perfectly gruesome but reasonable explanation, the story of a bad man who preys on children, whose own son believes he's guilty. It's the kind of explanation I need so that I don't have to believe in what can't possibly exist. I want to pounce on it, swallow it to ease the itch of dread, shove it down Sam's throat so we can both be free from what lurks in the woods. But I can't. My blood sings that it's a lie.

My gaze is level with Shane's. "What about hunting monsters? What about all the missing little girls? Don't you see? It couldn't be one man." My chin set, I'm aware of the flurry of fear in the back of my head. "You said that kids see monsters everywhere." I stare steely-eyed at him. "What if there was something to see? What if I saw it?"

His eyes half-lidded with exhaustion, Shane settles back. He rubs the heels of his hands over his eyelids. "I'm sure whatever you saw that day was unspeakable. A sick man hurting his child. Bad enough for your mind to hide the memory away where it couldn't hurt you. But that's all it was." His whole face crinkles with the pain of saying it. "Kid, there's no magic, no monsters, no mystery, no demons, except for Mr. Talcott's." Pity softens his eyes, and his words are delicately spoken. I can feel myself becoming someone else—a victim—sitting across from him. Tim Shane has never treated me like I'm glass already veiny with fractures. I want to crawl out of my skin to escape it now. I want to shout and riot until I've broken everything in the room so he can see how strong I am.

"Have I ever told you about my grandmother?" he says.

My mouth purses, and I shake my head once.

"My grandma, my dad's mother, used to scare us kids to bed with stories when she visited us in Florida. She grew up here, in these woods." He's quiet for a full minute, eyes focused on the space behind me, head tilted like he's watching phantoms play on the wall. Then he sighs. "How much do you know about Minnesota's history?"

"We studied state history freshman year," I say, letting my own thoughts stray from this frustrating beige room. I can still feel the warmth of Sam's knees grazing my lower back as he sat behind me in class. I fake smiled at him every time he spoke to me in Mr. Flint's fifth period, but it made something quiver deep in me when his jeans touched the inch of bare skin between my waistband and shirt's hem.

"Okay, so you know that in the seventeenth century fur traders from France came to this territory for a time, and then a couple hundred years later there was an influx of Scandinavian pioneers who settled here." He pauses, and I nod. "But hundreds of years before, a group of Norse explorers sailed across the Atlantic, navigated the rivers, and settled in this spot. The Norse are descendants of the Vikings." I search my mind for the story. Something about it tugs at threads here and there, but they fray when I try to follow.

"It started with one of their children waking up with the tip of a finger nibbled off to its knuckle. At first the Norse were certain that a starving rat attacked him. But a few days go by and another wakes screaming, a few of his toes gnawed off."

I swallow hard.

"The settlement descends into chaos. The Norse think the children have been bewitched by natives living in the hills and that they're hurting themselves. You see, for generations before the Norse landed here, the Chippewa tribe made this land their home. But when the Norse showed up, they ran the Chippewa out of their village. It made sense to the Norse that the natives would seek revenge. They believed the tribe to have supernatural powers. To stop the magic, they round up the entire tribe and burn them alive. Toss them into a mass grave."

"Your grandma told you bedtime stories about this?" I press my back against the chair.

"Imagine her stories when she really wanted to frighten us," he says, the corner of his mouth curving into a smirk that fades as he gets back to the story. "But then a child wakes up screaming from an attack with his nose bitten from his face, and the settlers realize that it wasn't the natives or their magic. There's a creature from the hills that's feasting on the children. A beast. *A monster.*"

Rubbing his thumbs along his jawline, he continues, hushed, "Panic spreads. More and more children wake up noseless, fingerless, toeless. They try to escape the creature and give up on the new land. The Norse return to their longships and set sail for home."

His stare drops to the floor. "But only a night into their journey, while they're still navigating the rivers that lead to the sea, they're awakened by whimpering. There, strung up from the mast, is a boy of ten, his hands and feet bloody stumps where all the fingers and toes have been removed, and a Norse man, someone who everyone knew and trusted, is crouched under him, eating the boy's appendages."

For a second I think I see my breath fog the space in front of me, until I remember that it's June and we're inside. "You see, the Norse were certain that something unnatural was preying on their children. First a magic that didn't exist, and next a beast that wasn't real. They slaughtered an entire tribe. They fled the New World. But all along, it was one man." He rolls his neck, making it crackle. "When Berry and I arrived at the Talcotts' that day, you were sitting apart from everyone, staring into the trees. You were so little, and we put you in the back of our car to wait for your parents to arrive. We weren't supposed to ask you anything until they got there, but you looked up at me and started in on chanting that one sentence over and over again."

There's a bloodlessness to his pale skin. "Stella, I didn't sleep for a week. I know what it is to be terrified by the unknown. You were so little and what you were saying . . ." He hooks his finger in his collar and tugs. "It was my first year here and as a cop. If I hadn't remembered this story, I doubt I'd have stayed on the force . . . or in Savage. It helped me remember that all evil is *human* evil." He raises an index finger. "There were no monsters or magic, only *one* psychopath, in the story. And there are no monsters, only one bad man who hurt Jeanie." He straightens up, a steely cop look hardening his features, shadows pooling under his brow.

I cross my arms, my spine stiff. Yeah, it was a grisly story. Yes, I see the parallels he's drawing. But I still want to slap the expression of resolve from his face. "So what?" I ask dubiously. "You thought you'd tell me one story about a sicko who tortured kids and it would change my mind about Jeanie's dad?" A messy half laugh, half sob squeezes out. "Spare me, Shane. You know me better than that."

He inclines his head slowly, methodically withdrawing the pack of cigarettes from his pocket, whacking its bottom on his palm, and sliding one slender smoke out to tuck behind his ear. All the while he keeps his narrow-set gray eyes locked on mine. I don't blink.

Finally, he says, quietly but firmly, "I'm going to investigate what you told me. But the rest of it is resolved. I know that it's hard to accept after years of not knowing, but you don't get to ignore the truth because you don't like it." He gives me a look to communicate that he thinks I'm being a willful child. "Mr. Talcott is a bad man, and he hurt his family. You were lucky that he didn't hurt you. What happened to Jeanie doesn't have anything to do with kids who went missing almost a hundred years ago. The bone found was a relic from the park, probably of Chippewa origin. And the rash of animal disappearances is unrelated. Those are separate, and I'll get to the bottom of them."

I throw my hands up in exasperation, opening my mouth to argue, tongue tingling to howl and fight. His sensible explanations are wrong. He snaps his radio off his belt and speaks into it. His words swim in my head. "Let the judge know that Kent Talcott is ready for sentencing. . . . Bring Zoey Walsh. . . . Yeah, the spirited girl throwing a fit out there . . . No, don't cuff her. . . . Thanks."

He returns the radio to his belt. "You and Zoey are going to leave out the back door to avoid the press. I'm going to figure out a way to smooth over what you said about remembering. I'll call your father, and we'll figure out a way to spin it so it's forgotten."

He waits for a response that never comes.

He tries to pat me on the back as he rises, but I push his hand away. "You're going to enjoy the rest of your summer and your last year of high school. You are going to move on from all this. Do you understand, Stella? It's over." His fist pounds his palm, like if he asserts it with enough force he can make it so.

The room revolves slowly. Everything is muddled. Jeanie's dad confessed. Daniel believes he did it. Jeanie's case is closed. Shane doesn't believe me. But I know. *I know* there's something just under the surface of all this, watching me with alligator eyes, hungry for little girls, leering through the water's skin, but I can't find *it* because my reflection keeps getting in the way.

Zoey gets to the office, and Shane fills her in. Her face is unreadable, even to me; I'm too bogged down in my own head. She takes my hand and leads me through the door, down a dimly lit hallway. Before we turn a corner, I call back to Shane, "Ask Jeanie's dad where he learned to French braid."

It's probably my imagination, but I think I hear him swear.

Chapter Twenty-Two

Back in Zoey's car, we don't talk for a long time. She sends a few texts on her phone and holds up a response from Michaela for me to read.

Meet @ S's in 30 w/backup.

Zoey steers toward my house. The unmarked cop cars are gone by the time we arrive, my bodyguards dismissed because according to the police, the killer has been caught. Moscow greets us, meowing as an angry sentinel at the front door, and Zoey delivers us both to the couch. She bumps around the kitchen for a minute, returning with a pint of Ben & Jerry's and two spoons.

I shovel up a bite with a large chunk of chocolate, but even that doesn't banish the sinking sensation in my stomach.

After a while Zoey lisps with a slightly numb tongue, "I made you choose because I knew you loved each other. We were only ten, and his whole face would explode with light when he looked at you. I knew you loved him back. And that I'd be the third wheel. It wasn't about being popular." She spoons up a giant red cherry and chomps down on it. "I thought you'd get over him. There are so many hotter guys. But it was like we were living freshman homecoming on an endless loop." She shrugs, licking her spoon.

"What do you mean?"

"Sam and that corsage. You sent him away, everyone laughed, and you looked like a puppy run over by a car the whole night. That's what it was like every time you rejected him. It was painful to watch. And out of all the guys you've messed around with or flirted with or gone out with, you haven't wanted any half as much as you wanted Sam when you were ten. I may be mean, but I'm not stupid or blind. Apparently you were." She stares at me, her eyes growing wet. "I'm sorry. I should have told you, but I figured you knew."

"No, I didn't," I say. "It wasn't your fault. You're right. *I chose*. Over and over again." It's true. I was stupid. I was embarrassed by how Sam acted like every little thing we'd shared as kids was so important. I didn't see that that's what makes Sam important. He understands that things matter. "I didn't think you remembered the corsage."

"I'm not the one with amnesia," Zoey deadpans. She looks down at her hands. "I think about it a lot." She doesn't sound remorseful exactly, just thoughtful.

I want to ask if what she did to the trio of junior girls from the dance—systemically taking their boyfriends and relegating them to the lower castes at school—was her version of reaping revenge on my behalf. Yes, popularity is a zero-sum game to Zoey. Yes, bringing down girls who claim it for themselves makes her glow like she has radiation poisoning. But she has a code of honor and rarely goes after other girls' boyfriends—that's for leeches and barnacles, as she would say. Those girls we were so eager to impress were served particularly cruel social executions by Zoey. And if we hadn't been with them at the dance, she would have done little more than rolled her eyes at Sam and we would have had no audience to prove ourselves in front of. I don't ask, though; she would have told me if she wanted me to know.

Zoey acts engrossed in shoveling through the pint, mining for cherries. "How was it? Messing around with a guy who isn't just drooling over your snowballs but who actually gives a shit?"

It makes me sad to hear how sad she sounds asking me. "I love you, Zo."

"I love you, too, Queen of Loserdom." She needles me in the side with her elbow. "So what are we gonna do?"

"I'm not giving up." I launch into recounting my memories for her and an explanation of my time line and the pattern of animal disappearances. Zoey loves furry little creatures and predictably thinks whoever hurt them should die a fiery death.

"I'm going to dig up those heaps of dirt in Mrs. Griever's yard tonight. If I can prove they're buried animals, Shane will have to believe that something bigger is going on."

Zoey salutes. "Aye, aye, Secret Agent Slut. I'm in, but let's not tell Michaela or Cole when they get here. I don't want them to know that we're *both* conspiracy junkies."

"We have to talk to Caleb. He was there that summer and the cops already know about me investigating, and I'm sure my dad is about to find out. I don't have anything to lose."

She jabs her spoon in the ice cream and leaves it standing erect. "When your man's teal abomination dropped me off yesterday, Caleb was showering. *Showering.*" She says it like it's the most preposterous thing in the world. "He never showers in the middle of the day. My mom was home from work and said she thought he was getting ready for a date. Call me paranoid, but I wanted to make sure it wasn't with Cole." Her features pinch together. "He took Mom's car and I tailed him. I was going to catch them in the act."

I'm pulling myself upright, feeling revived. "Where'd he go?"

"The butt crack of a library. I waited forty-five minutes in that gross parking lot with the windows up, practically suffocating on fumes just to make sure he wasn't trying to trick me or that he wasn't rendezvousing between the shelves with her."

"What was he doing there?"

"Def not studying, since he screwed up and missed registration for summer classes," she says, pleased and in an I-told-you-so kind of way.

"Do you think it had something to do with Jeanie? Like, was he researching past disappearances too?"

She flicks her wrist, unimpressed with the coincidence of Caleb at the library mere hours after we left. "Unlikely, 'cause you only knew about other girls since that hag told you, and no one told Caleb."

"Right," I say, but somehow I'm not convinced. Caleb was

worried about me hunting a killer. Could he also have been worried what would happen if he didn't do anything? "He couldn't be digging up stuff without us knowing?"

"Like I said: He doesn't have the balls. Night-light until he was thirteen. It had freaking unicorns on it." She flourishes her fingers at me. Zoey had the identical night-light.

A moment later there's a knock on the door. "It's about effing time," Zoey warbles, bounding to answer it.

We spend the next few hours watching lousy reality TV on the couch. The four of us smashed side by side, sipping pink wine—the "backup" Michaela brought. Zoey does a masterful job of filling Michaela and Cole in. She tells them about Jane Doe's scalp and the finger bone found in her hand, about Sam helping me uncover other missing girls from the 1930s, and about Mr. Talcott's arrest and Daniel going on record against his father. She avoids mentioning Mrs. Griever, the animal sacrifices, and anything monster-tastic that makes us sound insane and would only drag Michaela and Cole down the rabbit hole with us. It isn't that I don't trust Michaela; I do. It's that Michaela wasn't here for Jeanie; it isn't her ancient history to survive. By the way Michaela's brow furrows as she listens, she's holding back questions. I'm grateful and guilty that she realizes there are details that Zoey doesn't want to reveal.

Michaela's chin nuzzles my shoulder when Zoey finishes, and Cole squeezes my hand like it's a stunned bird she's pumping life into. I worried I'd feel like a freak show with an audience, but instead it's as if I have more company onstage.

Finally the conversation moves to safer, mundane topics. I try to soak up the warmth of Cole's blush as Zoey says that Taylor's back on the market since I've passed; and Michaela's hiccupy giggle as she dubs pink wine the greatest invention in the universe; and Zoey's vigor as she stands on the coffee table to reenact the Ds' fight over her.

We're closing in on five in the evening when the girls slip on their flip-flops and trudge out to their cars. Zoey kisses me on the cheek and whispers in my ear that she'll return at eleven before joining Cole and Michaela, who are arguing about who is the most sober to drive. Zoey crosses her heart and yells, "I was only pretending to drink that pink swill so Michaela would pluck the stick from her ass and have fun." Cole whines about leaving her car parked on my street as she climbs into Zoey's backseat. They all wave at me through the windshield as Zoey backs her SUV out of my driveway.

Back on the couch, I stare at the haze of colors on the TV screen, not really watching or following whatever junk is on. After the third time my eyelids droop closed, I stagger upstairs for a nap. With four hours until Sam is off and six until we go grave digging, I curl under my comforter. My head sinks into my pillow, my shoulder into the mattress.

"Stella, are you okay?" Sam whispers close to my ear.

"Mm-hmm," I murmur.

"Your front door was open," he says.

I sit bolt upright, throwing Moscow from the crook of my arm. He growls as he pads off the bed. Sam's profile is outlined perfectly against the brightly lit hallway, but everything else is dark. "What? It's unlocked?"

"Yes, and wide open."

"Dad isn't here?" I throw my legs over the side of the bed, knees wobbly as I stand, blood rushing to my head.

"His car is gone. Maybe you didn't close it all the way and the wind blew it open?"

"No." I shake my head into the dark space between us. "I walked the girls out."

"Maybe you left it unlocked?" he whispers.

"No way." I put my lips to his ear. "I'm a hundred percent sure."

I feel his eyes linger on mine for a half second before he breathes, "Follow me." He takes my hand and leads me soundlessly through my bedroom door. Even in the jaundiced glow of the hallway I'm shaky walking close behind him. We move from my room to Dad's to the guest room, searching. As I peer into the far reaches of the linen closet, it occurs to me that I really hope whatever ghosted the front door open is long gone.

The balls of my feet ache from balancing on tiptoe as we angle downstairs. I twine my fingers in the hem of Sam's shirt and hold my breath as we check behind curtains, inside my nana's antique trunk, and under the dining room furniture. Nothing other than lint and a decaying legless gummy bear. No doubt discarded by Zoey and nibbled on by Moscow before he decided that Zoey's favorite food group isn't real food.

"There's nothing here," I say, a trill in my voice. "Maybe I'm wrong about the door?" Sam doesn't respond. I scoop the amputee gummy from the carpet. "Zoey always leaves her mark." I look to see if Sam's cracked a smile, but he's staring hard at something behind me. I twist around to face the fireplace.

Mom had this thing about capturing moments, even ones she had to manufacture herself by ordering me to pose just so. That's why the mantel is crowded with photographs. But all those framed pictures are lying facedown. All except one: a photo taken during an elementary school picnic the spring before Jeanie vanished. Me, Sam, and Zoey, hand in hand, are lined up at the head of a wooden canoe, our mouths open wide, singing. Jeanie's blurry figure is off to the side, up to her ankles in Blackdog Lake, apart from the rest of us but still in the shot. I've never noticed her there before.

She isn't singing or grinning. Her face isn't exuding light. She's focused on what or who is to the right, beyond the scope of the lens. Panic makes her face resemble a three-hole light socket—her mouth and eyes gaping and dark at what she sees.

Chapter Twenty-Three

I'm calling the cops," Sam says from behind me. It takes almost a full minute for me to look away from the lonely photo and push Sam's phone from his ear. I can't get over the fact that suddenly I remember Jeanie sniffling and staring vacantly at the seat in front of her on the bus ride to the picnic. Zoey was bouncing next to me, the seat cushion jouncing me into the air each time she landed. We reached Blackdog, and Jeanie was still a husk of herself, refusing to do anything but gape and sniff. Zoey wouldn't stand for her ruining our fun and told Sam and me not to play with Jeanie.

Our silence was why Jeanie hovered on the outskirts of us, and it floods me with guilt and resolve in equal measure. I can't travel back to that day and invite Jeanie to sing with us or paddle in the same canoe or roast marshmallows sandwiched between Zoey and me or ask her why she was acting so strange. But I can be brave for her now.

"This is supposed to scare us," I say.

Sam tries to hit the send button again. "Mission accomplished."

"No, Sam." I cover the screen of his phone. "I mean, that this was done by whoever doesn't want us uncovering more missing animals. More missing girls."

He lets me take the cell from his hand but frowns. "That's why I'm trying to call the police, Stella."

I grab his sleeve and try to pat him calm, until I realize that he's still and I'm the one shifting from foot to foot. "We won't be able to go to Griever's if my house is crawling with cops or if Dad comes home from work because Shane calls him." Sam rubs his eyelids furiously and shakes his head, like he can't believe what I'm saying. "I won't give up because someone rearranged some pictures."

Sam gestures at the mantel, his eyes wide with disbelief. "It's a little more serious than that."

"Sure, but not as serious as figuring out who killed Jeanie. This is proof that we're on the right track." I swallow a lump rising in my throat. "If we weren't, whoever did this wouldn't have bothered. They're probably the same people who left rotten strawberries. It's going to take a lot more than some nasty fruit to scare me off."

I squint back at the photo. The reflection of a craggy mountain range traces a jagged line in the lake. All those endless trails that dip and climb into isolated crevices and peaks. "Where is Norse Rock?" I ask abruptly.

"I'm not certain I've ever heard of it." Sam sounds thoughtful, distracted—momentarily at least—from calling the police.

"One of the girls who disappeared in the 1930s was on a picnic with her family at Norse Rock, right? It's what you read in one of those clippings." I tingle from the crown of my head to the pads of my fingers. "And Shane told me a story about Norse explorers coming here ages ago. They had some kiddie cannibal with them."

Sam angles his head. "A child cannibal?"

"No. I mean someone who was eating the fingers and toes of children," I say, flustered. "That isn't the part that matters. It's just the Norse part. Another girl you read about disappeared hiking up in Blackdog, right? What if they have more in common than their age, the red hair, and what took them? What if they disappeared from the same place? Norse Rock?"

"Betty Balco disappeared from her front yard on Jeanie's old drive. You and Jeanie were picking berries," he says gently.

"For all we know, Betty Balco could have been up at Norse Rock the day before she vanished. And anyway, you can hike straight from the woods at Jeanie's into Blackdog. And maybe Jeanie and Daniel went there once too?" My pitch climbs. "Maybe they were at Norse Rock the day before or the month before and whatever snatched the others spotted Jeanie? Maybe it spotted her here. Maybe it's what she's looking at?" Two steps and I've snatched the photo and am waving it at Sam. "It could have been watching her on this day."

A strange ripple of emotion runs through me. I replace the photo hastily. I backtrack from the mantel. Rather than accept that Jeanie's killer is caught, I've uncovered more fuel for night terrors. I slip my hand into Sam's; his chilled skin on my feverish palm. My other hand taps search terms into Sam's phone, and I'm staring at a map of Blackdog State Park in an instant. I tilt the screen for Sam to see.

"I don't see a Norse Rock, but there"—my thumb hovers over a corner of the map—"Old Norse Trail. The Norse part can't be a coincidence. It could be named after the Norse explorers, and Norse Rock is probably on it."

Sam blinks at the rough map. "I don't know. I saw a special on the History Channel about Norse explorers who established a settlement here. Archeologists claimed to have found a rune stone, like a written record of their time, recounting some sort of massacre. But the rune stone turned out to be a hoax. Faked by a farmer. Shane's story is just a folktale." He pauses, holds his breath so his cheeks puff out.

"But what if it's true, except what if it wasn't really a Norseman picking the kids off?" I ask. "You said yourself that there are more redheads in this area because the settlers were Scandinavian. As in descendants of the Norse and the Vikings." I punctuate my point with my finger in the air. "What if this *thing* was here even then? It could have gotten its first taste of what it would crave for centuries." I look back at the map. "It would forever hunt little redheads in this one spot."

After studying the vague lines of Old Norse Trail, I tow a reluctant Sam into the kitchen. I don't know why, but it feels safer in there, surrounded by appliances and Dad's brightly colored serving dishes. I guess I'm not so different from my father in that way.

I ogle the fridge's contents and pull out a cooked lasagna. I'm not hungry, but this is what Cambrens do when they can't process stuff.

"Zoey texted me what happened at the courthouse today," Sam says.

"Zoey who?" I ask, sticking the lasagna into the microwave for reheating. I hop up on the counter, socked heels beating percussively on the cabinet doors to drown the racket of my pulse.

He manages a laugh that doesn't reach his troubled eyes. "Weird, I know. She told me to come straight over here after my shift. Also that she'd meet us at Jeanie's place tonight." Sam steps nearer, leaning against the counter between my knees. There's heat in my cheeks.

"She must be going somewhere before she heads over."

"Daniel isn't answering my texts," Sam says. The parenthesis mark deepens on his brow, and I want to smooth it out with my finger.

"I'm not surprised. He was a zombie version of himself today. All dressed up and polite to the same cops who used to throw him out of town. And then he acted like I was crazy." I pound my chest. "*Me.* You should have seen the way they looked at me." I try to shrug it off. Truth is, I can't remember a time when people didn't look at me with a question in their eyes. What makes me popular with my peers unsettles adults. Two little girls go out to play and one comes back, well, it's hard not to look at the survivor like she's an exotic species of bee rumored to have wiped out an entire Amazonian village. But this was different. "They were looking at me like people used to look at Daniel. Like, why can't I just let Jeanie go? No one was asking *why now?* All this time Daniel has never acted like he thought his dad could be guilty. Why all of a sudden?"

Sam's hand rests on my knee. "I guess people do weird things when they're sad." He sets his chin with a determined air. "We don't need his help to find Jeanie's killer."

"You're right. We can do it. You and me," I say, swinging my legs.

Sam's smile is slow, but it comes. He smooths my hair from my face. "I thought maybe after a whole day to think you might have changed your mind about *us*." I know he means boyfriend-girlfriend us and not grave-digging us.

"Us," I say, trying it out. It sends a little hum of panic down my spine. The good kind, though. Like what you feel with your hand up in class right as your name is called or in the instant you let go of the rope swing at the cove and you're momentarily airborne before gravity tugs you down. I think Zoey is right: It's always been Sam. And I was just too blind or stupid to see it.

I wrap my arms around his neck and slide until I'm against him. It's definitely mint shampoo. I inhale deeply. A tiny groan escapes his lips, and the microwave buzzer sounds.

"To be continued," I sigh, a little nibble at my conscience. Isn't saying that always tempting fate? Tempting the monsters to come out of the shadows to bite the living shit out of you? You'd think I'd know better.

As we eat, I can tell Sam's as desperate as I am to pretend that nothing scary is going on. Each time there's a pause, he rushes to tell a joke. I guess the silence is too empty and he starts to think about all those missing little kids.

At ten forty-five p.m. I change into black leggings and a black hoodie—because you obviously wear black for grave digging. I climb into Sam's station wagon after standing all the frames upright on the mantel. At least with my police guard disbanded, we don't need to worry about them following. Dad's working late again, although he takes the time to text about how relieved he is that I don't have to be afraid anymore, now that Jeanie's killer is behind bars. I stare, dismayed at the impersonal message, and reach across the car to hold Sam's hand. It's only hand holding, and yet a thrill shoots like a comet through me, leaving stardust and hope in its wake. *What a little fool I am.* For a moment I let myself forget that bad things happen, despite all the evidence to the contrary.

Jeanie's abandoned house is even more ominous at night. It's alive with the sounds of scratching rodents and creaking, rotten eaves. At least I hope that's what they are.

We sit huddled on the porch's front steps, waiting for Zoey. After a half hour I'm nearing nuclear with nerves. My phone rattles on the porch beside me, the sound ricocheting up into the cobwebby beams. I fumble for it.

Handling something. See u 2morrow. XO

"What does that mean?" I whisper way too loudly.

Sam's been drawing pictures in the dirt with the toe of his shoe. He blinks at the cell's screen. "Maybe she couldn't leave because her mom is home?"

I roll my eyes. "You don't remember Zoey's mom, do you? She'd probably supply Zoey with night-vision goggles and a shovel if Zo told her what we're up to."

"Maybe she's helping Caleb with something?"

"Yeah, I guess that could be. Maybe she's holding him hostage until he tells her what he remembers from that summer?" I don't say it out loud, but I think her not being here is a message to me. She's not okay with Sam. I groan loudly. There's nothing I can do about it now. "Let's go without her."

Sam knows better than to ask me anything else about it. He grabs a shovel from his backseat and a huge flashlight he bought at BigBox. We clasp hands and start down the lane.

"Now I really do feel like Hansel and Gretel making their way to the witch's house," I whisper as the lane narrows to a footpath. If it's possible, the barbed vines of the bramble have grown wilder, tendrils braiding with the strawberry vines and resting on the trail, lying in wait as snares to catch prey. No, no, and no. It's only elongated shadows from the light of the lowish moon. Still, I'm glad I wore running shoes.

The blaring screech of a night bird overhead and the beat of powerful wings. The sky is a milky black with tiny, twinkling tears in its velvet. The canopy interlocks above us and there's a new spectrum of darkness. Even the stars can't see us now.

"What if it's not just animals buried?" I whisper.

"It will be." Sam pulls me into his side.

"But what if it's not?"

"Then we'll call the cops," he says simply, like a phone call could really save us from what I fear. We round a bend, and clouds of heavy stench warm my nostrils. It isn't a rotten odor, but the smell of something hot and sweaty cooking.

"Dinner?" I say, gagging.

"We're close," Sam says. We slow our pace and creep forward as stealthily as possible. I move as if I'm hunting. We emerge from the tunnel of forest.

"Better switch that off." I tap the flashlight. The dark really is dark. There's no other word for it. The moon is good for only a stunted glow, revealing the outlines of things but none of the details. And as Dad says, the devil is always in the details.

My legs tremble. This is insane. What were we thinking? Jeanie's killer has been caught. Mr. Talcott confessed. Daniel accepted it. So why am I too brain-dead to move on?

I'm about to tell Sam I've changed my mind when the heaps of dirt come into view. A foot or so wide, two or three long. Tens, maybe hundreds of their outlines. They're too unsettling to not be something awful. My doubts are shushed.

"You keep watch from here and I'll dig." Sam's mouth brushes my ear, and I shiver. "If you hear or see anything, signal me."

"What kind of signal?"

"An owl hoot." I nod and press my lips to his before he moves through the shadows into Griever's yard. Sam stops at the mound closest to me and sinks to his knees. Very slowly and carefully he picks at the dirt with the shovel. It doesn't sound like more than a tiny mouse's scratching. Minutes pass—it could be two or twenty for all I know—and then silence. After a few seconds I can't bite back my dread.

"*Sam? Are you okay?*" I whisper as softly as I can.

Nothing.

"Sam?" A little louder.

Two things transpire next, and they happen at almost the same instant.

"I think I can feel the muzzle of a dog," Sam whispers, a split second before a deafening boom cracks open the quiet and fills the night with Sam howling in pain.

Chapter Twenty-Four

I move faster than I have ever moved and ever could move again. I fly in front of Sam, shield his crumpled form, and scream, "STOP. It's Stella Cambren!"

Old Lady Griever's raspy voice comes from our left, the opposite direction of the house. "I told you not to come round here no more, boy. Sneakin' round my house at night. You deserve to get a bullet in your leg."

"I'm not Daniel," Sam shouts, although it's more of a wheeze. I drop to my knees, panic radiating through me, hopeful that Mrs. Griever isn't homicidal enough for a second shot.

I fumble over him, hands searching for the wound, lungs filling with the coppery stink of blood. His right leg is warm and wet. "You shot him, you crazy witch. Call an ambulance!"

"Stella, it's okay," Sam groans.

"It's not okay—you're hurt. Can you walk?" I try to track Griever's movement as I duck under Sam's arm. I have to get him away from here.

He grunts, and I take it for a yes. I move to stand, but my knees shake and my back bows under the weight. We stagger a step forward, and Mrs. Griever starts barking—there's no other way to describe her halting laugh—like this is all a joke.

"You're not makin' it back like that, and I said that boy deserves a bullet, not that he got one. It's rock salt in your leg. Smarts more than a bullet, mind ya, but won't do no damage if we take it out quick."

"You're insane. I'm not letting you near him," I yell. "We're calling the police."

"Careful, girl. You're trespassin' on my land, and if I'm a day over twenty, you came here for answers. You leave tonight, you ain't ever comin' back."

I try to move us toward the path, but Sam resists. "Stella, she's right. We have to stay. I'm . . . I'll be fine," he says in a faint voice. I drag my cell out of my pocket. No service. No way to call for help.

"The longer you stall, girl, the longer he'll be in pain. I've got to take the salt from his wound. Bring him inside."

Her silhouette moves past us, seemingly gliding. It travels up the porch and converges with the shadows. Deep inside the shack there's the scrape of something heavy dragged across the floor, and then a warm glow seeps out the doorway.

"C'mon, this is the only way," Sam whispers, limping forward and guiding me rather than me helping him. The porch protests loudly under our weight as we lunge over the busted steps. We pause at the mouth of the door. The faint light wafts down a long hallway—longer than I would have expected, given how little and squatty the shack looks from outside—and smoke makes the air shimmery and thick.

"Sam." I catch his chin and make him look at me. His eyes have the look of pink-rimmed black marbles. And it's my fault. "I swear I'd get you to the hospital."

He swallows the pain and smiles feebly. "I know you would."

Without another word he lifts his injured leg over the threshold and tugs me inside. As we struggle through the last door in the hall, we see Griever hunched over a stone fireplace. Suspended over the flames is a giant cast-iron pot; she stokes the blaze, and the flames lick its sides. She sinks into a crouch and holds long metal tweezers into the heat until their tips glow molten. Sam hobbles to an empty chair.

"I tan leather at night." She clinks the tweezers on the cauldron. I can just make out a brown solid bubbling up from the water on the surface. It has the look of an empty sack of skin. "Boilin' rather than jus' soakin' keeps the hide from crackin'," she adds. It's the stench of cooking leather pervading my mouth, lungs, and nostrils.

She rises nimbly from the fire and hurries to Sam's side, where she squats at his feet. She doesn't move like someone who's ancient, about to break down. "Have you done this before?" I ask, eyeing the bottle of rubbing alcohol and strips of gauze.

"When I was younger, I nursed sick folk back to health," she says, wielding a pair of scissors. She cuts Sam's pant leg off at the thigh. I creep closer and gasp at what I see. Griever gives me a fierce stare, and I get ahold of myself. There are maybe ten or twelve wounds, seething and bubbling where large shards of salt like glass are embedded in the minced skin.

THE CREEPING | 287

"Why shoot me if you thought I was Daniel?" Sam asks, averting his eyes from his leg.

"That boy's been stickin' his nose round here since he was a scrawny li'l thing just off the breast. Empty stare. Stumbled on him in the woods that same summer your li'l friend went missin', saw his game diggin' the eyes from a squirrel he snared. I got a name for rotten ones like that." She wags her tweezers in Sam's face. "*Boys.*"

I prop my clammy hands on my hips. Griever's words are a line cast into my sea of formless memories. It snatches a few out with it, giving them shape. I remember Daniel sticking potato bugs in a glass jar and shaking once. I remember that he used to collect these spiders that had bloated bellies and wiry crimped legs. He trapped them in an old container with breathing holes drilled through the lid in order to keep them indefinitely. I even remember him going out of his way to step on crickets. Horrible, yeah, but boys are always messing around with bugs and mud. Torturing squirrels is another thing. A sick, demented thing. Not the kind of thing a boy who loves his sister as much as Daniel loved Jeanie has in him. A surge of anger rushes through me, and if it wasn't for Sam grinding his teeth to bear the pain as Griever sticks tweezers into the first festering cut, I'd lose it with her.

"Daniel's only after answers. He's lost his whole family," I say sharply.

"Is that so?" she clucks. I can't tell if she doesn't know or if she's being sarcastic. "Girl, get to askin' me your questions before I run outta patience with ya."

I look to Sam for help, but his eyes are scrunched closed, sweat shines on his forehead, and he's rounded forward like he's trying not to be sick. It's painful to watch him, so I pace. "What's buried in your yard?" I ask, failing miserably at delicacy.

Griever doesn't miss a beat. "Animals, but you already know that. I heard you diggin' 'em up and findin' a dog."

My stride falters. I try to tie my hair back from my face, but my hands are shaking so badly I can't make a knot. Instead I just wring them like some kind of OD'ing schizo. "So there's someone—or a group of someones—who are sacrificing animals in Savage, right?"

Half her face shadowed, she watches me, her good eye trained on mine, the tweezers lingering at the mouth of Sam's open wound. "Same families have been doin' it for generations. Only one of their bloodlines left, though. Don't know how it started, but we've been tryin' to stave off the evil for years."

My mind plods over her muddy words. "'We've?'" I breathe.

"Ahhh, there ya go, girl. That's right. I'm the last one." She turns back to the tattered skin on Sam's leg. "Mind ya, I don't get round like I used to. I got holes in my bones where the age has eaten through. Long time ago there were other families doin' it. Back-woods folks mostly. They've all died off or moved on. Now it's jus' me, sacrificin' the li'l things, givin' 'em proper burials, hidin' their corpses from pryin' eyes."

"You're saying that your family has been killing dozens—hundreds maybe—of animals? You're confessing to slaughtering house pets?" She doesn't call me an idiot. I'm right. But her smile is a half sneer, and it's like she doesn't understand what a gruesome confession her silence is. "And you're killing them in sacrifice? You believe you're appeasing the spirits or gods or whatever?"

She lurches at me, bloody tweezers clutched in her hand, still on her knees, and hisses, "Not whatever. *Whatever* is the thing that's sucklin' on the bones of those li'l lost girls." She jabs the tweezers in the air to make her point and then turns back to work.

Sam braces himself against the chair arms and straightens out of his slump. He pants under the effort it takes to stack each vertebra in a column. He's pasty, and his lips are blue by the time he finishes, but the pain's ironed out from his voice. "The animal disappearances don't just coincide with kidnappings. They happen after accidents, too. How could you think you could stop car collisions, or illness, or fires? Whatever took those girls isn't causing *accidents*."

She snorts, regarding him. "Who are you to say what evil can and can't do? And I said there used to be other families workin' on stavin' it off. Backwoods folks more superstitious than mine. I know who it's got an appetite for. But other families blamed it for every loss in Savage."

A cold current rushes through the room, and I start noticing things. I was so focused on Sam that I didn't wonder what kind of hide Griever's tanning to make leather; I didn't see the animal pelts nailed to the wall. There are seventy or maybe a hundred of them, covering every square inch of space. They give off this hot-animal-fur stench that turns my stomach into a roiling sea. Some are furry pelts and others are just leather hides. Dimly I register her saying, "My family's been the only one goin' round and collectin' their bodies to bury for generations. I don't take their coats off unless they're somethin' special."

I have to look away. I can't stand to wonder which are dogs and cats. I don't need to examine the hides she considers special. How could a woman who used to nurse people back to health be capable of this? How could *anyone* do this? *Unless* . . . I sweep my arms, encompassing the room full of animal carnage. "However awful all this is, whatever you're trying to stop is worse, isn't it?"

"There ya go, girl," Griever growls, grinning.

Despite the heat and the animal carcasses—or maybe because of them—I start to shiver. Griever drops shard after shard of salt onto the floor at her feet. Sam's brow gradually uncreases, his shoulders relax, his breath eases.

"It's been in the woods since before people settled here. Monster," I whisper, furious that my mouth forms the syllables but helpless to stop it.

"That's jus' a word we use for what we don't understand." She slices off a long piece of gauze and wraps it around the mangled flesh on Sam's leg. "You'll heal with some scars, but it won't get infected." She carries her tools back to the fire to sanitize them. I stumble to Sam's side, dabbing his forehead on my sleeve and pressing my lips to his temple.

Griever glides easily across the room and dips a glass into a bucket. She offers the cloudy water to Sam, who takes it and gulps gratefully. Then she crouches on the floor by the fire, watching us, her good pupil trained in our direction and the milky one veering sharply away.

"The Creepin'," she whispers hoarsely. So quietly I think maybe I misunderstand. "That's what you're after."

I shake my head, not getting it. "The Creeping?"

She raises one arthritic finger to her cracked lips, shushing me. "Be careful who could be listenin'." I look around to make it obvious that we're alone. She raises her eyebrow, mocking me. "It's the name my ma gave it. Other families had their own—those who spoke about it, at least. 'Cause some folks wouldn't for fear talkin' about it would draw it in."

Sure the room's temperature has dropped a few degrees, I lean closer to Sam, who's staring intently at Griever. She pulls a pocketknife and a thick stick from the folds of her dress and starts whittling absentmindedly, filaments of white bark scattering in front of her like snowflakes.

"What is it?" Sam asks, sounding stronger already.

The *shwet shwet* of her knife slicing at the stick doesn't stop. "Don't know exactly. I don't put creed in thinkin' it's a force causin' accidents. Best I can describe it is this: It's an appetite, a creature bent on feedin'. It craves a certain kind of li'l girl, and if it can't get its hooks into what it wants, anyone in its path will do."

My fingernails are blue from cold and gouging into the back of the wooden chair hard enough to leave claw marks. I chew the inside of my cheek, hoping to jolt myself awake from the nightmare I'm obviously trapped in.

"But what is it?" Sam prods. "Where did it come from? Is it an animal? A person?"

She shrugs, cool amusement playing on her face. "It might have started out as one or the other. But once it peeled the flesh from a babe's arm jus' to hear her blubber, it stopped bein' either."

"Like the devil," I murmur.

Griever appraises me, running her tongue over her gray gums. "There's no devil. Doesn't need to be, with what actually lurks high in those hills. Trust me, you don't wanna be after rememberin' it. When I was a li'l thing, folks in Savage wanted it kept secret. Maybe people are still after keepin' it quiet?"

"But why keep it a secret?" I sputter. "If parents knew, they wouldn't let their kids in the woods. The disappearances would stop."

Griever waggles a splintered yellow fingernail at me. "You see, when folks knew 'bout it when I was a girl, there were those who preyed on their fear. Did things to li'l girls and blamed it on the Creepin', knowin' full well they'd get away with it. Sure, the critter sank its latch hooks into some of 'em, but men and women took others. Folks thought it was better to keep quiet 'bout the monster they knew than to unleash all they didn't."

"That's why the graves in the cemetary were tampered with," Sam says. "Someone didn't want future generations seeing all those graves of little children and investigating what happened, finding out about the creature if it had been forgotten. Betty Balco and the other girls went missing, and they never found who did it. And you're saying this—this *thing* took some of them, but people took others because they thought they could hide behind the legend? And they were right. When this happened eighty years ago, they never made any arrests."

"But that's not happening now," I say. "If people were trying to cover it up, they wouldn't have let Jeanie's case go unsolved for eleven years, right? They would have found a viable suspect. Put the case to rest so people didn't ask questions."

"Maybe they thought it would go away?" Sam says. "One little girl's an anomaly after so many years. But Jane Doe showed up dead and they figured it's happening again and they hustled all the charges on Kent Talcott. Rather than letting people know there's something in the woods, they're sending an innocent man to prison."

"But how does anyone know about it?" I ask Griever.

She tilts her head back, regarding me. "Same way folks know 'bout anythin'. Someone told 'em. Stories passed down through generations. Even though a lot of the old families have died out or moved on, you got some who've lived here for years. I bet they know 'bout the Creepin'. How couldn't they know a monster's afoot with all those dead li'l girls turnin' up?"

Griever sets her jaw so her jowls twitch in the firelight. I want desperately to believe she's mostly crazy, brain turned to mush with age, spinning stories to justify a pathological violence against animals. Yet I don't.

I move out from behind Sam. "This *thing* is what took Jeanie? You helped her once, though, didn't you? You found her when she was lost in the woods a month before she disappeared." I recall the good witch that Jeanie said helped her.

Griever licks her lips. "I seen you kids playin' at huntin' lots of times. I told you and your li'l redheaded friend to be careful what ya looked for, ya jus' might find it. Yous were stubborn li'l brats who didn't listen." And there it is. A mystery solved. Griever warned Jeanie and me, and we didn't listen.

"You." I struggle to keep my bearing. "'If you hunt for monsters, you'll find them.' You told us that. Why didn't you tell the cops?"

"Police were lookin' for someone to blame. Someone to hold responsible for the missing li'l girl. I wasn't gonna admit to talkin' to yous out here alone."

I run it through my mind until it's smooth and shiny. All these months since I read the case file I've been parroting what Griever said to shoo us from the woods. To keep us safe and alive, but we didn't listen, and Jeanie died for it.

I rub my damp hands on my jeans. "Do you know where to find it? Is it at Norse Rock? Is that where it spots its victims?"

A wet snort. "I ain't tellin' you. You go up there"—she points at the west wall—"you won't come back. You ain't monster enough to survive."

"But Mr. Talcott confessed yesterday," I say, taking a step toward her. "No one's looking for it anymore, and I have to prove it wasn't him."

She juts out her chin, examining the sharp tip of the wooden dagger she's whittled. "Grief does funny things to folk," she says thoughtfully. A moment later she rises hastily. "It's time for yous to leave. Out with ya." She waves her hands like we're flames she'll fan out.

"But he can barely walk." I rush to support Sam as he stands unsteadily from the chair, wincing to put weight on both legs.

"Not my concern. You've brought too much trouble round already. Be off." She waves the pointed stick in the air. Sam takes my hand, coaxing me along as he limps to the doorway. We move surprisingly fast through the hall and back into the night. My eyes take a minute to adjust, and for a while we're in pitch blackness. Who knows what beasts could be stalking us from the shadows? I help Sam over the busted steps and we start toward the path.

"Girl," Griever hisses from the mouth of the shack, "best you jus' move on from here. Take your fella and thank your lucky stars it wasn't you."

With Sam's arm slung over my shoulders, I can see only her head as I glance back. A floating head with black holes under her brow where her eyes should be. *I should listen to Griever. But I am stubborn, and stupid, and brave.*

Chapter Twenty-Five

It takes ages for us to get back to Sam's car. Fear nips at my heels with every step, and I get the sense that we're being watched, followed, hunted even. The white disk of a moon casts enough light for us to see a few steps ahead, and the bramble on either side is black and impenetrable.

"We're okay, Stella. There's nothing out here," Sam murmurs when I whimper at the nearby crunch of leaves. Yards past the old Victorian house, the lane's only streetlight shines as a second moon.

Somehow we make it to the station wagon without being attacked by night creatures. I help Sam into the passenger seat and sprint to the driver's side. Once inside I slam my hand down on the door lock—that little click of the car doors being secured the most comforting sound in the world. The car rumbles to life, and I pitch it into drive. I accelerate down the lane and only slow when we hit downtown.

We don't speak the whole way home. Sam's arms stay braced

against the door and center console. His breathing is an erratic and harsh melody filling the cab. I'm sad and relieved for different reasons when I round my street corner and see Dad's car still missing from the driveway. "Can you stay with me tonight?" I ask, turning into the driveway.

"What about your dad?" he asks.

I point to the digital clock reading 2:05 a.m. "If Dad works past midnight, he crashes in his office."

Our second night together couldn't be more different from our first. I help Sam into a pair of Dad's sweats, bring him four Tylenol to ease the pain, and help him into my bed. He tells me three times that it's not too bad before I stop asking if we should go to the emergency room. Before I can say I want to compare my time line from last night with what Griever told us, his breathing has evened out.

I pore over it myself. I confirm that the accidental tragedies with corresponding animal disappearances occurred forty or more years ago. Those sacrifices must have been made by the backwoods families Griever said are no longer alive or living in Savage. Griever said she and her family only sacrificed animals when it seemed like the Creeping had taken victims. In the last few decades, the animal disappearances correspond with hikers and campers vanishing, what was assumed to be a bear attack, and Jeanie Talcott's kidnapping. Those recent sacrifices must have been the work of Griever and any relative of hers alive at the time.

Satisfied that I've gotten to the bottom of the animal disappearances, I change into a tattered T-shirt and slip into bed. I stare at the thin lines of light like pale chalk between the slats of my blinds. Somewhere out there a streetlamp is burning white and steady, guiding moths out of the night to its warmth while I'm shaking as the cold in my bones freezes me from the inside out. For the first time it occurs to me that remembering might be too . . . *too everything*. What if I witnessed more than Jeanie being taken? What if I watched as her insides, neatly tucked and coiled under thin pink skin, were pulled from her body? What if I heard the crackle and snap of her scalp's tissue parting from her skull? What if once I remember I can't stop replaying it, and it becomes all I hear? Jeanie's whimpering. Jeanie's bones breaking and her cartilage crackling. The hiss of Jeanie's last breath. What if it's so much *more* and I'm not strong, or certain, or able, or *enough*, and it breaks me?

Ultimately, though, I swallow the fear so it roosts somewhere smaller, darker, deeper in me, because of the whistle of Sam's breath between his teeth. Sam is here. Sam will help me bear it. I gently brush aside the hair sticking to his forehead. His long lashes are clumped together in little starlike sharp points. He got hurt tonight because of me. I dragged him there like I've dragged him everywhere, tethered by some invisible rope he calls love. Sam's uncovered nearly every piece of evidence that proves there's a creature lurking in the woods. That there's something so much more—or less—than human.

My hand hovers just above his forehead, so close my fingertips imagine the flutter of hair on their pads. A flutter of something else in the back of my head. It was Sam's idea to look for past disappearances in library archives, to search the graveyard, to investigate what we were doing in the woods as kids. Every hunch he's had yields blizzards of clues, and all that evidence has led me to one impossible conclusion: the Creeping.

My hand retracts carefully as I'm shaking my head into the swell of the pillow. No, no, no, what am I getting at? This is *Sam*. Too patient, too kind, too forgiving, too-good-to-be-true Sam Worth. I'm clinging to the edge of the bed before I realize I've rolled away, put space between us. I must be losing it if I'm even thinking . . . *What am I thinking?* That six-year-old Sam had something to do with Jeanie's disappearance? That now he's steering me away from human suspects by inventing monsters, by fabricating evidence and leads? Sam isn't just my Sam. He was six. But is there something he's steering me away from? Sam's been eyeing the supernatural all along. How could he have known?

I know Zoey and Caleb were home with chicken pox when Jeanie was taken, and Daniel was home with his mom, but I don't have a clue where Sam was. I've never asked. I figured he wasn't there because it was a girly playdate, but isn't it weird that it's never come up? I've heard loads of kids who barely knew Jeanie talk about where they were that afternoon. Everyone wants to claim a piece of history for themselves—even the Jeanie-shaped history of Savage. How has Sam never mentioned that he was sipping lemonade poolside, or thumping a ramshackle birdhouse with a hammer at Scouts, or taking a dreamless nap when Jeanie was abducted?

Suspicion sends my thoughts shrieking backward, bashing along memories like speed bumps until I reach the Day of Bones. Me: in the cemetery lying on the stone bench, eyes closed. Sam's head in place of the moon as my lids snapped open. No crunch of his footsteps, no blurry form coming into focus between the graves. I didn't see the direction he came from.

I twist farther from Sam as I wag my head no, no, no. He doesn't have anything to do with Jeanie or Jane Doe. *But I didn't see where he came from.* What if he was traveling from deeper in the cemetery? What if he stumbled across me after offing another little redheaded victim, and he's smart as hell, so he pretended to have followed me?

My hands drop limp at my sides. This is insane, crazeballs, nutso, borderline betrayal that as Sam sleeps vulnerable and unguarded a foot away I'm trying him of murder and finding him guilty. I need a straitjacket if I'm actually thinking that six-year-old Sam had anything to do with Jeanie and that now he's hungry for more. I push my palms against my eyes until fireworks take the place of the mangy scrap of skin that was Jane Doe's scalp.

A moment later I feel for the furry lump on the carpet, the stale polyester smell of my bunny's fur in my face and lungs as I squeeze him tighter, my whole rib cage cradling him. My eyelids are fat and heavy. I went grave digging tonight. An old woman warned us about an ancient monster that kills little girls. She accused Savage of trying to keep it a secret years ago; she warned that it might be happening again. I rock Bunny. That's all it is: exhaustion, ragged nerves, imagination drunk from the blurred line between reality and nightmare. Sam would never hurt anyone.

Before I let myself fall asleep, I list every time *I* hurt Sam in the last five years. Times I rolled my eyes when he wished me happy birthday or asked how my day was going in fourth-period biology. Times when I ignored him for other guys. Times when he was about to ask me out and I made an excuse—which we both knew was bogus—to dodge him. The list goes on and on. It could fill a book. And yet Sam has never injured me back.

Right then and there I swear that I won't doubt Sam. I'll accept that he really is as good as he seems, and I'll spend however long it takes, forever even, making all the times I hurt him right. After that sleep comes easier.

In the morning Sam's muddy-brown eyes, fringed with hazel lashes, are watching me from their place on the pillow we're sharing. Blinking carefully, purposefully, so they don't miss a thing.

I hide my intake of breath with a yawn. "Hey. How's the leg?"

He mimes rapping on his knee protruding from under the covers. "Still there." He smiles lopsidedly. "Stiff, but not so bad. You okay?"

"Fine," I say in a tense voice. "Have you been awake for long?"

"Twenty minutes or so. I've been thinking about the cat in the cemetery." He frowns. "Griever admitted to sacrificing all those animals, but she also made a point to say she buried them so people didn't come across their corpses. She's managed to fly under the radar for decades."

I shrug against the pillow.

Sam's brow knits as he focuses on me. "The cat in the cemetery was just left there. We found it." He waits for me to comment. I should. Sam is observant and smart, but I can't stop watching his hands like they're going to thrust out and strangle me. "That seems pretty sloppy for someone who's been at it for decades."

I blink once and focus on his face. "She must leave the animals out as an offering to . . . *it*. She collects their bodies later."

"But the cat was beheaded."

"She's deranged."

"The pelts on the walls had their heads . . . or at least the fur that would have been on their heads and ears."

"I don't know, Sam." I sigh, shaking my head. "Maybe she's going crazier?"

Sam pushes up on his elbow, eyes crinkling, studying me. "What's wrong?" His hair is plastered to his head, and his cheeks are lip-gloss pink. The covers, twisted around us, seem to tighten around my legs, binding them up.

He reaches to touch my shoulder and stops. I'm staring wide-eyed at the approaching hand like I'm looking for traces of blood. "Stella, talk to me," he whispers.

Heat creeps into my face. What am I doing? What am I thinking? This is Sam. I laid all this suspicion to rest. It was only a symptom of the horror of the night. But from the instant I opened my eyes and saw him watching, all I could think was, *You don't miss anything. How did you miss Jeanie being taken?*

"Look, I want to forget about all of this. Jeanie. Jane Doe. All of it," I say, fast and messy. If I spew enough words, tell Sam whatever lies I must to make him leave, the horrible things I want to accuse him of won't come out. "Even if I do remember, I don't know that a recovered memory eleven years too late is going to make a difference. I destroyed my believability once I lied in front of the whole world yesterday."

Sam rubs the parenthesis between his brows. "What about what Griever told us?"

"What about it? I didn't need her to tell me there's something unnatural in the woods. Decades of missing girls. Centuries more of everyone who ever settled here dying and fighting and struggling. It's always been here. The bone in Jane Doe's hand proves that it's been killing for a thousand years. Maybe more. Maybe it causes the darkness in Savage, or maybe all the darkness clotting here made it. Like a scab on the earth in this one place." My tone has the hush of sharing an awful secret.

"I don't need to know. Jeanie's gone. There's no bringing her back. Or any of them. And this is nothing but crazy, us hiking through the woods, talking about monsters and things that totally can't exist." I'm going on blindly, groping for words. "I mean, if whoever or whatever offed Jeanie has it out for me, they've had eleven years to get me. And guess what? They haven't." A shudder of awareness runs up my spine. If Sam is hiding something, he's had years to hurt me, and all he's done is proven that he won't.

"I have to ask, though." I rub my palm back and forth across my face. *No, no, no, what am I thinking?* This is Sam. I can't stop it, though. Here it comes. "Where were you, Sam?"

He half smiles, like he's not certain if I'm telling a joke and he doesn't want me to feel like I'm not funny. "Where was I when?"

"When Jeanie was taken." I exhale the words with a breath I've been holding. "Why weren't you there, at Jeanie's, with us in the woods? Why haven't you ever mentioned where you were before?"

Sam bolts upright, kicking the blankets away, swinging his feet to the floor. "That sounds like more of an accusation than a question," he says softly. His back to me, he bends to slip the sweats off and his pants and shoes on. I hear a soft grunt like he's in pain, but he doesn't stop until he's on his feet.

I will my body to free itself, untangle my ankles, but I can't make my legs cooperate through the trembling, and I only manage to sit. "Why aren't you answering me?" I plead.

Blood tie-dyes the white gauze around his revealed leg. "Because I shouldn't have to defend myself, Stella. Not to you. Not after . . . *after everything.*" I know he means every time I threw him away; every time he gave me another chance. Sam strides unevenly to the door and pauses at the threshold. He stares at his sneakers. "I was an idiot to think you're still that little girl who loved more and climbed higher and swam faster and laughed harder." I slump back onto my pillow. "I kept looking. Trying to find bits of who you used to be, but she doesn't exist anymore. *You're not her.*" He moves soundlessly from the room, down the stairs, and out of the house with barely a rumble as his station wagon accelerates from my driveway. Sam leaving me is the loudest noise I've ever heard. *You're not her.*

During the rest of the morning and into the afternoon, every time I think of Jeanie or Sam or Zoey or Daniel, my ears ring with Sam's words. I'm letting them all down because Sam is right; I'm not as fear-less as that little girl growling in the Polaroid, gripping a spear on the hunt for monsters. I'm surprised she couldn't keep Jeanie safe. I'm not as brave as the ten-year-old who pulled Sam in for a kiss. And I'm definitely not as honest. I should have admitted to myself sooner what last night and this morning were actually about. Sam got hurt because of me, and I was scared to death that I'd lose him like I lose everyone else, like I lost my mother, who is the one person in this world you're not supposed to lose. I guess making him leave by accusing him of something unforgivable was easier than waiting around for it to happen naturally. How could I doubt Sam for even a second? I take refuge in the shower, hoping the water will pound away the aching in my chest.

I can't stop thinking about how everyone else changed because of Jeanie, her absence, and the mystery around it. Is Jeanie why Zoey is the high school equivalent of a Viking raider when she covets something? Did Zoey learn early on that you lose what you don't fight to keep? Is Jeanie why Mom left? Did Mom wonder if there was a reason I came back and Jeanie didn't? Did Mom wonder what it said about me that I survived a monster? I dunk my head under the pounding water.

I won't stop looking for who or what took Jeanie. *I can't.* Everyone else stopped, and she deserves better.

I check my cell after drying off. A text from Zoey:

Come 2 Cole's bash tonight. We've got 2 talk.

That's it. No *Sorry for flaking on watching your back last night.* No *Did you survive?* I throw the cell at my bed; it skids to a stop at my stuffed bunny's feet.

"Can you effing believe that?" I ask in a tizzy. The bunny doesn't answer. So this is how it's going to be. I'll get whiplash trying to keep up with Zoey's bipolarness over Sam. I throw myself on my bed. I completely forgot about Cole's party. Playing host at your first bash is kind of a rite of passage for newbies at school, and now that the whole town thinks the psycho serial killer on the loose has been caught, there's no reason people wouldn't show up. Still, I feel burned that Cole didn't at least try to cancel.

After texting Zoey ten times with no response, I text Cole and Michaela the same message:

Not up for 2night. Soorrryy xoxo

Michaela responds before the screen turns dark from the sent text:

Miss u. Let's hang 2morrow. Call if u need me.

Cole responds a minute later:

Tried canceling. Z says party must go on.

I blink at the screen as I'm walking to the kitchen to scrounge up a piece of fruit or a yogurt. I'd probably spend most of the afternoon wondering what Zoey's motivation is for not letting Cole cancel, but a fist pounds on my front door.

I peek through the peephole and see Caleb raking his floppy hair from his eyes.

"Hi, stranger," I call.

He jumps a little as I swing the door open. "Hey, can I come in?" His voice sounds tight, nervous. He ducks his head and shrugs deeper into his jacket as he slips past me. It occurs to me that he might be upset that I've been secretive and absent since we spoke the day at the cove.

"I'm really sorry we haven't been able to hang out much since you've been home," I say as he hovers in the middle of the living room. He's shifting by the recliner, as if he can't make up his mind whether he's staying long enough to sit. "Are you mad?" I ask.

His eyes meet mine for the first time. They're caught off guard. "No, sorry. I need a cigarette or something. I'm freaking nervous." He flashes an apologetic smile and drops into the recliner with a groan.

I settle cross-legged on the end of the couch nearest him. My eyes drift to a muscle pulsing in his jaw. "Why are you nervous?"

"Look, Stella." He rubs his dry palms together like sandpaper. "I've got to be honest with you about something."

My hands wrap around my ankles and I squeeze, willing away dread. "Okay. You're kind of scaring me."

He hazards a quick smile that doesn't reassure me. "It's just that Zoey cornered me last night and had a million questions about the summer Jeanie went missing, and I realized I kind of left you guys high and dry without talking to you. Saying I'd tell your dad and all . . . well, it was a dick move. Snitches get stitches and all that."

I smirk and relax. "Did you learn that from a Jay-Z song?"

"Probably." He smiles at the joke, but the lightness of his expression fades fast. "I remember hunting monsters." I'm instantly angled forward. "I told Zo last night I didn't want to talk about it. I wouldn't give her answers. There's a reason for that. There was so much in the year leading up to Jeanie that you guys are too young to remember." His face is thinner and sharper than usual; his cheekbones like blades as he continues. "Boys always talk about supernatural shit. In the second grade we'd yell 'Bloody Mary' three times in the mirror. At the beginning of third grade a couple of kids saw two bums beating on a mangy-looking dog in the woods. It inspired all kinds of crazy stories. Kids were going on about camps full of drifters who were cannibals or dog eaters. That same year Jeremy Bellamy—he was that kid who walked with a limp from shattering his right leg when he was a toddler?" He pauses and I nod. Jeremy graduated last year from Wildwood. "Anyway, he pissed his pants in the woods behind the elementary school and came out crying about a ghost with empty wet sockets instead of eyeballs. For weeks we tore through the trees, searching." He takes a deep breath. "None of it was true. Boys want to hunt shit and we didn't have anything real, so we hunted make-believe."

I bob my head encouragingly. None of this is new; it's more detailed than Sam's account, but there's nothing earth-shattering. "The spring before Jeanie started that same bullshit way. We—Daniel and me—overheard his dad talking to a ranger buddy about some town legend no one remembers anymore." His chin juts out, giving him a slight underbite as he thinks hard. "This ancient animal thing lived in the woods. There was some history to it, I think. I couldn't remember what, and I went to the library the other day to see if they had any folklore-type books about Savage."

I'm leaning forward, practically falling from the couch I'm so intent. "Did they?" I whisper.

"No. The librarian looked at me like I was high." He snorts. "Ironic, 'cause it's the only time I've ever been in a library when I wasn't." A clipped chuckle. "So anyway, it was springtime, and we started hunting this monster in the woods. We made spears and bows and arrows. I mean, we really got carried away. And it was more fun than doing it with the boys at school because you, Zoey, Sam, and Jeanie were only six." A bolt of pain snaps across his features at admitting how young we were, and I realize where this is going. Caleb suffers from guilt over how he contributed to Jeanie's disappearance, and he wasn't even there. "You all got really into it. And at some point, we forgot that it wasn't real." He sniffs. "Or maybe kids know what's real better than adults do?" He focuses on my expression. "Maybe we were smart to believe in what lives in the dark?" My pulse is in my throat. He gives his head a jolt and starts massaging his hands with the look of someone trying to rub the cold out of his knuckles.

All the years fall away, and there's this childish quality about him sitting sunken in the recliner. He's been skipping meals, and his black bomber jacket swims on him. His skin is pale porcelain; a lattice of blue veins shows through on his neck. No, not childish, fragile. "So that's what we did all spring and into the summer, until Jeanie was taken," he says. "We hunted the monster."

"Caleb, why didn't you tell anyone this? Why not tell the cops once Jeanie disappeared?" It isn't that I think it would have made a huge difference; Jeanie was gone, and who would believe a nine-year-old crying about monsters?

"You wouldn't have been out there if not for us." A tremor builds in his voice. "Me and Daniel. We're the ones who got you so comfortable going into the forest. If we hadn't, you and Jeanie would have stuck to the front yard. You don't know, Stella. Jeanie goes missing and everyone's parents and the cops are talking to kids about staying away from strangers. Parents get carried away and they scare the shit out of their kids." He looks frightened now. "Most clam up. They worry about getting in trouble for playing in the woods. But some talk. You don't remember, but kids were going to school counselors and teachers for almost a year after, crying about how they saw Bloody Mary in the mirror or a ghost in the woods who must have taken Jeanie. The whole town needed therapy or meds after it happened. Daniel and I were afraid that everyone would know what we suspected: It was our fault."

I'm on my knees at his feet in a flash. "You were a kid. It's not your fault." I force his hands from his lap and hold them in mine. "You had chicken pox, and I was the one with Jeanie. I'm the one who couldn't help her. I'm the one who didn't remember."

Caleb goes gradually still. "Didn't? Do you remember Jeanie's dad hurting her?"

I sit on the coffee table so our heads are level and close. I don't know why I feel the need to whisper in my living room. "It wasn't him, Caleb. I've been getting flashes from that day. Not of who or what took her. Not yet." Cold fingers grope at my heart as I voice how inevitable I believe it is that I will remember. "Do you ever talk to Daniel?"

Caleb shrugs. "Not really since we were kids. He was sent away, you know. Maybe off and on each time he'd come back to town."

"Could you talk to him, for me?" I ask, scooting to the edge of the coffee table until our knees touch. "Could you remind him about what you overheard his dad and the other ranger saying? I don't know why he told the police he thinks his dad is guilty, but if one of us could just talk to him about hunting in the woods . . . Maybe he's too afraid to face what he suspects really happened? Just talk to him and get him to call me. He might listen to you, since you were friends." He looks away. "Please, Caleb. Jeanie deserves better than this."

There's something in his eyes I can't identify as they move back to me.

"What?" I ask.

"The way you just said her name . . . I've heard you and Zo talk about her in the past." He pauses and I brace myself. "You aren't talking about her like she's gum stuck to the bottom of your shoe anymore."

I want to cover my face in shame. "The more I think of Jeanie, the clearer my sense of her becomes; it's like my idea of her is being distilled over and over again." I shake my head, frustrated. "She was this black-and-white outline to me before."

His hand covers mine, resting on my knee. "And now she's being colored in. I get it. And yes, I'll try to find Daniel and talk to him."

I sink back on my spine. "I'm glad you came over. I miss you. You're like my less bitchy best friend," I add with a grin.

He presses his lips to the crown of my head as he rocks up from the chair to leave. "You're my less bitchy little sister."

Chapter Twenty-Six

Dad actually comes home—by five, no less—and bumps around the kitchen making enchiladas. Dinner is more awkward than normal given Sam's recent sleepover (the one Dad knows about) and my little outburst at the courthouse yesterday.

"It's normal to have a difficult time accepting resolution," Dad says after serving himself a second helping of Spanish rice. "Don't beat yourself up. You'll need time to adjust."

I nod agreeably like I usually do with Dad, *but on second thought* . . . "It would help if you were home at night more," I say. He stops mid-bite and stares at me. "I miss you, and I'll be leaving for college next year."

He places his fork down and removes his wire-rimmed glasses. He thumbs his chin in the way he does whenever he's puzzling something out. "I have been working a lot lately. I guess I've been trying to cope with your mother remarrying."

I move the food around on my plate listlessly. "I know. But I am too."

He reaches across the table for my hand. "You're one hundred percent right, Pumpkin. It'll take some creativity, but I'll cut back. Maybe we can finally find time to go furniture shopping like we've been talking about? I can get to know the Worth boy again. That is, if you think I should."

"I don't think he's going to come over anymore. I said something and I don't think he'll forgive me," I admit.

"Sure he will. Who wouldn't forgive you anything? How about once you two are better I'll make dinner for the three of us? You pick the night and I'll make it happen."

The rest of the evening is our old normal. Dad lies on the sofa watching the national and international news. Moscow follows me up and down the stairs as I make a trip to the laundry room with my hamper. It's not until Dad goes to sleep, calling softly down the hall for me to have sweet dreams, that things get weird.

I sit at my desk for a half hour trying to compile a list of people who might know about the past disappearances of little girls. According to Griever, people tried to keep it a secret when she was a kid. But do I believe it's happening again? The term "cover-up" conjures up tinkering conspiracy theorists in basement laboratories, accusing small-town mayors of concealing UFOs. I don't relish being in that company. It is undeniable, though, that several redheaded girls went missing in the 1930s, and at least two of them visited or disappeared from Old Norse Trail or Norse Rock. A very long time ago, likely in the years immediately following the disappearances, someone concealed the names and ages on several graves in the cemetery. Some of those graves could belong to the three missing girls we know about from the thirties. The others could belong to additional missing children.

I believe Sam was right when he theorized that the vandal was attempting to stop the spread of the Creeping's legend by destroying the evidence of its kills.

But how would the police not know about the cold cases from eighty years ago, and if they knew, why stay quiet about them? Why wasn't Jeanie's case—or Jane Doe's, at this point—connected with them?

I need to find whoever in Savage knows—however few or many—and convince them to act, shine light on the secret so that the FBI, or CIA, or NSA, or whoever deals with paranormal wackiness can hunt the Creeping down. Revealing the Creeping—the actual predator taking lives—is the only way Mr. Talcott will be exonerated. I know I'd make more progress with Sam or Zoey to bounce my craptastic ideas off of, but Zoey blew me off when I needed her last night, and I'll be lucky if Sam ever speaks to me again, so it's all me.

Any people in jobs positioned to see that there's a pattern of missing girls have to be aware that similar disappearances occurred eighty years ago in Savage. That means police department employees or anyone with access to cold cases could be involved. Archivists either from the newspaper or the library who have access to all those articles we saw. Any local historians. Probably the mayor? Sam said Mayor Berg's family has been here for seven or eight generations. Any groundskeeper of Old Savage Cemetery; they'd see the graves. I'm sure I'm missing people, but this is pretty damn good for me all by my lonesome.

I chew my lip for a good fifteen minutes before deciding to take a big risk. I snatch my cell and dial Shane before I lose my nerve.

"Hello?" a groggy voice croaks.

"Shane? It's Stella," I say meekly, the courage draining out of me.

A creaking mattress and whispers. A moment later and I hear the whoosh of cars, like Shane's stepped outside near a highway. He must live in the apartment block near the interstate.

"Stella, do you know what kind of week I've had? This is the first time I've been to bed before midnight in a year. What is it?"

I take a deep breath, here it is, do or die. "How long have you known?"

"Known what? It's too late for guessing games."

"Known about the Creeping or whatever your name for it is. *How long have you known?* When you learned about it, did you realize that it's the creature in your grandma's story?"

"What—what are you talking about? Is your father there?" Then a furious whisper. "This is inappropriate, and I don't think he'd approve of you dragging me out of bed and accusing me of—of—"

His voice faltering gives me an extra boost of courage. "I bet you didn't know for sure until the day Jeanie was taken, huh? I bet you had a load of questions when I came back talking about hunting monsters, and Detective Rhino Berry wanted to keep it quiet." Pieces of the puzzle click into place. "I read a lot, and I know that cops usually keep details of the crimes to themselves." (Actually, I know it from *Law & Order* reruns, but how embarrassing to admit that.) "Like something in their back pocket for when they have a real suspect. But you didn't even question anyone about it. Instead you kept your mouth shut about monsters."

"Now wait just a second." His tongue is sharp on the consonants. "You're making some serious allegations, young lady. I think we should meet to talk about this."

I can't help the hurt seeping into my voice. "How long are you going to help them keep it quiet, Shane? How long are you going to lie to me? Why would you give me my case file if you were just going to act like I was having a nervous breakdown? You sent Jeanie's dad to jail even though you know he didn't do it. You're just letting Daniel think his dad is a killer."

"Kent Talcott confessed," Shane snarls.

"So effing what? His wife and daughter are dead. Surprise, he's messed up in the head."

"I really think we should talk about this in person." From his uneven tone, I can hear the effort it's taking him to stay calm. "We've been getting noise complaints about a party at Cole Damsk's house. Are you there? I can come meet you."

I have never for a second been afraid of Detective Tim Shane. I've trusted him more than anyone other than Zoey, but alarm threatens to make my voice quaver as I lie, "Yeah, I'm in the upstairs bathroom. But I'm not going to stay here for long, so maybe tomorrow." I hang up before he can reply. I was right, but there's no wave of satisfaction, only a sickly sense of losing the solid ground I was standing on.

I crawl under my covers and curl around my bunny. "I wish Sam were here," I whisper into its floppy ear. Eventually, I stop jittering and push everything to the back of my mind for tomorrow. I'm half-asleep, in that sticky middle world of distorted shapes and tie-dye colors, when my phone buzzes. I expect it's a still angry Shane, but instead it's Caleb.

"Caleb?" I answer.

"Stella." Caleb's voice is almost drowned out by thumping music. "I need you to come meet me." Then louder and muffled, like he's pressing the cell to his mouth. "I'm at Cole's. Zoey got hammered.... I tried talking to her about Jeanie.... She freaked out ... ran off into the woods." The shouts and bass fade as he moves away from the house. "If she hears you calling her—"

Before he's finished I'm out of bed, pulling leggings on. "I'm on my way. Meet me in front of Cole's."

"Thanks, Stella," he shouts, and then the line goes quiet. I fumble with a pair of Converse tennis shoes and pull a hoodie over my head. I hope Zoey really is having a full-on attack, because if she isn't already, she's going to once she sees that I'm wearing zero makeup in public. I pull my hair into a ponytail as I tiptoe down the stairs. No sense waking Dad for this drama.

My car sputters curbside as I turn the key. Once the engine's roaring, I speed off across town. Cole lives on the opposite side of Savage like Zoey, but in a newly developed neighborhood, with giant grassy backyards butting up against Blackdog State Park. The houses are mini mansions with waterfall pools, movie theaters, and snaking driveways.

I roll through stop signs and hold my breath for luck as I speed through red lights. The idea of Zoey, alone, drunk, and vulnerable, in the woods while this Creeping or whatever you call it is on the prowl, is too much. I will not lose anyone else. Especially not Zoey; I would never survive.

I sail through a fork in the road. To the right is the highway leading straight to Old Savage Cemetery and Blackdog Lake. I go left, and a mile down is Cole's serpentine driveway. Cars are parked along it, most haphazardly, taking up more lawn than drive. Cole's house looks about to burst at the seams, it's so jam-packed with kids. Brightly colored lanterns hanging from the awning make it look etched in hard candy. A glittering gingerbread home bright as a lighthouse on the edge of the dark forest behind it. I desert my Volvo cockeyed, blocking the four-car garage, and dash toward the multitiered front porch.

Caleb paces furiously at the bottom of the stairs, eyes glued to his cell, oblivious to the yips and hollers of the tipsy partygoers just above him on the steps.

"Caleb!" I shout.

He jerks his head and waves for me to follow before I even reach him. As I scurry past a pulsing blob of juniors and seniors encircling a keg—a mass of holding hands, bumping shoulders, swaying hips, lapping tongues—I pull my phone from my pocket and scroll to Sam's name. Too many pairs of blinking eyes sticking to me for someone not to mention me being here. Sam will hear that I came to a party tonight. I'm probably already tagged as attending this sloshfest or in the back of someone's sepia-tinted picture.

My thumb jabs the send button. I don't want Sam to think I felt like going to a party after everything we said to each other this morning. But calling him to explain why I am where I am in the middle of the night when I'm not even certain he'll answer my call (or worse, he will answer because he's still Sam, and that means he's impossibly good) right after I accused him of an unspeakable crime doesn't seem like a great idea. I hit the end button after the first ring and slide the cell into my hoodie pocket. I'll call in the morning. I'll apologize. I'm sure he won't forgive me, but I'll try. I reach Caleb lingering at the tree line.

"Where's Michaela?" I ask. The forest floor vibrates with bass.

"She went home already. Zo was playing beer pong with some guy and she called for a ride. So I show up and she loses it. Screaming and crying. Bitch-fest. And I try to talk to her, answer her questions from last night, like I told you." He throws his arms in the air. "I've never seen her so out of control." Caleb's blond hair is dark with sweat, and his cheeks are bright red. He must have chased after her.

"Which way did she go?"

Caleb shines the beam of a flashlight he's holding to the right, in the direction of the swamps and Blackdog Lake.

"C'mon," he says, taking me by the elbow.

People say there's a little tickle of intuition right before something bad happens. You know, like an imp whispering, "Lock the door!" or "Don't let that person in!" or "Run!" Victims regret not listening to it. I always thought that was bullshit, victims blaming themselves for not being clairvoyant. But in that instant, when Caleb touches me, I feel a tiny trill of panic at the base of my skull. I shake my head and it's gone. Only goose bumps from loud music and cold air.

We jog deep into the woods. Poplars, birch, and hemlock knit together, framing token-size bits of sky illuminated by moonlight; the northern air thick with summer mosquitoes. I leap over knotted black roots bursting through the soil. Caleb works the flashlight right to left, scanning every clearing. The beam leaves long shadows from trees crisscrossing everywhere.

I shout, "Zoey, it's me! Come out!" again and again.

After ten minutes I hunch over to catch my breath. "Do you really think she went this far? We're halfway to Blackdog, and she'd never go through the swamp alone," I pant.

Caleb stops at my side. "She didn't go back to the house. We would've seen her." His eyes dart right to left with the beam of the flashlight; his pupils swallow up the pale blue of his eyes, and his lips are so distorted by a grimace they're near cracking.

"Hey," I say, placing my hand on his shoulder. His sweatshirt is damp under my palm, and he's shivering. "Caleb, look at me. We'll find her."

He takes a hasty step back. "I'm fine," he says, a tattered edge to it. He nods to himself, mutters under his breath, and then adds louder, "We can't stop hunting for her."

The distant caw of a night bird makes the hair on my arms stand on end. I squint through the beam of the light he's aiming at me. "I can't see with that in my eyes," I say.

"Sorry," he mumbles. The beam drops away, and silver spiders blossom in front of me as I blink to adjust to the dark. "You didn't see how out of control she was, Stella. I bet she's too wasted to find her way back—or—or even know how far she's gone," he adds. We're only a foot or two apart, and his eyes don't rest on anything for long. He's frightened for Zoey.

I rub at my arms. "We'll find her, okay? You don't need to worry. If anyone can take care of herself, it's Zo." I want to believe it, but I don't think anyone walks away from what might be poaching in these woods—other than me. I got away from the Creeping, or else it didn't want me.

Caleb scratches the back of his head, continuing to scan the space around us. "Yeah, I guess. Let me try to call her," he says.

I nod, reassured by the idea. I should have thought of that. I assumed that because Zoey ran off during a fight, she left her cell and purse at Cole's. The phone could be tucked into her pocket, though.

Caleb transfers the flashlight to his left hand. In the instant his right hand passes under the shaft of light toward the pocket where his cell must be stowed, shadows like black sores are cast on his skin.

"What's on your hand?" I ask, alarmed. I reach as if to brush away the dirt or insects that have landed on him, but as he retrieves the cell and holds the top of his hand up for me to see, there's nothing there. It was only the angle of the light exaggerating every little pit and imperfection of his skin. "It looked like something was on you," I murmur, frowning.

"They're scars," he says with a shrug. "From the chicken pox. I scratched too much." He shines the light on the faint blemished tissue for me to see. When shining straight on, the beam illuminates them as the pale, pinkish scars I've seen a million times and hardly noticed. When the light comes from the side, his skin has the look of a pot-holed membrane, a leper's hand, *a gnarled hand.*

He holds the cell at his ear. He shifts the flashlight, and I squint into it again. My throat is siphoning off my air supply. My body's reacting to what my brain is limping to grasp. "I have this memory"—I only know I'm talking after I hear myself—"of someone's gnarled hands in Jeanie's hair."

He takes a step forward. The light shines brighter in my face, and I can't see his expression. I try to visor my eyes from the light. "But it wasn't you. You were home sick," I say, breathless. I shake my head to clear it.

A sharp crack of a stick behind me—or maybe I hear the electronic chiming from a few feet away first? It's a phone, but it isn't Zoey's ring. I spin around just in time to see Daniel closing in, his face flash-illuminated by the shaft of light. He wields a thick branch above his head and before I can duck, he brings it down on me.

Chapter Twenty-Seven

The knotted branch smashes into my arm and sends me crashing to the ground. It has something barbed at its tip; its spiked cluster burrows deep into my shoulder. My nerves take a few seconds to catch up, and at first I scream because I anticipate the pain. Once I feel it, there's no more screaming, or air in my lungs, or noise over the buzzing in my ears. Fire spreads from the gash to my chest and down my arm.

Daniel twists the stick free; it doesn't come out easily. I hear the jagged splitting of my skin and muscle tissue like the parting of a zipper.

"What the hell was that?" Caleb yells.

Daniel laughs—actually laughs, like Caleb's told a joke—and says, "The little bitch deserves it. This was all her fault. Jeanie was *her* fault."

I lie writhing on the ground, reduced to one sensation: pain. Hot, goring pain ripping my arm apart. Pain so bad it has its own pulse.

Even maimed, my broken body the proof of the danger I'm in, the threat doesn't feel real. What does is the pain and confusion. I don't understand how we got here—not *here* in the woods but entrenched in this awful fantasy where Daniel and Caleb are arguing in whispery voices and I'm collapsed on the ground.

My vision tunnels, and I battle to stay focused. Instinct tells me that staying awake means staying alive. Then I have laughter bubbling up from nowhere, because how absurd that I'm worried about staying alive with Caleb—even Daniel. I bite my tongue, shocking myself alert. I focus on my shoulder; my sweatshirt is already black with blood. I'm bleeding. My insides are emptying on the outside. The manic laughter dries up in my throat. My hands search the ground around me, fingers splaying in the dirt, desperate for anything to be used as a weapon. Then I remember. My cell is in my pocket, and the last number I dialed was Sam's.

I slip the phone from my hoodie, hit send, and bring it to my ear. Sam calls my name on the other end. I want to cry out for him. I choke down a sob and replace the phone quickly without them noticing.

"Caleb! Daniel!" I shout, and the pain magnifies. "My dad knows I'm at Cole's. He knows Cole's house backs up against Blackdog Lake." There. That has to be enough for Sam.

Daniel's head snaps my way. He's glaring. "Shut up," he orders. "We're wasting time. Let's get her moving." They lumber toward me. I shrink back, hands tearing at the slippery topsoil behind me, but I know there's no escaping two full-grown guys, especially with a wounded arm.

They drag me to my feet and wrap both my arms around their necks. My shoulder kills as I'm jostled forward. They stride hurriedly through the woods; my feet don't touch the ground, and I'm yanked back and forth. They struggle to keep in step with each other, and it feels as if I'm being torn in two. As we career down a steep grade in the forest floor, my phone bounces from my sweatshirt pocket and clips my knee, tumbling to the ground. The boys barrel forward without noticing. There goes my only chance of keeping Sam on the line, of calling for help once we arrive wherever we're headed.

They avoid the bogs, moving toward the lakeshore in a deflected path. Our trajectory keeps us on solid but uneven earth. The thumping bass is long gone. How I wish I could trade places with anyone in that party, even loose-lipped Janey Bear.

We were closer to the water than I thought, because within ten minutes the moon's reflection winks up at us. It's full and white and obscured only by the tattered strips of clouds. Our pace slows on the shore; the boys pick their steps carefully over the rocks.

"Why are you doing this, Daniel?" I whimper. "I was helping you. I haven't given up looking for Jeanie's killer. I won't, I swear."

"God, you're a stupid bitch," he snarls right in my ear. "Don't you get it? That's the problem. One of these days you're going to remember that it was *me* who killed Jeanie."

His confession slaps me in the face. I trusted him. I protected him. For years I defended him. For years I defended myself to him. *I hate this boy. I hate this boy.* I try to squirm away from Daniel, but he holds my arm, digging his fingers through the tears in my sweatshirt and into my gash. I scream until my voice is a bloody wail.

"Caleb, please," I rasp. "Help me, Caleb."

They drop me where the water laps rhythmically against the pebbled shore. My knees hit first, the rocks gouging through my leggings. "Oh, sweetheart," Daniel says bitingly. "Caleb isn't going to help you. Caleb killed Jeanie too."

"No, you're wrong," I say. I try to get to my feet but stumble backward. The icy water sinks like fangs into my skin. The cold helps me focus. I splash some on my shoulder to extinguish the fire burning there. "We were just little kids, Caleb." I can't drag my eyes from his hands. They would have been blistered by chicken pox the day Jeanie was taken. "Caleb." My voice becomes more desperate. "Even if you were there somehow . . . none of it was your fault. It couldn't be." How could it? "I was there too. We were little kids."

Caleb stands a foot up the shore. His silhouette reminds me of the flickering flame of a candle—one that's about to be blown out. "It's more than feeling guilty over playing in the woods. I lied to you earlier," he mutters, resigned.

I reach out to him, hoping he'll help me up, walk us away from Daniel. "The police will understand. You were only nine. Whatever you did, it must have been an accident. It'll be okay," I insist.

He keeps the divide between us. "It's too late for that." His voice cracks. "It's not just Jeanie. If they find out what we did, they'll blame us for the girl in the cemetery, too." Caleb sinks to his knees. The flashlight clatters from his hand onto the rocks. Its thin beam juts into the sky. "I didn't touch her. I swear it, Stella. I wasn't even back in Savage. I didn't come until I saw on the news that you found the body. That thing got her. I had nothing to do with it. She just . . . showed up dead and brought this whole thing back to life. The way she looked . . ." His eyes stretch wide and his mouth contorts as he pounds his fists into the rocky shore—once, twice, three times. Dark liquid oozes from his knuckles, but if they hurt, he doesn't show it.

Caleb rocks back on his heels. "*Whatever* killed her ruined our lives. No one was looking for us. Not until that body showed up. Maybe it's the goddamned devil making us pay?" He covers his mouth with his mangled hand for a beat. When it drops away, there's a smear of blood on his lips as red as cherry lip gloss. "You don't think whatever it is was pissed that we'd gotten in on its game, do you? Like we took something it wanted? Like it killed that little girl to rip this whole Jeanie thing open again so we'd be caught?" Caleb's voice becomes less human with each word. He's gulping, choking on tears or air. This is what becomes of those who believe, of those who see monsters in the shadows.

He sways, rocking himself from hysteria to calm like you'd rock a baby. "No, it's just a coincidence," he mutters to himself. "But who will believe that? They'll want us to pay for what was done to her." He bows his head, lips moving. He looks up abruptly and whispers, "That's it. It's just a coincidence." Caleb's rant sends a current charging up my spine. By the time it reaches my brain, it's screaming, *There are no coincidences.*

I search for anything that won't make it so. "Daniel, your dad confessed—to—to everything." Daniel paces, kicking his boots with every step and scattering the pebbles that cover the banks of the lake. Caleb's a lump on the shore, but Daniel's a mounting storm. I point at him and cry, "You told the cops you thought he did it," shaking because I'd rather it be Mr. Talcott than Caleb and Daniel.

Daniel recklessly swings the branch he bloodied me with back and forth like a pendulum. "He's the reason we were out in those woods hunting a monster in the first place." He stills abruptly. "*And he knows it.* He knows he put it in our heads." He stabs the stick in the air between us. "Don't you get it? It was hunting the monster that got Jeanie killed. *It was his fault.*" His volume climbs. "He knew he was the reason I did it—*all of it.* That's why he confessed. And I let him, because if it wasn't for him, it wouldn't have happened." His jaw clenches and he shakes his head. "It wasn't the plan. Griever was. It was her fault too. If we hadn't seen her put a dog down, we wouldn't have thought to try it."

"It *needed* a sacrifice," Caleb whispers—the sort of whisper you use for telling vile, dirty secrets. "It was hungry for more than some flea-bitten mutts."

Daniel's lips press into a puffy, uneven seam. I can't tell if he's grimacing or smiling. "You and Jeanie were in the woods. We were shooting arrows. Caleb said we needed to leave the thing a little blood." He gives Caleb a look that could make a tree wither and die. "I aimed an arrow at you. It was just supposed to nick you." He stands rigid over me, his chin on his chest as he looks at his hand. There's blood on it from my shoulder. He rubs his fingers together, staring at the human smear—most likely contemplating the universe's symmetry that here we are and he finally has a bit of my blood for what we hunted.

"But the arrow hit my sister," he continues in a distant way. "It sank into her stomach." His eyes cut from the blood to me. "I told you to stay with her. You didn't. We couldn't lead my mom back. The woods were too big, and without you to mark where she was . . . You showed up an hour later at the house . . . sniveling."

I can't hold Daniel's eye contact anymore. He's too removed from the pain of Jeanie's death; his stare is too hungry for something I can't identify. "But Caleb, you couldn't have been there. You were home with the chicken pox. Zoey had it too." I'm arguing more with myself than with Daniel or Caleb. I know what I saw in the light of the flashlight. It doesn't stop me from needing to see it again. This is *Caleb*.

I pick my way over the rocks to him. I lift Caleb's hand to my face, wipe the smattering of blood away, and squint through the moonlight. It becomes all so horribly clear. I've seen the faded scars a million times before. They were seething red blisters when he held Jeanie's head. Now they're almost unnoticeable. Everything seems larger when you're a kid. Kids make monsters out of everything.

"The wood connects your two houses," I say. "You snuck out and snuck back in without anyone noticing." How could I have been such an idiot? Believed even for a minute in something that couldn't possibly exist? *There's no such thing as monsters.* Only bad people. Shane told me: You can be *that* wrong about people. He said you can miss what's really inside. He was right.

"Caleb . . ." Saying his name brings on a deluge of memories: Caleb building blanket forts; Caleb boosting me up to look at the bird's nest in the porch eaves; Caleb grinning through the window as he idled in front of Mom's house last December—staying with him felt like being home. "Why did you come over earlier? Was the whole thing an act, Caleb?" I shove his chest, try to force him to look at me, but he won't. "You wanted to know what I knew?" I scream into his ear. "You want to know what I know now? You fucking lied to me. You're my family." I hammer my fists into his chest, but he never raises his head, and eventually, I can't bear both the pain in my shoulder and the pain in my heart. My hands drop to my sides. At some point I start to cry. Tears trickle down my cheeks like icebergs carving their way through the North Sea.

Finally, Daniel answers for Caleb. "We needed to know if you were letting it go after my dad was arrested or if you were going to keep being a problem." I played right into Daniel's hands. I told Caleb I wouldn't stop; I swore I'd remember everything.

My tears slow. I have to pull it together if I'm going to survive this. I have to outthink them or devise a way that makes it okay for us to walk out of the woods together. Jeanie was an accident. A tragic *accident*. "Why didn't you tell the cops it was just an accident?"

Daniel paces, hand raking through his hair like he means to pull it out. His eerie calm has blown over and the storm's returned. "There's no body, no proof that it was. But really, my mom kept it from the cops because she thought we did something so bad to Jeanie that we had to hide her body. I couldn't even prove that I hadn't meant to hurt my sister, because *you* didn't stay with her like I told you to." He swallows like he's going to be sick.

The Talcotts' stares, all those years stuffed full of them, were never because I survived and Jeanie didn't; they were watching me like a slow-motion car wreck, guessing at what I'd seen Daniel do to Jeanie, wondering when I'd remember, when I'd steal their other child away with what was lost inside my head.

"My mother never looked at me the same," he says louder, planting his feet on the rocks. "And then Jeanie was everywhere. She was a vindictive little bitch at six. Always disagreed with me. Never shut up. I tried to *teach* her." His empty hand fists at his side, and I know I've heard similar words before. *Don't make me teach you.*

Daniel said it to Jeanie when he thought no one was listening. I can see the afternoon as if I'm there, reliving it. He had that rusted coffee tin, the tiny holes in the lid so the bloated spiders could breathe. The three of us—me, Daniel, and Jeanie—were just beyond the strawberries. Daniel wanted us to search for owl pellets, the gut-shaped masses of bone fragments and membrane that owls vomit. Daniel liked to dissect them, to reconstruct the tiny skeletons. Jeanie told him we wanted to play dolls instead. In response he pushed the tin into her arms like she'd been begging for it. She bit back tears. Now I recognize it as the same tin Jeanie wore on a string as a necklace in the Polaroid. I recall that nothing frightened Jeanie as much as spiders did.

I was six. I didn't understand it was Daniel's way of punishing her, of *teaching* her to do what he wanted.

Daniel snorts. "Guess I'm not shocked she's fucking with me in death." He says it like he's watching the memory play in my eyes. "I see Jeanie everywhere. Crowds of people wear her face. I catch her reflection standing behind me. I hear her froggy little voice. She's taunting me. She's waiting for me to get mine." He closes the distance between us, hovers over me as I shrink back. "She's waiting for you to remember," he shouts. "It gets worse near the anniversary. I can't close my eyes without her there. She's wherever I am, laughing, watching me, walking down the sidewalk alone. . . ."

He straightens up. Something's changed in him. He's bigger against the inky sky, as though he's drawing on its vastness. "You can't imagine all the times I worried about what you knew or suspected or dreamed." He raises the branch so the barbed end is inches from my face.

"For years I tried to make you tell me; I tried to frighten you into keeping your mouth shut. Then I realized something. You would remember. There was no if, only when." He tilts his head and continues in a whisper, "I needed to beat you to it. Reopening the case was my only shot. You were going to remember and tell them what I did." He makes me sound like I'm the villain, the killer out to steal his life away. "I needed to come back here. I needed to find Jeanie's body. Never finding it had me fucked up. It's somewhere." He nods. "It's in the woods where *you* left it. Or Griever took it, buried it. I thought if I could find it, prove that Griever had it all these years, the cops would arrest her. No one would give a shit about a memory you came up with in the face of physical evidence."

He angles closer, the branch's spike nudging my temple. "Do you know my mother blamed me once the redhead showed up in the cemetery? She didn't believe I wasn't responsible. Some neighbor called to tell her that a body had been found. She was waiting for me when I got home, hours after the bonfire. She was going to tell the cops what she thought we'd done to Jeanie. Can you believe that?" His mouth twists in disdain. "Her own son. She wasn't even going to wait until morning. She just wanted to tell me to my face first—she cried that she owed me that. Jane Doe was all the proof she needed that I was the pervert she always thought."

Daniel muffles a wet sob that comes out of nowhere and draws the branch back like he's winding up to strike me with it. I recoil, but at the last second he hurls the bloody stick into the lake. "I begged her to listen. Dad was sleeping." His fingers rub hard against his cheeks, contorting his features.

This is the moment when I realize that there's no going back; the three of us aren't walking out of these woods together. It's so much more than Jeanie and the accident.

"She had the phone, she was crying hysterically. And then . . . then she turned her back on me, dialing the cops. Weird how hard it was to keep the phone cord around her neck," he says, almost as a side thought. He covers his own neck with his hand and mimics strangling her. "She was stronger than she looked."

My mind races. *This can't be happening.* Not Daniel. Not Caleb. *Especially not Caleb.* "But my hair . . . it was braided." It's such a stupid thing to say. As if that one little detail can save me; as if I can prove to Daniel he didn't do it and we can all return home.

"Mom got you to shut up," Daniel says. "You were blubbering from being lost. She didn't figure on your mom noticing. But now I've spent too much goddamned time worrying about what you suspect or what you remember." He smirks lopsidedly with the admission. "You're a loose end. Zoey was a loose end."

Zoey. I figured Caleb's whole story had been a lie. An ugly ruse to draw me out here alone. "Caleb, where's Zoey?" My tone climbs with alarm.

Caleb's features are slack as he stares at me, a mournful ghoul's face carved up by long shadows. "I told her to shut her mouth. I warned her. She kept saying, 'How could you keep this from me?' She wouldn't stop asking how. How? How? How?" The word is like the dying caw of a crow. He reaches for me, taking hold of both my arms, shaking me in rhythm to his quivering bottom lip.

I hold myself stiff under his tremulous grip. "Caleb, what happened to Zoey?"

"I—I didn't mean to hit her, but she wouldn't stop. In my face, drunk, brought me out back from the party, slapping me." Caleb releases me, bringing his palm down hard on his cheek. "She said, 'I know you.' She said it like she could see my insides. 'I know what you're hiding.'" His nasally pitch imitates Zoey. "'I can see the guilt all over your face.' I didn't mean to hit her." He's on all fours now, crawling away from the lapping water to the tree line. This isn't the Caleb who baited my fishing line when I was small because I couldn't stomach touching worms. Not the Caleb whose face is as familiar as a brother's.

I move to go after Caleb—Caleb, but *not Caleb*—but Daniel seizes my wagging ponytail and drags me to my feet. "What did you do to Zoey, Daniel?" I whimper.

He grins, turning me around on the sweep of rocky beach so that we're facing the water. "Nothing. She did it all to herself, and it's fucking beautiful. That nosy bitch wouldn't stop asking questions. Caleb hit her and she lost it. But then the most wonderful thing happened." Daniel pulls me tight to his side. I look down the length of his extended arm. At the center of the lake is a small square dock for swimmers. I know that it's barely long or wide enough to lie on. Zoey and I sunbathed there freshman year when seniors took over the cove. We'd swim out and sit all breathless and bleary-eyed from the distance.

"She ran from us. Probably meant to run for help, but she was drunk, ran into the woods rather than away from them. I give her credit because the twat was fast," he whispers the vile words right into my ear. "But then she ran out of land and went thrashing into the lake. Heard her gulping for air most of the way to the dock. Probably choking on her own puke, she was so hammered. Then nothing. She got there and passed the eff out. It won't take long for her to roll into the water." He smiles wide and wet, with spit glistening on his chapped lips. "She'll drown."

Chapter Twenty-Eight

You're going to kill us both?" I try to be brave, but my strength crumbles and I sob. I drag my good arm across my face to wipe the snot away.

"No, sweetheart, *you're* gonna kill yourself." Daniel tightens his hold on my ponytail, twisting my neck so I'm looking at him out of the corner of my eye. "It's simple. Swim to save her." He exhales in my face, filling my nostrils with rancid breath. Hot, moist lips turning my skin green with their poisonous words. I run my hand over my gash. My hoodie is soaked with blood. I'm woozy on my feet, and I won't last long in the water. That's the point, though. That's why Daniel injured me, isn't it?

The light flashes in Daniel's eyes as he smirks. "You know what they'll say about the two of you? Zoey was a whore, always getting wasted at parties. No one will be surprised she swam out too far. You're her lackey, so of course you fell in the woods going after her, drowned trying to reach her. You're lucky that it worked out this way.

I wanted to jump you, make it look like that freak show that Caleb's pissing his pants over got you." If I wasn't already shivering violently, I'd start after hearing their twisted plan. What's worse is that it will work.

"What if I won't do it?" I bluff.

Daniel raises an eyebrow. "That's your best friend, isn't it? All that sisterly love and pussy power. I tell you what. If you reach her—and it's a big if, since you're not looking so hot, princess—I swear we'll row out to get her," he says, grinning wickedly, crossing his heart with his free hand.

"And me?"

"You we'll knock out and throw into the water. You drown no matter what." He releases my hair and shoves me. I catch myself at the edge of the obsidian water. "Drowning is better than getting eaten or torn up or—what's your monster do to those little girls, Caleb?" Daniel laughs like it's all a big joke.

"Shit, he has mush for brains." Daniel takes a few steps away and jabs his finger at Caleb, who's standing with his hunched back to the trees. "I couldn't believe my luck when this idiot rolled into town. Fucking coward was pissing his pants when I told him what I did to my mom to keep *us* out of jail." Daniel advances on Caleb. "What'd you tell me about Jane Doe?" he taunts. "It was the monster that did it to her?"

Daniel looks over his shoulder at me, smothering a contemptuous laugh. "He actually thinks that creature tucked a finger bone into the little redhead's hand." His grin widens, and he winks just as he did the afternoon at the cove—as if we're sharing a joke. He faces Caleb again. "You think it sliced the girl's scalp off, took a bite, and put the rest of it back? Your monster's got self-control, does it?" He spits a fat wad on the ground. Caleb stares at his shoes even as Daniel closes in on him. "Hey, look at me. Shit," he snarls, sending a spray of saliva at Caleb. "You're a fucking idiot. You wanna know what goes bump in the night?" A pause. "I do. I'm the monster."

I have trouble looking away from Caleb. He looks too much like his sister. *Zoey*. My legs twitch with a shot of adrenaline. They're twitching to run, to escape, to survive. I whirl around to face the lake, pressing my palms hard against the thudding in my chest, a wild hummingbird heartbeat near exploding. I order my feet to move for a minute before they get the signal. When they finally do, I stagger forward, stumbling, splashing up to my ankles.

I could make a run for it. I'm injured, though, and I'm not sure how fast I'd be. My gaze flicks back to Daniel and Caleb. Daniel shoves his fists into Caleb's chest. Caleb pushes back. They're distracted. With a head start I could hide in the woods. I could swim out a few yards and tread water, or float if I'm too weak, at least until Sam and the cops get here. Really, there are a dozen ways I could try to stay alive. But with every passing minute of Zoey knocked out on that bit of an island, it's more likely she'll drown. Even if I reach her, I won't be able to do more than keep her on that dock. Even in better conditions—sun shining, tepid water, and my shoulder not bleeding and split open—I'm not strong enough to tow her limp body to the opposite shore. Daniel and Caleb bet their whole plan on my love for

Zoey. On my willingness to die in order to save her. And I'm helpless but to play right into their hands.

My shoulder spasms as I throw my hoodie over my head; its angry buzz threatens to pull me deep into a soupy haze. I kick my tennis shoes from my feet and peel off my socks. I finally step deeper into the lake. The water's so cold it burns. It won't be swimmable until July. Great. I'll add hypothermia to the list of things that might kill me tonight. The dark water laps at my knees, my thighs, my waist. I shove off, closing my eyes and baring my teeth, reaching forward in a breaststroke.

I dunk my face, trying to bear the pain and cold all at once. I surface, mouth gaping open, a silent scream rising from my frozen lungs. The chill tears at my skin, hammers into my spine, drills into my head. I dunk back under and reach forward to propel myself again. I do it ten more times and the numbness begins setting in. The less sensation in my arms, the more I can move my injured shoulder. I pick up the pace, aware that I don't have long, aware that death is chasing me.

Ten more strokes and no matter how I gulp air, I can't catch my breath. My legs kick slowly, suddenly too heavy to move through the water. I get stuck under, unable to lift my head above the surface, like Jeanie really is weighing me down. No, Jeanie is dead. Daniel and Caleb killed her. *Like they're killing Zoey.*

A little surge of panic electrifies my limbs, and I hit the surface. But I don't stop. I never stop. Not until my outstretched fingers jam into the dock. I grip its edge and scream, "I made it!"

There are muffled voices from far off, but they're dwarfed by the thrumming in my head. I feel blindly on the dock above me; my icicle hand jabs at empty space. I kick to move around the dock's perimeter, dragging myself to its other side. As I round the corner, Zoey's tiny silhouette slides into the water. I dive forward to catch her before she descends too deep to be found. The water is thicker now, harder to cut through with a kick, as if it's freezing to a solid. Or maybe I am?

Pins and needles attack my wide-open eyes as I catch her; her skin scalds mine. *She still has blood flowing through her veins.* I fight to bring our heads out of the water. Hers hangs to the side at an awful angle; her lips are parted, with buckets of water spewing out. I hook my bad arm under hers and reach with the other to grip the dock. It's smooth. No handles. No seams. My nails claw at the planks. A few nails splinter, but I don't feel them ripping away from the skin like I should.

"Help," I cry, spitting up water and bile with the words.

A curtain of clouds drifts over the moon. There are only flickers of its light on the tips of waves that keep getting higher. A voice shouts above the buzz in my head and the lapping water. It's a ghost's wail, carried to me on the current of the wind. "Hooooold ooooon!"

The words float out in front of me, and I see them bright violet against the darkness that surrounds me. They shimmer and dip into the water, sinking down, like Zoey's body wants to. I try to keep my hold on the dock, but my fingers slip.

Rather than Jeanie weighing me down, Zoey is. I hold her tighter, even if she's an anchor who's drowning us both. This is my Zoey: savage, hot-tempered, and loyal. I won't let her go. My legs are dead as we slip under the surface. I can't keep us afloat, so I just keep us together.

Bubbles escape my nose. We sink deeper into the inky depths. Burning-hot fingers wrap around my neck. Nails dig into my skin, and I open my mouth to scream but gulp water instead. It's the Creeping come to finish me off before a peaceful death can find me. It tightens its grip. I gag. A backdrop of hellish red is all there is.

I close my eyes just before I break the surface, too tired to see what sort of monster has me now. *No, no monsters.* Monsters don't exist. Bad people do, so they don't have to.

The hard lip of a boat scapes down my back as I'm hauled over it. I feel Sam's warm lips pressed to mine. *I'd know them anywhere.* He's breathing air into me. Water runs from the corners of my mouth, and I cough until the pith of my lungs feels shredded and dry. Sam is staring at me as my eyelids flicker open. The relief does something beautiful to his face. He goes from gaunt and pale to strong and determined with the oars of the boat in his hands. My tongue is numb as I try to hack the words out. Sam is here. Daniel and Caleb are here. Sam is in danger because of me.

"Daniel killed Jeanie," I gargle through fat, clumsy lips. Sam's smile corkscrews, and I know he heard me. The words make me dizzy. My head clunks against the bottom of the wooden boat. Zoey's slumped against me, the flurry of her heart rapid and light. Her head rocks with the boat's rising and falling, knocking against my temple, hammering an SOS into my skull.

At times I know what's happening, other times I don't. Shane is here. He came to Cole's. Sam found him, and they ran through the woods searching for me. In the same woods as the Creeping because of *me*. In the same woods as Daniel and Caleb. Monsters everywhere and nowhere.

Shane stands grimly on the shore, fists propped on his hips, bracing himself against the wind. I'm aware of my mouth moving, vomiting a jumble of warnings, accusations, pleas, and nonsense sounds. He should have known it was Daniel. He should have kept me safe. He should never have given me Jeanie's case file. He sent an innocent man to jail. I try to clamp my lips shut as I cry something about the Creeping.

Sam with his hands in my hair, stroking it, husky voice cooing in my ear. I'm rocking, ranting, raving as Caleb was in this very spot only minutes ago. Caleb left blood on the rocks; I'll leave behind everything that kept me immune from what happened to Jeanie. Shadowy faces of men with twisted appetites who snatched her from the woods. Vaguely imagined monsters who stalked her from tunnels in the understory. They shielded me from a truth I couldn't handle. As I twist my hands in Sam's shirt, as the shrieking propellers of a helicopter descend on us, I come unhinged. Finally, here it is, the wound that Jeanie left ripping me open.

I kick and spit when I'm loaded on the chopper without Sam. I howl to him that I'm sorry. That he has to forgive me because I need him more than he needs me. The giant bird goes airborne. The only reason I stop rioting is that Zoey is beside me. Sleeping peacefully. Sleeping beauty. She doesn't need to be awake for this.

Dad's waiting when we get to the hospital, pacing in striped pajama bottoms and a sweatshirt. He forgot his glasses, and he's blinking into the fluorescent lights. His eyes water when he sees me; I look bad even in his bleary-eyed state. I must appear haunted, the fury drained out of me, a ghost betrayed by someone she loved. I don't say anything about what happened, and he doesn't ask before I'm rushed to intensive care.

Zoey has her stomach pumped to get the booze up. I guess it was suspecting that Caleb was hiding something that caused her to drink enough to pass out; she couldn't stand reality and so she tried for alcohol-induced nothingness. The entire time the doctors work over me, musing at my tissue's rapid recovery from exposure to detrimental temperatures—their mumbo jumbo, not mine—I consider asking them to slice me open. Crack my rib cage. Take a peek at my heart. Fillet my scalp. Drill a hole in my skull. Look at my brain. I want them to diagnose the fatal flaw in me. The thing, however buried in my flesh, that made me blind to the monsters around me. I want them to remove it as they would a tumor.

Once the doctors have left, I stare hypnotized at the fifteen black stitches sewn in my skin. They remind me of the bramble growing through the strawberry vines. They're meant to piece me back together. Fat chance. I'm the relic of a child who saw brother kill sister. Child kill child. No wonder I didn't remember.

A nurse bustles around me, tucking me into a hospital gurney. She lets me borrow a compact mirror. I run my fingers over the skin of my bloodless lips.

"The stiches look worse than they are," the nurse clucks, attempting a reassuring smile.

She's wrong. Everything is much, *much* worse than it looks. But why bother telling her? She wouldn't understand. She didn't half drown saving her best friend from said best friend's brother. She wasn't attacked by a man who killed his sister and his mother.

Eventually, the doctors decide that I'm stable enough for visitors. Dad, Sam, and Shane are ushered into the hospital room. Dad hugs me until he catches me grimacing from the twinge in my shoulder. I take shallow breaths and promise him it doesn't hurt badly. It does, but not so much as the razor-sharp puzzle in the soft gray matter of my brain. Monster. No monster. Daniel and Caleb. The Creeping. Jeanie's killer. Jane Doe's killer. Betty Balco's killer. It's so many shapes, it's shapeless.

"Looks like you put that through a meat grinder," Shane says, pointing to my right hand and torn-off fingernails. Two cigarettes are tucked behind his ear, and his whole face is carved up with worry lines. His big oven-mitt palm pats me on the head. "I'm glad you're okay, kid. You told me enough of what happened for now. We'll talk about everything once you're up to it."

Shane turns and heads for the door, broad shoulders collapsed forward.

"Shane," I call. "Did you find Daniel and Caleb?"

He turns partially around, half his face shadowed. "No, but there were traces of blood. Signs of a fight. We were able to re-create what happened. Caleb and Daniel chased Zoey out onto the water. They held you against your will. They confessed to killing Jeanie and Bev Talcott. Caleb and Daniel fought. There are signs of an escalating struggle. We're not sure if they fled into the woods when they heard our sirens or before. The boys will turn up," Shane assures my dad.

Dad nods, satisfied at the promise of justice. After Shane leaves, Dad claps Sam on the back and kisses my forehead. "I think I'll go see if we can find you a decent cup of coffee and a muffin in this place." He kisses my cheek. "That will fix you right up, Pumpkin." He pads out of the room, relieved to find some way he can help.

Sam leans over the hospital gurney, his round eyes dilating as he studies the bruises on my neck. I have the imprint of his hand from him fishing me out of the lake. "I'm sorry I did that to you," he whispers, skimming the injured skin with his fingertip. "If—if something had happened to you . . ."

I duck my head and kiss the top of his hand. "I'm so sorry for what I said this morning. You got hurt, and I was scared that something worse could happen to you. And then you were asleep and I was confused and suspicious. But Sam, you saved me." He probably thinks I mean by rescuing me from drowning. I mean more than that. I lace my fingers in his. Blisters forming on his palms from rowing across the lake catch on my palms.

He inches farther onto the bed. "The day Jeanie died, my dad had too many beers on his lunch break and dropped a piece of canning equipment. He broke his leg in two places, and my mom and I were in the emergency room with him."

I hide my face in the crook of my elbow. "I shouldn't have asked.

I shouldn't have needed you to tell me," I say, my voice muffled by my skin. Sam pulls my arm down and kisses my cheek. I blink, surprised. "You forgive me?"

His eyes crinkle at their corners, and he laughs softly. "What do you think?"

I appraise him, trying to understand what I see. I am the lucky one. I have Sam *and* Zoey. They're both alive. "Daniel and Caleb killed Jeanie," I whisper, closing my eyes. Caleb's face flashes across the inside of my eyelids; I see him every time it's dark. Caleb on his knees, bloodied knuckles dragged across his mouth, rocking and ranting. Caleb wailing that it was the monster setting them up. That it was the appetite that haunts Savage, crawling out of the darkness to enact its revenge because Caleb and Daniel had taken something that it craved—Jeanie—that reopened the case. How could I have been so wrong about them? *I trusted them. I loved Caleb.*

"But what about Jane Doe?" Sam's eyes search mine.

There's an idea germinating in my head; it hasn't taken shape enough for me to explain it to Sam except to say, "Daniel sees Jeanie everywhere. He said crowds wear her face. He thinks Jeanie was there waiting for me to remember, waiting for him to get his. He hates her. He has Caleb believing it was the Creeping who took Jane Doe."

Sam bites his lip, appraising my expression. "You don't think so," he says.

I shake my head. "No, Sam. The timing is too much of a coincidence. Daniel hasn't been here in years, and when he finally comes back there's another body found? And it isn't just that. Daniel said something. He said that Caleb thought the monster had taken a bite out of Jane Doe's scalp and put the rest back. We didn't tell him about the missing piece, did we?"

The corners of Sam's mouth tug downward. "No, but someone in the police department could have when he was questioned. Or Zoey might have told Caleb, and Caleb could have told Daniel."

"I guess." I shake my head. "But it was more the way Daniel said it. He was bragging and gloating over how gullible Caleb was. He even winked at me. He said, 'I'm the monster.'"

"But what about Betty Balco and the others?" Sam asks. He isn't skeptical, just thoughtful.

I struggle to lift my head from the pillow, and he moves his arm to prop it up. He flanks me on the gurney. "They were taken almost ninety years ago. The police know, Sam. *Shane knows*. There's no appetite or force or monster. Whoever did it is human and dead," I say. I guide his face closer to mine. "Promise me. Swear to me that you won't go looking. That you'll stop believing in the Creeping or monsters or devils." Yes, it feels dangerous to tempt fate by staring into the dark for too long. But also, I don't need another mystery eating away at my edges, making me more like Caleb and Griever.

"What about the Norse folklore?" Sam asks. His eyes glow; he's determined to solve the puzzle. "What if there was something other than a man nibbling on those kids? What if it's still here? Two of the girls who were taken decades ago visited Norse Rock. What if that's where it lives? Norse Rock could be named because that's where the original settlers camped. That can't be a coincidence, can it?"

There are no coincidences. "Is it a coincidence that all the victims are redheads—that even Jeanie was a redhead? That those early Norse settlers who were maimed were probably blond or redheaded?"

My heart hiccups at his determination. I can't bear watching him eroded by believing. "There's no way for us to know if there's any truth to the Norse lore," I say, pressing closer to him. "We're not stalking through the woods in pursuit of a mythical monster. We're not six anymore with bows and arrows. We know better." Better isn't really how I feel about knowing that people do monstrous things; that even those you love are capable of them; that monsters aren't half as scary as human evil. "It doesn't exist, Sam. It's only a story. When Griever was young, more people told it. Someone, a bad man or a few of them, knew the story—or a version of it—and he thought he could use the superstition and fear to take little girls and get away with it. He's dead. The victims' families are dead."

The arm I'm on bows around me, and Sam shifts me closer to him. "You're saying the story was just a legend and someone used it as inspiration for their crimes?"

"Yes." I nod into his chest. "Stories have their own kind of power."

"Small towns are prone to panic," Sam admits reluctantly. His free hand absentmindedly smooths my hair. "There weren't actually any witches in Salem, but it didn't stop them from burning women. Savage in the 1930s wasn't exactly seventeenth-century Salem, but Savage was more isolated than it is now, and people would have been more superstitious."

"Exactly." I pull a little away to meet his eyes. For Sam's sake, I need to sound full of the conviction I want to feel more than I do. "Griever is what you become when you believe in what can't exist. This is over for us. Please. Promise that you'll stop looking too."

Sam tilts his head, doubt skittering across his eyes, but he says, "I promise," anyway.

Forty-five minutes after Dad's left, I convince Sam that I'll be fine alone until morning. He turns at the last moment on the threshold, propping the door open with his tennis shoe. He smiles and says something sweet—probably that he loves me—but I don't hear him. Because in that moment a family passes through the hallway. They're framed by the door for only a split second. The last to pass, a small girl lagging behind, cranes her neck for a better look at me. She scrunches up her freckled nose and smiles, revealing gaps from missing front teeth. As her mom ducks back to tow her away, her mop of red ringlets looks green in the fluorescent light. The door swings shut and she's gone, and I hear Daniel's voice on a loop in my head: *I see Jeanie everywhere.* I wonder if I will too?

I spend two days in the hospital. Hours spent staring at the yellowed, sagging ceiling tiles while Dad is at work and Sam is at BigBox. Hours of restless sleep where I awake sputtering for air and clawing at my pillow. Hours where I struggle with what Sam said. I know there is no ancient beast; I know who killed Jeanie and Mrs. Talcott. I think I know who killed Jane Doe. I know that Betty Balco's kidnapper must have been human; I know that he likely took the other missing girls and that he's dead, rotting in the ground.

The knowing doesn't stop the wondering. Not only because it's more painful to accept the very human appetites haunting Savage. It is. Also, there's a restlessness in my blood, making my veins itchy. I can't shake that elated and wild grin I wore in the Polaroid any more than I can shake Jeanie's bleak stare. I can't stop wondering if I was braver and more alive before Jeanie vanished and if losing her snuffed something out in me.

But mostly, I'm restless because deep down at my roots, I fear what Sam does. How do you disprove an ancient evil lurking in the woods? Even if we search Norse Rock, we can't search every dark nook and cranny of the forest. We can't traverse every narrow passageway in the undergrowth. We can't explore every mine shaft and every cave and every aerie in every treetop. How do we know that the Creeping isn't there, suckling on a little girl's finger bone?

Chapter Twenty-Nine

I sit swinging my legs along the side of my hospital gurney. Strike that. Not *my* hospital gurney anymore, since I'm waiting for Dad to pick me up and bring me home. The leg swinging makes me look upbeat and less like a traumatized schizo than cowering under the bed would, and if I'm going to get out of here, I can't look like I'm twitchy with PTSD. Trust me, inside I am.

Zoey went home yesterday. Before Caleb showed up at Cole's party, Zoey did a keg stand. After he arrived, she tried to drown her suspicion in Jell-O shots. Zoey knew Caleb was hiding something. It's why she bailed on Sam and me the night before. She waited all evening for him to leave the house. And when he finally did, she went through his drawers and came up with a strange black candle and a hunting knife he hadn't cleaned. Right there, barefoot in the middle of Caleb's childhood room, Zoey realized her brother had taken the head off the cat in the cemetery. As children Caleb and Daniel had seen Griever sacrifice a dog. It was the event that made them want to offer a smear of blood to stave off the monster.

Eleven years later, with the decapitated tabby cat in the cemetery, Caleb was still trying to give the monster its sacrifice. Sam was right: It wasn't Griever.

Zoey waited to confront Caleb, but he never came home. The next day she texted him about Cole's party; she told him Cole was asking about him, and he took the bait. After he arrived, Zoey dragged Caleb outside to confront him. She probably could have handled herself with only Caleb, but he had called for backup once he realized that she wasn't going to quit. Zoey said she didn't feel afraid until the moment Caleb's knuckles crunched against her face. When his fist came away, she saw how Daniel was looking at her, like he was going to finish the job.

For two days I've tried not to picture Zoey flailing through the woods, alcohol poisoning setting in, running for her life from her brother. I asked her why she didn't tell me about Caleb. She said she couldn't say what she was thinking about her brother out loud until she spoke with Caleb about it, until she knew for sure. I get that.

I was supposed to be released with her, but the skin around my stitches was swollen. They kept me another day to be sure the gash wasn't infected. I close my eyes and rub my temples. No infection, but I do have a bulldozing headache. Daniel's face flashes across the inside of my eyelids. *I see Jeanie everywhere.* So do I.

"You sleepwalking?" Shane interrupts my nightmare train of thought.

My eyelids snap open. His clothes are rumpled, and the lavender bulges under his eyes rival my own. "Yeah right, as if I sleep anymore."

His mouth sets in a bleak line. "Your dad said I could pick you up."

I shrug and jump off the bed, my sneakers slapping the tile floor and my head spinning.

"Should I call a nurse?" Shane grabs my elbow as I teeter.

"No, the painkillers make the room spin," I explain hastily. I want out of here.

Two minutes later Shane's holding the passenger-side door of his car open for me and placing my small overnight bag, stuffed with the few items Dad brought to the hospital, at my feet. I manage to buckle the seat belt across my chest without yelping. Shane's cleared away all the fast-food wrappers from the floor, but the upholstery still reeks of cigarettes, and there's a new coffee ring on the dash that shines sticky and fresh.

"So you and that Worth kid are a real item now?" Shane asks, steering out of the almost empty parking lot. A droplet of sweat runs from his hairline down his temple. I crack the window to let the June breeze in.

"We have ten minutes before my house and you want to waste it on who I'm dating?" I raise a quizzical eyebrow.

"No, I'm stalling." He looks at me for a long second, trying to determine my condition. Am I too broken to tell the truth to? I wave impatiently for him to continue. "We found Caleb."

"What?" I strain against my seat belt.

Shane keeps his gaze on the road. "A fisherman spotted tracks along Blackdog River early this morning. He followed them and found Caleb huddled in the hollow trunk of a fallen tree. Hadn't had water or a thing to eat for two days."

I sit up straighter. "What did he say?"

"He hadn't had any water or food while he was out there," Shane parrots himself.

I knock on the dashboard. "Yeah, hello, I heard you the first time. *What did he say?*"

"It's more complicated than that. He can answer our questions, sure, but he's . . . unwell."

I can tell by his reluctance that he doesn't want to continue. "Whatever it is, I can handle it, Shane."

He takes a deep breath. "He's painted a detailed picture of his involvement with Daniel. He reached out to Daniel on his way back to Savage. He only came back because he saw the coverage about Jane Doe. Daniel told him shortly after he arrived that he killed his mother to keep her quiet. Caleb made no effort to tell the police. He and Daniel conspired to frighten you off trying to remember Jeanie's death. He confessed to having Officer Reedy, who we've learned is a previous acquaintance of Caleb's, help by distracting his partner from watching your house when Caleb left the strawberries on your porch. Apparently, he knew Caleb and Daniel were on their way, and he insisted on a coffee break."

I drop back into the seat, wincing at the sting in my shoulder. Daniel and Caleb were pulling the strings all along. They left the lifeless strawberries on my porch. Caleb could have used one of Zoey's many misplaced keys to let himself into my house; Caleb and

Daniel rearranged the photos. Caleb threatened to tell my dad and the cops if I continued pursuing Jeanie's killer. They were trying to scare me off the investigation. Now that I really think about it, the only time Daniel cooperated with me was to bring me to Griever's. Daniel believed Griever had Jeanie's body; he hoped she'd implicate herself. He didn't know she'd tell us about the others or send us after monsters.

"Reedy's claiming he was blackmailed. Caleb has some incriminating pictures of him smoking marijuana at a party. Daniel learned about them and seized the opportunity," Shane rumbles on. "There's something else," he warns, sizing me up again out of the corner of his eye. "Under the stress of recent events and confronting you and Zoey, he's showing signs of a psychosis. It's situational, meaning that he's capable of having lucid conversations on some topics, but when discussing others, he's delusional. He's talked a lot about a monster. He doesn't have a name for it like you do. He said the monster chased them through the woods when they left you at the lake. It attacked Daniel."

I slump back. That's what happens to those who believe in what couldn't possibly exist. Caleb rocking and ranting. Caleb crying that it was the monster setting them up. He was always more fragile than Zoey. Daniel let him believe that Jane Doe was proof that it existed. Daniel called me a loose end; Caleb was one too. I don't want to give Daniel too much credit, but I think he was handling Caleb. As long as Caleb lamented a beast, no one would believe him if he confessed about Jeanie. Manipulating Caleb was Daniel's fail-safe.

"Stella," Shane says gently. "We found Daniel about a half mile up the river in a ravine. He'd been dead for a day. Impaled by a branch. The techs who recovered the body found hair and blood on it. They believe it'll confirm that Caleb killed him."

I exhale shakily. "Daniel is dead? Caleb killed him?" My voice is hollow. The words are eely, hard to grasp in my head. In a way Daniel killed himself. Daniel fed and stoked Caleb's belief in the monster by lying to him about Jane Doe. "Did you search the Talcotts' old house? Did you find the missing piece?"

Shane looks at me sideways and then back at the road as we soar through a yellow stoplight. "It'd be healthier if you stopped thinking about this stuff, but yes. You came up with a hell of a theory as to why Daniel killed Jane Doe and removed her scalp. The missing piece was there in a backpack that was covered in Daniel's fingerprints. He must have worried we'd find it at the Talcotts' current residence."

It occurred to me the first morning I woke in the hospital. The night before, I'd told Sam that Daniel was gloating over Jane Doe, smug over the handiwork no one suspected him of. Then all night I dreamed of Daniel hissing that Jeanie was everywhere. She was a mistake he couldn't outrun or outlive. I saw Daniel so clearly that morning: driving toward Savage, having already decided to come home, tired to the bone from waiting for me to remember and certain that it was only a matter of time that I did and implicated him. Maybe he cut by a park or school yard? And there she was: a familiar stranger. He thought fate was dangling a Jeanie-size solution in front of him; there was no better way to reopen the case and pin it on someone else than for a little Jeanie double to show up dead. Maybe he thought the search for Jeanie's body would be renewed and that the police would find her remains at Griever's? Griever would be blamed for both deaths. Who knows, maybe at the time he really thought Jane Doe was Jeanie? I imagined Daniel hovering above her, scrubbing his palms over his eyes, waiting for the resemblance to Jeanie to fade with her life. It didn't. So he took her hair. Without her red hair, she wouldn't resemble his sister as much.

Shane's eyebrows draw together, and he says softly, "But why keep a portion of her scalp? And why bother returning the rest to her head when he dumped the body?" I called Shane that first day in the hospital to tell him where I thought he'd find the missing piece.

I'm aware that my heels are tapping in place, and my organs feel like they're pinballing inside me. "He left the hair on Jane Doe's head like it never happened. Maybe he felt bad when he realized she wasn't his sister? But he took the piece—it was the proof he never had of Jeanie being dead. He needed proof or else he'd see her everywhere too. She'd haunt him as he thought Jeanie was haunting him."

We accelerate on to the highway. In three exits we'll be in Savage. Bristly pines line the road, and I avert my eyes. I don't want to stare into them. "We've identified the little girl," Shane says.

"How?" I turn to face him.

"The evidence told the story." He frowns at the horizon. I don't think he's shaven since Jane Doe was found, and there's a fine dusting of white in his beard. "Daniel's backpack contained a couple of crumpled receipts. They're from cities between here and Portland,

Maine, where he was staying with his aunt. Using them, we charted the route he took to Savage and contacted local authorities. Her name was Becca." He allows an intentional moment of silence. "He snatched her the evening before the bonfire, only hours before he arrived in Savage. She was a foster kid. The group home didn't even realize she was missing for several days."

Daniel chose his victim perfectly. We'll never know if he realized he could use Becca's body to frame someone for Jeanie's disappearance before or after he killed her. Was the murder calculated, a means to an end? Daniel was full of hate for Jeanie, his little sister who he tried to *teach*. Perhaps killing her once hadn't been enough? Mrs. Talcott's death wasn't as ambiguous. Daniel's mom saw through him; he hadn't planned on killing her. But it was an opportunity that he didn't waste; it made Mr. Talcott a likelier suspect.

I catch the tail end of a very paternal-sounding pep talk from Shane. "Savage will heal. This isn't like when Jeanie was taken. We know who to hold responsible. We don't need to be afraid. The newspapers will get tired of writing about Daniel now that he's dead. Caleb will get the help he needs."

We've exited the highway and turn right on Main Street, and I see how close his words are to being realized. Storefronts have thrown open their shutters; kids swing and whoop on the monkey bars at the jungle gym across from city hall; the bible-thumping pick-eters waving their rapture slogans have vanished. There's even a line of kids streaming from Powel's Candy Shop.

I touch my fingers to the window as we drive past; where three of my nails should be, there are patchy violet scabs. For me it's too soon to heal. It's too soon to forgive myself for what I couldn't remember, what I could have prevented if I only had. It won't happen again. I'm working out all the details; the devil won't be able to hide in them. "Daniel's motivation for everything was Jeanie," I say.

Shane nods. "That jells with why we think Daniel placed Becca's remains in the cemetery."

I nod; working through the details and laying them to rest makes my insides solid. "He knew she'd be found at the bonfire on the anniversary of Jeanie's disappearance," I say. Not only was it the most dramatic way for Daniel to reveal the body, but the timing would serve as yet another link to Jeanie. We round the corner on to my street. I hold my breath until I see it's mostly deserted. Any news vans camped out for a glimpse of the "girl who was left behind" must be at the police station where Caleb was taken.

"So what about the finger bone?" The thousand-year-old bone is one of the last remaining pieces without a place.

"It's likely he found the bone in the woods near Mrs. Griever's, and he assumed it was Jeanie's," he says. "Daniel was smart. He must have known that Becca looking so much like Jeanie would link the cases, but the finger bone would solidify the link. The bone is likely a Chippewa artifact, as we first suspected." Shane exhales a long, whistling breath. "Why do you think Daniel came back? We weren't looking for him."

I sink lower in my seat as we pass a clump of neighbors standing on their lawn. I'm not in the mood to be gawked at. "He thought it was only a matter of time until I remembered. He just wanted someone—*anyone*—to be arrested for Jeanie," I say. "He thought Griever must have come across Jeanie's body. He wondered if she was still waiting to be discovered in the woods. He probably planned to find Jeanie—well, the rest of her, if he thought he already had her finger—and phone in an anonymous tip or something. He didn't care who was arrested for the crime. He blamed everyone else—me, his father, Griever, and Caleb."

He was wrong, not only because he shot the arrow. If Jeanie had survived that summer, there would have been more games in the woods. I keep coming back to the tin of spiders around Jeanie's neck. My stomach twists over it. With every kink, I remember what I couldn't make sense of as a child: Jeanie despondent when she learned that Daniel was riding on our bus for the school picnic at Blackdog; Jeanie petrified that Daniel would kill the ladybugs on the strawberries because he killed every little critter or pet she ever loved; Jeanie spooked, guarding against the woods, because Daniel was watching her. He was always watching, I recall. He liked seeing her squirm and cry. He liked making her cave to his will.

Who knows, maybe Daniel was lying about aiming the arrow at me. Maybe his violence against Jeanie had escalated, and when he saw what he'd done, he realized he couldn't take it back and ran for his mother? The concerned-brother routine was all an act. Daniel didn't care about justice for Jeanie. He cared about escaping what he'd done to her. Maybe it was the woods? The monster? The hunt? Or maybe Daniel was rotten, fated to maim from the start?

I splay my mottled fingers on my thighs. Tying up the loose ends of the mystery surrounding Jeanie is all I've thought about for days, but there's no great satisfaction in solving it. "What about Betty Balco and the others from the 1930s? Why wasn't Jeanie's case connected with theirs?" I ask. It's the last of the blurry details plaguing me.

Shane drags his hand across his mouth. "You gotta understand that was a long time ago, kid. There's no one alive now—or even when Jeanie was taken—who was on the force then. Hell, the children of the men on the force in the 1930s aren't even alive today. It was decades before records were stored on computers and at a time when people didn't talk like we do now about criminals who hurt children. Generations pass and crimes get left behind." The car bumps up my driveway, and he puts it in park. He twists to face me, his forehead pleating. "But between you and me, I think people wanted those disappearances forgotten. They were unsolved and ugly. Savage was a small town at its beginning. I bet they tried their best to keep it quiet after they didn't make an arrest. The tampered graves appear to be evidence of that. I took a look and agree that they were vandalized a long time ago."

It's painful to meet his red-rimmed eyes. I've been pushing him hard to solve the coldest of cold cases for the last two days. I want to be able to wash my hands of it. I want to bury the tiny seed of doubt and not have it sprout into a sapling. "There has to be a way to find more details on the investigations."

He fiddles with the lid of a Styrofoam cup of coffee in the console. "There's an old warehouse south of Minneapolis where police records are stored from the surrounding counties after they've been closed or retired." He takes a sip of the brown liquid. His mouth purses, and he replaces the cup in the console. "I'm heading down tomorrow to look through them. I'll be able to see if there were suspects they never made public. That's what I'm guessing I'll find. Sometimes the police know who did it, but they can't prove it, and crimes go unsolved officially." He looks more resigned than hopeful.

I unbuckle my seat belt, carefully drawing the strap over my shoulder, but I don't move to leave the car. I blink up at him. "Griever said it was the creature in the woods."

He smiles ruefully. "I'm sure she did."

I squint at him. "There isn't even a part of you that wonders?"

"Stella, you're the one who figured out a way to prove Daniel killed Jane Doe. You cleared up all the mystery surrounding Jeanie. If a beast killed those kids in the thirties, where has it been? What's it been up to? Why hasn't it taken anyone for so long? I don't wonder. I told you the story of the Norse settlers not to create doubt in your mind, but to eliminate it." He pinches the bridge of his nose and shakes his head. "Is that why my grandmother told the story to me? Maybe not. She could have believed like Griever. And why did her mother tell her the story when she was a girl? And why might you retell it to your children someday?" He inclines his head. "Do you see what I'm getting at?"

I pull the door lever and kick one foot out. "The same story can be used to prove and disprove that the monster exists." I don't mean to sound so petulant.

"Interpretation is everything," he says in this maddeningly rational way. "It's only real if you let it be."

I know Shane's right. I want knowing that monsters don't—can't—exist to be enough. Instead those missing girls are like flypaper sticking to my thoughts. "It's crazy," I admit. "I just need to know for certain what happened to all those little girls. I need that to move on." Shane's crescent eyes pool with liquid watching me as I heave out of the sedan. As I bend to wave, he nods his head ever so slightly, an echo of the nod he gave me last September when I asked for the case file, the nod that started everything. I hope this one finishes it.

Chapter Thirty

When she gets to my house, Zoey looks smaller. Okay, so no one packs on the freshman fifteen scarfing hospital food, but even I didn't waste away living off green Jell-O. Every time she catches something moving in her peripheral vision, she recoils like a turtle trying to take cover in its shell. She arrives a few hours after Shane dropped me off, while Dad is still cooking my welcome-home dinner, and Sam and his mom haven't arrived yet.

Zoey's wearing yoga pants and tennis shoes—an ensemble she'd usually consider too casual for the school gym. The plum bruise on her right cheekbone is fading to a sickly yellow. I get bleary-eyed watching her ferret through a box of assorted truffles Dad picked up on the way home from work. She nibbles on the corner of a caramel, then places it back in the box.

"What?" she snaps as I watch her. "It's not like I'm contagious." She selects another truffle and licks it before replacing it. "I'm just not hungry." She smiles a crooked smile that fades too quickly. It feels like a performance; Zoey playing at being Zoey.

I shrug. "I've never seen you resist stuffing your face when candy is involved is all." She crosses her arms against her chest as she leans back into Dad's recliner. The cushions practically swallow her. "How was this morning, you know, since he was found . . . ?"

She swipes at a tear escaping the corner of her eye. "My mom had a shit-ton of questions. What did I do to Caleb to make him pissed at me? Why would Caleb try to hurt me? How could I believe Caleb could hurt anyone? Once she heard that they found him, she ran down to the police station like she was going to save her innocent baby. It was so freaking obvi that she blames me. Big surprise, right?" I reach for Zoey's hand and lace my fingers with hers.

She blinks faster, trying to keep up with the tears. "What are those loose-lipped bitches at school going to say? Who is going to take me to senior prom now? Those dickless guys will treat me like I've got a safety pin through my eyebrow or like I wear fat jeans." She half laughs, half sobs.

"No, they won't." I squeeze her hand. "I won't let them."

Zoey was right about more than Caleb: I did need her protecting me, dragging me forward, dragging me farther from the day Jeanie disappeared. And now I'll do it for her. Now I'll protect her from what people might say about Caleb; from what Caleb might say about her; now I'll protect her from sideways glances and sharp-tongued whispers. I lean forward and brush her shaggy bangs from her eyes. "You are going to have the best year ever. I swear. And besides"—I wink at her—"Sam can set you up with someone for prom."

Zoey's mouth winds up like she's struggling not to smirk. "I am not going to prom with Dirty Harry."

By the time Sam and his mom arrive, Zoey's polished off five truffles. Her lips are stained dark with chocolate and lip balm as she takes a second portion of Dad's macaroni and cheese. I watch her closely through dinner anyway. I watch Zoey, and Sam watches me. Every gesture, every word I measure out perfectly, like it's one of my nana's recipes. If I'm too chatty or too quiet, Sam will worry; he'll suspect I'm still thinking about the others. I want Sam to be unburdened from wondering.

When he kisses me good-bye on the front lawn, his mom in the car trying to give us privacy by studying the contents of her glove box, I lose it and whisper, "Sneak back once your parents are asleep." Screw it, maybe he'll hear me crying out in my sleep, shouting back at the nightmares, but tonight I cave to wanting Sam. He stays with the tip of his nose touching mine for a moment, grinning.

"Give me an hour," he whispers before pulling away and heading to the car.

Zoey leaves soon after, the box of truffles tucked under her arm. An hour later, when the glow of Dad's reading lamp from under his bedroom door goes dark, I tiptoe down the stairs and twist the lock open. Sam's sitting on the porch with his hands shoved deep into his pockets.

"I'll have to leave before your dad gets up for work," he murmurs into my ear as we move soundlessly up the stairs.

I lead Sam into my bedroom, the door clicking softly behind us. My childhood night-light casts rainbows on the ceiling. I chart the fractured bands of light, waiting for his lips to meet mine, and then smile into their warmth.

He pulls back a fraction of an inch. "Am I hurting you?"

I shake my head and wrap my arms around his neck. My shoulder stings in protest, but I don't care. I want tonight. I want to know what it's like to hold Sam so close there aren't even atoms between us. For as much as tomorrow's uncertainty scares me, there is nothing uncertain about the way I feel for Sam.

I untwine my arms and drop down to the bed. I'm so glad Zoey doesn't believe in buying dumpy bras and that I'm wearing something black and lacy—it even matches my stitches. I pause for only a moment. He thrusts his hands into his pockets, watching me pull my tank top over my head. I crawl backward so my elbows rest on my pillow. I try to give him a sexy come-and-get-me look, but I chew my lip, fighting back how vulnerable I feel. Other guys have seen me in my bra, so it's not the nakedness factor. It's that I love him. That I know exactly what I want from him: everything. He moves slowly to the bed, crawling over me on his hands and knees. An arm slips tentatively under me, supporting my head.

"Is this okay?" he asks, sliding his hand down my back, leaving a trail of sublime heat on my skin.

"Yes," I whisper in his ear. His eyes are wide and questioning as he moves his hand to the back of my bra.

"This?" he asks, unfastening the hooks.

"Yes. Do you have a . . . ?" I'm too embarrassed to say "condom" out loud. He jerks away, so startled he almost falls off the bed. He grabs hold of the headboard just in time.

"Overboard," I say with a giggle.

His cheeks are glowing red apples. "Stella, we don't have to do anything you don't want to do. I'm happy waiting for you. I don't expect that," he says.

I reach for his hand and place it on my waist. My pulse quickens. A thin strip of his skin shows between his jeans and his undershirt. "I've never had sex before. You were my first kiss, and I want you to be my first at this too," I whisper. "I want it to be special."

A grin spreads over his face as he pulls his wallet from his jeans pocket and slips out a packet.

"Do you always come prepared?" I tease.

"I've been carrying this around since I was thirteen," he jabbers. "Not this exact one—not that I've been using them, just because they expire, you know." A beat later. "I've never had sex either." My grin is even wider than his.

He tugs the undershirt up and over his head. I reach for him. He kisses my neck, brushing his lips over my collarbone. I arch my back. I quiver. But mostly I smile. Through every single second, through every kiss, through every half moan, even when it's uncomfortable at first, I smile because despite everything—monsters and men—I love Sam.

It's still dark when Sam lifts his weight from the mattress.

"Hella Stella," he murmurs, sending warm currents through me. "I have to go. Call me when you wake up in the morning." Eyes half-lidded, I nod into my pillow, still smiling dreamily, completely unafraid of what tomorrow will bring.

Chapter Thirty-One

Four weeks later Sam parks the wagon at the foot of Jeanie's old drive. We keep low to the ground, moving along the edge of the wood. Zoey's a shadow at my heels, and Sam's close behind her. Outstretched branches catch and pluck at my hoodie. It's a half hour before the sun breaks over the horizon. You'd think sneaking around in the small hours of the morning would have me clutching Sam. It doesn't. Thanks to Shane, I don't wonder anymore.

Three weeks and six days ago Shane found six case files for missing girls in the warehouse where old police records are stored. One of them was Betty Balco's; all were from the 1930s. All girls were taken from the Old Norse Trail or in the woods near their homes. Shane was right: There were suspects never made public. One was a history teacher. The other was a naturalist working for the forestry division in Blackdog State Park. Both could have known the Norse story, and both hiked Old Norse Trail frequently. The investigating detective was so certain of their guilt that he spent weeks trailing them, waiting to catch them in the act. He never did.

The files were thick with notes and interviews. A few were given by the missing girls' friends and relatives. Although none witnessed the abductions, they were with them in the minutes before. The interviewees spoke of a quiet falling over the woods, except for rushes of movement in the undergrowth. They said their friends felt they were being watched for days leading up to their vanishing. The detective concluded that the men stalked their victims before taking them. Several more interviewees, neighbors and adults, mentioned a legend they grew up hearing. It told of a predator living in the woods, craving a certain kind of little girl. Another recounted almost verbatim the Norse story Shane's grandma told him. Dottie Griever, Old Lady Griever's mother, told the detective that Betty wasn't the first to go missing. She said another was taken when she'd been a girl; the detective could never substantiate the claim.

As Shane and I pored over those yellowed case files, I kept thinking about him telling me that the monster's only real if I let it be. That's true, you know. Caleb gave it life. Griever gave it life. Even Daniel allowed it to breathe a little. Shane did more digging on the suspects. The same warehouse had a file on the schoolteacher. On his deathbed he confessed to all six kidnappings and killings. I decided not to give the monster life even before Shane told me.

Zoey and I are wearing black, because you obviously wear black while sneaking around town like phantom menaces charged with restoring modern-day sensibility. Sure the hatchet I took from Dad's toolshed looks medieval, Sam's toting what amounts to an iron sickle, and Zoey has a shovel, but we're here in the name of reason. Caleb's arrest and Daniel's death caused a unique sort of aftermath; a distinctly different shape from the lost years.

Someone has to stop the monster hunters and tourists from flooding our small streets with busloads of "believers" fresh from whatever haunted amusement park or Sasquatch safari they've come from; the hour-long news specials airing about Savage; the tabloids printing salacious front-page stories about "Monster-Gate" and "the Savage Killers."

Dad and Shane say people aren't always rational, and the sensationalist news coverage is whipping up fervor for horror stories. Sam got all historical: "Think about McCarthyism or the Satanic Panic of the eighties and nineties. If you can make people think their neighbors are communist super spies and their teachers devil worshippers, it's also possible to make them believe there's an ancient monster in Savage, feeding on redheads." He has a point.

What really gets me is that the hysteria came *after* we proved that Daniel and Caleb were responsible for the recent deaths. Newspapers picked up the story of the manhunt while I was in the hospital. Headlines read SAVAGE TWO RESPONSIBLE FOR MURDERS OF THREE. At first most of the coverage was about Daniel. Then Caleb was found, and as he stood before a judge who would gauge his competency to stand trial, he muttered about the monster. The judge declared him unfit and committed him to a mental health hospital in Minneapolis. A reporter bribed someone there and interviewed Caleb. The next day all hell broke loose. In the article Caleb swore the monster exists; he claimed to have seen it; he said Jeanie's body was taken by it; he ranted about it killing Jane Doe and Daniel. I think Caleb held fast to his conviction because without the monster, without the need for a sacrifice, the boys were just unjustifiably and unforgivably guilty.

We crouch halfway up the drive and listen. There's only the repeated lilt of birds and deserted front lawns. There's no one to see us commit murder. "Let's go," I whisper. We start forward, slower this time and doubled over to make ourselves smaller.

It wasn't long after Caleb's interview that tabloids joined the ranks of the reporters in Savage. At some point the officially unsolved disappearances from the 1930s were uncovered. The archivist who pulled the articles at the library for Sam gave copies to reporters. Front-page stories were printed about the multigenerational murders of redheaded girls. Newscasters called it proof of an inhuman force ravaging Savage's youth. The police were backed into a corner. They couldn't make the case files available without making the interviews available. A judge forbade them from coming out with the deathbed confession on the grounds that it was hearsay, since no charges were ever filed against the teacher and you can't try a dead person for a crime. All the police could to do was attempt to control the panic and go on record that there was no willful cover-up.

Newspapers and tabloids reported more on the origins of the "imagined" monster than on the real crimes committed by Caleb and Daniel. Even though Caleb never denied that Jeanie and Mrs. Talcott died at the hands of Daniel, there are still those who insist that the

Savage PD is trying to keep the existence of the monster quiet by forcing Caleb and Daniel to take the heat for the murders. Daniel must have told Caleb what I said 255 times the day Jeanie was taken, because he shared it in his interview. Zoey said she didn't, because it wasn't her secret to tell. Predictably, tabloids used it in the headlines of articles "proving" the monster's existence. Reporters also learned about Mrs. Griever. She disappeared before they descended on her cottage and the miniature graves of the sacrificed animals. Wherever she is, I hope she doesn't find peace.

Mr. Talcott, on the other hand, deserves a new start; I hope he gets it in Portland, where he's living with his sister. When Kent Talcott was released, he told Shane that Daniel had admitted to killing his mother and Jane Doe the day before he walked into the station and confessed. He saw how broken his son was and felt that he'd failed him. He took the blame after making Daniel promise that he'd leave Savage and never hurt anyone else. Savage's district attorney decided not to prosecute Mr. Talcott for the false confession. I bet we'll never see Jeanie's dad again.

The mob of a town is just as hungry for the monster as they were for Mr. Talcott. Sightings of beasts in all shapes and sizes are reported regularly. The rosaries and talismans against evil have popped back up on front lawns. People want to believe in hazily imagined beasts rather than accept that someone who looks like you and me could be capable of monstrous things. They'd rather believe in what goes bump in the night.

Yes, there are loads of serious newspapers that dismiss Caleb's stories as the rants of a sick boy. But here's the thing about whack-jobs who believe in monsters: They don't read serious newspapers. They read the stuff that claims to be uncovering the truth others are hiding from you; they search for yeti footprints.

The strawberry vines and bramble take shape a few yards away. Somehow they stand out in the weak light. They're all sharp angles, wild loops, and jagged fringes, like the outline of a dragon or the Creeping itself. I sniff. The Creeping is the name Griever gave the creature, but I can't think of it by any other. I pull my hoodie tighter around my neck as the wind picks up. It's only July, but the suggestion of fall is in the air.

"How do you want to do this?" Sam asks, rubbing his hands together in anticipation.

Zoey lifts her shovel above her head in a stretch. "I'm going to harpoon this beast."

"Make sure we get the roots," I say. The silhouette before us shudders like an animal preening its fur. A squirrel squirming in its nest or the wind, I'm sure. Instinctually, I move to a crouch. Something primal runs from the cold, wet soil into my hot fingertips, like I'm hunting prey, like I can feel the earth's memories of people in this exact spot and position creeping up on a predator eons ago. I can practically hear the wind singing in a silken whisper, *Do it. Do it.*

During the day there are tourists hovering around the straw-berries. They snap pictures and nudge the glossy green leaves with their shoes and pretend to prick their fingers on the thorny bramble. No one's ever brave enough to eat a berry. I'd eat every single one if it would get rid of the tourists for good. You know how when some super-religious person spots Jesus's face in a grilled cheese sandwich? And all the other religious people from miles around come and stare at it? That's what these strawberries have become—that but opposite. The strawberries are proof that evil exists. An entire spectral tale's spun around them. I've come here a few times, wearing sunglasses that mask half my face, to listen to the awed whispers. *Why couldn't Kent Talcott kill them? Are they possessed? Does the monster feed on them? Did nature send the bramble to protect the berries or snuff their life force out?* I swing the hatchet and swipe it left to right, its blade slashing through the web of vines with the precision of a guillotine. Branches snap as necks would.

The strawberries are innocent, as much a victim to the aftermath as we are. But there's no other way. Sam hammers the earth with the sickle; with each strike its curved blades puncture the hidden root systems of the vines and bramble. Zoey uses the shovel to uproot the thickest stalks from the dirt. We go on like this for ten or fifteen minutes. Berries red and round as inflamed eyeballs tremble on their stems. One after another they fall, popping, splattering their blood. We stomp them out. I drag my sleeve over my mouth. Sam's chest heaves; his eyes are as wild as a rabid dog's. I'm sure I'm foaming at the mouth too.

I watch Zoey's fervor. Her hair sticks to her slick forehead. Her lip gloss drifts to the corner of her mouth. She curses under her breath with the effort. I know Michaela thinks she's pursuing the glory that lasts and that Zoey's kind—the popularity, the social chairs, the prom crowns—is transient. Zoey has something else, though. It's not that Zoey is as fierce as warriors used to be or as beautiful as an unscarred forest or as complex and wending as a tunnel that burrows to the center of the earth. She's all those things. Zoey is loyal, and there's no glory that outlasts that.

Ten days ago Caleb tore a piece from his T-shirt and stuffed it down his own throat. He suffocated on it as orderlies tried breaking down his door, where he'd wedged a chair under the knob. He left no suicide note, but I don't need a note to know that Caleb couldn't live with what he'd done to Zoey. Yesterday Zoey's mom had a memorial for Caleb. Dad, Sam, Mrs. Worth, Zoey, and I were the only ones who went.

I swing the hatchet faster, elbow straining, a pain shooting into my shoulder. Not surprising. The scar tissue throbs when I brush my teeth. There's wet earth rot in my mouth and nose. I tug a pair of black knit mittens from my pocket and jam my hands into them. I drive my fingers into the dirt where the stalks disappear, and their fat stems turn to colorless roots like obese earthworms. I claw deeper as Zoey does the same. We're up to our wrists in dirt. Finally, I feel where the roots turn from snakes to spindly veins. We pull every last one of them out.

I survey the pile of butchered vines. Only now am I aware of the pinprick stinging. Some of the thorns from the bramble embedded themselves in the fabric of my sweatshirt, their points sticking into my flesh. Rather than grimace, I smile down at the massacred shrub. It had to be done. I had to prove that there's nothing preternatural about this pile of sticks.

"I dare you to grow back now, you hose-beast," Zoey pants to the ground.

I jam my muddy mittens into my back pocket and pull the Polaroid from my hoodie. We leave the garden sickle and hatchet on the heap. Let people see what finished off their supernatural berries. Next we move into the woods. The sun's just breaking over the horizon, giving everything a scrubbed-clean look. Jeanie's abandoned house fades from view as we hike deeper. Sam's arm is around my waist. The brittle grasses crunch under our feet; it hasn't rained for weeks. Moss like tinsel garlands frost tree branches sucked dry of green. Oak leaves scatter the ground with the look of dead cockroaches curled in on themselves. Prehistoric crane flies hover in the shade, their droopy legs twitching.

Zoey ducks each time one flies near. "I don't get why we couldn't have done this in Jeanie's front yard," she whines. She glances over her shoulder, hand on her hip, an icy-blue eye blinking at me above dirt like warrior paint on her cheek. "It's uncivilized out here. And besides, it's not like Jeanie will know."

I look down at the Polaroid. I've left sweaty thumbprints on the glossy finish. "I know, Zo. But this just feels right." I shake my head to clear it. If I'm going to find the right spot in this expanse of woods, I have to focus. Even though I don't remember exactly where it happened, my body wants to move in a certain direction. I'm trusting instinct. "I think we're too far west." I pause and survey the copse of trees around us. "Yeah, let's move east," I call up to Zoey.

"Okay, Wilderness Slut, which way is east?" Her head turns from side to side.

"Left," Sam says without missing a beat. He gives my hand a light squeeze. The broken blood vessels like red spiders against the white of his eyeballs are gone. He had trouble sleeping for a couple of weeks after I got home from the hospital. He was afraid that the nutcases spilling into Savage would come looking for me. There are knocks at the front door and letters from those who believe Daniel and Caleb are innocent, urging me to come clean about the beast I saw make off with Jeanie. But we've managed. Dad works from home most days, and Shane checks in when he doesn't. I sneak Sam into my room most nights to hold me under the covers. I think Dad and Sam's mom are onto us but have decided to give us a pass.

Zoey flurries her pink polished fingertips at us. "Sam's going to have to do the digging, because I've already chipped two nails." *Sam.* Not the King of Loserdom. Only Sam. She turns for a beat, like she can sense what I'm thinking, and grins at the two of us.

She wades into a sea of electric-green ferns. In a forest of waning brightness, they illuminate the ground under a tightly woven canopy of hemlock. I grip the photo—the one of us kids on the monster hunt—a little tighter as their fronds brush against my thighs, the topsoil and our feet disappearing.

"You okay?" Sam's head is level with mine. His owl eyes flick over me.

I rub my thumb along the curve of his jaw. "I was just thinking about how lucky I am to have you." His lips brush my cheek. I think about it a lot lately. I used to measure love in terms of Daniel's love for Jeanie. I thought Daniel's limitless desire to figure out what had happened to his sister was the product of a love unbounded by this world or the next. Jeanie could have been dust and Daniel would have found her, made her whole again.

I was wrong. Daniel could have put Jeanie to rest years ago by coming clean, but he was too worried about the consequences for himself. Now I'll measure love differently: in terms of Zoey and Sam. I'll love them come hellfire, monsters, secrets, and Weirdowood—and they'll love me the same.

We're looking for the spot where Daniel shot Jeanie with the arrow; where I sat with her until she died. I want to bury this picture, the nearest thing I have to something that belonged to Jeanie, in the dirt that might still be coppery with her blood. It's as close to a funeral for Jeanie as I can get. A tribute to Jeanie was Shane's idea. He thought focusing on her being in a peaceful place would give me closure and help me stop imagining her face everywhere. Shane's the only one I've shared that with. He's as haunted as I am. When I told him I wanted to do it where Jeanie died, his cheeks puffed out like a blowfish until he whooshed with resignation.

We invited him along, but he has his hands full. The police are worried that with the amount of news coverage the crimes and the monster are getting, there will be copycats, sickos hoping to prove the monster's existence by committing crimes, and pedophiles flocking to Savage in order to pin their dirty work on phantom beasts.

As we pass over the edge of the goblin ferns, I freeze. Sam's side presses to mine. Zoey turns when she doesn't hear our footsteps following, the wind rustling her short hair. With the light behind her head and her hair like that, she could pass for Caleb.

"Is this it?" Sam prods gently. Zoey is there on my other side in a flash, and before I confirm or deny, she has the shovel in her hands and she's thrusting it into the parched soil. Eight unchipped nails be damned.

I release Sam and crouch down with my palms pressed to the earth streaked with red clay. It's cool and soothing against my skin. The clearing extends ten or twelve feet wide and long, with a fallen tree dividing it. From where I squat, I see shiny black beetles scurrying over the trunk, plump brown mushrooms with caps like umbrellas, nodding white flowers like a picnic blanket of snow tinged with lavender, and a luminous blue-winged moth fluttering by. I don't know how, but I know I've been here before.

"Yeah, this is where it happened," I murmur. For some reason I expected death to be thinly veiled here: trees shriveling, decomposing animal carcasses, crimped spider legs, a sulfur stench, and a bank of moss growing over her skeleton. I thought I had to face this place for Jeanie. Stare it down to tame it. Put her to rest. Find her bones to bury. It's where it all happened. But it's already peaceful.

"Her body isn't here," Zoey says, out of breath.

Sam frowns, scanning the clearing. "Animals likely dragged her away. It's been years," he says. "I'll dig." He reaches for the shovel and Zoey hands it over, her forehead shining with sweat. She stands behind me, hand resting lightly on the crown of my head, playing in my hair as I let the peace of the place sink into me, loosen the knot in my chest. When the hole is wide enough for the photograph and about three feet deep, I lean into the earth and place the picture at the bottom of the grave.

In the instant it leaves my fingers, *I see*. I see petunias nodding in the breeze, their fuchsia and gold funnels big as teacups. A pile of lizard tails scattered around a crumbling pinecone castle. The cicada chirp of the TV through the open windows of Jeanie's house, where her mom is snoring on the couch. Jeanie and I go tearing through the jumble of strawberries. The ruffled hem of my skirt rips as I climb over a fallen trunk, but I don't care.

We run full speed toward the witch's lair. Jeanie wants to see her cast a spell, but I told her good witches don't cast spells. Halfway there I squat down to watch a glistening black centipede roll an acorn between my sneakers. One of my laces is untied, and it takes the crawly thing forever to roll the acorn over the obstacle of the lace. I look up to see if Jeanie's watching, but she's bending over a fallen sparrow's nest, a cascade of multicolored candy beans exploding from the depths of her pocket. I pop up to see if there are eggs in the nest.

I hear a laugh, and then an object buzzes through the air, stinging my arm as it whooshes past. I spin around as Jeanie staggers back, mouth pursed like she's sucking a lemon drop, hands red with finger paint. She lands on the ground like a pinned butterfly, wings spread and quivering, an arrow sticking from her tummy.

Caleb and Daniel charge through the trees. I don't know where from. Daniel spits and shouts. Caleb cries. The ferns are tall, their fiddleheads swimming at my waist. Jeanie disappears under them, her cry sharp, loud, whiny as a fire engine. Daniel tugs on the arrow as Caleb holds her head still, winding his fingers in her hair. Jeanie cries louder, so I clamp my hands over my ears. "Take it out," I shout. "Take it out. Take it out." Once I start, I can't stop. Jeanie's got a splinter. Jeanie's hurt bad. Worse than skinned knees. Her mom will be mad. Daniel and Caleb jostle and shove.

"We gotta leave a little blood for the monster so it doesn't come outta the woods," Caleb bays, still gripping Jeanie's head. "We gotta feed it."

Daniel shoves him off her and lunges at me; he grabs my shoulders and squeezes until his dirty fingernails make me whimper. "Stay with Jeanie or I'll make you eat worms." His fingernails dig into my skin and I nod. He drags Caleb away by the shirtsleeve and hollers for his mom as they run toward home.

I tiptoe closer to Jeanie. I want to see if she's sleeping. She isn't. She stares back at me, glassy eyes blinking as she spits up. Red liquid curls down her forehead from her scalp, and she smells like pee. A triangle of geese fly over us, and my head snaps up at their honking. I look back to Jeanie—Jeanie has a parakeet, she likes birds—but she's crying. I crouch and let the ferns tickle my face. I close my eyes and listen for the boys. The forest is humming with life. We left a pile of berries for the monster last week, but it must not have worked. Daniel says it's getting hungrier. Caleb says it'll come out of the woods.

Then there's a sharp *pop* from behind, like one of Daniel's cherry bombs. I hop up, craning my neck to stare at the dense thicket across the clearing. I take two steps and stop. Everything's gone quiet—the birds, the wind, the brush, even Jeanie's gulping. The thicket's fronds knit together in a wall, and there's the hazy outline of a form crouched behind it. I whimper—can't keep it in. Daniel says the monster smells us when we're out here; it smells Jeanie's blood. There's an abrupt rush of movement behind the fronds, and the shadow flits a few feet to the right.

"It's hungry," I whisper to Jeanie. My chin quivers. I turn to see that Jeanie's whole front is soaked red; the paint's dripping onto the dirt. She makes dying animal sounds, turning screechy.

"Shhh," I whisper as I back away from her and the shadow in the thicket. "It'll hear you." Her gurgle-choking gets louder. The shadow shifts. "Jeanie, *shhh*." She wails.

I keep repeating the plea, begging her to quiet down, pleading with her to shush. "Jeanie, *shhh*." I back away. I want to stop. I want to stay with her. But Daniel and Caleb are right. The monster's hungry, and I don't want it to eat me, too.

I jerk away from the memory feathering before me, before the panic can yawn and stretch inside me. Jeanie was alive when Daniel and Caleb went for help. She was alive when I backed away from the shape in the brush, begging her to be silent. What was it? Was it a bear or a mountain lion drawn in by Jeanie's wounded animal noises? Is it the reason her body's no longer here? Dimly, I register Zoey and Sam talking. Don't know about what. If I'd stayed at her side, would Jeanie's mom have found us? Could I have scared the animal away? Daniel shot Jeanie with an arrow, but could she have survived? He ran for their mother; he tormented Jeanie but didn't want her to die.

No, that came later, after years of dread that someone would discover what he'd done; after seeing Jeanie everywhere, taunting him, waiting for him to get his. Only then was he capable of murdering a little girl for having a face close to his sister's.

I teeter on the rim of the makeshift grave. Zoey kneels beside me, the warmth of her arm scalding mine. All that make-believe, us in the woods with bows and arrows, howling about witches and monsters, is what turned them—*us*—savage. How could I have been so afraid that I walked away from my dying friend? Caleb and Daniel said it needed a sacrifice. The monster was hungry. The forest went quiet—a deafening noiselessness—before I saw the shape behind the ferns. There was a rush of movement in the thicket. Jeanie was staring into the woods for weeks before she was taken, as if she knew she was being watched. It happened just like it was described by the friends of those who were abducted. I wag my head hard. No, no, no, monsters don't exist, at least not the sharp-toothed and taloned kind. Only bad people. Jeanie guarded against the woods and acted strange because of Daniel. Jeanie wasn't afraid of the things that tap at your window at night. She was afraid of the boy who lived in the bedroom down the hall.

Jeanie died because I was a little girl frightened of something that couldn't possibly exist—because I *believed* in it, if only for that moment. Never again. There's no such thing as the Creeping. The echo of a laugh flits to me from a mob of trees. My head snaps, searching. My hand flies to my mouth. It's me who's laughing nervously because a shadow of doubt faltered through my head like a one-winged moth before I could swat it away.

Dimly, I register Sam's arms hooked under mine, hauling me to my feet, guiding me away from the clearing and everything it witnessed. *What* did it witness?

I float forward, tethered to Sam, wading back into the ocean of ferns a step behind Zoey. I see the choice I have; it is hellish red dazzling against the forest's earth tones. I've seen what happens if you spend too much time thinking about what hides in the dark. You become a monster yourself. You become a lonely old woman in the woods with stories; a killer who sees his victim everywhere; a boy who'd rather believe in monsters than live.

You become the keeper of a graveyard, real and imagined.

Rather than monsters, this is what I'll focus on: Zoey alive for the best year of her life; Sam and Dad sitting across the table from me eating Dad's amazeballs macaroni and cheese; Shane beating back the chaos threatening Savage; Jeanie sending me back to Sam; Jeanie resting in peace.

Acknowledgments

I am indebted to many people who made this book possible. These brief acknowledgments do not express the immeasurable gratitude I feel to you all. A very special thank you to:

My mother, who filled my childhood with library visits, books, and love. Thank you for being so very present for me. My father, who encouraged me to think critically and work harder. My sister, Elizabeth, who makes me feel like the funniest person alive. No one does make-believe like you. My brother, Andrew, who is always in my corner. Thank you for being nothing like the brothers in this book.

My childhood friends, for the adventures we had and the adventures we didn't. My grad school chums, who "networked" tirelessly with me as I worked on this manuscript. And thank you to all my friends and family who were good to me in countless ways and expressed so much enthusiasm and optimism for what was a long shot.

My agent extraordinaire, Brianne Johnson, for your guidance, hustle, and believing in me and this creepy little book.

All writers and early readers who offered up support and critique. A special thanks to Debra Driza, whose eyes were the first other than mine on this manuscript; the Fearless Fifteeners, who supported me in a way that only other debut authors can; Olivia Valcarce, for all of your feedback and help; CB, for making me believe; and Melissa Palmer, librarian and lifelong friend.

The extraordinary team at Simon & Schuster, with great thanks to: Valerie Shea, copy editor, who spared me loads of embarrassment; managing editor, Ellen Grafton; and production manager, Heather Faulls. Thank you to Lizzy Bromley for designing a cover that is as sexy as it is unsettling. I cannot stop staring. And thank you also to Caryn Drexl for her stunning photograph.

To Navah Wolfe, stellar editor, who shares a love of monsters with me. In many instances the characters in this book deserved better than I could give them alone. Thank you for your guidance and for asking all the right questions. Thank you for understanding that this book is about loyalty and friendship as much as it is about deceit and wickedness. You have made it immeasurably better.

And finally, thank you to my husband, Joe. Thank you for always making me laugh, letting me read aloud, celebrating the small victories, dismissing the defeats, steadying me throughout this crazy, wonderful ride, and never wavering in your belief that I could do this. I did it because of you.

Thank you, thank you, thank you.